IZZ OF ZIA

THE GOOD THE BAD AND THE NOBLE

TOM ICON

Let The Adventure Begin

UNLEASH THE ADVENTURE

WHERE FANTASY AND REALITY MEET

For further information, contact us at:
izzofzia@gmail.com
Or visit us at:

IZZ OF ZIA

Published by TomArtCom
902 Delrey, College Station, Texas
www.tomicon.com
Book design copyright © 2017 by TomArtCom, All rights reserved.
Front and back cover illustrated by Tom Icon.
Photographer Cory Dobson
Cover design by Tom Icon
Interior design by Tom Icon

Published in the United States of America
ISBN: 978-0-9987089-1-1
1. Fiction / Action & Adventure
2. Fiction / Romance / Fantasy

I would like to dedicate this book series to my wife, Andrea,
without whom this book series would not have been possible.

Contents

Introduction

Izz of Zia is where fantasy and reality collide. This work is a multi-faceted epic written with a poet's hand. The Good the Bad and the Noble is the first novel of a five part series too big to be a trilogy. This epic venture can be interpreted on two separate horizontal stratum, as an exciting, fantasy, adventure, thriller, or as a deeply spiritual journey of love. Izz of Zia is set in a parallels universe; in the First Age of the Noble Kings, in the Middle Era of the First Millennia, in the year One Hundred and Eleven, in the days of King Ozzdon, in the Empire of Xylenia, on the magical planet of Zia. The reader is given glimpses into each captivating character's innermost personalities that are easy to relate to on many levels. As the reader assembles the puzzle, they will find themselves caught in a circle of many powerful mixed emotions of love, hope, and sorrow.

This read is a magnificently spun tale of romance and exploration that creates an intricate web in which two young heartthrobs that are as different as the East is far from the West learn the fathomless meaning of passion, devotion, and the significance of true love.

Prepare to be inspired by a love that refuses to be denied no matter how tragic—hope rises from within. Fantasy fans who crave medieval fantasy, castles in the sky interwoven with intriguing characters, action packed escapades, death defying quests, and humor, in a magically imaginative world, will fall in love with Icon's compelling writing style. Be prepared to be drawn in and held until the last page. Are you ready for a read so thought provoking that after reading it, you will be left enchanted? This is that book.

One

The Arrival

A dreaming dreamer of dreams, dreamed he dreamt a dream within a dream—therefore—for now, our story must wait until the dreamer wakes. For the moment, in the dreamer's deepest sleep, the dreamer perceives a sequence of images and ideas in the dreamer's mind's eye. Illusions never imagined before sparks a succession of new emotions and sensations through his nervous system. In his brain, pons and neurons send unfamiliar signals through his unconscious mind. He imagines that he is his own apparition, envisioning wonderful impossible things, creating a tale out of his fragmented thoughts. He was, at once, in an unearthly scene. He enters a heightened state, in a neutral realm, somewhere between the surreal and the impossible. Here the tangible and the intangible collide. And it provoked the most astonishing images that he had ever thought of in his whole life. The dreamer sees himself enclosed in the middle of an enchanted meteorite like enclosure floating about weightless, silent, and unseen. In his dream, he sails among the stars, racing through the realm of time and space at an incredible speed, greater than his imagination can comprehend, on an endless voyage, to an unknown destination. His journey carries him across the vastness of space toward the origin of all creation where time was born.

As his dream plays out on the stage of his inner soul, he drifts in an endless flow, passed great clusters of galaxies, stars, planets, and moons. It seems like a realist's brilliant painting on the canvas of his imagination with colors beyond the rainbow. Galactic solar flares erupt into multihued arches and coronas that fountained thousands of miles like blazing tongues across endless space. On the outer edge of eternity, the tails of comets flicker like wafting, flashes of luminous, incandescence halos carried away on streams of rushing solar winds. It is beautiful beyond description. It is as if a dream painter is stirring and splashing his brush with vibrant colors of living light so intense it exerts a measurable force upon his mind.

The dreamer recognizes the stars for what they are, but the hue colored spheres he did not recognize. As he rides upon his chariot of fire, his destination is seemingly guided by a single pulsating star. The guiding star shines with a white heat that flickers like a beacon in the vast deep continuum of perpetual darkness. Finally, after what seems like an eternity that passes by with the swiftness of thought, he finds himself somewhere between the geneses of time and infinity. He is deep within an unknown galaxy in the southern sector of an immense infinity, in the center of the cosmos. In the distance, he sees what has been calling out to him. It is the brightest star in the heavens, a great round yellow-white sun shining brilliantly on the seven round planets that orbit around its realm. He is amazed by the marvels that he sees with his eyes wide shut.

As the dreamer approaches the solar system, he is drawn by a strange magnetic force to the seventh planet. From a distance, it appears to be a small blue globe, surrounded by a bright, glowing aura of illuminating luster. Reflecting white swirls eddy over a panorama of radiantly deep blues. Amidst the colors, there are areas shaded in patches of greens, browns, and grays. As he enters the shinning globe's orbit, the whites become pillaring milky clouds drifting upon peaceful currents of playful winds. The blues become vast oceans teeming with life of every shape, color, and size. And the greens become great landmasses covered with lofty mountains and enormous plains. The land is blessed with natural beauty and rich fertile soil where rains often fall. There are thick forests and lush meadows rippling with a multiformity of living things. As he touches down, he finds himself within grandeur beyond conception, surrounded by the brightness and color of such beauty that it is beyond the reach of interpretation. The scent of beautiful flowers fills the air. The dreamer's self thought wonders, *What is this strange, nameless place that has come from within the depths of my mind? And what could it all mean?* He somehow recognizes from some faraway memory that the seventh planet had been his home in a life before life. It was unearthly beautiful and beautifully unearthly, a place that was always now. The dreamer of dreams suddenly finds himself treading on a path paved in gold. Everything is springing into dazzling life before him in a spectrum of magical hues that he has never seen before. Even the bugs and worms are beautiful in every golden, fluorescent detail. He can feel the land beneath his feet, gently turning toward the East. He steps through a meadow of wildflowers, bigger than any he had ever seen before. The tall green blades of grass around seem to wave at him as he passes; each tiny, subtle green leaf seemingly shivers at his presence. And each flower burst forth, appearing to turn that he might admire its beauty from every angle. He never imagined that such colors, smells, and shapes, existed.

The sunlight is warm upon his face; a flirtatious breeze dances around him like a gentle caress. As he converges on a rainbow's end, he turns his gaze toward the top of a flower crowded hill. He sees a young girl of untold beauty standing at the end of a flawless path of bliss. The beautiful young noblewoman reaches her hands out in greeting as if she has been expecting him. A full head of long, golden hair drifts around her face in the gentle air currents and then cascades down around her waist. Her glorified form is dressed in a glimmering white, luxurious hand spun fabric that drapes her stunning body and flows down to her beautiful feet. Her face is pure and unblemished as fine porcelain flawlessly shimmering like that of an angelic being. Her eyes are a piercing blue with striking hints of emerald. Her countenance overflows with joy, and she gleams with happiness as if she has been longing to see him for the longest time. As they came together, love and truth meet. She wraps her arms and smile around him, and he returns her embrace, wrapping his heart and soul around her. Beautiful thoughts seem to be radiating out of her eyes like an aurora of sunshine. In a dreamy echoey utterance, the young maiden whispers in the most beautiful and harmonious voice, "I have missed you so much," as a magical smile playing across her lips. The dreamer looks deep into her unfathomable blue-green eyes and sees the significant meaning of his dream rising from their depths. He somehow knows then and there that he is reuniting with his soul mate. Suddenly at that moment, the vast web of life all around them erupts into an eternal restlessness of glorious rapture. The dreamer feels everything around joining in animation and himself moving within it.

The flowers sing, and cheerful blades of grass hum their beautiful melodies as the soft wind wafts past their scintillating presence. Nearby, gentle brooks carried the same resounding tune as they cascade down waterfalls into waiting ponds that drink up their refreshing waters. Even the stones within their midst unexpectedly make a joyful sound. Choirs of snow white doves have landed close by solely to pour out their hearts with song for only them. He enfolds her closer to him as her hands moved over his muscled shoulder. She is more precious than fine gold, and her skin is smoother than fine silk. They close their eyes, and the dreamer begins to lower his lips to hers. His head begins to spin; a shiver runs down his spine and midsection to his feet. His toes tingled as they start to curl.

Then suddenly, out of nowhere, he feels an unexpected pull on his big toe! Again and again, he feels the persistent tug that by now had become a forceful jerk! In an instantaneous flash, his jubilation buckles and collapses as he comes crashing back to reality. With bittersweet regret, the dreamer laments over the evaporation of his beautiful dream. Fleeting fragments are swept away on the whispering breath of a waiving puff of air until even its echo had faded into the Gulf of Forgetfulness. Slowly, the waking dreamer opened one eye and then the other as he loomed in and out of his profound, blissful slumber. He slowly sat up sluggishly, requiring time to adjust his mind to what was real and what was an illusion.

All at once, the dreamer woke right in the middle of the vivid dream that was so real that at first, he thought as he awoke that he was instead drifting into a dream. The seafarer rubbed his eyes and yawned as he stretched out his arms as far as they would go and flexed his fingers blissfully as if without a care in the world. It took him a moment to awaken enough to realize that there was something hooked at the end of the fishing line. A line he had tethered to his big toe before drifting off to sleep. The sleepy dreamer pulled in the foot he had dangled over the side of his small boat and reached for the line. There was strong resistance as the creature at the other end of the line struggled to live, but it was well hooked and doomed to be a morning meal. The splashing fish was pulled up into a world it never knew existed up until that moment. The young sailor hauled the plump sea trout into his hands under the dim light cast by his flickering candle lantern. A cumbersome firefly might have provided more light in the predawn darkness. Half awake and half asleep, the ocean crosser staggered from one end of his small boat to the other like a drunken sleepwalker and threw the fish into a woven basket. It was still a good while before dawn, so he flopped back down, huddled up against himself. And once again, he drifted back to sleep, eager to continue the beautiful dream. But the dream in which he had seen things he had never dreamed of before, only faded into a faint remembrance until his divine vision was overthrown by nothingness. And thus here is where the dream ends and, as it must be, our story begins.

Once upon a time, long, long ago, there was a kingdom known as Edawn in the empire of Xylenia, on the planet Zia. It was a kingdom outside of time, as we know it, in a parallel universe not of this realm in the days of King Ozzdon. It was a time when magical things filled the whole great world of Zia. It was at a time when stories were still written in stone when men still believed that their world of Zia was flat. Yet it was a golden era that held the best of everything throughout the face of Xylenia. The kingdom of Edawn was the birthplace of Zia's greatest civilization. It was the foundation of awakened imagination, a culture tilled into the wealthiest and most dominating power the world of Zia had ever known. Its treasuries were filled to overflowing. Edawn's milestone marker was the stone from which all distances were measured throughout the community of kingdoms. Edawn was the megalopolis heart of the entire nation, the terrestrial center point of Zia, positioned in the hub of the universe itself. The Edawnians were a people of a new Golden Dawn, a handsome people who lived far beyond the average span of a lifetime. Love was their most significant power, honesty was valued more than silver and gold, and virtue sought more than treasure. Most citizens were extraordinarily wealthy; even their servants had servants. It was beyond imagination; it was the wine and fabric of Xylenia, a beacon of light to all.

At the summit of the communal system was the upper crust, headed by the noble king, Ozzdon, the distinguished emperor of Xylenia. He was the most reputable of the Noble Kings, was a strong, admirable, pleasant man nearing old age. He ruled the entire empire from the central government of Edawn. He was the unchallenged head of the chain of command, the supreme monarch who held legislative and judicial as well as executive powers over all the land. His rule was absolute, administrated on the authority of his word alone. Yet he was a compassionate man. He allowed each king under him to rule his kingdom independently. Under the kings were appointed governors and administrators. The councils of city elders were in charge of local administration and so on.

The king loved one woman, his lovely wife, Queen Zahra. They had one child, Princess Zuree, who was a rare young girl, as spirited as she was beautiful. She was the fairest maiden in all the land. It was said that King Ozzdon's power to rule came from the mystical crown that he wore. The crown had been handed down through the generations from king to king. Legends of old proclaimed that great authority had been bestowed from above to whoever bore the crown. No one knew exactly where the crown had come. Its origin lost in time vanished from memory. It had been said that the ancient prophets spoke of an age old era when spirits walked upon the world of Zia, and seers held ceremonies on the mountaintops to the northernmost dominions. It was widely believed and recorded through word of mouth that the unknown God, the Great Creator of All Things, had bestowed the magical crown on Xylen. And thus he became the first king of Edawn, by virtue of the fact that he was the first of the Noble Kings to walk in the light of a virtuous heart. By virtue of the crown, King Xylen conquered vast lands, and in his day, he ruled from sea to sea.

There were long forgotten myths of the twelve crowns of Zia no longer told. Tales of the existence of eleven more crowns, when all people from every major race and creed were ruled as one, were now forever gone from the remembrance of men. It was said that the other eleven crowns had disappeared during the Great Wars between the Light and the Darkness. The secret of their location was taken to an eternal grave by the defeated Dark Kings. But the perceived power of the crown was not enough to make Xylenia the most prosperous empire in recorded history. The land also required great wisdom and administrative skills of the mind, and King Ozzdon was wise beyond compare. He was responsible for the binding of all the Zian kingdoms into one global empire and named it Xylenia in honor of his great grandfather, Xylen, the founding father.

Kings from every kingdom in the empire sought out King Ozzdon's presence and wisdom. And every king in the realm paid homage to the earthly king of kings. The entire dominion continuously sent him tributes of gold and silver, spices, horses, and yakoxen. The allegiance of the empire made Edawn opulent, and wealth meant supremacy and strength, and Edawn was the most powerful kingdom in the realm. The throne of kingdoms was built on the beautiful southernmost coast, surrounded by lofty foothills that rose above spacious plains. The mighty Megacon River watered the vast lands to its north. The plentiful river water was distributed throughout the interior valley by an extensive network of irrigating canals and aqueducts. The earthly paradise it provided was bountiful, green, and lush with growth. Children were born into the Ziaian world in unmatched numbers. The kingdom seemed to grow bigger daily as farmhouses sprout up far and wide across the countryside like mushrooms. Small townships sprung up everywhere, creating great cities, which merged into kingdoms, which centralized into the great Xylenian Empire.

The mighty Megacon River, with its life giving power flowed through Edawn, feeding its many internal fountains, wells, and gardens. Eventually, its reservoirs and finally emptied into the Bay of Tranquility, creating a deepwater harbor surrounded by a natural land waterfront. The bay was the nerve center of their world and the lifeblood that connected Edawn across the adjoining seas. It was the most important kingdom of the superb world of Zia, and its influence was felt throughout an empire that stretched out to every corner of the planet. Its distribution of goods and products to the marketplaces throughout the Xylenian Empire was unsurpassed. Edawn was the place to be, a breeding ground for scribes, poets, and thinkers, who described Edawn in their writings as heaven on earth. It was indeed a blissful age; perhaps the closest humanity had ever come to spawning a paradise.

The civilized world of Zia was united in tranquility under King Ozzdon as one. Everyone in the empire lived happily and in harmony with their neighbors in an era of wisdom, knowledge, and understanding. Society was based on high merit and interconnect-edness, celebrating the dynamic energy patterns of fundamental life at every level, emotionally, physically, and intellectually. In a land where everything was obtainable to any hand that could grasp it, made Edawn an ideal place to live. Throughout every kingdom in Zia, safety and opulence flourished as one. It was an awesome time to be alive. As the empire expanded, through proud toil and sweat and foresight, its citizens spread throughout the world and became more prosperous and more powerful with every new gen-eration. The magnificent rhythm of the Edawnian world was the product of inventive minds and the devotion that poured out of the bottomless hearts of its people. Future generations built on the suc-cess of past generations and learned from the errors of their ancestors. Expansion bore down upon the world of Zia, so fast that sometimes King Ozzdon felt as if he would not be able to cope with the acceleration of its increase. For many centuries, all was well, and the empire had lived in peace since time out of mind. It had become a civilization that created a golden era greater than history could get a handle on. Oh yes, it was far from perfect, but it was close enough. Most people were reasonably fulfilled, and nearly everyone was happy.

For nearly a thousand years, Edawnians had enjoyed the good life, and engaging in recreation was part of it. They had to have ways of expending their extra energies, to keep from becoming soft from indulging in too many pleasures. Thus the Totalitarian Games were born to satisfy their most human primal urges for competition. Although Zia had not known war for a generation of generations, taking part in stringent athletic competition was enforced for every able man regardless of their social class. Competition and conquest were considered the ceremonial rite of passage for all young men. Every man in their youth aspired to be the best they could be, and for the privilege and honor of representing their respective kingdoms. Even the most peaceful members of the harmonious society were driven by the primitive yearning to experience an expression of self preservation. Thus was born the Totalitarian Games, an annual event that quelled Edawnian's insatiable propensity for entertainment and stimulation. Every kingdom was represented by a cross section of their best, strongest, fastest, and most cunning competitors. It was regarded as the ultimate way of becoming ideal physically, spiritually, and intellectually. To satisfy and keep in check, this most urgent need to pit oneself against the strength and wits of another. The empire simulated combat battles by hosting campaign games at the annual gathering of titans. The games filled Edawn's monumental stadium with enormous crowds of people that overflowed onto the surrounding hillsides. Competitors and spectators alike could feel pumping through their veins the thrill of absolute victory or the agony of unequivocal defeat. The victors were given golden crowns studded with precious stones and were lavished with honor and glory. Their names and the names of their kingdoms became part of the very fabric of history. Training for this nationalistic rivalry required constant drilling, preparation, and ruthless discipline, and was of the highest importance in the education of young Ziaian men. But to become a champion required years of grueling training, in a system designed to weed out those who were not totally committed. To provide a tremendous spectacle, the game overlords supervised most athletes' training, all year around. A strict set of criteria chose competitors physical performance, overall character, and morality were all keys for consideration by the game overlords. Above all, competitors were required to demonstrate high endurance, courage, and skills in mock combat. The running races were the oldest event, both short and long distances. The lance throw, wrestling, bare knuckle boxing, archery, swordplay, were among the other many events. Horse racing was the event of kings.

The high point combat events included the thinking man's game. In this competition, whole armies of different kingdoms were pitted against each other. Strategizing generals were handpicked by their kings exclusively for their skills to executed precision catapult targeting and complex war maneuvers. But the favorite and most spectacular event of the games was the Tournament of the Conquerors wherein the champions of champions competed, one on one, in hand to hand combat. Face to face combat was perhaps the most violent of competitions where almost anything was fair. The winner of this event was made famous, his name passed down from generation to generation, recorded for all time. Officially, the winner was given the top honors. One never had to work again. Their home kingdom donated piles of riches, lifetime retirement funds, even kingship. However, the highest honors were reserved for the competitor who won the most individual events. They became as close as one could come to deity in this worldly life. It was as close as you could get to be immortal in a mortal world. One especially gained incredible status, wealth, and notoriety from becoming the next Totalitarian victor. Massive monuments were erected in their honor, and many times, as was often the case, they were accepted into marriage contracts with the rich, the influential, and sometimes the ruling elite. The reigning Totalitarian champion of champions was Rizan. His strength and exceptional valor were legendary. For his conquests, he had been awarded incredible prestige, troves of treasure, and kingship over Ziyontopia, the most beautiful kingdom in Zia. But best of all, he had been hand picked by Emperor-King Ozzdon himself, promised the hand in an arranged marriage, to his only daughter, Zuree, the princess of Edawn.

South of the kingdom, where the land met the sea, in the Bay of Tranquility, the midnight watch atop the southernmost lighthouse sounded the bell in the fifth hour. On the horizon where the eastern sky met the land and sea, further than the eye could see, there was an approaching dot nearly hidden in the dark waves of the watery tide. The speck gradually became a dot, and the dot soon became a tiny outline of a miniature sailboat. Onboard the small sailboat lay the young dreamer of dreams, with a motionless hand upon his boat's rudder. Once more, he is again trying to pick up on his farsighted vision among his first waking thoughts. His sleepy head lay upon his leather satchel, where he kept far more than his simple earthly possessions. They were those few valued things that he truly cared about. They were a few things that symbolized his someday, sometime, somehow wishes, dreams, and treasured memories. His little sailboat was the only thing of value he needed in the whole world. The travel worn garments on his back were practically the only necessities of life that he owned along with a few otherworldly belongings. He pulled up on a long, woolen scarf he wore over his mouth and nose. The scarf was precious to him because his mother had woven it. The loner did not know how he knew that he assumed that someone must have told him once, but he could not recall the telling.

The visionary's name was Izz of the Isles Zollerzon, a young man who was just on the threshold of life barely beginning to navigate through that tricky limbo world of adulthood. He had become self dependent while still a boy; it was a life that was well matched to his circumstance. The nomad was a born adventurer who went anywhere the four winds blew. Always eager to set out for the unknown on a journey of self discovery, with enough courage to face whatever life offered on whatever terms he was allotted. He imagined that someday he would be a great hero. He was the kind of soul that created his own world and ran free in it. On whatever spot he stood, that ground, he owned, occupying its breadth of space from the core of Zia to the outer reaches of the heavens in the sky. No burden of care did he lug upon him only the bare essentials of life.

He was lord of the sea, continually changing his whereabouts. Izz was the owner of every moment that he lived, and did his best to make each new day a wondrous adventure. He was as free as a bird, disencumbered from those nagging questions and uncertainty with the future, which weary most other earthly lives. He blazed a trail through life solo, fearing little, spreading merriment around him everywhere he went, and everything he put his hand to seem to flourish. Never, anywhere, at any time, had there ever been a young man quite like Izz. He was an honorable young man, wise beyond his years. He was tall and lean, with copper colored skin and thick, glossy raven hair that fell like a mane in curled waves to his shoulders. The striking bone structure of his gallant face was extremely handsome. His expression was always animated, happy, and he was seldom ever seen without his infectious charismatic, porcelain smile. His exposed chest rippled with muscles. He was in the prime of his physical strength, a perfect specimen, strong and healthy. His attire was simple, his clothing modest, and unadorned, nevertheless well made of the highest quality cloth.

Caring little for material wealth all he had to offer was the knowledge of the lands he had traveled and a few tokens of their wonders, which he would always carry with him. The only thing of real value that he owned was his own life. But he possessed what few men could boast of, a pure and loving heart, which profoundly influenced his moral values. He was a young man with a deep soul, his primary focus was on what was right and good in life, and he did not lie, cheat, or steal. At every opportunity, he went out of his way to uplift the downtrodden and the less privileged. He was a giver, not a taker; the kind of person that never held back his meal from anyone he knew was hungry. At every available opportunity, he defended the weak, comforted those in need, and never knew how anyone could wish to do otherwise. He was a worthy young man through and through.

One might say that Izz was a rich—poor man that existed only for the moment; he had a zest for life with a curiosity that strives to know everything. Izz seldom complained and lived a full untroubled life. However, if one looked deep enough, they would see that there in the depths beneath the layers was hidden a profound sadness in his soul. His young mother had died giving him life. He had been displaced when he was just a newborn; fate had deprived him of something that was meant to be his birthright. In the middle of the very following winter, his father's will to live lost its fight to a heartbroken beyond getting over the loss of his beloved companion. His heart aches now buffered by time as a mollusk covers an irritating grain of sand with coatings of pearl. The sea had become his mother and the sun his father.

Gentle waves lapped against the boat, rocking the peaceful sleeper back and forth. Hoping to catch another fat trout. The listless dreamer had once again hung his leg over the edge of the boat. At the tip of his foot on his big toe was tethered the line that was cast into the deep. At the end of the line was a piece of cheese that concealed a finely honed, curved hook. Fishing was an activity that he engaged himself in many times while sailing long distances across the sea. A multitude of enthralling curiosities bounced around in his mind. He knew that he would never be able to get the dream that had filled him with a sense of good fortune out of his head. He felt a significant change coming, though he did not have the slightest clue what it could be or in which direction it would take him. But what did it all mean? He searched for something from his memory, something from which to envision his future, but he could not begin to guess what that could be. Izz tossed and turned, hopelessly trying to recall the details of the dream that had felt so real that it left his heart fluttering. All he could remember was that it had been a very peculiar dream, and Izz could not seem to shake loose of it. He searched his mind over and over and over seeking out the dream that teetered on the tip of his memory. But each time his train of thought only ended with an inner crash of confusion. The more he tried to recall this enchanting vision, the more it seemed to recede and shuffle itself deeper into the back, dusty corners of his mind. Perhaps it would never to be remembered again. All that lingered in his memory were vague shadows and unrecognizable reverberations without significance or connection to his waking life.

Zia turned in its place, and the sun slowly rose, increasingly radiating its light across the rotating world below. As the first glow of dawn became visible, the first shafts of light found their way through the misty horizon. The sky above turned gray with the approach of first light. Gradually, the sky became a prism of a thousand hues quickly changing from dark blues and deep violets into tones of oranges and yellows. As the day developed into a beautiful spring morning, Izz looked across the sea, gathering his waking thoughts. As beams danced hand in hand with shadows over the restless sea, dazzled by the refracted patterns of the passing moments, Izz painted imaginary illusions on the undulating surface of the water. He felt as if he could live this way forever, immersed in the pure magnificence of living free in a world he saw his way. He seldom squandered a glance looking backward or forward. He adjusted his sail with the prevailing winds and set his rudder toward the approaching land of Edawn. Izz looked toward the shore and focused on the shoreline ahead. He turned his head toward what at first was a thin line of unbelievable brilliance budding on the horizon. Edawn's skyline could be faintly seen glimmering in the distance like a dark, opulent jewel under the rising sun. Izz had come a great nautical distance over the rippling cadence of the vast sea.

The early morning sun at last burst forth, blossoming into brilliant golden light as the edges of the sky burned with its fire. With enthusiasm, Izz greeted the warmth of the dawning sun that had helped guide him across the sea as its earliest light smiled on his arrival. It was a new best day of his life, a great time to be alive. Izz smiled back and said, "Good morning, my trusted friend. Yet, another day, you shower me with your bright kindness."

More than ready to seize the day, Izz turned his attention to the basket that held his prized sea trout. He took the slippery creature and quickly prepared it. He stirred the ashes that seemed long dead and gone and found live coals beneath that had held their glow through the night in his small cast iron cooking pot. Izz tossed a handful of fuel into the stove from his coal sack. After a few expectant moments, the coals burst into flames, and he threw the fresh trout on the crackling embers. He watches the fish with the minutest care and attention as if cooking it to perfection would somehow affect his eternal happiness. When the fish was broiled to his liking, he allowed it to cool for a moment. Then took it with his bare hands and tore the soft, succulent flesh away from the bones in an eager eruption of appetite. The fresh meat was delicious, and he did not stop until he had gobbled the whole fish, he even licked his finger clean.

The gentle winds continuously moved the small sailboat closer and closer toward the mainland of Edawn. The colors in the morning sky were by now changing from shades of yellowish-reds into tones of light blues along the eastern horizon. Izz sat back and unwound. Sailing on the spring currents, drifting in a peaceful, quiet moment, he closed his eyes and romanced the sea, his first love. The sweet smell of the North wind carried an invigorating breeze that soothed his tanned face, and he felt the excitement of adventure stir deep within him. On the open high seas, the fresh winds blew, and Izz felt more acutely alive than anywhere else on Zia. It seemed as if nothing could go wrong. The fish sat well in his belly. It was the rich nutrition he would need throughout the exciting day to come.

Izz of Zia

Of all the adventures in dazzling far off lands, this would be the most marvelous. Izz was on his way for the first time to the national games. He came seeking the opportunity to leave his mark; a scratch would do. He looked forward to competing against the strongest runners from all around Zia, eager to test himself against the legendary kingdom champions. Izz had every right to be optimistic. Izz was a natural athlete and had mostly trained himself. From early in life, he loved to run and compete against anyone any chance he was given. Soon he was running faster than all his friends, even those that were many years older than him. He dreamed that one day he would be the fastest footed man in all of Zia. Not one of the fastest footed or next to the fastest footed, but the fastest footed of them all. The competition would be fierce, but his mind was focused and determined. He had already easily beaten the top runners on Zollerzon, the isles of his birth. And now he longed for the chance to challenge the ranks of the best of the best runners in the whole world of Zia.

Izz was a young man of many talents, from diving for pearls to craftsman, but carpentry was his favorite trade. He loved tinkering and working with his hands and was quite skilled at it. There was little that brought him more pleasure than taking apart a complex piece of machinery only to figure out how it worked. He had managed to earn a small fortune of wealth diving for pearls and treasure in his spare time and had worked as an apprentice in a carpentry shop. Izz was in the prime of his life, strong from hard work and full of ambition, hopes, and dreams. There were simpler paths in life he could have taken. But the hunger for exploration always led him to set his sail to catch the shifting winds of adventure along the route less traveled. He was filled with boundless vitality, a tireless rainbow chaser, sailing the high seas on his own, following after the call of distance romance and glory. He was the spirit of loving kindness and was born to add value to the world. His eyes beamed with promise. It was this bright light inside of him that attracted young maidens to him everywhere he went. Many times he had tossed his wild and free heart around simply to see where it would land. And his memory was etched in many a girl's hearts. But falling in love was the last thing on his mind. Izz was in no hurry to do anything fast; he was more interested in enjoying the journey of life everywhere and anywhere, rather than racing to its finish. Day in and day out, he changed the compass reading of his life. He was as yet uncertain where home for him would be. There remained inside the boiling curiosity of so many of life's most profound, unanswered questions. He had as yet not lived their profound answers, but he meant to keep searching until he discovered them. Until then, a home would remain a question with no answers.

Finally, Izz could now see the seven high towers of the legendary Kingdom of Edawn as they pierced the vault of the clear blue sky. They were gleaming like beacons, yielding a dazzling white sparkle as they reflected the light of the early morning. It seemed like an unbelievable dream. It was more breathtaking than he had ever imagined it could be. He drank in its astonishing splendor as inch by inch, the distance shoreline rose out of the haze. Izz lowered his billowing sails as the craft caught the incoming tide and drifted toward the sandy shore where waves expanded in toward the heart of the harbor. All along the coastline, the land glittered with foliage like a green transparent gem. The sun was by now shining over Edawn, and from a distance, Izz could now clearly see the astonishing skyline of the kingdom. He gazed at Edawn in what could have been only a look of utter wonderment. The older sailors he had once sailed with had not exaggerated its grandeur. If anything, their descriptions had failed to capture Edawn's true magnificence. It was a place one could only have imagined in one's dreams. In its glimmering and glittering splendor the dazzling, kingdom shone like an adorned halo cresting the sacred seven mounts, a truly magnificently jeweled crown in the sun. Edawn, at the edge of the warm sea, was blessed with deep harbors, which were by that time bustling with multitudes of merchant ships. Izz watched in amazement at the ships coming and going, bearing fine goods from every corner of the empire. Seafaring men were mooring their vessels. Massive mechanical ship crane loaders, of such that Izz, had never seen, were loading and unloading the burden of their cargo. The harbor was the kingdom's lifeline, its window to the world beyond.

As Izz entered the Bay of Tranquility, he was confronted by seven monolithic statues built on a monumental foundation, carved by the most exceptional artisans of the kingdom. The stately figures were the colossal statues commemorating the seven greatest Noble Kings of the Great Ancient Wars of the territories over the rule of the empire of Xylenia. Upon entering the port of Edawn, Izz saw more merchant ships from distant lands. They were here in peace, for trade and comradeship, heavy laden with spices, silks, glass, pottery, and riches from across the furthest reaches of the empire of Xylenia.

With a few final oar strokes, Izz pulled onto the shore, lined with thousands of other small boats. He cast his anchor, jumped into the breakers, hauled his boat onto the white beach, and pulled down his sail. He dropped to his knees and kissed the sandy shore. This debarkation ended a long voyage that began from a far off land in the southernmost kingdom on the edge of the empire. With a thousand zettas of open sea between him and his home soil, he faced everything anew. It felt good to be on dry land again. The sun now was high overhead and dazzling, the air crystal clear, almost glistening in its transparency. The sky was intense indigo. Izz walked along the shore with his satchel, diving dagger strapped at his hip, and the clothes on his back as his only possessions. With a whistled melody on his lips, looking as brisk as a spring breeze, his footsteps left tracks in the sand that soon vanished in the ebbing surge as sand crabs ran in front of him. He looked into the sky and saw black headed seagulls flying all around high overhead, while waves crash onto the glimmering shores. He heard the laughter of little children as they ran passed splashing water at each other. By the time Izz had reached the front walls of the kingdom between the docks and the gates of Edawn, the kingdom was already a bustling beehive of activity. The hustle and bustle of carts and loaded wagons, rushing to and fro, echoed with the clatter of horses' hooves. Izz had come from the edge of the Zia to reach its center finally.

Izz felt the rising surge of excitement as he approached the larger than life walls and gates of Edawn. As he drank in every sight, exhilaration filled him the same as the restless ever whirling winds that filled his sails. Finally, he was before the gates of the glorious Kingdom of Edawn, here to take part in the pinnacle event of the year, in the most magnificent kingdom of the empire. He was there on his own merits. He had no wealthy sponsors. Still, what he lacked in promoters, he hoped to make up in natural physical ability and determination. He was, as yet, virtually unknown, but Izz believed that all of Zia would know his name soon enough. For a moment, Izz looked toward the distant horizon from where he had come. He could make out the curvature where the sky met the sea and had an unexpected, fragmented flashback of part of his strange dream. He wondered if the land he walked on could in actually be round as he had dreamed it had been? How could that be? Anyone could see that the world was flat, but then why could he only see the mast tops of the ships far out at sea. For a moment, he reasoned the moon, and the sun is round. His dream was turning into a master conundrum that harbored ever deepening mysteries. This riddle would require more profound thought at a later time. For now, he had the new world of Edawn to discover.

In the bay, men and beast hurried along with their early morning tasks. Merchant ships that made Edawn the busiest port in Zia endlessly unloaded their merchandise from around the empire. Exotic good filled Edawn's many stores, shops, taverns, meal stands, and emporiums. Shipmasters moved their enormous vessels into their docking positions as yard workers scurried about directing and mooring the great ships. An armada of heavily laden ships belonging to various kingdoms was anchored along the piers to load and unload their heavy cargo. The huge cranes and hundreds of flat wagons used for the cumbersome task of loading and unloading lined the port. Barrels, crates, and bulging sacks of assorted sizes could be seen piled on top of one another all over the shipyard. In a realm where everything throbbed, overland supply chains of camel caravans added to the growth engine that boosted the Edawnian economy and revenue. Izz drank in his surroundings; it was magnificent, a cause for awe.

When Izz reached the kingdom's entrance, its massive gate arches reared up to a center point to tower before him. His mouth gaped open in silent awe as he was filled with wonder. The enormous size of the two oak doors, he found disquieting and even a little daunting. The great gates of Edawn must have been so massive that it could have hardly been open or shut by a score of strong men. Massive iron bands secured the two colossal door sections fastened deep into the centers of the solid stone. Each gate door was decorated with golden and silver clad symbols that told stories of great feats, epic conquests, and mighty heroes of long, long ago. Each panel was carved elaborately with intricate designs, bearing a message of peace and prosperity, embracing a sense of splendor and brotherhood. They were covered with seven kinds of metals: iron, tin, zinc, copper, brass, silver, and gold, the handiwork of some very skillful artisans. On the upper middle part of the gate was the Great Seal of Zia. The ornamented emblem depicted a White Crowned Eagle with outstretched wings. The giant White Crowned Eagle was the national bird and graced every Zian flag. It was the biggest bird in Zia, almost as big as a fabled dragon, and had long been esteemed as a species of power and wonder, prized as a sacred bird.

The outer walls, unbreached for centuries, wrapped around the kingdom and were built with giant blocks of white granite that each weighed over a ton. Its massive structure was breathtaking. The walls were a complex interconnection of stone, carved and fitted with the most impressive masonry skill, and lined with structures of art. Master stonecutters noted for their talent perfectly fitted the beveled joints of the massive stones. Carved pictures told of many accounts in the history of Zia before the written word. Up close, these walls were also covered with symbols of hidden mysteries and knowledge of earlier times. Prophecies that could be traced so far back that they had ceased to keep pace with the present understanding. From Izz's approach, the high wall towers pointed sharply toward the sky. When other parts of the Ziaian territories were building timbered and sod cottages, Edawn was constructing the most wondrous kingdom of the great Zian world.

The gate doors were swung wide open, shouting out an invitation, as if extending a welcome to the whole world of Zia to come into the enchanted kingdom. And everywhere, from every direction, new visiting multitudes continue to arrive crowding into the streets of Edawn. Izz was just one more nameless entity of a vast moving throng. Standing at each door were two gatekeepers. The guardians of the gate stood at their posts, greeting and welcoming anyone that passed through. Izz entered through the gatehouse, steel portcullis, and beyond where thousands of people went about their own daily lives. They all seem to be moving in different directions, all at the same time enjoying the tranquility that was their peaceful existence.

Izz entered, tall, broad chested, and so noticeably in control of his life. Inside the walls, Edawn was a place of marvel, a mosaic of breathtaking, lofty buildings wondrously structured in exquisitely crafted stone. Inside the entrance was filled with loaded carts lined up along both sides of the street. Shops throughout were constructed in the traditional style with massive stones. Izz whipped his head this way and that, endeavoring to take in everything at once, but there was no way to take in all the grandeur that was the magical Kingdom of Edawn. There were soaring buildings everywhere. To the right, there was a large building used by shipping officials. Just beyond the shipping sector, there were hundreds of workshops, maybe thousands. Craft men were making candles, baking bread, weaving fine linen, and producing embroidered carpets of many colors. A cobbler fashioned a pair of shoes. Tailors hung out their wardrobes. The smell of leather goods and the fragrance of scented oils wafted in the midmorning haze.

To his left, shops were selling the best of all kinds of spices and precious stones, colored marble, and golden jewelry. There was a family of potters creating their goods. Practiced spinners and weavers produced a diverse range of products varying from silkily delicate garments to heavy tapestries.

A blade grinder sharpened a cutting utensil. To his right, Izz saw wine shops on either side of an old red bricked brewery. A blacksmith hammered his iron, and a butcher's cart jingled along. The wheels of a rickety hand cart clicked across the cobblestones, overburdened with the weight of a huge swordfish caught in the bay. The owner of the fish trudged along untroubled, proud of his prize. On both sides of the street, Izz saw merchants opening the shutters of their shops ready to start a new day. A grand adventure lurked at every turn. Wherever Izz looked, something exciting and beautiful attracted and held his eyes in amazement. Even the walkways were fixed into the streets in thoughtfully laid out patterns of brick and stone in such a way that rainwater overflow was directed away into stone lined drainage ditches. The glory of Edawn was all there in front of him like an enchanting dream. But it was not a dream. It was all real. There before him, a wondrous kingdom filled with a multiplicity of other humankind from all walks of life. Thousands, perhaps hundreds of thousands of people, of every description, personality, and culture, beliefs, and ideals, strolled along its glittering streets and avenues beaming with excitements over the coming World Games. More and more crowds continually entered the walled kingdom to be swept along in the tide of people milling about different shops and eateries. Amazement filled his eyes as he looked through shop windows to see the display of an astounding variety of goods.

Izz followed the aroma of an enticing meal being prepared and found himself in front of a dining hall built into the wall right in front of a group of small brick shops. Under the shaded roof hung the carcass of every farm and game animal that Izz could ever imagine. Big, dark sausages swung in the open air, and fowl of every variety dangled from support beams. Upon entering the eatery, Izz thought, *There has to be someplace to sit in here.* Most of the booths were filled with athletes. As was his habit, Izz sought a table in the corner from where he could see everything that took place inside. There in the corner was one table. He took a seat and settled in with his back to the wall to survey the room. Frequent, good natured laughter warmed the room. And even though the place was packed with athletes, trainers, and fans of the games, he received fast and friendly service. He ordered a bowl of Yakox soup, half a loaf of barley bread, and a large tin of new blueberry wine. The meal was enormous, yet relatively inexpensive. The meal server was pretty and a very friendly temptress. As he smiled his most pleasant smile, Izz asked, "And what might your name be?"

When the serving girl saw Izz, she stopped to straighten her posture in a maidenly way. She tucked in some wayward strands of hairs that had escaped from underneath her head covering. "My name is Zophie," she replied as she set the table with fresh bread and silverware.

"What a pretty name for such a pretty girl." Izz raised his eyebrows. "Can you tell me where I can find the home of Lott the Master Carpenter?" he asked between mouthfuls of bread and butter.

"Lott, yes, of course, he made the table and chair you are now sitting in. His shop is just across the street, but these days, he has been seen there less and less. Do you know him?" she asked with an expression on her face that told Izz that she liked him.

"Yes, he is my uncle. I will be staying at his home." He reached for another piece of bread and spread it thick with butter and honey. The maiden smiled as if pleased with what she had just heard and walked away. When the server returned with Izz's meal, she added, "We have heard of your uncle's plans to retire and move to his little cottage in the country at the edge of the Ebony Forrest." She then turned away to serve other patrons.

When Izz had finished his meal, he smiled as he stood to pay. He pulled some coins from his pouch and gave the meal server more than the cost of the meal, as was the custom when one was pleased with the meal and service.

"Your uncle's home is beyond the market, passed the King's Court and palace, between the metal smith's shops and the foundry. A modest walk north. You cannot miss it. Just follow the smoke. "

Izz drained the rest of his blueberry wine drink, thanked the kind lady, Zophie, with a big smile, and stepped back into the streets of the kingdom. He drifted back into the swift moving crowd, where he once again becomes part of the thronging sea of people who were flowing every which way. With the hearty meal he had just eaten percolating through his insides, he felt a sudden buoyant vigor. Izz looked to the sky and saw the smoke of the foundries and headed in that direction. He followed the wriggling and rolling flow, moving swiftly past roll after roll of small storefronts among the crowds of people. The crowds on the street were packed so close together that they looked like one giant creature headed toward the main market. Every tavern he passed displayed a sign on its door that read No Rooms Available.

Around the corner, Izz could see the market just ahead of where copper pots bubbled on open fires, and the smell of baking pastry filled the air. The market was the heart of the city, the busiest place in the kingdom. The shipping lanes and the bounty of the sea provided the kingdom's primary market with every imaginable thing necessary for life. Every morning, as usual, it was crowded with its regular morning grind. Thousands of merchants and consumers came from near and far to the market's square to buy or sell their goods and wares. The streets and marketplace echoed with the sounds of clanging shop grates and shoppers and merchants haggling over prices in dozens of different languages. In the morning mist, the unfamiliar fragrance of hundreds of exotic aromatic oils and the enticing scents of many imported spices and aromatic incense overwhelmed Izz's sense of smell. Each merchant repeatedly called out to the world to come to see their superb display of goods. Gold, silver, and copper coins, all bearing the Zian eagle emblem, exchanged hands. Women thread their way through the crowds acquiring their morning goods with babies in colorful slings slung on their backs. Some carried bundles of vegetables wrapped in their robes as they hurried to their homes with their purchases. With an expression of wonderment, Izz wound his way past the market place through the unbounded, hustle and bustle of early risers pressing around him on the verge of sweeping him away in their whirl.

Izz might have blended in better, dressed in the humble homespun garments, yet everywhere he went, he seemed to draw a curious glance from those he passed. With nothing in his outward appearance, apart from his sun kissed skin, and without doing any-thing to attract attention to himself, Izz still stood out. He drew stares from passersby. Nearly everyone who noticed him had to take a second look. Perhaps it was because seldom would a man be seen in the kingdom who had cause to bear such a finely tooled leather scabbard and dagger at his side.

Suddenly, up ahead, a swirl of dry leaves danced in the corner of the street chased by a strange, unexpected wind. The air was thick with the smell of curious herbs. As Izz reached the outer fringes of the grand marketplace, some detecting sense seemed to click on that produced an alerting emotion from within. Izz was unexpectedly struck by an odd feeling that crept over him, seizing his attention like a foul smell in the air.

Two

Encounter

There was something fiendish there just up ahead. Izz felt a defensiveness rising within him as he discerned a chill in the air as though an icy shadow had suddenly fallen over him. Troubled and exceedingly ill at ease, Izz set his feet apart, and without thinking, at once set out to unearth the threat that had suddenly flustered him. He quickly glanced around, searching out the ambiance of wrongness that had so profoundly set his nerves on edge. Somehow Izz sensed a presence as if someone was looking at him and turned. The first thing that caught his eye was a sign hanging above a merchant stand that read: "YOUR FUTURE TOLD, HERBS ENCHANTMENTS." He had long rejected the belief that cards and bones could tell the future any more than could the entrails of an owl.

As Izz continued to read the public notice, "POTIONS, SUPERNATURAL CURES. FREE SAMPLES." Izz fought back a laugh. Then Izz's full attention was mysteriously drawn to the unusual, little older man standing behind a table topped with bottles, jars, and tins of different sizes, shapes, and colors. The spindly shriveled old man looked as if he was in desperate need of a healer himself. Izz looked directly at the unusual peddler and met his gaze without fear. He found himself staring straight into the most chilling eyes that held no warmth within them. There was something so uninviting and somehow sinister about the person. At that moment, Izz could not have turned his eyes away if his life had depended on it. He saw something wicked in the stranger; he wished he had not. There was an emanation of darkness about him like a distinctly unpleasant aura that he had never seen around anyone else. Izz's awareness seemed to have provoked something profoundly dark and wicked in the elderly man. The most bizarre little man looked away as if Izz was unworthy of his notice. A sudden sense of intensifying premonition swept across Izz, and he drew back, wishing he had not been noticed. Izz's foreboding could not be short of utter doom to come face to face with the decrepit, old man. The strange gray haired man in the long black cloak was the one called Baddlock, born one day when the sun refused to shine, known to one and all, near and far, as the Grand Wizard of Edawn. From time to time, Baddlock came into the kingdom to sell the strange concocted remedies that he claimed could cure any one of anything.

Finally, Izz was able to tear his eyes away. There and then, he was suddenly overcome by an overwhelming urge to avoid the peculiar old man at all cost. He tried to inconspicuously skirt around the crowd trying to steer clear of the disagreeable geezer who seemed so repulsive and somehow so very sinister that it made Izz's skin crawl. He hoped that somehow, someway, he had not drawn the strange, old man's interest. He took a glance toward the weird, rickety man from behind the crowd. The creepy fossil of a man looked disgruntled, seemingly incapable of cracking a smile as if a smile might have fractured his weasel like face. He wore a weird pointy cloth hat on his head from which his long tangled hair cascaded down to the middle of his hunched back. His eyes were hard and cold, hollowed, reddened with deep dark shadows around them. His long, grizzled, unkempt white beard hung loosely down to his sunken chest, which seemed was the perfect tomb for his evil heart. He wore a long black robe that fit loosely over his stooped shoulders and around his thin frame. The pale skin on his skeletal face was crisscrossed with so many lines that he looked like a sun bleached prune. His very pale cheeks had an unhealthy bloodlessness to them. His bottom lip drooped with gloomy discontent, which made him look much like a vulture waiting for something to die. His appearance could have startled a slum rat. So disconcerting was he to look upon that Izz had to cast his eyes down at the street immediately as he tried to get the unsettling expression off his face. Almost at once, he felt a tinge of guilt, for so suddenly passing judgment on someone he did not even know.

But in truth, Izz had a good reason for his ominous apprehension. Little did Izz know that the wizard known as Baddlock would be his most evil of nemesis sooner than Izz could have ever imagined.

However, the fact was that the purported wizard was two faced, with a double identity, and living a double life. He was a master of illusion, a skilled conjurer of cheap ploys and deceptions, who made a habit of deceiving the minds of the trusting with smooth talk and flattery. In reality, he had a short and violent temper, hotheaded, and his heart was as dark as a dungeon. He was ever on the lookout, like a leech, for human prey. He was a master of disguise and had little trouble concealing the deceit in his spirit and the evil that lay invisible in his heart hidden from most people. His scales were even loaded with incorrect weights to wrongfully profit from his transactions with the desperate and fool hearted that believed in his mystical potions.

As much as Izz wanted to bypass this unpleasant fellow, he could not avoid him, because Baddlock's makeshift stand was on the corner that led to his uncle's house. If only he could edge on passed while the old man was busy with a client, he could slip on through without attracting his attention. As he made his move, he came close enough to overhear the charlatan's deceptive sales ploy rolling off his tongue. Izz mistakenly paused to see as the deceiver smiled the kind of smile one puts on for show, as he exchanged a flask of his foul tasting concoction for an absurd amount of coinage. The older woman whose only illness seemed to be old age reached for the bottle with a shaky hand. The wizard spoke words well worth nothing with the soft voice of a snake charmer. "This is going to make you feel so much better, my dear." Sounding very pleased with himself, he concluded callously with a brazen lie. "But if you want the very best." He pulled out a brightly colored bottle of so called miracle tonic, just another prop in the little charade he was performing. "This is what you want if you want to make sure you get the very best value for your hard earned money." The false message he proclaimed was that of care, health, and good fortune, and his smile seemed sincere enough, but his beady eyes were shrewd and as cold as two cubes of black ice. The old cheat remained patient and charming until he had finished their transaction. He could have hustled lamp oil to a snake oil merchant. But as sure as right was from wrong, fraud was written all over his face. Izz knew the woman had wasted her hard earned money to the astute old swindler.

Suddenly, Baddlock reacted with annoyance, and his thin counterfeited expression abruptly collapsed into a grimace of apprehension. As he seemed to realize that he was being watched, the old geezer's head suddenly whipped in Izz's direction. He flashed a hideous expression of contempt and loathing for the young man who dared to look upon him with a calculated gaze. Izz quickly looked away from the eyes that shot their deep barbs. Not wanting to make eye contact with the old man, he pretended not to have seen him as he hurried along. But he could feel Baddlock's eyes searing coldness on him, studying him from head to toe as he passed. A strange kind of fear suddenly filled Izz, and for a moment, he had the strongest urge to run. Out of the corner of his eye, he could see Baddlock's hooded eyes narrow as they bore into him. It was as if an unwelcome stranger had unexpectedly invited himself into his domain, and he could not think of a graceful way to make him leave. Izz stiffened when he heard the sleazy old man beckon him with a gravelly voice.

"Young man!" Baddlock called as he studied the newcomer.

His voice was tinged with a gruff tone that Izz found unsettling, sinister, and even a little threatening. Unnerved, Izz hesitated as his eyes slid in the old man's direction for the briefest of moments. He tried to act as if he had not heard and turned to enter the corridor that led to his escape. Again Baddlock called out, "My fine young man!" This time his tone had a bitter edge to it. "I seek nothing from you but a short moment of your time."

Izz could not keep from responding to the voice that froze him in his tracks. Izz glanced at the disturbing old man and regarded him suspiciously. As he turned, he suddenly saw Baddlock's face metamorphose, shifting one external expression and transforming into another as his face exploded in a wide, tooth stained smile. His grin grew fixed with a welcoming expression, yet a different mask on the same face. The innocent look did not deceive Izz. Behind his smile, more of his mindset was hidden than revealed, where something hatefully dark, diabolical, and mysterious burned.

His jewels sparkled brightly from his skinny neck, concave chest, and spiny arms. There was something extraordinarily strange about this man, something about him that gave Izz the creeps. He looked like an emaciated owl with the heart of a vulture. His old schoolmaster had once said that if one could not discern immediately who his friends and enemies were, then that person was bound to live a very uncertain life. The wizard shook back his stringy white hair that poked out from his skull like head like twisted wire as recognition seemed to light up his face. Suddenly, his inscrutable smile broadened, showing too many teeth without reason. Scratching his bony chin, he abruptly recoiled as he choked down a dry swallow. He stared intently at Izz, seemingly straight into his being as he searched his mind. And just as suddenly, his smile soured, dying on his lips and running away from his face. Then, as if Baddlock had long anticipated, the inevitable day of this meeting, his sunken cheeks at that instant twisted as if he had just finished sucking on a lemon. All of a sudden, clearly intimidated by Izz's very presence, Baddlock wrenched and twisted for an instant. Then bit by bit, hideously, his visage took on the unmistakable countenance of pure evil. His hate filled eyes were unnerving, stabbing. Izz had managed not to tremble under the disturbing, long hard stare from two narrowing slits that seemed to peer into his inner essence. At that moment, the old goat could have terrified a grotesque goblin. It was like dragging a repulsive sack of putrefying death into an unspoiled place.

While Izz's presence seemed to disturb his peace of mind increasingly, Baddlock was somehow abruptly able to conceal his insightful expression to hide the fact that he had perceived Izz's true identity. Trying not to betray any concern, the manipulator of men knew how to seem pleasant. The wizard's talent was an illusion, counting on the gullibility of good and upright souls. Izz, too, quickly wiped his expression to hide his repulsion. Keeping his apprehension to himself, he met Baddlock's gaze squarely and nodded his head with respect in greeting as was his custom. Both allowed the silence between them to stretch as the air in the background echoed with the cries of shoppers and merchants. The clenched jaw and faint scrawl Baddlock periodically flashed made Izz, however, continued to feel ill at ease.

Again, Baddlock spoke, "I see that you are new to the kingdom," fishing for information. Izz offered none. "I bid you welcome, my friend." His gaze was direct and unwavering, but the darkness in his eyes did not reflect the sentiment he expressed. "Please allow me to introduce myself. I am known to all as Baddlock, the Grand Wizard of Edawn," he said as he continued to take a long, icy, scrutinizing look at Izz.

Izz carefully studied the puzzling mask pasted on Baddlock's face as he approached the stand and did not like what he saw. By now, Baddlock was eyeballing Izz as if he was something disgusting he wanted to scrape off the bottom of his boot. Having seen what had happened to the elderly lady, Izz assured himself that he would not be the next one to fall under the wizard's spell. Izz did his best to bear the indignation of having to endure the very presence of this foul human being. Izz's face bore no expression and did not indicate his displeasure. Baddlock's evil grin stretched to reveal even more of his crooked, yellow teeth, baring them up to his swollen gums. His skin was rough and warty as if weatherbeaten by a century of storms. As Izz reached the merchant's stand, Baddlock forced an even wider grin as Izz came closer. But the sorcerer could sense that his disguise did not fool Izz. Baddlock's smile waned slightly as he continued to study Izz.

A shadowy reflection of evil and repugnance gleamed in his red and puffy eyes as his lips twisted with arrogance. For a long time, the two eyed each other without warmth. They stared at one another, neither one ready to be the first to back down. Up close, Izz could see that the so called wizard's eyes were heavy laden with thickly creased eyelids as if shrouding some evil and unsightly thing that lurked within. There was more silence for an extended moment.

Finally, Baddlock's gaze wavered and was the first to look away, saying, "Today is your lucky day. You, my young man, are at the right place at the right time." He spoke as if his wordiness would lower Izz's guard. He then flicked out his oily tongue, licked his dry lips, and asked, "What can I offer you, and what are you willing to trade for it?"

Izz just let him rattle on; the more he allowed him to say, the less he would have to, and the fewer questions he would have to answer. Undoubtedly the most bizarre old man he had ever run across was just a fraud, as bogus as a carnival soothsayer who was simply crafty with the use of words. Izz remembered what his old schoolmaster always used to say: Listen more carefully to what people meant, rather than what they said. Nonetheless, Izz tried to give the alleged wizard the benefit of the doubt. Izz drew closer, even though the feeling of wrongness persisted. He concealed his mistrust as he stood before the unscrupulous con artist.

As the good and the bad stood face to face, a plumpish, hunched back figure stepped out from behind the wizard. While all this time unseen, the little urchin had been brooding over Izz with an unwelcoming curiosity. He was dumb looking, short, locked into a stooped, twisted, misshaped, and knotted malformation that rendered him less than capable fo making it on his own. The side-kick's uneven face with a flattened nose regarded Izz, staring up at him through hoggish eyes set too close together on a lopsided face that was throwing Izz a sour almost poisonous look. It was clear from his vacant expression and an unfocused gaze that there was not too much going on in his upper room—no common or intuitive sense, addled brain, and mentally slow. His roly-poly cheeks were framed by an evil grin that bore a mouth of loose and missing teeth. The odd kind of figure was dressed in black, dirty, tattered rags like those on a scarecrow and looked as if the dwarf should be touring the Zian Empire as a circus sideshow.

He was called Tigbone, Baddlock's longstanding servant, more like a serf than a servant. Unwanted, named worthless, cast aside by those that should have loved him most. Baddlock had taken him in when he was just a child. No one else seemed to be that interested in the abandoned, disfigured orphan, and so the wizard took him under his wing and raised him. He was made to earn his fare, or starve; he was treated with unkindness and with extreme mental abuse and even brutality. The truth was that the disfigured boy would have been better off destitute and alone, for soon after he came under the warlock's care, he was entangled in bondage that was more absolute than being shackled in chains. Tigbone knew little and cared less for the things of the world. He distrusted his own thoughts and would rather do as he was told. Exploring the murky depths beneath reasoning was best left to others.

All in all, Baddlock had his vassal entirely under his thumb, and even though he thought his helper a little better than a half wit, he knew that the simpleton was the only one he could trust completely. Baddlock suddenly held out a hand to Izz in a mocking gesture of false friendship. Izz reached out, and as he shook Baddlock's withered hand, he felt a cold mental chill. He stared at Baddlock as if he had suddenly sprouted a pair of pronged horns; then he drew back his hand abruptly. Again against his better judgment, he cautioned himself not to jump to imagined conclusions.

Baddlock, with a lopsided grin, said, "As you can see, there is nothing I like better than helping those in need." He said as he patted Tigbone on the top of his little pointy head. "You see some heartless no account left this precious, unprotected child alone here in this brutal world to fend for himself. I...took this vulnerable little bird into my heart and home. Why? I live to do good to those less fortunate. And you seem like someone who could benefit from some of my special elixirs of life." Baddlock's eyes narrowed, watching for the slightest sign of weakness.

Izz did not look convinced as he drew himself up and choked back the reply that wanted to leap out of his mind, *You should take some for yourself because you looked like death worn over.* Instead, he asked, "What is in it?" Trying to remain courteous, trying to avoid a negative confrontation.

"You need not concern yourself with such matters. It is a sacred secret handed down to me from the days of old." Baddlock tried to assure Izz with a hint of loathing. The stranger's attitude infuriated Baddlock. The exchange soon ran dry. *How dare this tramp to question my integrity!* He thought, even though Izz had good reason to mistrust him. He was not used to being challenged. Up until almost everyone in the kingdom had been easily drawn under his power and twisted by his will. Tightening his mouth into a thin line, Baddlock fought to keep his voice low, his expression friendly, and his anger under control. He jeered silently behind the smile he kept in place for Izz, which suddenly turned into a harsh laugh as if he had just been told a bad joke.

"I see you are suspicious." Baddlock persisted in trying to gain Izz's confidence. "And you lack the proper trust." Baddlock leaned forward as he spoke, "If only you knew who I was. You would understand the fault of your mistrust. Why I am the most honest person you will ever hope to meet." His warm breath, like stale cheese, escaped into the air as he spoke. Raising his eyebrows in mock innocence, Baddlock argued, "I am offering you a free sample of my finest mystic tonic for whatever may ail you."

For a moment, with questioning eyes, Izz debated with himself whether he ought to take offense as the wizard held out an insistent bony hand offering Izz the small bottle of dark cloudy liquid. "Everything you could ever want is right here waiting for you."

The offer sounded like an insult to his intelligence. Baddlock's face was grinning out at him like a heinous gargoyle;

his black beady eyes were full of dishonesty and hate, reflecting the darkness in his soul. "This will lighten your burdens, not add to them. I swear on my life, this is the truth." His words were soft and as mesmerizing as a hypnotic snake luring in its prey just before striking and devouring it. Izz shot a sidelong glance at Tigbone, who was bobbing his head like a toy doll with a broken spring in its neck.

Izz wrinkled his forehead suspiciously as he could practically hear Baddlock thinking, *Do not make trouble for yourself, share with me the secrets of your dark side.* Izz suddenly grimaced as if he had just tasted a bite full of foul fruit. He then thrust Baddlock a look of mistrust as though he thought Baddlock was not entirely right in the head. And after a long awkward moment, Izz said, "No, thank you. There is nothing that is ailing me." From that point, the conversation soured.

"How dare you turn down such a generous bequest." Baddlock's disappointment was evident as he held up the vial and spoke in a gruff voice. "Do you think I hand the best of my elixirs to every downtrodden soul I meet? Today is...your...lucky day!"

"Give it to your little friend here. He looks like he could use it more than I," Izz spoke in a tone he hoped would indicate the end of the discussion.

"Indeed," Baddlock snickered with bitterness in his voice. He did not seem to appreciate Izz's opinion. He eyed him arrogantly as his expression grew loftier. The two stared at each other across the table at an impasse of wills as Baddlock sought to bring Izz under his yoke to do his bidding or crush him utterly. Time froze as resentment poisoned the air. Izz fixed his gaze. He wanted to look away but could not.

Izz stood his ground, and ultimately, Baddlock shifted a defeated little grin as he seemed to lose his footing. Then he took one stumbling step back as if he was backing away from a blazing fire that had suddenly become too hot. His smile, which now looked like a twisted frown, fell from his face. His eyes shot back and forth quickly as sparking anger showed in his malice filled eyes blazing with rage. Bitter enmity entered his soul and filled it to its depths as bolts of loathing imploded in his heart, and Baddlock despised Izz from that moment. Trembling with rage, overwrought with frustration, the peddler of concoctions angry eyes ignited with the passion of hate so intense that the glare he cast on Izz could have set a fire. The look was pure poison, which seemed to burn into Izz's soul like a red hot poker.

"Your damnation is waiting for you." Izz thought he heard a strange wind whisper. The wizard stiffened, threateningly rigid with anger and snapped. "I am not the fool you have taken me for. If I were you, I would hope that we never meet again," Baddlock concluded.

Baddlock's glare drilled into Izz so intensely that Izz felt that Baddlock had melted a hole right through him. Izz's heart grew stone cold, sending a shiver down his spine as he felt the air around them grow thicker and thicker with tension with every pounding heartbeat.

In a condescending tone, Baddlock at long last hissed and said dismissively through his clenched teeth, "Then go away and may our paths never cross again." Baddlock added for good measure.

Izz took a step backward with the feeling of an uneasy truce, turned, and tore himself away. All of a sudden, he wanted to put as much distance as quickly as he could between him and the most unpleasant man he had ever stumbled across. As Izz turned, he breathed a sigh of relief that the confrontation was at an end, yet he could not help feeling somehow wronged by the chance encounter. As Izz continued to distance himself, he thought, *I must have reminded this unfortunate soul of someone who ruined his childhood, in this life, or perhaps somehow, someway, somewhere in a former life.* He had met Jackals before, hyenas that smiled in your face while cursing you in their hearts. But never, ever, had he met anyone with such a sinister presence about him. He was, without a doubt, no one to trifle with. If he never saw him again, it would be too soon. If Baddlock had had a poisoned throwing knife to hurl at the moment, Izz would have been carrying it in his back as Izz crossed the street. Even from afar off, Izz could feel Baddlock's bulging glare burning a hole in the back of his head. He hurried along as the words he had spoken to him became tracking dogs haunting and snapping at his heels.

Baddlock sniffed in disdain; his thin, wilted lips sagged in a vicious, revengeful scowl. He had used the best tricks he could to achieve the desired results, but Baddlock knew he had failed to sweep Izz into his web of deception. From the moment his hatred first sparked into life, an unyielding yearning to utterly wipe Izz off the face of Zia began to breed, fester, and spread like a malignant virus through his dark soul. Baddlock immediately sought a way to destroy Izz. He mumbled to himself, "Your days are numbered, my new little friend." He looked about to make sure that no one was listening. Then he instructed his assistant, Tigbone, talking out of the side of his mouth, "He does not know it as yet, but he is already a dead man. Tigbone, I want you to follow our new friend. Tell me where he goes, who he talks to, and where he is staying."

Tigbone, who always stood by to do his master's bidding, eager to obey with a dog like loyalty as he listened to Baddlock's every word with great concentration. He was utterly enslaved to his obedience, ready to comply without hesitation or question. As Tigbone sprang to fulfill Baddlock's request, he hobbled around and out from behind the stand, edging around the table as clumsy as a three legged yakox, nearly knocking over everything on the tabletop. "Oh! You imbecile! You are a worthless good for nothing! You are worse than useless," Baddlock snarled, shooting him a murderous glare as he steadied the rattling jars of concocted potions.

"I sorry, sorry, sorry...I too, too, so sorry, my muster." Tigbone winced at Baddlock's tense, icy scorn just as if he had been struck. The chastisement was deserved.

"To be cursed with such a bumbling oaf," Baddlock grumbled to no one in particular as he grimaced in annoyance and rolled his eyes skyward. "You are so dumb that there is nothing to compare. To say you were dumber than a dumbfounded mule would only be insulting the mule. You are worth less than a pinch of salt."

Tigbone trembled at the thought of displeasing his master and stood there with his head bowed to one side, ready to receive his punishment. He squirmed inwardly and turned to slouch away. The commotion drew the attention of some passersby, and the wizard resisted the urge to rush over and give Tigbone a few swift kicks to hasten him along his way. With pure indignation, Baddlock flashed those that had turned away to look a pretentious smile as he lashed out of the corner of his mouth. "Just follow him and report his every move!" Then he waved him away as if he were a bothersome, insignificant mote of dust.

Tigbone scurried off sluggishly, awkwardly, almost like a misfortune waiting to happen, moving, seemingly like someone who had the knack of breaking things merely by being in the same proximity.

For the longest time, it would seem that Izz could not get the bitter aftertaste of his encounter or the image of the old geezer's hate filled eyes out of his head. It was a recollection he wanted to hold over a flame and see it reduced to ashes. The farther Izz moved down the street, the better he felt, and at long last, he began to feel relieved. So why did he still feel as if he had suffered multiple stab wounds to his back? He was amazed that, in this one brief encounter, the strange little old man had made himself someone Izz would from that moment strive to avoid at all cost. Soon the landscape of dreams that was the kingdom of Edawn and its people gradually washed away the memory of the chance meeting to the point that Izz thought at least now that he might be able to forget the whole matter altogether. And Izz was once again lost in the wonders of his new world, without an inkling of the unpleasant encounter.

Then suddenly, Izz came upon the rising line cut into the sky of the tallest and proudest structure that soared above all the others within the walls of Edawn. Nothing could have prepared him for the marvel that came into view like a precious jewel. The bright white walls of this vast building glimmered and shimmered as if buckets of diamonds had been cast upon it. There, in the distance just ahead, at the end of the main avenue that led to the grandest sectors of the kingdom, stood the King's Palace. It was a building that spoke of supremacy and power. The architectural design was a perfect thing of beauty, constructed by the empire's most skilled master architects. It gave Izz a sense of the grandeur and durability in one of man's noblest creation. It was built entirely of the finest white marble, quarried from the local mountains. The shimmering walls seemed to glow in the light of the bright sun, fixed at an angle that captured its rays and reflected them perfectly, especially at this hour of the day. Its entire construction stood on a raised, square foundation, built of massive megalithic stones. The central vault of the palace was crowned with a glass dome that glittered in the sunlight like a multifaceted gem. The central belfry rose to a height where it seemed only eagles dared to fly. The corners of the palace were flanked by seven high towers of lustrous white stone. Each tower rose like a sleek javelin reaching for the sky, whose splendor and massive form took Izz's breath away. At the top of each observation tower, spiral rods of gold adorn each of the seven pinnacles. There flew, majestically, flags bearing the king's crest, and the Ziaian golden eagle emblem snapping in the wind. The exterior of the palace was lined with rolls of crystal windows framed in red, honey colored hardwood. The walls were decorated with designs perfectly integrated and interlocked throughout its entire outside surface, cut deep by the empire's most talented hands.

Precious gems were used to accent the dazzling patterns so exquisitely that Izz had to stop and admire it all for the longest time. Wherever Izz looked, there was something extraordinary and striking to capture his eyes. To the right and left, the King's Palace was flanked by elegant emporiums and great exhibit halls for the refined, offering treasures of art from every kingdom of Zia. The palace was surrounded by fragrant groves and flowing gardens where brilliantly colored peacocks added to the exotic beauty of its surroundings. Singing fountains, never ceasing, warbled and sang out with their flow to fill radiant, reflecting pools that sparkled like a metallic liquid in the bright mid-morning sun. The massive outer walls that surrounded the meticulously groomed gardens were laced with wrought iron gates, the height of five tall men. Thousands of people, conceivably tens of thousands, never feeling more peaceful and safe, filled its well dressed interconnecting boulevards and avenues.

It had been some time before Izz had spotted the strange, drab looking, pudgy urchin following him, almost close enough to spit on. There was something peculiar about his flatfooted, hobbled walk as he wobbled along, muttering under his breath. The fact that he was being followed wherever he went meant that there was no logical or probable explanation except one. The sinister old man was having him spied on. It was almost comical, the way the natural born simpleton stared belligerently then slumped his shoulder and turned away every time Izz looked in his direction as if that was somehow going to hide the way he stood out like a sore thumb. Izz pretended that he had not noticed that he was being followed, then moved along and turned the corner. At the end of the next street, Izz could see the billowing smoke coming from the foundry chimneys. Izz knew that he was close to his uncle's home, and he hurried his pace. Ducking into a crowded street, he easily gave his clumsy shadow the slip.

Now that Izz had put considerable distance between himself and Baddlock, why did he feel like someone was standing over his grave? Izz reached the metalworking sector of the kingdom, where gold, silver, and copper were hammered up into objects of decor and utility. He passed blacksmiths, silversmiths, and coppersmiths fashioning their wares. Finally, Izz was standing in front of his uncle's front door. A knock brought his eldest cousin, Lana, to the door. She was overwhelmed with joy when Izz introduced himself as her cousin.

"Izz, how wonderful it is to meet you finally," she exclaimed excitedly.

Izz announced, "I have come seeking conquest in the land of fortune and fame, to test myself against the finest runners in all Zia."

Izz swirled her around as he said, "And look at you, you are all grown up now!"

The rest of the family came running into the front room, led by his uncle Lott. Next came aunt Azira with little versions of herself settled on her hip and was followed by a brood of another five young daughters. The room quickly filled with excitement. Uncle Lott held Izz's face in his hands and gave him a long, compassionate look. Izz could see that his hair was graying, his aging face was creased with deep laugh lines, and his eyes were filled with kindness. Lott gave his brother's son a robust and manly embrace with arms that were still muscular from hard work. Aunt Azira also gave him a tender hug and a peck on the cheek.

"How good it is to at last meet everyone," Izz said with a slight bow.

Izz had never known such kindness and contentment all under one roof. Every one of his seven younger cousins came pushing forward to be the next to hug him. Amid the excitement, Izz announced, "I have special gifts for everyone." As the older children pressed around him, Izz felt someone tugging at his leg. He looked down to find Dacia, the youngest member of the family wrapped around his leg, looking up with her huge, bright eyes. Dacia was in the third season of her life, the baby of the family, her father's favorite. Izz whisked her up and gave her a big kiss on the cheek. She, in turn, hugged and gave Izz a sticky kiss. With an innocent inquisitiveness in the child's expression, she asked, "What did you bring me?"

On that cue, two of the other youngest girls left their mother's side, their little feet pitter-pattering across the stone floor, to flock around Izz with their eyes beaming. With his free hand, Izz reached into his satchel. His hand probed around in a hidden pocket inside where his fingers found what they were looking for. The three small objects he had bound together with colored ribbon. He pulled, pushed, and twisted the objects up out of the pack. It was three beautifully hand carved dolls.

"She is beautiful!" exclaimed the youngest, who was still nestled in Izz's arms. "I will love her forever." Her face was a picture of delight. Izz pulled out of his bag gifts for everyone. He had made jewelry boxes, inlaid with different colored woods for the older girls. A fine new pipe for his uncle Lott and a flower carved brooch for his aunt, Azira.

As all the excitement wore on, Aunt Azira announced that the evening meal was set on the table. She was a woman who could assure that one would eat, and this time, she had outdone herself. Izz moved to his place by his uncle Lott at the head of a long dining table that glistened from dutiful cleaning. There were chunky loaves of freshly baked black bread, ceramic dishes of stew, and plates of broiled meat with an assortment of pickled vegetables and candied fruits. There was a huge platter of praiseworthy bread pudding, nibbling sweets and cheeses, and even a streaming crock of sweet beats that had been dug from the ground that morning. There was much to be thankful for. Izz sat before his bread trencher and pulled up his chair. They ate while the stone wood stove crackled, and the candlelight radiated in all its richness. Izz ate heartily. The house became cheerful with heartfelt feelings of warmth, making the meal with his family the highlight of Izz's day. It had been a feast to please crowned heads. When Izz could not eat another bite, he thanked his aunt.

"Aunt Azira, you are by far the best cook in all of Zia!"

Azira was the embodiment of a fine wife and mother. Her clothes were always tidy, her house in order, she at all times was well groomed.

After the meal, Izz and his uncle Lott retired to the main living quarters. And as usual, Izz made himself at home as he did everywhere he went, especially now in his uncle's home. And this would be his abode until the games were over. Lott walked to the far end of the room where the granite hearth crackled with a smoldering fire. There was a pleasant smell of wood smoke in the air.

Lott stirred the embers with his poker, then reached into the wood bin and picked up two split pieces of wood and threw them on the dying fire. The flame almost instantly jumped back to life. Heavy with the fatigue of travel, Izz leaned toward the flame to feel the welcoming heat upon his outreached hands. Lott burrowed into his breast pocket and drew out a battered, old hard root pipe from his inter shirt pocket and began to clean its bowl with his small knife.

As Lott continued to clean his pipe, he asked, "Well, my brother's son, are you indeed ready for tomorrow's great athletic exposition? Rizan the Noble will be your greatest competition in the dash race. He is the fastest man in Edawn."

As Izz felt the heat of the growing fire warming his soul, he answered humbly, "I have as much hope as any other man."

"You are your father's son, and you will be a force to be reckoned with," Lott said as he reached for a burning twig from the hearth to light the pipe he had tightly packed with his favorite leaf. The glowing embers in the pipe bowl rose in wisps of smoke. Lott pulled deeply on his pipe and exhaled a lungful of smoke blowing out the flame on the stick and waved his hand to dispense the billowing haze he had unleashed. While he smoked reflectively, lost in recollection, a sad expression shadowed his face. Knowing that his father had always been a painful topic for his uncle, Izz quickly changed the subject to keep the tragic memory from dispiriting the moment.

"I ran into the strangest little man today on my way here." Izz gave a little shudder to shake away the haunting recollection.

There was only one man in the kingdom that could fit that description. "Baddlock," Lott said, making the name sound like a wicked disease. "Yes, I know that devil well." The thought of the so called wizard brought a deepening grimace to his face. He is fabled to have the strange power of invading people's deepest dreams. Thought by all to have supernatural powers, which enabled him to look into the future, evoke marvels, call up potent spells, and heal the infirmities of the sick through the use of his nasty narcotic concoctions. Why even the king holds the graybeard in high regard. "I say hogwash. He is a fake, a conjurer of lies and craftiness. He is unquestionably the most unpleasant man in all of Zia," he added in a weary graveled voice tainted with resentment. "Wizard indeed, falsehood is the root of all his power. He is clever at wheedling and cajoling and has always been unashamed about gaining whatever he has sought by deception and quackery without the need to get dirt under his nails. He never lifted a finger to help anyone, never worked an honest day in his life, and never offered a kind word to anyone. If he possessed anything, it was sure to have been ill gotten spoil. Rumors have floated around that he has sold his soul to the darkness. He is a skilled liar who could tell a lie on top of a lie twisted over another lie with added turns and trickery. If truth be told, he should be known as the Wicked Warlock Wizard!"

"I am sure he is harmless," Izz said with a cautious smile as the firelight reflected in his dark eyes. "But yet, there was something exceptionally odd about him. It was as if he could read my mind, and for a moment, almost controlled me. I am sure that I overreacted."

"Your trusting nature is going to get you in trouble one of these days," Lott said with fatherly admonition. "He is a wolf in sheep's clothing. He is the sort of person who prefers to hide what he does in the dimmest of shadows. Stay out of his way, if you do not want anything bad to come upon you." To emphasize the gravity of his warning, Lott added, "Everything Baddlock does is a deep, dark evil. Most do not see it, but I can see him for what he is." Lott spoke in hushed tones and muzzled words so that his wife and children would not hear. "From as near as I can tell, he derives his dark powers from ancient mystic writings, from a creed long forgotten and outlawed in Zia. Whispered circulations have reached us that the savage Norticlan tribes from beyond the Noragore Rim still practice these forbidden rites. There has even been the talk of human sacrifices. They are things I know nothing about, nor do I care to know." Lott stopped talking long enough to take another long pull on his pipe. He exhaled a snowy shroud of smoke that obscured his face and then drifted up into the air.

"There is a wise old man, an excellent client of mine, whose name is Ammiz the Seer. He is always asking me to make these odd contraptions I know nothing about, nor have any idea of their uses. Some think him crazed, but I know he is a brilliant and honest man. So I do not ask too many questions about these gadgets, and besides, he pays extremely well. As far as I am concerned, his studies in these mysterious areas have caused him to lose touch with the real world. However, he is the only other person I know in all of Zia that can see that weasel Baddlock for what he is."

At that moment, Izz's aunt Azira entered, carrying a tray bearing two tall earthenware flagons of wine.

"My finest wine," Lott boasted as he picked up the drink and thanked his lovely wife with a kiss. Izz did the same, without the kiss.

Lott cleared his throat and continued, "To tomorrow! And may the best man win."

"To tomorrow!" Izz Echoed.

They clinked their jugs together in a toast, and both took big gulps of the fruit of the vine. The sweet berry wine soothed Izz's stomach, if not his brain. As they enjoyed their wine by the warm fire, they sipped from their drinks and smacked their lips. They spoke of plans, dreams, and hopes between laughs and chuckles well into the night.

Three

The Totalitarian Games

The next day at first light, after a hearty breakfast of fruit jams and delicious cream filled bread, Izz was off to register for the Totalitarian Games. It was a brand new day, and Izz felt fully alive. He had trained rigorously, and he was ready for the grueling competition to come. Accompanied by his uncle, Izz reported to the officials' table to register for his events. The scene around him was an exciting festive occasion filled with athletic contestants, dance, and music. Izz had spent his whole life dreaming of this moment, and now it was finally upon him. The crowds were already starting to arrive in droves, swarming in from every corner of Zia, coming to see the biggest event of the year, and to show themselves off in their most elegant attire. By that time in the morning, the whole nation was filled with a reverberating sound and the rising pitch of rumbling voices, all with the same obsession. Regional champions, star athletes from every kingdom were all signing in for their assigned events. There were runners, archers, hand to hand combatants, Catapult Masters and their crews, mock battle lords and their troops, and many, many more.

The Edawnian Totalitarian Games were organized and being run by groups of noble judges. To provide the most magnificent spectacle, the supervisors had selected competitors on the advice of their regional handlers. Above all, the athlete was selected based on endurance, courage, and skill in mock combat. The local judges choose the best of the best from every respective kingdom. Spirituality and intelligence also played a significant role and was considered the most venerated way of becoming a perfect citizen. A competitive instinct was paramount in the character of these young men.

Tom Icon

Last year's winner of the champion of champions award was Rizan, crowned Totalitarian Warrior. He was a middle aged man with a fine looking scare of valor upon his cheek. He had won top honors by overcoming all challengers in seven events: the disc throw, the javelin throw, the dash run, the wrestling competition, the weight lifting competition, the sword competition, and the war games competition. Rizan was expected to return as lord over the games this year, as well. He was the greatest warrior ever. He was born into a prosperous landowning family whose holdings were well known throughout Zia. Rizan was the youngest king in the Xylenian empire, and he was the hero of the people, not to mention Zia's ruling classes. Rizan was a man after King Ozzdon's own heart. He was handsome, strong, and brave. Subsequently, he was handpicked to be betrothed to the king's only daughter, Zuree, the princess of Edawn. But above all, Ozzdon hoped that Rizan would someday be his successor. Zuree had nothing against marriage, but she was not sure she was ready to enter that kind of commitment.

As Izz was signing in for the dash and long run events, he caught sight of the distasteful old man, the one known as Baddlock, whom he had encountered in the marketplace the day before. There was something about him that gave him the creeps. At Baddlock's side was his ever present, cumbersome looking, tangle haired shrew, Tigbone. Boastful and boisterous with his nose up in the air, Baddlock arrogantly approached the sign-in table, stroking the edge of his greasy beard with one hand as was his habit. When he saw that Izz had signed in for the long run, he laughed out loud and looked up and searched Izz out. When he finally spotted him, he said in a loud, giddy voice, "I hope you like the taste of dust." And then he chuckled a dark sound that made Izz's skin crawl. Then the rest of Baddlock's party joined in nodding, heckling, jeering, and finally, they all ripped into raucous, unruly hilarity. Tigbone was bobbing his head in confirmation, hackling harshly through a few teeth short of a wide smile.

The competitor, Baddlock, was signing in just smiled, seemingly lost in thoughts of self importance. He was tall and sinewy, all knees and elbows, without one ounce of fat on him. His long, dark, hollow face was stretched as tight as a drum over his skull. He seemed bundled up with tension and twitched repeatedly. Lott leaned toward Izz and whispered, "The word is that the wizard gives his competitors forbidden, stimulating potions." He squinted one eye as he declared his suspicion.

By midmorning, it seemed to Izz that everyone in Xylenia was in attendance. All were welcome, the lowest commoner to the highest noblemen. Young unmarried maidens were dressed in their most elegant gowns, strolling in front of the muscular athletes, giggling and trying to look pretty. The contestants flaunted their prowess as they displayed their strength and weaponry skills. They flexed their muscles and smiled and elbowed each other as the young women paraded themselves before them. Children ran from cart to cart, searching out their favorite treats. Edawn's hillsides had turned into a kaleidoscope of colored tents, with each kingdom's banner dotting the hills that overlooked the site where the games would be held. More flashy tents along the banks of the river sheltered both athletes, handlers, and other spectators. Anyone could recognize the king's quarters. His tent was gigantic and far more elegant than all the others. It sat atop the tallest hill, the best vantage point in the kingdom. From here, the king, if he chose, could see the entire games, especially the mock War Game maneuvers. The first event was the dash run and was also the oldest competitive event in memory. Already, the overflowing spectators had filled the amphitheater wall to wall to brimming capacity. The overcrowding fans spilled onto the grass covered hillsides.

Emperor-King Ozzdon sat reclined in his shaded imperial podium on his richly ornamented pedestal of honor made of gold, silver, and ivory. Four columns supported a canopy over the royal podium. Each surmounted by a statue of a past glorified champion. Poles were positioned out over the royal family so that the fabric could be rolled out as a shelter to protect against rain or the searing sun. It was the first level of the amphitheater, which was reserved for the most elite Edawnians, including the emperor and his host, nobles, aristocrats, elder seers, visiting dignitaries, and past Totalitarian champions. Naturally, the raised first level provided the best views of the arena. In the midlevel, marble seats covered with cushions were reserved for the non-noble aristocrats. The higher level was reserved for educated Edawnian citizens. These seats were rows of stone blocks. The highest level was reserved for the commoners, consisting of wooden seats, which were set up around the very top wall of the amphitheater. But no matter where one sat, all seats offered an unobstructed view. Altogether, the stadium was designed to accommodate one hundred thousand spectators. This day's capacity was a new record and was estimated at over three hundred thousand participants. There were probably another ten thousand vendors, ground crews, judges, handlers, scribes, and artists, not to mention the competitors themselves. It seemed that the only one in all Zia that was not in attendance was Ammiz the Seer. Ammiz, regarded by many of his peers to be the wisest man alive perhaps ever to live, thought that such a spectacle was a trifle barbaric, an exploit for the thrill seeker, and only encouraged hostility. With or without the seer, it was standing room only.

Scribes readied themselves. They were the key historical figures, the intellect, the analyzer, the thinker who documented the meaningful events that surrounded the most significant community figures of their time. Soon, quells would race across parchments in loops, squiggles, scrawls, and scribbles. The world would know who had won and what they had done this day. Anyone who won top honors earned the passage into immortality.

The competitors for the first run of the day gathered in front of the imperial podium, where they greeted and wished each other well. The race consisted of one single rotation around the track of the arena. From start to finish, the race was seven hundred paces. This race demanded natural speed, fixed focus, power, and incredible form. Izz would go head to head with Rizan, the champion of champions. It was sure to be a clash of titans, a race between the fastest runners from each kingdom. Each runner had worked hard all season, and there were some great competitors in the arena. The outcome of this race would crown the fastest human in Zia. Izz felt confident. He had never been beaten. Competitors stretched and worked their arms and legs, trying to pump blood into their muscles. In the background, a young minstrel played the lute and sung a tribute about Rizan's days of glory.

As Izz warmed up suddenly, triggered by the tension of the race, thoughts filled his head like actors on the stage of his mind. And for a moment, a memory long forgotten flashed in Izz's thoughts. He tried to recall the details of events that had long lain dormant, interred among his remembrances. He remembered how he had trained himself to run as fast as he could. He remembered how the older boys from the orphanage would chase him down to take his sweets. One particular boy, much older than he, who was exceptionally cruel, enjoyed collecting the rigid, sword shaped spines of the local agave plant. This malicious boy found a sadistic pleasure in chasing Izz down while throwing and piercing the spiny shafts into Izz's back. Once struck with several prickly darts, Izz had to force himself to run faster and faster or suffer the pain of these razor sharp arrows. He wiped his eyes with the palms of his hands as if that could erase away the unhappy memory. Letting the last vestiges of the memory fade from his mind, he walked to his designated starting spot.

As he continued to limber up out of nowhere, his gut alert system desperately attempted to get his attention, seeking to make known that something required his immediate attention. He looked all around him, but he could not fathom what was escaping his awareness. Izz tried to focus on the unfolding events of the race that was about to start. Cheers shook the stadium as the runners approached the starting grooves. It was the loudest crowd Izz had ever heard at any completive event. He could barely hear himself think as Rizan, the former champion of champions, stepped forward. Above all else, the nagging within his moral fiber like a barb in his mind was intensifying relentlessly. His spirit man was trying relentlessly to bring something to his attention. What was he missing? Rizan, who was standing ready, turned as he kissed the palm of his hand and flung a symbolic kiss in the direction of the crowd. Out of the corner of his eye, Izz had been sizing Rizan up, when Izz took notice of Rizan's gesture, and his eyes quickly slid across in the direction in which Rizan's imaginary kiss coursed. His kiss had been cast to his beloved enchantress, Zuree, who was seated next to her parents, the king, and queen, waving back jovially. The princess of Edawn reacted nervously and lowered her eyes modestly. She was young and shy and had always kept Rizan at arm's length. All the while, Rizan was feeling confident. *I've never felt better; I am sure to break my old record,* he thought as he continued to limber up.

Izz's eyes rested on the object of Rizan's admiration for a time, and then he started to look away when, suddenly, Izz's head snapped back up and turned as if of its own accord to stare in fascination at the most beautiful woman he had ever seen. His breath caught in his throat. He felt his heart missed a fluttering beat when his eyes beheld Princess Zuree for the first time. What felt like the strike of a thunderbolt had struck him. Its power and intensity could not be denied. The arrow of love had finally found him, penetrating right through his protective body armor, lodging itself deep into his heart. Izz felt as if his chest had split open, and his soul bled out for the whole world to see. At the same time, he felt a joyous sense of distinct recognition. He did not realize it then, but from that same moment, he was irrevocably changed. His eyes widened questioningly, riveted for an instant, and then opened a little wider. Izz's eyes twinkled as pictures of thin ghost remembrance danced through his head, and something from within sparkled in the deepest depths of his soul. He had seen that face before, but where, how? Like a whirlwind, confusion twisted his mind. She was like a heavenly vision to him, dressed in shimmering blue, the ultimate embodiment of perfect human beauty. Her face was like that of an angel. She was a beautiful woman, yes, but what captivated Izz most of all was her piercing blue-green eyes and her genuine internal smile. It was a face Izz unquestionably knew, yet had never seen until this twinkling. He stared at the princess, bearing her in mind for what seemed like the longest frozen flash of his life. Her long golden hair was braided in a circlet that sat like a jeweled crown atop her head. Izz did not consciously realize it at the time, but in the farthest recesses of his mind's murky depths, a small piece of his puzzling, cryptic dream fell into its place. The remembrance he had been searching for rushed to the forefront of his mind. "I know you," he whispered to himself. The girl in his dream was real! From that split moment, Izz was smitten. And just as quickly, he realized the ridiculousness of such a line of thought.

The princess could not help but take heart in the odd stare she was receiving from the strange young runner looking up at her from down below. He was looking at her as if he knew her. At first, Zuree pretended not to notice the dark eyes methodically probing over her. She remained composed, removed, even regal. But then her eyes somehow could not help open fully in his direction as an ember of recognition flickered in her mind as well. At that moment, she could not turn away from the eyes that held her in that pulse of time. Everything in the world around them virtuously seemed to vanish. For a twinkling of an eye, there was only her and only him. In an immeasurable instant, faster than perceptible thought, the trancelike vision blocked out the sights and sounds of the immediate world from their senses. Then out of thin air, like a faraway echo from a parallel universe, the arbitrator in charge of this organized stampede, which was about to begin, called the runners forward. Each runner stepped up to the starting line. While Izz stood there with an astonished smile pasted on his face, lost in a dream within a dream. The starting judge's voice suddenly called out, like a slap to the face. "On your marks...Get ready..."

Izz tore his eyes away, took a deep breath, trying to refocus. A good start was critical; there would be no time to make up for any mistakes in such a short race. From an upright standing upright position, he readied to launch himself forward from the grooved stone starting sill where he dug in his toes. The runners would explode out of their starting places when the arbitrator dropped his arm at a trumpet's blast. Any athlete moving before this was immediately disqualified from that event. The judge's right arm went up and then came down as the trumpet blast sounded. Each contestant heaved and thrust themselves out of their toe grooves. Everyone in the amphitheater lurched at the same instance, somewhat easing the anxious pounding of their hearts. All camaraderie was tossed aside at the sound of the starting signal as runners elbowed for a position. Izz let out his held breath as he shot forward. He was now totally focused. The crowd and its fervor fluctuated relative to the actions of those running on the track. Izz threw his arms forward in a way that propelled him ahead. It was an explosive start, perfectly timed and executed. He was leaning forward so far that, for a moment, he feared he might fall flat on his face. He fixated his focus on driving on until he reached the first turn of the race. He kept his head down as he concentrated on leaning forward to build up speed. Izz gradually allowed his body to come upright as he came out of the first curve. He pumped his arms forcefully, intensifying his increasing pace. He brought his hips and legs back under his body smoothly transitioning himself from a leaning acceleration posture to an upright position as he reaches full stride. At the halfway point, Izz's main focus was on maintaining his maximum speed by staying relaxed and deepening his concentration on his running strategy and technique. Izz found he had surged into the lead. He had put all his heart into the race, and he was winning. The feeling was indescribably amazing. It was the world's greatest race at the highest levels of competition with the fastest runners on the planet. Izz ran to the best of his ability, faster than he had ever run in his whole life. *Soon I can say I am the fastest man in the world!* Izz thought. With legs pounding, he pushed to the finish with his heart pulsing strong and steady. He wanted to look back, but he resisted the temptation. He concentrated on the finish line ahead that was nearing with every stride.

Izz leaned into the final turn as he focused his attention on taking deep, full breaths and blowing out the air forcefully, being careful not to pant or gasp for air. As he came out of the last turn, there in his outskirt vision, he spotted Rizan just outside of his tunnel vision. Then he saw Rizan pulled up alongside, forcing him to run faster. They ran side by side, stride for stride, jostling elbows and shoulders. The roar of the crowd increased in volume exploding in the bowled stadium, its waves ebbing into Izz's ears as if he was on the inside of a bell rumbling up into the heavens. No one was willing to lose between the two of them. Slowly but surely, Rizan made his move and began to pull ahead. Izz's heart sank, feeling a plunge of disappointment as he fought to suppress rising panic. The crowd roared. Resounding cheers came from thousands of voices as they yelled, stomped their feet, and roared with the thunderous sound of Rizan's name.

You need to stay focused on what you are doing, Izz thought to himself. Keep on your toes, relax, so you will not slow down or get tired. Maintain your stride. The finish was coming up fast. Everyone in the eager crowd seemed to scream out until their voices rose as one into an ear splitting roar. Izz allowed his natural speed to flow, keeping his elbows bent and arms straight, he swung them front to back. Izz focused not on the finish line, but beyond it, at a dead run, pouring himself out completely. Rizan was just inches in front of him. The crowd was by now jumping with the excitement of the race of races. Three more long steps and Rizan would be across the finish line. The greatest of many races have been decided at the finish line, and this race would be no different. Izz gave everything he had left, and the crowd's riotous noise vanished entirely from his hearing. Izz dug in and pushed himself faster than ever, and at the very end, he relaxed utterly, letting the momentum of his body carried him across the finish at a blistering speed.

Thinking he had won, Rizan pulled up ever so slightly in that last stride, while Izz held desire above despair. Izz stood up tall, letting his shoulders sag back. With his lungs full, he stuck his chest out and leaned his body forward as far as he could at the end of the line. Even the unruly crowd fell silent for the longest moment. Izz fought to hide his disappointment. Rizan's foot seemed to have crossed the finish line first. But the judges were focused on the men's upper torso. The crowd fell silent as the arbitrators and judges gathered and compared among themselves what they had witnessed. The hush of silence continued to hold the multitude in suspense. Some judges wanted to proclaim Rizan, the winner, but the head judge had to stay true to his oath. The smallest measured blink sometimes decides the difference between winning and losing. The awarding judge approached Izz, and Izz had no idea until that moment that he had won by the skin of his teeth. The decision was final. Eternal truth prevailed. The record had fallen, the champion had been beaten. The head judge stepped forward and placed a golden crown of victory upon the top of Izz's head. The uproar of the masses once again was deafening, oscillating into pandemonium.

As it was Rizan's honor and pleasure, he stepped forward wholeheartedly to congratulate Izz, the new winner. He was a mountain of muscle, the manliest of men: square jawed and straight nosed, with sturdy features and penetrating eyes. He reached out his long haired arm and huge, hairy calloused hand. Strong chinned, Izz clasped Rizan's hand and submitted to what he thought would be a bone crunching handshake. Rizan's grasp felt solid as if he had the strength to tear off the limbs of a man, yet he did not crush down on Izz's offered hand as he easily could have. Izz felt the gentle strength in his presence and decided at that moment that he could get to like this man. He might have been his stanchest challenger, but Izz knew from that instant that he was a good man.

"You had me, you know," Izz whispered as they both threw their arms around each other and staggered into the mob of congratulatory athletes.

"The lean at the finish," Rizan whispered back, as both men strived to regain their breath.

Baddlock, surrounded by dogs of evildoers, watched from a distance and became angry and jealous. He hungered for Izz's demise, murmuring, "You are nothing but an insignificant bug to be squashed underfoot. I will crush you, and you will forever remain broken. I swear on my soul to make your life a living nightmare."

Unaware of the hate filled storm brewing against him, Izz sat in the stands, resting and enjoying the fierce field of competition of events. His eyes were on what was going on in the arena below him. But his mind was lost in thoughts of the devastatingly beautiful princess he had seen in the stands. He could not seem to get her out of his mind. In his heart, he knew something he did not know. He wondered what his dream could have meant. Were they predestined to have met? Were their destinies somehow intertwined? That possibility made him smile. She could not be any older than seventeen summers, which was all right; he was just in his nineteenth sun rotation himself. He smiled at his flight of fancy. He found himself wanting to see her again. He felt as if somehow, his dream could come true. He had dared not mention his vision to anyone as if fate might overhear.

But, of course, he knew in his mind that his feelings had been an illusion like the dream that would always be just that: a figment of his imagination. What would such a woman of royalty possibly see in him? He was just dreaming, and this had been just the kind of damsel who could cause a man to dream, to wish, to grope for hope. And unless he found a vast treasure, he was always going to be a drifting dreamer. But after all, that was the life he wanted for himself. The excitement faded out of Izz's eyes. No matter what, as soon as the Totalitarian Games were over, he would go on his merry way. Izz tossed the fantasy of her away. But it just kept returning again and again up until the appointed time, the banner displaying the bow and arrow emblem was hosted, signaling the first call for the bowmen to assemble for the preliminary elimination competition.

It was impossible to tell when bows were invented, or who created them. In the past, the bow and arrow were considered one of the most devastating weapons of death. But in these times of peace, archery no longer was looked upon as an implement of war and destruction. It was now nothing more than a useful hunting tool, and as an organized sport, it was a true test of precision and accuracy. Izz gathered himself up and headed for the archery range. With several thousand spectators packing the east stadium and overflowing onto the grassy hillside, the bowmen gathered. Izz had learned to enjoy the virtues of archery as a youth while at the orphanage where he grew up. And even though Izz had undergone hours and hours of practice, achieving the muscle memory needed to become an excellent archer in his own right, yet he did not feel worthy enough to go up against the best archers in Zia.

Nonetheless, he wanted to see this event up close. As Izz watched the competitors warm up for the competition, he noticed a group of men huddled at a distance, murmuring among themselves as they glanced his way. Izz might have guessed Baddlock was at the center of the group. Out of the bunch, Tigbone was staring at Izz, and as usual, he was bobbing his pointy head and showing off his missing teeth as he grinned, seemingly knowing something he would never tell.

The first round of competition included more than three hundred archers from the farthest reaches of the empire. The shooting distance was one furlong, which was roughly one hundred paces. Each archer was allowed to shoot three arrows at targets that were made of straw bands folded round to the center and sewed together. Its face was canvassed and marked with ten evenly spaced rings. Each ring was given a value from one to ten. The innermost ring, the size of a grapefruit, was called the King's Ring and was given the highest mark. The circles were colored from the inside out gold, silver, bronze, red, orange, yellow, black, white, blue, and green. After each round, the archers walked toward their targets to retrieve their arrows as judges marked their accumulated points. If that the arrow hit the boundary line of any ring, the higher of the two points were awarded. The score of each archer was the sum of the values of the rings hit by his arrows. All the values scored by each player were immediately recorded on a score sheet by the event scribe. In the case of a tie, the archer closer to the center was declared the winner. Winners of each match moved on to the next round as one by one, the competitors were eliminated. They continued through the quarterfinals and moved into the semifinals until there were only eight finalists, including Dandork, the king's master at arms, who was considered a renowned bowman by many, having won top honors for three years in continuing order.

The talk circulating among the fans was that Zandor, a young, up and coming contender, was the only one that had a shadow of a chance of beating Dandork. He was a tall, endlessly good natured young man who had risen rapidly through the ranks of the hierarchy. He was a man who could take care of himself, who quickly advanced to a position of prominence in the king's service. He was one of two identical twins. Kondor was the younger of the two, born a few moments after Zandor, and because he had been, within a few moments, the firstborn, Zandor had always considered himself Kondor's big brother. The close knit twins were two faces of the same coin. Zandor was the more aggressive of the two and was fiercely competitive.

Reckless, quick tempered, and stubborn were all far above average on the list of Zandor's faults. He concealed no fault and faked no virtues. On the other hand, he was a dedicated soldier, honorable, and loyal to his very soul. There was a powerful masculine strength about him, which added a rugged vigor to his appearance. At present, Zandor felt very fortunate to still be in contention, barely edging out his competitors in the preliminary rounds. To get this far, one needed to be more than a good archer; one required a steady hand, a good eye, and the ability to keep calm. One little flaw and one's arrow went way off from where one intended. The ranking in the opening rounds determined which archers would face off in the final elimination round. Winners of every event moved on to the last round, and the losers moved down to compete in the lesser honor's competition. Zandor held his own, managing to edge out each opponent until he was one of only four contestants left. Zandor was seven points behind his match with only one arrow left to shoot. He stepped up to the line and studied his target.

He breathed in deeply. With his chin lifted with determination, he focused his sights for a few seconds, and as he exhaled, he took aim and released his arrow. The arrow whistled through the air and hit the nine point ring, giving him the victory and the right to face off against Dandork, who had won his round convincingly. The crowd seemed pleased with the display, showing their approval with loud applause. Zandor had been faithfully committed to the same skill that his forefathers had taken onto the battlefield of the Great Wars centuries before.

According to archery rules, the last round would be scored on the same target. Only after the scoring and when each hole was marked would the arrows be removed. The two archers were given a few moments to refresh themselves. Kondor, Zandor's twin, encouraged his brother and wished him luck as he readied himself for the finishing round. Zandor chose the three straightest arrows from his quiver and checked them for balance then checked the feathering of each arrow. Satisfied, he stepped to the shooting line and signaled the judge that he was ready. Most of the excited fans were rooting for Zandor. Zandor placed the first arrow in the well marked nock point of his bowstring. He took his bow securely in his right hand by the handle and let his bent arm rested against his side. Zandor brought his bow into position, hand clenched into a fist. He held his arm straight and aimed with his body. He confidently released the arrow and saw it slice through the air to hit the nine-point mark. The crowd cheered their approval. He was well pleased with that shot, but he knew, to beat Dandork, he would have to do better. He picked another arrow from the quiver hanging at his side, took the second arrow, and with the same technique, he drew back. He closed his eyes. *Calm down,* he thought to himself. He breathed in then breathed out and shot. The arrow arched on its trajectory, and he was surprised to see his arrow hit within the border of the ten-point mark. The crowd roared. One last shot and Zandor would be done. It would have to be his best effort ever if he expected to win. He placed his bow in his left hand and wiped the sweat from his right palm along his pant leg. He lined up the lower end of the bow against the inside of his right foot and brought his left foot forward. Slowly he drew back the bowstring to full draw to the right corner of his lips, feeling the bow's awesome power at his fingertips. His left wrist locked as he braced his arm. *Don't flinch* or freeze *when you release,* he instructed himself. All the spectators seemed to be holding their breath as Zandor held his shot. Zandor felt a jolt vibrate through his powerful arm as he released. Swift went the arrow with deadly accuracy as it produced a clear, shrilling sound through the air. Every eye went to where the arrow hit a perfect bull's—eye. The crowd came to their feet and erupted into a boisterous shout of congratulation.

"How did you do that?" Kondor asked as he ran up to congratulate Zandor.

"Practice, practice, and more practice," replied Zandor. Dandork raised an eyebrow and sneered in contempt as he tauntingly whispered so that Zandor was the only one that could hear, "Is that what you call shooting. I have seen cross eyed
men do better."

Zandor only leaned over to spit on the ground in response. Zandor respected Dandork because of his office, not because of who he was. Dandork approached the shooting line with his bow strung across his chest. He placed his two hands behind his neck, stretched in a backward arch, and then interlocked his hands in front of him, with his palms facing out as he cracked his knuckles. He looked extremely relaxed, perhaps a little too relaxed to be natural. Dandork nocked his arrow and drew his bow back to full draw. He brought his bow down to eye level and aimed. He exhaled, relaxed, and executed his shot. The arrow screamed through the air and struck just outside the ten-point mark. Dandork let out a quick burst of air from his nostrils as if in a gesture of taunting humor. Calmly, he took his next arrow. Knowing that the two next shots would be critical, his face took on a stern, serious look. As he loaded his bow and positioned himself, his body became strangely rigid, yet unusually relaxed. He used three fingers to hold the bowstring with his index finger above the arrow. With one fluid release, the whiz of the shaft was heard. The crowd let out a long collective sigh when the bolt struck an absolute bullseye, splitting Zandor's arrow in two. The crowd was stunned into silence. Slowly they recovered from their astonishment and began to grumble in amazement among one another. Zandor bowed his head and shook it in disbelief. *How could that be possible? H*e questioned himself as he forcefully smothered a curse.

Dandork had one final shot, one last chance to win. He had to hit the center mark. Not only would he win, but he would break his own, current world record. No one seemed to notice when Dandork caught Baddlock's eyes and exchanged a knowing smile. Tigbone stood off to the side, grinning crookedly like an imbecile, as always baring the few teeth he had left. He rubbed his knobby hands together, seemingly chilled, though the day was hot. Dandork took some dirt and rubbed it between his hands. He nocked his third arrow, remained calm and unmoved. He raised his bow and adjusted it down to the target. The crowd gasped in unison. Dandork held his place; the tension thickened as the suspense mounted, and the air crackled with anticipation. He leveled his bow, held it for the longest time, but then lowered it unexpectedly. The crowd groaned their nerves seemingly as taut as the string on Dandork's bow. The suspense was unbearable, and the crowd's rumbling began to rise again but was quickly hushed when Dandork once again raised his bow, took a long deep breath, and aimed for the needle's eye. He exhaled slowly, let go, and sent his arrow in flight, speeding toward its target. Time seemed to hang as the arrow followed its course. Zandor's hopes of winning were blown into eternity as Dandork's arrow hit its mark with a perfect bullseye, splitting his very own arrow in half. In reaction, the crowd seemed to implode and then explode in complete disbelief. And with that, Dandork was raised to the ultimate pedestal of champions as Zandor's eyes rolled in silence.

Four

The Ulitmate Fight

One of the most exciting competitions was fast approaching. Athletes were competing in the disc and lance throw. But everything and everyone came to a standstill as the call for the battle of the Titans was announced. It would be the crowd's favorite event, especially among the men. There was nothing quite like the electrifying excitement that took place in the games when two of the biggest and strongest men in the empire met in the arena. The idea of Rizan, the crowd's favorite, and Pongo, last year's champion, going at it in a fight to the finish certainly brought out its own brand of excitement. Knowing that the encounter could end in sudden tragedy at any instant, it attracted more attention than any other competition in all the games. The hand to hand combat was particularly brutal, and the only rules were that there were no rules. But generally, as a gentleman's decree, biting, eye gouging, and blows to the groan were so frowned upon that no fighter ever used such tactics. The sport was viewed with mixed opinions, among many intellectuals considered as barbaric human cruelty by some. Izz had decided not to attend.

There was a part deep inside of most Edawnians, primeval, and driven that Izz's peaceful counterpart did not understand. Many of the commoners considered it a test of ultimate manhood, a final ritualistic rite of passage for every young male. The king, even though he would not admit it publicly, enjoyed the thrill of a well matched fight. Every year during the Leagues of Council, the banning of this event was voted on, and every year the ban was narrowly defeated. Perhaps the primitive event was preserved only to satisfy the primal urges of humanity, the blood soaked passion and fire that every zealot harbors within their chest. As each fight started and ended, the crowd around the arena became louder and rowdier. There were plenty of action packed battles, but what everyone wanted to see was the greatest fight of all time, Rizan against the reigning champion, Pongo. Rizan was the only man in all of Xylenia brave enough to face Pongo in the arena. The man who challenged Pongo the year before died in the match, brutalized by Pongo. It was the most thorough and vicious beatings ever delivered by one human being on another. Pongo toyed with his defeated adversary like a cat with a mouse, blow after blow, chewing away at his opponent's liquefying face. Then he lifted his semiconscious victim in the air, swung him around three times, building up momentum, and then slammed his body against the hard ground for the sport of it. The spectators were horrified as Pongo took great pleasure in pulverizing his helpless victim. Just before the judges could put an end to the fight, Pongo lifted his adversary off the ground and landed a ruthless head butt that crushed his opponent's face. The blow virtually pushing the bridge of his nose bone into his brain and splitting his skull in two. The unfortunate fighter was dead before he hit the ground. He lay there, to the disgust of all, bleeding out of his eyes, ears, mouth, and nose. So utterly destroyed was the combatant's face that the mortician had to reconstruct his nose back into the center of his face for his burial.

Now Pongo had been mouthing off for several weeks about how he was going to put Rizan down in the opening round. Rizan, however, had little to say to anyone about the upcoming match. Rizan's soft hearted manner disguised a warrior's strength. Rizan did not usually participate in this event, but he had known the man that had died at Pongo's hands. Despite Rizan's kind nature, revenge was seething in the back of his mind. Nonetheless, his main concern had been only in trying to make sure he was the best he could be when he stepped into the amphitheater.

The introduction to the main event finally arrived, and with pulses racing, the two combatants entered the arena. Pongo was from the Northern provinces, a bear of a man, almost as wide as he was tall and immensely muscular. He was massive, the biggest man Rizan had ever met, and there was not one ounce of fat on him. His skin was so stretched tight that he looked as if he might split open at any time. He looked like he could charge right through a solid stone wall without breaking his stride. As Pongo flexed and stretched his toned and rigid muscles, they glistened with sweat in the noonday sun. Rizan was as tall, not quite as widespread, but strong enough to go up against a bear. He was not as muscular as Pongo, but in the arena, it was more about stealth, agility, and speed rather than forceful strength. The multitude went wild as the two giants moved to the center of the ring, looking like two ancient gladiators about to do battle. Rizan was clearly the crowd favorite. Pongo only received jeers and scoffs from the spectators. The only ones cheering for Pongo were Baddlock and his sinister looking group of associates. Even Tigbone could feel the high intensity in the air as he laughed and drooled in anticipation.

The two giants faced each other. Rizan stood out like a finely hewed corner pillar of a mighty fortress. Pongo stood tall and imposing. His broad chest powerfully muscled with impressive chiseled features. There would be only one way to fight this battle—toe to toe. After a few pleasantries, the two men squared off and waited for the blast of the brass trumpet. The sound of the first trumpet came, and pound for pound, the two best fighters in the world of Zia faced off. Zuree's heart was gasping and skipping beats, thinking that Rizan had taken leave of his senses as Rizan stepped forward, ready to come out fighting. Zuree had adamantly objected to no avail. And she wondered why anyone as intelligent as Rizan would subject themselves to such brutality. Pongo circled Rizan, weaving back and forth like a one man army while Rizan only slowly rotated like a mountain of massively muscled flesh. Pongo was fighting for the prize and the glory. Rizan was in it for his fans, his family, and his king, but especially for his beloved princess. In the first tense moments of the fight, both fighters moved in. Pongo tried to provoke Rizan, "Let us see how I can break that pretty face of yours."

Toe to toe, both fighters cautiously jabbed at each other, finding their range, looking for the fight ending opportunity. Each man's hands were wrapped around with leather straps not to protect the combatants, but only to prevent them from breaking their hands. Pongo suddenly reached out, wrapping his powerful fingers around Rizan's wrist, but Rizan shook off the grip almost with ease. After a quick exchange to open the first bout, Pongo landed more hits, but Rizan's strikes were harder and quickly reddened Pongo's face. Pongo went for the takedown and was met by a pulverizing right fist that sent him backing away. "You must do better than that," Pongo taunted as he spits out a drivel of blood.

In the next exchange, both men pummeled each other, landing blows to the head that would have incapacitated a yakox. The two seemed to be evenly matched, each able to absorb or fend off each other's hard hitting thrusts. The pace quickened, with Rizan a little more under controlled in his movements. However, Pongo held an early edge behind his bone crushing leg kicks as the first round came to an end. But the match was far from over. The end would come only when either combatant seceded or could not continue. The first round had consisted mostly of Rizan pursuing Pongo around the ring. Both men had delivered devastating strikes, but Rizan had taken several severe kicks to his midsection. The leg kicks had had little immediate impact. It would not be until later that Rizan would feel the damage inflicted on his body. Rizan had connected a few kicks mostly thrown to keep Pongo on the defensive and off balance.

Between rounds, the on site healers examined the fighters, focusing on the face and hands where most fractures occurred. They did not want a repeat of the previous year's disaster. Two healers worked at a feverish pace on several bleeding cuts on Rizan's face. Several welts began to swell. Rizan's trainers doused him with a bucket of cold water and toweled him off. The knot in the pit of Zuree's stomach tightened. It was not an easy thing for her to watch, and she was not sure how much more she could stand to see. She wished with all her heart that it could all be over so that she could question Rizan's sanity for having put himself in such a dangerous predicament.

The second trumpet sounded, and the next round was underway. The big men faced off slowly, but suddenly, the bout turned into a fast and furious encounter, and both fighters looked even more energized than they had been in the first round. Each competitor connected one flurry of commanding shots after another. The pair continued to exchange punches, with Rizan the more accurate of the two, landing a hard left fist against Pongo's jaw in the swap. A cheer came from thousands of voices as the crowd came to its feet, rising with the bloodlust and excitement of a mob that demanded revenge on Pongo. Blood gushed down over his mouth and chin, but Pongo fired back with a kick to Rizan's ribs, causing him to double over briefly. Zuree put the back of her hand to her mouth as she sucked a short gasp. She could see the sweat beading and glistening off Rizan's back as his powerful muscles twisted and bulged with every assault he launched and countered. The second round came to an end as the condition of the fight was growing uglier by the moment, and if it kept intensifying, something heartrending was sure to happen. One and the other fighter showed signs of exhaustion and pain, but no signs of letting up. And its ugliness was sure to keep building in the next rounds.

Rizan and Pongo went straight at it from the first sound of the third trumpet. The eye contact was intense. The bout quickly escalated in ferocity with both men taking turns landing severe strikes on the other. Each man trying equally to prove that he deserved to be called the greatest champion of Zia. Blood splattered in all directions, but neither combatant stopped throwing one venomous punch after another. After a series of unanswered blows, a wild, murderous rounded right found its mark on Pongo's jaw. His face rattled as the strike sent a shockwave through his skull. Seemingly un-phased, Pongo hurled a counter shot that struck Rizan with a numbing impact to the temple with a skull crunching force. Rizan possessed the physical fortitude beyond ordinary men, and thus, swift, powerful, and cunning Rizan struck back, smashing

Pongo with a devastating hard right to the face. Blood from his nose spattered the ground, and the crowd went wild. Even though Rizan almost shattered his right hand from delivering the shot, Pongo somehow was barely shaken by the wicked bell ringer. The blow that would have killed a lesser man only seemed to infuriate Pongo. With a bloody fist of death, Rizan followed up with a thunderous right to the heart and a crushing left to the temple, and Pongo staggered back. Rizan stepped forward with catlike grace and kept up the assault, drawing blood from several gashes in Pongo's face. He was hitting Pongo almost at will, practically knocking Pongo out. Then out of nowhere, Rizan unleashed a blinding right to Pongo's left cheekbone, and speckles of bloody spittle flew from his mouth. Rizan immediately followed up with a crippling uppercut that snapped Pongo's head violently back and sent Pongo reeling and bleeding on his way down to the ground for the first time. Pongo must have momentarily blacked out. He stayed down on his back for a long moment, with his eyes rolling around like two peas at the bottom of an empty gourd.

Right there and then, Rizan could have ended the contest with a barrage of well placed kicks to the head, but instead, he crossed his arms and waited to see if Pongo would get up. The crowd exploded to their feet and screamed, urging Rizan to end it. But Rizan only stood there waiting until unbelievably Pongo came to and scrambled to his feet, lunging at Rizan, hoping to catch him with a succession of wild swings. In desperation, Pongo clung to Rizan and tried to gouge Rizan's eyes, which brought a hiss of disapproval from the spectators. Pongo broke away, and Rizan went wild, chasing him around the arena. Sensing that the round was nearing its end, Pongo went on the offensive, throwing a combination of kicks and blows, but not connecting much. The third round ended, and Pongo stumbled to his corner, almost falling before he reached his stool. He slumped into his corner. While the healers struggled to stop the bleeding gash on the brow of Pongo's left eye, Baddlock stepped in as if to encourage his fighter. He secretly slipped Pongo a liquid filled wax ball, which he popped in his mouth while he pretended to wipe the blood from his nose. Then Baddlock returned to his shady group now joined by Dandork. They all looked very aristocratic and haughtily confident as they exchanged arrogant, knowing smiles. Tigbone displayed his acknowledgment with an almost imperceptible raising of an eyebrow and bobbing of his head as he rubbed his grubby hands together. Suddenly, the dark countenance in Pongo's eyes sparked, coming to life with renewed alertness.

As far as Rizan was concerned, the blast from the fourth trumpet came much sooner than he wanted or expected. No sooner did Rizan stand when Pongo was all over him with punches and kicks seemingly coming from everywhere. Pongo rushed at Rizan with one single intention, to batter him into the ground. A sizzling right hook landed, and then a crunching left uppercut, thrown with all the brute force in Pongo's body, followed by a crushing left-right combination to the jaw. Rizan's knees buckled! Then Pongo wrapped his hands behind Rizan's head and brought it down hard, smashing it against his upraised knee. Rizan was visibly hurt as Pongo, without letting up, continued to pound Rizan with body shots. Rizan's eyes began to swell shut from Pongo's quick handed straight punching and combinations. Pongo seized the advantage as Rizan fought desperately to stay on his feet. Pongo grabbed Rizan from either side of the skull and delivered an incapacitating head butt to the face that left Rizan's hands trembling wildly. Zuree's stomach did a flip, and she turned away, unable to look any longer.

The crowd's eyes were wide with astonishment as a hush of alarm swept through them. Pongo mercilessly moved in to finish the wounded challenger. He unleashed such a terrible beating to the body that left Rizan freakishly twitching and bleeding profusely from the nose and mouth. When Rizan appeared to be broken down and maimed, Pongo intensified his onslaught, cruelly toying with Rizan. Rizan staggered back and crumbled awkwardly, dropping flat on his back. Sensing a kill, Pongo pounced over the fallen champion with a cruel predatory follow up. The mind boggling assault was inhumane and would have undoubtedly killed three ordinary men put together. From his mounted position, looking for the finish, Pongo grabbed Rizan by the hair ready to loosen the beast from within. And just before he released every ounce of strength, he had left in his right arm mercifully the bout came to an end. Knowing that he would be disqualified if he did not stop immediately, Pongo slammed Rizan's head against the ground. The questionable move brought staunch warnings from the judges and loud, prolonged jeers and condemnation from the crowd. Pongo had to be pulled away from Rizan's mauled body. Rizan remained motionless. Zuree winched in reaction, letting out a gasp and had to be restrained when she tried to go to him. What business did he have foolishly thinking he could stand toe to toe with a monster like Pongo?

Everyone, including Pongo, thought it to be the end. But somehow, after what seemed like a breathless eternity, Rizan managed to reach deep into the well of his profound will to pull through. He rose drawing to the surface a fixed resolution of purpose and determination, daring the imagination of everyone and nearly defying reality. Somehow enduring, as if willing to fight to the death, Rizan, the lionhearted challenger, tottered, swayed, and reeled himself to his feet. Rizan took a few steps toward his corner, almost falling and had to be dragged to his bench. Rizan had come as close as he had ever to death. Blood was spewing from his mouth and nose, but he refused to allow his trainers to stop the fight. The adrenaline that surged through Rizan's body limited the agony that would have disabled any other man. The king thought of stopping the match, but knowing that sometimes this event got very violent, and out of respect for Rizan, against his better judgment, he allowed it to continue.

The trumpet signaled the start of what would be sure to be the last and final round. Both men stepped to the center of the ring. One or possibly both of these titans could breathe their last breath before this match was settled. With the fight in his grasp, Pongo came out hastily picking up where he had left off, seemingly possessing the physical endurance of a raging bull. Pongo came on with a two fisted body attack, capitalizing with some dangerous strikes that drove Rizan back. Rizan absorbed the damage as he tried to clear his head. He was seriously hurt, but yet his mental and physical faculties, which, when tested to their limits, proved able to deal with the threat that reached far out of the ordinary laws of limitations. His speed of foot, his agility, and his reach advantage allowed him to come back repeatedly with a series of counter blows like the true champion he was. The two giants moved around the arena as agitated as two hornets in a jar. The momentum of the fight was relentless, neither warrior held anything back, absolutely pouring themselves empty, giving everything in their hearts, utterly. It was a vicious toe to toe war, not one or the other man backing down. It was a monumental clash in the skills of hitting and not being hit, giving and taking. Looking like two men twisted into one, each fighter trading momentum shifts with knees, elbows, and wits, both struggling in a savage battle of attrition. The winner of the most brutal and fiercest conquest ever witnessed would prove himself as the greatest, undisputed, living legend of all time. His name would become immortal, to live on the lips of every man forevermore. This challenge would be remembered for all time and celebrated as the greatest contest of backbone and guts ever recorded in the history of Edawn, Xylenia, or Zia. The entire crowd was on its feet and roaring, screaming themselves into an electrifying frenzy at the spellbinding, awe inspiring spectacle unfolding before them. It was a fight like no other, the most thrilling, awesome, breathtaking centrifugation of action ever. Zuree had both hands over her face, fearing that something tragic was about to happen, unable or not daring to look. She tried to turn her attention away from the arena. Her nerves were not about to let her stand much more, but somehow, she could not bear to tear herself away. No matter what the outcome, the promise of glory and fame gained would never in her mind be worth the price.

Rizan, almost desperate, bobbed and weaved, sidestepping and blocking his opponent, who was putting everything he had into every deadly punch. Rizan lumbered out with a shrewd, controlled move, bobbing in and out. He drove with a staggering right and then a left pummeling Pongo's face to a bloody pulp. Pongo's followup barrage came up empty as Rizan used his quickness to thwart Pongo at every turn. Pongo's efforts to deal with Rizan's attack met with failure. The tide was decisively turning as Rizan regained the initiative. In frustration, Pongo lunged forward, firing a reckless, wild catapult like right at close range. But just in the nick of time, Rizan used his quick hands and feet to deflect a blow that, if landed, would have ended in disaster for Rizan. The narrowly missed knockout punch left Pongo off balance and exposed. With the crowd roaring, Rizan countered with fast and accurate strikes, making Pongo pay for his mistake. Then there came an incantation, over and over the crowd chanted, "Rizan, Rizan, Rizan!"

Encouraged Rizan, hastily dropped his upper body down as he took a powerful step forward. He twisted, and darted up at the last possible moment, and nailed Pongo with a tremendous left hook that would have brought down the front gate of a fortress. Pongo's legs seemingly disorderly dangled like that of a jerking puppet waddling on strings at the hands of a drunken puppeteer. But not even this seemed to deter Pongo from his crazed effort to win. Not hesitating this time, Rizan narrowed his eyes combatively and quickly followed up with a tremendous fisted shot to the liver that instantly dropped Pongo to his knees. Pongo was stunned. His battered carcass swayed back and forth like a big tree in the wind. He steadied his head long enough for Rizan to rip a running, searing, hip level, a fistful of fury. Rizan's fist made a whistling sound as it wedged through the air. As the mighty right hand landed solidly, Pongo's face exploded, whipping around, spilling out a splashing arc of blood across the arena. Pongo made a last ditch effort to counter his backward motion, only to fall forward flat on his slaughtered face, collapsed, sprawled, and unconsciously twitching horrifically on the ground from the onslaught. Rizan's hand speed had proven too much for Pongo to handle. Everyone, including the king, was on their feet, clapping and thundering prolonged, deafening screams of acclamation. The noise from the crowd made

Zuree's heart pound, but at least now she could finally relax and smile a little.

Pongo's inability to continue fighting brought an end to the brutality. The high and mighty Rizan battered black and blue raised his massive bloodied fists in triumph, and shook them in the air. He had once again proven to be the greatest, and the entire arena went wild for the longest time in jubilation for their returning Totalitarian Champion. As Pongo was dragged away, he came to and dug in his heels in; he kicked and screamed, "No! You cannot defeat me! No man can defeat me!" Pongo struggled and fought so much that extra trainers had to hold him down.

Zuree tried to pretend she was enjoying the celebration of the brutal victory Rizan had just narrowly won.

In the distance, Izz had found a secluded spot overlooking the field where the Catapult Games would be held. He heard the loud, long triumphant sound that came from the amphitheater, and he knew that Rizan must have won. Izz took the meal his aunt Azira had packed for him. He ate his banquet of round cakes sweetened with dates and sipped sweet pomegranate juice as he watched the cumbersome tripod catapults maneuvered into their strategic positions. Catapult masters and their crews on both sides prepared for their part in the war games. Teams of catapult handlers awaited the command to load and prime their well oiled weapons. These catapults were mounted on turntables, which made their casting arm easy to swivel and could be aimed in any direction. They were specially designed to launch a quarter ton projectile up to one thousand paces or one zetta. Target balls were piled alongside each catapult. The large balls were made of big sea sponges with large wooden globes sewn into them. Each wooden ball encased dense lead centers. These target balls were then painted with bright pigments to mark wherever they hit. The lighter than stone sponge balls could easily be launched over six zettas. It was all more a matter of amusement than anything else. In a mock battle, opponents were not permitted to hurl actual stones at each other, to

Baddlock's frustration. No one was supposed to get hurt, however, winning defiantly mattered, and there was always the element of danger. Catapult masters anxiously waited for the opening trumpets while they checked and rechecked their designated targets. Two opposing cavalries stood ready, backed by their foot soldiers. The game combatants were provided with helmets, breastplates, suits of armor and weapons, ancient spears, swords, and axes from the royal armory. Even the horses were armored. The king's staff had been more than willing to polish every bit of armor for their warriors. As a result, they glistened in the bright sun with white radiance, which scattered their illumination everywhere.

Flag bearers proudly held their blue colored banners in the cooling breeze. At the front of the king's army atop his warhorse sat Zandor dressed in chainmail that fit like a second skin under his armor. Rizan, King Ozzdon's top general, was unable to take part due to the severe beating he had endured. After the fight as the adrenaline and excitement wore off, exhaustion and pain took hold. There was not one single muscle in Rizan's whole body that did not ache. Zandor was called forward. He was someone that could carry out commands, was swift to improvise, and able to organize large groups of men. And so Zandor, who was next in line, took his place as the Blue team's commander. Zandor appointed his twin brother, Kondor, as his second in command. Both men were young and inexperienced, but the king had full confidence in both. Even though there had not been a war in a thousand years, the war games were a tradition handed down from generation to generation. The mock battles were used for training, planning, and testing military operations, but mostly for entertainment, education, and simulation. The mechanics of the war games were developed from careful study of actual ancient military maneuvers and battles.

On the opposite side of the field, flag bearers proudly held their yellow colored banners. Baddlock and his top general, Dandork, a formidable war strategist, made final preparations for the upcoming mock battle. Many men are clever at making things with their hands. Some are talented in the ability to compose beautiful music. Others have a knack for mathematical equations. Dandork had a special gift for military maneuvers. It was in his blood. Dandork made sure their targets were correctly ranged. Baddlock was going over their multifaceted troop maneuvers, studying his board game maps. His full concentration was directed toward solving the enigma of moving all the pieces to the right place at the right time. The preliminary trumpets sounded. Both sides ordered their crews and troops into their pre-attack positions.

The attack trumpet blasted! Connecting pulleys creaked as they drew catapults into their final firing positions. Armies on both sides suddenly sprang into spectacular action. Waves of riders and foot troops charged forward all at once. The would-be combatants wielded their swords and lances shelved in wooden scabbards wrapped in a cloth dipped in paint to mark strikes against their opponents. Judges dotted the field to declare direct hits and what would be considered mortal wounds. Catapult crews fired their test shots that arced through the air, whistling overhead on their way to their destinations. Judges watched sponge balls hits and estimated their impact damage and the simulated casualties they inflicted. Mock kills and incapacitating injuries were scored per the amount of blue or yellow paint splattered on the opponent. A direct strike on the opposition's headquarters scored a defeat for that opposing competitor. The first barrage of sponge ball hits sloshed paint everywhere as they bounced all over the rocky terrain. The objective was clear for each command post, delivering replicated destruction from a distance, across the lines of battle, toward the heart of the opposites command center. Front line observers for each team sent runners back to their catapult masters to report the accuracy of their volleys. Catapults were reloaded and spun on their axis, ponderously swiveling into new calibrations in reference to their runners' reports. Baddlock was hoping for a quick win by concentrating three of his best catapult teams on Zandor's headquarters. They walked in their shots toward their target with every new recalibration, adding range and accuracy with every volley.

The two charging mounted and ground troops came together with a sudden and tremendous clash. First, the horsemen, then the foot soldiers, while field judges scored the startling mock kills. Sword drilling resulted in other massive simulated casualties. As warriors were declared kills, they were directed off the field of battle. Those with minimal paint splatters remained and fought on. A sudden, smashing yellow target ball landed next to Blue's command tent, splashing yellow paint on its outer wall. Yellow's judges were quick to claim a direct score on Blue's headquarters. Blue's judges insisted that Yellow's aim had been off and had not caused substantial damage. The head field judge was quick to conclude that the shot had not scored a victory. And the war games continued without skipping a beat. As Zandor directed his field troops by way of a complex series of flag signals, he dispatched seemingly aimless maneuvers to craft confusion. He used decoy attacks and fake retreats to lure Baddlock into his snare. The target of his strategies was not the army he faced, but the mind that controlled it. Zandor flanked his forces, trading space for time, hoping to bait Baddlock into a rash attack up the middle, which would leave his troops in a weakened position.

Greedy for conquest, Baddlock ordered his main forces up the middle as Zandor had hoped. This maneuver was risky because it left Zandor's troops exposed to the onslaught of the paint soaked target balls. As soon as his main forces were out of the line of fire with speed and suddenness, Zandor concentrated his catapults on the oncoming Yellow attack. The massive loss of players angered Baddlock for having made such an irrational and most costly error. While Yellow stiffened their resistance to the catapult attack, Zandor ordered his flanking forces to turn and assail Yellow from their exposed, unguarded sides. By doing this, they denied Baddlock a target since splashed yellow paint even on Yellow troops meant Yellow loses. At the height of the confrontation, when the complete effort of brawn and brains were at the fullness of battle, Zandor called his finest warriors and gathered them in a tight circle.

"Now is the time to strike when they least expect it." He kneeled in the center of his inner circle of men and with a long twig, he scratched out a diagram as he spoke, "We will circle wide under cover of the groves, and attack Baddlock's command post from their rear."

Zandor's twin brother, Kondor, spoke up, "Baddlock's camp is sure to be heavily guarded with sentries and outposts that are sure to spot us."

"That is to be expected, but I am counting on them being preoccupied with their seemingly unopposed frontal attack. And the last thing Baddlock and Dandork will expect is an assault so far behind their lines."

"I like the way that sounds," Kondor responded. "But you do realize that if your plan does not work, we will be risking a humiliating loss."

"I am willing to take that risk," Zandor said confidently. *Now, if only our reserves and catapults can hold Yellow's troops at bay long enough for us to complete our mission,* he thought to himself.

Kondor smiled as he looked down, shaking his head. His twin was rarely cautious about anything, often jumping into the heat of the fire and then worrying about the flames as they dance around him.

Zandor had preselected his elite force for their ability to move swiftly, conceal themselves, and strike quickly without forewarning under any condition. They were the king's best scouts, disciplined to be phantoms with the ability to melt into their surroundings. The detachment stripped down to the bare essentials for combat. They mounted the fastest horses in the kingdom and spurred their beasts forward, heeling them into a gallop toward the North, bolting through the kingdom's groves, and unseen around the countryside. Meanwhile, Baddlock turned to Dandork and commanded, "Prepare our main forces for an all out assault."

Dandork had an uneasy feeling come over him. He turned and questioned, "Why would Zandor expose his front lines like that?"

Irritated by the interruption, Baddlock snapped, "He is young and stupid. This bungling move is his big chance to lose. So let us accommodate him and ask silly questions later."

Shutting out all thoughts except for the objective before them, the phantom riders circled wide around Yellow's camp Riding on quick legged beasts seasoned for the hunt, and trained for silence They approached a roundabout their target. While Baddlock was busy sacrificing his mainline attack unit to Blue's catapults in an all out effort to get to the Blue's command center, Zandor's horsemen were encompassing Baddlock's headquarters. The elite riders slipped along the grove in silence concealed in the shadows. As they reached their target, Zandor lifted a hand to signal a halt. The riders dismounted in silence and left their horses behind. They advanced on foot without stirring a leaf. There was no sound except for the buzz of insects as the elite guards rubbed mud over their faces and wound leafy vines around themselves for camouflage. After rubbing the scent of potent wild herbs over themselves, as not to alert their Baddlock's dogs, they quietly advanced toward the sound of catapults firing in the distance. They moved with such secrecy that not even the birds detected their presence. Zandor was the first to slither to the top of the ridge and then signaled the others to follow. Crouched, they moved, like mighty hunting cats soundlessly pressing in on their prey. Reaching the top, Zandor looked over the camp and measured the situation. Zandor signaled his men to spread out. He pointed and motioned for the outside men to peel off and circle the outer rim of the enemy's camp. From there, their advance was unhurried. Zandor halted his men when he thought he had been spotted. They fattened themselves to the ground relaxing every muscle, seemingly merging with the ground cover. Again, they moved in liquid motion so smooth they seemed to melt in with the terrain like a ripple less tide seeping overland. Every man moved into place and waited for Zandor's signal.

Zandor sensed that the eyes of all their adversaries were glued on their expected victory on the battlefield. He gave the signal to move in. Seemingly coming out of nowhere, the phantoms leaped from their secret hiding places right under their adversary's noses and struck without warning. Those that did not surrender were tagged with paint. Zandor approached Baddlock, who was unarmed and marked a big blue X on his breastplate as Baddlock could only stare belligerently in disbelief. Zandor tapped his chest armor and said, "Strategy does not win wars." The heart does." Powerless to retaliate, Dandork submitted reluctantly. Rivals shook hands with each other, and the defeated congratulated the winners, but Baddlock only seethed with anger. A great cry went up from the judges declaring Blue the victors, and with that, the mock battle was over.

Several races had been run, but Izz would not run again until the last event of the Totalitarian Games. It would be the longest race of the games, the bronze man's run. This foot race was the distance of thirty zettas; each zetta equaled one thousand paces. Only the hardiest of runners could endure this grueling contest. Only a Bronze Man runner could understand the obsession of running in this race. The first call went out to the runners. Participants stretched and limbered their leg muscles, readying themselves for the torturous competition to come. Baddlock reached out to Tigbone with an open palm. Tigbone only stared blankly at Baddlock's boney claw as if he had had a temporary lapse of memory. Then it came to him, "Oh yes, yes, yes!" But before he could react, he was struck by the hand he did not see coming.

Tigbone whimpered and bowed his head submissively as he handed a small vial to the Wicked Warlock Wizard. "Stop that whimpering, you spineless wimp!" Baddlock barked as he snatched the vial out of Tigbone's trembling outstretched hand. "As incompetent as you are, you are worse than useless." Then he dismissed his whining servant with an annoyed wave of his hand.

Artax, Baddlock's long distance runner, swallowed a little laugh as he took the small vial mixture of the warlock's enhancing concoction. Artax grimaced and coughed violently at the taste of the narcotic that would give him the extra energy and endurance he would need. "Bear in mind that you are to win at any cost," Baddlock instructed. "I am tired of being played for a fool. Someone will be waiting at the midway mark with another vial to make sure your victory."

Izz's plan was pure and simple—to win. *I cannot hold anything back. I will be racing the best runners in Xylenia, but most importantly, I will be racing against myself,* he thought.

The runners were called to their marks, and without delay, the trumpet blasted, and well limbered runners charged out, scrambling for position. Izz moved full speed ahead. The momentum was intense, carrying him into its wake like a runaway herd of horses. Right from the start, a group of strong looking runners took a very decisive lead. Then shortly afterward, they outdistanced the rest of the runners, leading by at least three hundred paces with Artax ahead of the pack. Upon seeing the early speed of these runners, Izz began to question his chances. He controlled his emotions and did not allow himself to get carried away. *I must run my race;* he reminded himself. *I must stick to my plan.* His strategy was to conserve enough energy to finish strong. The starting pace was grueling, and before he had wanted to, Izz found himself running at full capacity. There was no way he could keep up this tempo. A quarter into the race, the leaders were at least a half zetta ahead of him, and Artax was nowhere to be seen. *Are these men for real? How can they do that? Can they keep up this pace for thirty zettas?* Izz asked himself repeatedly. Just over a quarter along the way, he saw one of the front runners drop out in disgrace. He passed another one huffing and puffing, yet Baddlock's runner was still nowhere in sight. Izz could not afford to panic. *I have to stick to my pace and trust that I will somehow catch up in the next few zettas.* Izz gradually increased his rhythm sooner than he had anticipated and pulled away from one front runner after the other. Keeping up this pace became his strategy over the next several grueling zettas. By now, Izz was almost at his full capacity, which was much too early in the race.

As Izz approached the halfway mark, he saw his nemesis, Artax, in the distance and knew he was gaining on him. As Artax reached the halfway marker, Izz saw someone hand Artax something which he quickly drank. Water bearers were allowed to give runners water along the way, but that was no water bearer. Suddenly, Artax staggered, stumbled, and almost doubled over. Baddlock had tripled the potency as an added assurance. Moments later, Artax stood back upright and darted like a spooked gazelle. He shot ahead with a fresh explosion of speed, his spiny arms and legs pumping, his accelerated stride gobbling up the distance. Izz could not believe his astounded eyes.

By this time, Izz's legs were starting to hurt. It was a dull, burning ache that seemed to intensify with every muscle extension and contraction. Izz had been running faster than he had wanted, faster than he ever had for any second quarter of any race, and he still had over halfway to go! There was a steep hill ahead and more hills coming up. He began to outpace more runners on the uphills. Izz's mind started to question him, *what are you trying to do, kill us?* Most of his energy was now being spent just trying to talk himself into going on. By the time Izz reached the third quarter marker, he just wanted nothing more than to step off to the side of the course, walk to the shore, and sail back home with his tail tucked between his legs. Izz fought to change his train of thought, knowing that the minute a runner loses the fighting virtues of courage, then that is the same moment he has lost the right to compete among the best runners of Zia. He managed to control his thoughts somehow and quickened his stride, and getting over the next few hills became his only motive. Finally, Izz caught his second wind. His fatigue seemed to fade, and his lungs stopped burning. His heart kicked into a steady rhythm, and his spirit soared with a renewed sense of intestinal fortitude. He ran and ran, settling into a cadence, chewing up the horizon with his long strides as his long, black hair streamed in the wind behind him.

Over the next hill, Izz was met with a half glimpse of Artax going over the next hill. Feeling a surge of excitement, Izz broke into an even faster pace, voraciously consuming the span between them. At long last, Izz saw that his challenger was within striking distance. But the battle was only half won. By now, there was no amount of enthusiasm that could compensate for his loss of breath and the prolonged exertion that was taking its toll. Nor would any amount of willpower drive away the pain developing in his legs. Izz put his head down and kept grinding through the nagging ache in his side. Once again, his lungs began to burn with pangs of misery as he struggled to catch his breath with sharply indrawn hissing sounds. *I am almost there, he thought to himself. I can do it, just one more quarter to go.* By this time, Izz was running on sheer instinct. He had come too far to give up now. He forced his rubbery legs to pick up the pace a little. He planned to stay within striking distance, edging his way closer and closer. His legs felt like gelatin, and he had no idea how he was still picking up his feet and putting one in front of the other. Every man has a particular threshold of pain, a different snapping point, and Izz was closer to that point than at any other time in his life.

Every muscle in his body was screaming, but he just continued to pump his arms and lift his knees and push himself forward. The next thing Izz realized was that Artax was just ahead of him. And not before long, Izz pulled up alongside Artax and was shoulder to shoulder with him. Artax then tried desperately to pull away from Izz as they neared the stadium where the finish awaited the victor. Izz started to fall back a bit, but he knew that there was only one more zetta to run, and then this nightmare would be all over. Izz crested forward and was once again elbow to elbow with Artax, trying to read his relentless adversary's strategy, his condition, his breathing. As they entered the amphitheater, the grand entrance was lined with anxious people cheering and urging Izz on. Izz was confident that now was the time to break his opponent.

Both entered the first turn, bumping and nudging, each trying to cut into the inside of the oval arena first. *One more corner, and it will be all over!* Izz told himself over and over, grasping at the least bit of self encouragement he had left. They each exchanged the lead several times, testing one another with brief surges as they raced toward the finish line. Every time Izz pulled in front, Artax would then speed ahead with bestial energy and endurance. Even when Izz thought there was no way he could go on, time and time again, he dug in deeper, managing somehow to keep up stride for stride at Artax's side through the last turn.

On the straightaway, the finish line was in sight. *Sprint! Sprint now!* Izz urged himself as they entered the final stretch. Dashing at full speed, Izz moved on instinct, allowing his body to take over as his muscles seemed to shift into some primordial survival mode. His breath, or lack of it, was choking him, and sweat was pouring into his eyes. His heart was pounding so fast that he thought that at any moment it would mushroom out of his chest. His legs were on fire and wailing out at him to stop, but there was no way he could stop, not now! The crowd's screams were louder than they had ever been during any other race. But Izz was concentrating so hard that the crowd noise became but a distant echo.

Like a hallucination, all of a sudden, the memory of his boyhood tormentor flashed in his mind. He felt like he was reliving a nightmare of being chased by the dart wielding maniac. The pain in his legs, arms, and back became the darts he once felt penetrating his flesh. A chorus of agony wracked mind and body. In his dazed state, he could not move, except in reality; he was moving faster and faster than might be humanly possible at that stage of the race. Izz poured out all his insides, heart and soul, into his last minute thrust for the finish line. He pushed himself up to the edge of his limits and then attempted to go beyond that. But after pushing himself too hard, too early for too long, he found himself an empty and depleted shell, without anything left to give. He felt his heart implode as he saw Artax pull away. His arms and legs felt as if they were made of lead. He could no longer hear the boisterous crowd urging him on as its sound vanished entirely from his audible range. The dream of winning the greatest endurance race on Zia faded along with the feeling in his limbs. Izz had overextended his heart rate and felt faint, his mind coming in and out of a dizzy spin. His hands went numb as he struggled and staggered to finish.

Just ahead, Artax was steps away from victory. Baddlock started clapping his hands and virtually on the edge of dancing, when unexpectedly, to everyone's surprise, his runner clutched at his chest. Suddenly, a strange expression of anguish shrouded his face as an odd look of puzzlement glazed his eyes. As Artax stretched his trembling left hand forward with his last ounce of drug induced willpower, he collapsed. He fell forward on his face, just inches from the finish line, his hand still clawing the dirt. He hopelessly tried to pull himself forward with his long nails reaching for the line that marked the finish. Izz, barely able to breathe, staggered over the finish line just one step ahead. Stumbling over his own two feet, he tripped, fell over, and landed with a grunt, crumbling in a heap of heat exhaustion. The crowd gasped as it came to its feet and raised its voices to glorify Izz, among them, was Princess Zuree. Artax's outstretched hand looked very much like that of an emaciated skeleton's hand. Baddlock's champion, overcome by the narcotic induced exertion, just lay there, motionless like a rag doll that had been wadded up and discarded. While Izz lay face down, blowing small plumes of dust, sucking in air like a fish out of water, physicians rushed to the aid of both men. The crowd fell into stunned silence. Artax was turned face up, an expression of twisted torment was screwed on his blueish face. The attending healer put his ear to his chest. After a while, the physician stood and solemnly shook his head. Artax was dead. The purple spot on his chest indicated that his heart had exploded from overexertion. Tigbone stood over Artax with his thick lips frozen into a rounded O of surprise. Then Tigbone called to the wizard, "Muster, he be dead?"

Baddlock shot Tigbone two poison tipped barbs with his eyes then turned away. His frown was grim yet seemingly impervious to Artax's condition. And as he walked away, he mumbled, "I can always depend on you to point out the obvious, you pinheaded little moron." His voice came out sounding uninterested, void of any empathy.

Izz was raised to his feet after regaining his strength and crowned for the second time that day. In the jubilant commotion that followed, women threw up their handkerchiefs, and the men flung their head covers into the air. Zuree was clutching her hands to her pounding breast, appalled at the tragedy that had befallen Artax, but at the same time, relieved that the young runner was well. She turned to her mother, the queen, and said to her own surprise, "What an extraordinary young man."

"Truly, he is," Queen Zahra replied.

Suddenly, without any apparent reason, Zuree turned her eyes back to the oddly intriguing young man. Then all at once, she felt a cold knot tighten in the pit of her stomach. A cold chill coursed through her veins, stirring her blood and unsteadying her nerves. An enigmatic tinge of emotion, a peculiar mixture of bonding, remembrance, and premonition made her heart stand still, like the calm before the storm.

Five

The Inheritance

That evening after dinner, his uncle Lott called Izz to sit with him by the fire. Izz watched yellow sparks dance over the fire as Lot spoke.

"My fine young nephew," he said as he lit his brand new pipe. "Izz, you have brought your family great honor this day, and we are all exceptionally proud of you, my son. You have achieved the right to enjoy what glory you have earned." Lott exhaled a snowy puff of smoke and continued, "You are well on your way to becoming an extraordinary young man with all of your life ahead of you." Lott took the pipe out of his mouth and cut through to the heart of the matter on his mind." Life, for me, has tapered off to a comfortable crawl. I am an old dog who has had its day. I wish nothing more now than to spend the rest of my days as an old dog resting in the shade. Carpentry has been an honorable trade for me and one that I am proud to have chosen. It has kept bread on my table. My father, your grandfather, spent his whole life working with wood, and his father before him, and his father before. It is in our blood. Your father himself was the most excellent carpenter of his time in the Southern Territory." A glazed look flashed briefly over his eyes as his last words left his lips. Izz respectfully listened as he raised his wine filled silver goblet to his lips. "And it is my greatest wish that my sons continue in my footsteps after me, but since I have no sons..." With pipe smoke whirling around him, Lott resumed, "The thing is...life is full of unexpected opportunities that vie for our time and energies, and sometimes fate requires of us to make rigid choices."

Izz wondered to himself where his uncle was going with all of this as he watched him draw deeply on his pipe, letting the smoke seep from his mouth while it twisted lazily upward.

"I am afraid the years have caught up with me, and I wish to pass on the virtues of my hard work to the next generation. We are all remembered by the legacy that we leave behind to our children." Lott paused to relight his pipe, drew a mouthful of smoke, and blew it out slowly. "The fact is, I have done well for myself, and I wish to retire now. As you know, I have been blessed with seven beautiful daughters, but no sons. You are the closest thing I have for a son. Therefore, I wish to leave to you my shop."

Izz was stunned by the offer. Still, he said nothing. Lott knew he had to offer Izz an inheritance for his brother's sake. Honor demanded it. But the truth was that Lott had long harbored a nagging tinge of guilt for not having taken Izz in when his parents had died at such a young age, but at the time, he was barely starting out in life. And with a growing family to feed, he had convinced himself for good reason that Izz would be better off under the supervision of the orphanage in Zollerzon. Yet, that had not kept him from often wondering over the questions that stayed with him: what could he have done, what should he have done, that would have made a difference all those years ago? But now, the opportunity to lie to rest the vexing inquisition of his conscience had finally presented itself. Only in this way could he finally be a real father figure to his brother's only son. A serene expression came over Izz's face. Trying to keep the weariness out of his voice, Izz responded tonelessly.

"Uncle Lott, you are far too kind, but—" Izz started to say when Lott stopped him with a raised hand.

"Do not make your decision now...sleep on it tonight before you call your final decision, and in the morning, you can give me your answer. Get a good night's sleep, for tomorrow I will show you where my new home can be found," Lott concluded as he set down his emptied goblet.

That night, Izz lay awake, staring up at the ceiling, picturing images of what the beautiful young princess had looked like, of all things. Her attributes flickered through his thoughts in an endless succession. He could still feel the warmth in her eyes, and the radiance of seemingly beautiful thoughts shining out of her face like brilliant sunbeams. But why was he thinking of her in this way, arousing illusory feelings of adoration? Such immortal admiration was clearly beyond the realm of realism. It would be his secret, secret. Izz struggled to focus on something else, wishing the memory that haunted him would fade, but the wish to forget only fixed the memory of her more intensely. But to what purpose? Such thoughts would only lead to trouble at best and destruction at worst and would be better left forgotten. Throughout that night, Izz tossed and turned, wrestling with questions that as yet would have to remain unanswered.

The next morning, they left early by cart, drawn by his uncle's faithful donkey. "What an absolutely glorious day!" Uncle Lott declared as they started towards the countryside.

They spoke of things they had in common, as they rode along on the cobble overlaid avenue that led them toward the northern gate of Edawn. As they passed the foundries, the cart's wheels clicked over the cobblestones to the rhythm of the steadily clopping hoofs and the creaking old leather straps and jingling buckles. Izz was glad his uncle had not pressed him on what he had decided about his offer because he had pretty much made up his mind. He had already determined the path of his life. He had decided long before that a free spirit needed space, a wide range, and a continuous change of scenery. Can a nonconformist be tempted to linger in one place? Why should he make himself a slave to a life of wood and sawdust? He saw more clearly every day that he was meant to live free, to tread on the sea to places he had never been before. Adventure was the center of his life, to live everywhere, and nowhere was his creed. He was in the heyday of his youth, with his best days before him. He was hungry to discover the entire world of Zia. He could not settle for a lesser, trivial life. They passed through the northern gates of splendor, staffed with gate guards, and flanked by two powerful towers that were stationed with ceremonious tower watches. The gate guard on his uncle's side called out to Lott as they passed, "My wife loves the new table you made for us, Master Lott!"

Uncle Lott gave him an acknowledging nod and said, "Give her my best."

Beyond the gates of Edawn lay an early morning mist that covered the immense Wazoo Valley before them. It was one of those flawless midsummer days that arise more often in memory than in life. All along the way, a jumble of little farms, cottages, and shacks stretched to the horizon in every direction. Izz took his time to observe and enjoy the scenery. It was a beautiful day, and the scent of spring was in the air. A warm breeze blew leaves across the roadside as they moved steadily northward. The vast countryside unfolded into an expansion of fertile lands as far as the eye could see to the North, east, and west. The flagstone road they were on was a well traveled route used by camel caravans and heavy laden wagons, bringing goods from around the northern empire to trade in Edawn's many stores and shops. Izz absorbed the tapestry of life, watching all its scenery go by as it wound out on the wayside. The two lane road stretched and unwound through the valley overflowing with the radiant colors of the sunny season.

A two wheeled cart loaded to the hilt went passed them, making squeaking sounds as it was drawn by two lumbering yakoxen. A chain twisted around their jaws was used to steer them along. Lott guided the donkey with a snap of the reins as the two yakoxen drawn wagons rattled, and harness chains jingled and clattered to the slow surge of the Yakoxen's trudging cloven hoofs, plodding along with the rhythm and resolve of two giant tortoises. Once the wagon steadily moved down the road, Uncle Lot flicked on the reins urging his donkey on. Yet the beast of burden hobbled along with the constancy of a swinging pendulum, going neither faster nor slower. A delivery wagon drawn by four mules, carrying large wooden casks and sacks filled with grain, stirred and churned up the dust as they passed them on the road. A flock of goats scurried past them, filling the air with the clanging of bells, leaving their thick, pungent scent hanging in the air. Lott brought out his new pipe from his shirt pocket and lit it. His puffs of smoke filled the air with its sweet, stimulating aroma.

As the day wore on, they rode past magnificent gardens waving green in the sunlight, embracing the promise of a bountiful harvest of cabbage, peas, and melons where hardworking cultivators hunted for weeds among what promised to be a bountiful yield. Fields of golden corn rippled across in wide curving swells. They passed vineyards with heavy vines filled with bright grapes hanging ripe with delicious nectar and orchards that grew fruits of every shape and color. The air was crystal clear and only intensified the beauty of the lands around Edawn. In the outer fields they passed, villagers were gathering wild honey, apples, peaches, and figs. Warm, easygoing people exchanged pleasant, hardy greetings as they met along their way. They were every bit a part of the land as the land was a part of them. Neatly kept farmhouses dotted the landscape. Izz watched milkmaids vigorously emptying her cows, young farm girls bore crocks of milk, and diligent hands churned butter in hand cranked butter churns in the middle of their long, busy day.

A group of young women gathered wild blackberries, ripe and juicy, with purple stained fingers. One young maiden settled the weight of a full woven basket against her hip as she prepared to carry it to the waiting wagon. Cheerful children herded a flock of geese along the road. To the left, a young woman was making her family's daily bread, pounding grain in a stone mortar with her heavy pestle. She smiled up at Izz as they passed, making Izz's feeling of welcome all the merrier. *I could get to like this place*, he thought to himself. Then his thoughts turned to Zophie, the café server, and he smiled to himself. He considered himself somewhat of an expert on the subject of women's hearts, and the look in Zophie's eye's told him that if he so wished, it would not be long before he could be romancing her. His thoughts inevitably turned to the memory that called out to him. He remembered the face with the polished alabaster complexion. The face that he could not get out of his mind since his eyes first gazed upon it. It truly began to shake his mind up. He had his place in life by birth, and she had her noble station. He tore his soul from the thoughts of her as he had done so many times before. He made himself see how far he had wandered from what was real and what was unreal. He had been born a commoner, a part of the unwashed masses, and nothing was ever going to change that—ever. Izz grimaced at the uncharitable thought. He forced himself to block any thought of her and tried to focus on the ocean of white blossoms that sprang up in vast clusters to decorate the entire hillside. Izz had been quiet for the longest moment, just watching the farmlands as they rolled on by.

Beyond the meadows lay the rolling hills, blanketed with blue-green grass, shrubs, jeweled with blossoms, and honeybees. Flowers of every color crowned the rim of the green valley, and their fragrance filled the air. The road meandered northward on the right banks of the mighty Megacon River that flowed southward from the extended upper valley, filled to the top of its banks by countless high mountain streams. Man made canals brought in fresh cool water from faraway artesian springs that continuously fed the thirsty farms, orchards, and public reserves that supplied water to every citizen in the kingdom. The approaching rolling hills were spotted with great flocks of sheep, goats, and herds of a type of cattle known as the yakoxen, ancient icons of the Noragore plains, a powerful bull like creature with massive beautiful horns. The first impression one gets of them is their size and alertness. Often there are many scars on them, wounds from battles with other rival yakox bulls, or mauled by marauding wolves.

Beyond the fertile farmlands in the meadows, they met hunters armed with bows, slings, and spears who were hunting after wild boar, deer, hares, and game birds. The realm of Edawn was indeed a place of splendor beyond anyone's imagination. It was, in truth, the most magnificent kingdom of its time, perhaps of all times.

The mountain rim that surrounded the hillside towered their craggy, jagged snowcapped peaks majestically skyward like massive sentinels. Beyond that, in the towering, silent world of mountains lay the unnamed, unexplored Northern Noragore Range, the territory of the notorious Norticlan tribes. They were a fierce people that had broken away from the world of Zia in the ancient times of the Great War.

At long last, they reached a fork in the road. With a tug on the reins, Lott diverted the donkey off the main roadway and onto a smaller, less traveled, dusty, weed cracked, rutted road that had more faults than road surface. The cart collected another layer of dust as Lott negotiated the uneven dirt trail. They traveled eastward with the picturesque Noragore Mountains climbing steeply to their left, followed by a trail of dust. The narrowing dirt road became a smaller bumpy path that led to the outer borders of the eastern Ebony Forest. There around the bend on the path that looked like what could have been a turnaround or dead end, nestled peacefully in an open green meadow, surrounded by wildflowers, a white stone house came into view.

"There is my new home," proclaimed Uncle Lott proudly as he brought the donkey to a stop. The cottage stood, with vegetables and herbs hanging on its walls, at the outer edge of the forest looking across the valley. It was a peaceful, conspicuously quiescent location well north of the kingdom of Edawn. A squatty, unmortared stone wall encompassed the well manicured yard, pruned fruit trees crowned with their ripe crop, and meandering hens that pecked and scratched about.

"It's a wonderful place, Uncle Lott," Izz exclaimed.

With a snap of the reins, Lott turned the donkey again to the East, down a narrowing, twisting trail on a steadily worsening path that led toward the forest. Approaching the outskirts of the clearing lay the fringes of the savage wilderness known as the Ebony Forest. Its vast boundaries swept across the great Wazoo Valley from the Great Noragore Rim to the vast southern sea. A cluster of millions of poppies gave the grassy savanna a radiant coppery shimmer along an ever constricting trail that had become an obscure pebbled track as it seemed to have last been used by the first founders of Edawn. From a distance, Izz could see over the canopy of the forest a group of hovering treetops that towered majestically over all the other trees. Astonished, Izz asked his uncle, "What is that?" As he pointed to the grove of trees, he saw perforating the skyline above the forest's roof.

"That, my son, is the Ring of Giants, the biggest, tallest, and oldest trees in Zia."

"That is unbelievable! Can we go there? I would like to see them up close," Izz exclaimed while rising to his feet, almost falling off the recoiling cart.

His uncle steadied him then pulled him back down into a sitting position as he warned, "The path that we will travel is well known, and it is not safe to leave it for any reason. To go any deeper would be extremely dangerous. Legend has it that beyond the point where we go is a cursed place, where people disappear, never to return to tell their tale, never to be heard of again. I have heard personal accounts of disappearances. One particular incident happened on an ordinary late afternoon like any other. The children of the folks I know vanished without a trace. No one saw or heard a thing. In the last year in Edawn alone, there have been several citizens reported missing within the radius where we venture. The kingdom has launched investigations and searches, but up to the present, they have been unsuccessful in solving the mystery behind these disappearances."

Izz had heard old sailors tell tales of such things before. Repeated variations told and retold. Not believing, Izz refuted, "My dear Uncle Lott, are you asking me to believe in evil spooks, legendary myths, and misconceptions!" Izz thought out loud without thinking, and even though he meant not to say anything more, the words just kept tumbling out by themselves. "Only fables told to children to keep them from misbehaving. Nothing more than fragments of superstitious nonsense that have been repeated often enough that they have put down roots in the minds of those that gather to hear any terrible tale. My dear Uncle Lott, if there is anything I have learned in life, it is that we must separate the facts from the fantasy."

Uncle Lott gave Izz a disgruntled look and asked, "How do you define real?"

Izz could see that Lott had a grave expression pasted on his face as he cautiously answered, "Well...if you can see it, touch it, feel it, smell it, and taste it...it is real."

"There are always some who do not believe. Have you seen the wind? One cannot see the force that keeps all things bound to Zia, but it is foolish to think it does not exist." Lott's serious expression eased. "I was as skeptical as you when I first heard of these accounts long ago from my father. I, too thought, they were nothing more than scary stories, folklore, myths told to timid individuals to frighten them. But I have seen things with my own eyes that have given me many sleepless nights. Once, while gathering wood for a special table, I ventured too far into the forbidden zone. While there, I saw standing before me an abnormality of nature. I saw what looked like a half man and half demon wolf beast."

Izz wanted to laugh out loud, but his uncle's strange expression lodged his laughter in his throat. Izz gave his uncle a skeptical sideward glance. There was no reason for him to believe that his uncle's departure from reality was anything more than some rare natural phenomenon he had witnessed. Finally, he spoke, "So what? Now am I supposed to believe that perhaps the ground will suddenly open up and swallow us up, or should I also believe the legions of the undead?"

Uncle Lott shook his head, and solemnly said, "All I am saying is that you should avoid the forbidden zone of the unseen world at all cost."

At that point, they neared the edge of the Ebony Forest. Its borderline stretched boundlessly from horizon to horizon, of which Izz could not see its end. As they entered the heavily wooded world, Lott said, "Be about your wits at all times, these woods are enchanted, filled with dreams and mysteries."

"Illusions can do us no harm. They are only visions from the past kept alive by fears of the unknown," Izz reasoned.

"It's much more than that. Bewildering tales have been told about this place. And at the core of every tall tale, there must be a kernel of truth. The place we are about to enter is rarely visited. It is considered by many to border the center of ghostly activities where evil spirits enter the world to tempt humans into folly."

As they continued into the forest, great groves of evergreens stood like guardians at attention on every side. Along the ground, wild quail were turning over leaves and scratching the earth in search of insects. From a high branch, an owl stared down at them, blinking its eyes against the bright sunlight as it followed the intruders, turning its head in almost a complete circle.

The drone of insects in the trees resounded throughout the forest. The croaking of frogs could be heard above the dull, continuous whisper of the wind and buzz of insects. Out of the blue, suddenly A startled flock of blackbirds exploded out of nowhere into the air, leaving even Izz a bit shaken. The track they were on or was it a footmark, caused the old cart to jolt and shake with every unfamiliar bump, lump, and hump. Strange woodland creatures peeped out of their hiding place to see what was coming. The hidden track obscured by overgrowth and grooved with ruts seemed to wander directionless as it led them into the depths of the forest. The forest's canopied ceiling glinted bleakly as whirlpools of dim light filtered through leaves in all the shades of gloom. It was as strangely awesome as it was awesomely strange. The path wound around trees, tree trunks, and under downcast branches. A vicious looking weasel with something between its teeth scurries away back to its den, and then came back out with some mangled baby animal between its teeth, to see Izz and his uncle pass by on their bouncing little cart. Uncle Lott's donkey nervously rotated her eyes and ears, continually searching the forest for hidden dangers. Izz could see through openings in the forest canopy in the distance, soaring above the tree line, the group of trees taller than any trees he had ever seen. And in the center of the giants was a single tree that was a giant among giants. Uncle Lott abruptly pulled on the reins and ordered the donkey to come to a halt.

"We must walk from here," he told Izz. From the back of the cart, Lott produced a longbow and an arrow filled quiver. "In recent months, strange occurrences have doubled, and the reports of multiple sightings have become more consistent. I am convinced that this is a place of spooky things, ill omens, spirits, and demons," Lott said as he slung the quiver and bow across his chest. "Besides that, we might run across a bear or a pack of wolves, or better yet something for the pot."

"Spirits and demons," Izz whispered to himself as he rolled his eyes skyward and thought, *Hellions conceived by unlearned peasantry touched with madness.*

Before long, they were on a trodden track that was kept in existence only by the deer and elk of the forest. They walked along the obscure trail across a crystal clear stream that had cascaded its way down trickling from snowcapped mountaintops, until they had reached the clearing where Uncle Lott had been gathering select wood for his shop. The unique wood came from a fallen giant that had long ago crystallized. It was the finest of all woods for making furniture. When they came to the center of the clearing, his uncle Lott said, "This is as far as we will go."

From this point, Izz could now clearly see through the opening the clearing of the Ring of Giants. He was utterly captivated by their existence. He could hear his uncle saying something above the far off chatter of forest animals and pretended to be listening. With outstretched arms, acting as if he was standing in the middle of a treasure trove, Lott announced, "This is the finest wood in all of Edawn! This special wood is the secret to making the most beautiful furniture in Xylenia. Nowhere else in the world can wood of this quality be found. I have managed somehow to keep it secret for all these years, and now it is all yours."

When Lott noticed that Izz seemed entranced, oblivious to anything he was saying, he walked up to him and followed his gaze to discern the object of his fixation. He pointed to the trees with a wagging finger and said, "Those trees are the oldest living thing in the forest, perhaps in the world."

Izz turned to his uncle with pleading eyes. "Uncle, we must go and see them up close."

"NO!" Uncle Lott snapped. "It is much, much...too dangerous. See that dead oak?"

Izz's gaze shifted to the old oak tree that appeared to have never had the power of life in it. "See the strange marking on it? That is a warning written in the ancient script. Men that have ventured beyond that point have disappeared, never to be seen again."

As Lott spoke his ominous revelation, a light breeze rustled the foliage away from the direction of the ancient oak. The dead tree's branches rattled in the wind as if they were sensing the present or the past, and seemingly whispering a dark story among themselves. From somewhere beyond the treetops, a soft, fluttering throb reached their ears, the beating of a feathery like clatter that grew steadily louder and closer. All at once, Uncle Lott grasped Izz by the collar and threw both himself and Izz into the bushes at the edge of the clearing. As Lott pushed Izz's head down, he pulled his bow from around his chest and drew three arrows from his quiver. As he lay on his back, he nocked an arrow in his bowstring and took the other two with his teeth. Lott slowly raised his head, his eyes scanning the treetops. Izz tried to raise his head, and Lott only shoved it back down the more and cautioned, "Shhhhhhh!" as he raised one finger to his lips then spread every finger out slowly as if to halt every sound. There came a distinct flapping of wings; something airborne was descending upon them, approaching fast— very—fast. The two listened intently as the flapping sound came even closer and became even louder. The winged creature circled once and then sailed toward them. Moments later, Izz heard a rapid flapping wave of feathers, a heavy setting down with a crunch, then a clatter of large claws landing firmly nearby. For a moment, there was a heavy rustling and crackling of branches and then silence. The birds stopped singing, the forest animals stopped chattering, and all wildlife took refuge, hiding among the greenery of the forest in their secret places. Even the insects seemed to stop droning.

After a few moments, Lott eased his grip on Izz's head. Izz slowly raised his head. He peered up with his eyes stuck to the roof of his skull. Lott returned a single finger to his lips, signaling silence, and then slowly pointed to the skyline of the tree canopy. Izz's jaw dropped. What met his eye filled him with awestruck amazement. It was a giant White Crested Eagle bigger than life, bigger than any fairytale dragon, perched, clinging with hoary talons on the tallest outcropping of a large, sagging oak branch. Izz, as a young deckhand, had heard the exciting stories of their existence, but never had he seen one in real life. The older sailors told stories of the supernatural, powerful wizards, and strange flying beasts, but Izz had always thought them to be fables made up by men that had been out to sea for too long till now.

The eagle was beautiful. There was a bright, white sheen of hackle feathers on the top and back of its head as white as the silver lining on a cloud in full sun. This cap, apart from its size, distinguished the eagle as a White-Crested giant. There was also white at the base of its tail. Its bill was black with a yellow cere, and its massive talons were also black contrasted by its bright yellow feet. The nationally recognized bird's image was used on the empire's crest and many company logos. Suddenly, the eagle ruffled its feathers then unfettered its impressive wings, displaying their massive span in all their glory. Its enormous wingspan at least the width of seven tall men blocked out the light. The colossal bird cocked its head extending from its massive form and scanned the clearing with its keen eyes as the sun glistened off its white feathers. Its eyes appeared to flash an ominous warning, reinforced by the fierceness of its beak and talons, to tread carefully when intruding on the territory it overshadowed. Out of the blue, Izz seemed to hear its imposing thoughts in his head as if the mighty eagle was speaking to him, *I see you there. But you look too stringy to taste good, so I will not bother with you. Perhaps another day.*

The feathers on its neck ruffled audibly, and then with a horrible bloodcurdling screech that echoed throughout the forest, it suddenly thrust its wings out and billowed upward. Lott clutched at his bow and tightened his fingers tighter on his nocked arrow as he clenched down on the arrows between his teeth. The eagle suddenly slapped its wings, creating great swishing whirls that stirred the forest floor and showered Izz and Lott with oak leaves, small twigs, and acorns. As the eagle launched off its perch with its thick talons ready to pierce, it shot itself straight up into the air. Its wings were a blurred canopy, big enough to fill the sky, just above them. The majestic master of the sky flew from the clearing and out into the midst of the heaven above its haunting shriek echoing back.

Izz stood to his feet, looking up into the heavens. In flight, with outspread wings, the eagle had to be the most impressive creatures in the world. He tried to trace its path overhead, but it was impossible to follow it through the tree canopy. For a moment, Izz wondered about the voice he had heard in his mind and how, in the past, he had had other similar, uncanny experiences with animals and sometimes people. Perhaps there was something to the world just beyond the one he knew. As soon as Lott was satisfied that the eagle was gone, he quickly relit his pipe and took short, nervous pulls on it. Lott put his arm around his nephew and said, "The great birds are not common in these parts. It must have a nest nearby." Lott scanned the air above. "They are known to hunt in pairs. Come, let us leave this place."

As they walked back through the knotting, greenery along the narrow trail, Lott warned, "The main rule of survival in these woods is this: you must never allow yourself to get so caught up with anything that you neglect to notice the out of the ordinary sneaking up on you."

Izz could now see how easily over imaginative folks might, without difficulty, imagine that ghosts lurk in every shadow. And how, with each repetition, the wild tales would grow like a malignant tumor. On the ride back, Uncle Lott spoke mostly of the legal matters of transferring the woodshop into Izz's possession, and how much he was looking forward to his retirement. But the truth was that Izz was desperately trying to figure out how he could graciously decline his uncle's offer. His creed had become a literal dance with life wherein he led and did not follow. But the greater truth was that he was born to chase the sky, yearning to rush off to any new horizon where the latest adventure awaited him. Izz knew he was only postponing the imminent confrontation that was anything but expected.

That night, Izz stayed in the loft above his uncle's carpentry shop, where fate offered him a home. Weary from the long day, Izz dropped onto the bed and lay on his back, Izz suddenly smiled broadly, laid back on his piled up pillows and rested with his hands behind his head. The words of his uncle's offer swamped around in his mind. But he had been self dependent since he was yet a boy, and his natural force of will was adaptively suited to roam, and nothing this side of life could hold him down. The future was wide open, and as of yet, he had only explored a fraction of one corner of the world he wanted to see. Nevertheless he toyed vaguely with the possibilities until like an unwanted visitor, the memory of the princess intruded into his thoughts to wreak havoc like a stone in his boot. She was of royal blood, someone he had nothing in common with. He tried to push those thoughts and memories to one side, but they were seared into his mind. He wanted to take the heel of his hand and pound it against his temple to knock the reflections out of his mind. However, his heart seemingly had a mind of its own and feeling hopeless; his mind resigned to the fate of its thoughts. He yawned once, balled his fists, and rubbed his eyes, then fumbled for the edge of the blankets and pulled them around himself. First thing in the morning, Izz planned to leave Edawn without a word to anyone. His uncle would understand that he just could not stay. Exhaustion finally claimed Izz as his thoughts wafted into the gray haze that existed somewhere between sleep and consciousness. He closed his eyes, and rest took him immediately, like a falling star through the night.

Izz's sleep was deep, and at about the third bell past the midnight hour, Izz began to dream. He surrendered himself to the rush of visions one more time, a willing participant in the cosmic drama of fantasy. Once again he found himself in the enchanted place he had visited in his earlier unfinished dream. He walks through the same magical meadow filled with chirping birds and golden butterflies that float effortlessly in the breeze. He can feel the soft wind caressing his face and dancing in his hair. Suddenly, he finds himself sitting on a throne shaped rock at the top of a high mountain. He is looking down the face of the receding slop at a long, winding, pebbled path. It is a very peaceful, solitude place. At a distance on the downward pathway, out of nowhere, appears a life form walking toward him. The personage had the outward appearance of an angelic being moving toward him like a brilliant slow moving comet traced by a glimmering trail of white fire. She is shrouded in exotic beauty and wears a long white flowing gown that glows as it waves gently in the waft of a delicate wind. The angelic being approaches, smiling up at Izz. Izz finds himself looking into the eyes of pure power, most splendorous, and holiest that he has ever seen before. Suddenly, the angelic being is before him, flooding him with overflowing magical energy. With an outstretched hand, she offers what appears to be a flat stone polished to a brilliant shine. Izz looks up at the gift bearer. Her eyes are filled with loving kindness. He takes the stone tablet from her hand and hears her say in the voice of an immortal being.

"Your destiny is upon you. Accept your uncle's blessings."

Izz looks up to ask what she means, but she has vanished and is gone as if she had never been in his dream. He looks back at the flat stone. On its surface, he sees what appears to be a boiling cauldron of many individual images, each playing out scenes from his past, visions of when he was a newborn, child, then youngster appearing and disappearing simultaneously. Each episode bubbles up from the depth of the stone. As it reaches the surface, it plays out and fades away, only to be replaced by another, and then another, and yet another until they reached the present. And then a strange thing happened, the phantasm transmuted into the future yet to come. The scenes he gazes upon play out his whole life from birth's first cry to his last dying breath. The cauldron of images quickened, like an attack on his senses, as if its contents of images were on the verge of boiling over. There within the kaleidoscoping scenes, he sees the hauntingly familiar image of the beautiful young princess, The pattern of images shifts into a course of pre and future existence, so profound that Izz cannot relate to or fathom their meaning. Visions in Izz's mind collide and flash quicker that he can observe them. Scenes intertwine with faces, spoken exchanges, and episodes. He feels his mind stretching to its outer limits. He struggles to capture his fragmented thoughts before they escaped him, but at this point, questions are reproducing faster than Izz can keep up with. Suddenly, his dreaming self registers a knock at the front door downstairs that will not go away, and as he stares at the blitz of unfurling images, the looking stone abruptly vanishes in his hands. Izz woke to find himself begging out loud to the weaver of his dream.

"NO! NO! PLEASE STAY!"

The insistent knock continued to sound at the door and persisted as Izz came fully to the surface of wakefulness. Izz lay in bed, looking at the ceiling playing and replaying the outpouring of his mind over and over while the dream was still fresh. He remembered what the angel had told him, and then tried to recall every exact moment he had dreamed or heard in his mind. Then Izz tried desperately to make sense of it all. The dream had been different, yet just as realistic as the first. Up to that point, his childhood had been for the most part a blur. Yet in his dream, his childhood, his life in the orphanage, his tutor, his friends, had been vividly familiar. That was all there, and he understood that to be correct. The parts of the future were vague, lacking definition, and unbelievable at best. But the part about prelife and afterlife was a complete blanked void in his mind. However, he did remember with crystal clarity the angelic messenger and what she had said to him. He remembered the beautiful girl in the looking stone, who had been in his first dream. He asked himself, *If she genuinely does exist, then where?* "Where?" In both dreams, the beautiful maiden looked strikingly similar to Edawn's Princess Zuree. But how could that be?

The pounding at the door that would not quit came to his ears again and again, louder and louder. Down in the streets, someone was knocking on the front door, and this time the banging knock was loud enough to wake the dead. Izz finished untangling himself from his bedspreads and came to his feet abruptly. With disheveled hair, he looked out the upstairs window, eyes still blurry with sleep, trying to refocus his attention. It was his uncle, Lott.

"Get dressed, sleepyhead. We must go to the Hall of Law to transfer the shop into your name."

Izz had already decided to turn his uncle's offer down. He had already packed his awards and his other meager belongings, ready to leave that day on the outgoing tide, but his astonishing dream had caused him to have a change of heart. By the time Izz was washed and dressed, below on the street everywhere, the kingdom was already coming alive in the predawn light with morning activities. Merchants were sweeping the sidewalks in front of their shops. The air was dense, rich with the scent of breakfast cooking in pots on open flames. Shopkeepers were already at their doorways competing for the attention of passersby. As they walked, Uncle Lott stopped briefly to buy two fresh, out of the oven fig cakes from a street vendor and handed one to Izz as he said, "Let us hurry before the record keepers get too busy doing nothing all day. Those of us that work with our hands should be so lucky."

Along the way, people that recognized Izz on the street stopped to congratulate him. The narrow flowerpot lined street turned into the main avenue that led them to the heart of the city, where the King's Palace and the Halls of Law stood. Along the main boulevard, artisans were already diligently at work like so many ants, constructing, repairing, cleaning, dismantling, and rebuilding the ever changing charmed kingdom at the heart of Zia. Eventually, the two men found themselves ascending the formidable flight of wide, granite steps that led to the grand entrance of the Halls of Law. The building was made of cut stone and built on the grandest of scales. The outside doors and walls were covered with reliefs that told the story of Xylenia from the dawn of recorded history. They approached the arched front entrance, which was flanked on each side by a projection of massive pillars. They went through the solid double doors, elbowed on massive brass hinges. As they entered the courts and palaces of kings, Izz felt a little intimidated by the imposing size of the halls as they passed through them. The inside walls were covered with intricate carvings that told of kings, queens, champions, and seers, testifying to the glorious past of Edawn. Izz took in every detail in the brightness allowed in through stained glass windows. This sector was the center of government for the whole empire of Xylenia. The inevitable citadel of supremacy at the center of the Xylenian universe was knowledge and power, which were in like manner the same. From here, King Ozzdon ruled the empire assisted by the heads of the Inner Council.

The king held court sessions with his elder academicians, issued imperial laws, and initiated new trading expeditions and expenditures. Here, the Edawnian intellectual establishment of royal minds met to collaborate and exchange ideas, courses of action, resolve conflicts, select delegates, administer oaths, and pursue their own aspirations. They also wielded considerable influence over the arts such as music, poetry, drama, dance, and so forth. Each year their powers were enhanced by newly elected members from the ranks of educators, scholars, artists, intellectuals, and spiritual seekers. It was an aristocracy in which any citizen from philosophers, magistrates, and aristocrats to merchants, laymen, and farmers, from any sovereignty, could attend, vote on new laws, systems of rule, ordinances for social conduct, and submit proposals as well. Within these chambers was a whole different world from the world outside its walls. It was a place of controversy and contradiction where men worked together and bicker all at once. It was the most hostile part of the kingdom, where members spent more and more time at odds, fighting perpetually for power among themselves more so than the issues they resolved. When the Halls of Law was in session, it was always in a state of confusion with clashes of opposing ideas, interests, and opinions. Disagreements varied from the uppermost philosophical arguments down to the most inconsequential of petty feuds. Most debates ended in all out quarrels, turned into unresolved bickering contests.

In many cases, the leading intellectuals of the day were no more virtuous than the babbling uneducated commoner. Baddlock was a personage of marked influence and was often at the heart of such controversies, unique in his ability to control and manipulate men's minds through evil means. He had the knack to influence other men to start up squabbles he had inadvertently initiated in such a way that they believed the clash originated with them. Baddlock only worshiped power, driven by and transfixed with wicked and cruel acts. Greed, pride, and dishonesty were his only gods. Preying on the weaknesses and the good nature of the good intentions of men were his greatest pleasure. His ultimate goal was to infiltrate the uppermost seats of power. He secretly sought to destroy or bring those with the uppermost influence under his direct control to fulfill a long held dream of subjugating all of Zia under one single supremacy, one rule—his.

As Izz and Lott walked through the central corridor looking for the Halls of Records, Izz was amazed by the meticulously polished marble slabs, so glossy that he could see himself staring back as he walked over them. The ceilings were three stories high with clusters of crystal chandeliers hanging from their lofty heights. On the walls, hung tapestries and thick velvet coverings worth their weight in gold. Through the thick walls around them, they could hear the latest embroilment of frantic arguments over debates within debates, minds clashing with minds. Lott turned to Izz, attempting an explanation.

"Oftentimes, when they are not asleep, here is where a group of educated elders organizes to conduct and report on accounts usually of no consequence. Finally, when, if ever, a conclusion is reached, they then file it away under established rules. Eventually, another group is organized, whose duty it is to investigate whatever it was that the first group buttoned up, then they all get together and take a vote on what was concluded. Then, at an unspecified time, yet another council is formed to check the ballot. The results are rechecked and amended and rethought out. The next day, the whole process is set in motion again, endlessly updating and revising with a few new twists. Thus they spent most of their waking energy disputing their own internal disagreements. It is a kind of a dog chasing its tail fiasco."

As Izz and Lott made their way, they were directed toward the proper authorities. They came to an intersection of corridors leading up to a variety of entrances. One such entry was prominently marked Halls of Records. From somewhere within, a loud, indistinguishable disagreement was intensifying. They entered the office complex to find an assemblage of bearded men of all ages, dressed in gray colored robes, working at desks and worktables of all shapes and descriptions. Occasionally they woke each other's daydream to bore the other with the monotonous repetition of the countless ceremonies of their office. Scribes were busily writing, looking through files, balancing accounts, and checking the records of the Revenue Laws. Pages were coming in and out, bringing and taking large record books with them. One carried a file so full of paperwork that it threatened to rip open its bindings. Filers were carefully filing and refiling documents, books, and records. Lott stepped up to the reception desk. Behind the barrier was positioned an administrator at his oak writing desk, rustling papers from a ledger he was reviewing. He was a middle aged man poring over a stack of records. Lott cleared his throat, trying to gain his attention.

The administrator looked up from his oversized ledger, looking as if he was too busy to be bothered. But knowing that the king was in council in the next room, he went out of his way to be more courteous than he might have been otherwise. He forced a smile at the edge of his mouth, and asked, "Yes? And what can I do for you today?"

Well acquainted with public and private affairs, Lott drew a crumpled document from an inner pocket. He unrolled it and laid it on the counter, saying, "This is my nephew, on my brother's side, and I wish to transfer some property into his name."

The overseer stepped out from behind his desk and approached Lott. From across the counter, he took the document and looked it over for a moment, and thereupon disclosed, "Everything seems to be in order." He laid the document on the reception desk and slid it to Lott as he rotated it right side up toward Lott. With his finger, he indicated where Lott should sign as he handed him a freshly dipped quill.

An unexpected outburst of malicious complaints and bitter disagreements came from beyond the closed door of the next room, where the overhead sign reads The King's Court. Izz and Lott looked toward the door and then looked at the administrator.

"Matters of an internal nature, nothing to concern your selves with."

Somehow the administrator did not seem convinced. The administrator then slid the document to Izz, indicating where he should sign as he said, "The original copy will be sent to you after it is properly recorded." When Izz was in the process of writing his signature on the document, the administrator gave Izz a long quizzical up and down look and asked, "Are you not the young man who outran Rizan the Great? "

Izz looked up from the document with a smile. "It was just luck," he replied humbly.

"No. That was more than luck. That was a magnificent display of athleticism," the administrator corrected as he signed and sealed the document in the presence of his two witnesses.

Lott let out a warm chesty chuckle and threw a proud arm over Izz as they turned to walk away, and as they did, Izz turned to his uncle and said, "I appreciate what you are doing for me, and I will never forget your kindness."

"Not another word," Lott quickly responded. "I know you will make me proud and will carry on our good name. This momentous occasion calls for a drink."

And so it was that Izz became the sole owner of the most popular carpentry shop in all of Edawn. As they reached the door on their way to the nearest tavern, they heard the heated conflict taking place behind closed doors suddenly erupted into an all out war of words. And as Izz and his uncle Lott walked out and down through the hallway, the raising voices from within the King's Court could still be heard echoing down through the cavernous hall.

Meanwhile, behind closed doors, in the King's Court, the controversy continued, while the court scribes were striving to record every word that was being spoken, so it could be written in the Eternal Book of the Law. With each noble lord, clinging to their individual interests, the situation was becoming so intense that King Ozzdon began to fume. His fingers drummed an impatient cadence on the armrest of his throne as he glared into middle space. The king, who had the last word on everything, felt his patience snap and had to call the meeting back to order.

"SILENCE," he commanded abruptly, cutting off their heated exchange. "Enough!" Unsigned papers, unread scrolls, and wax sealed parchments surrounded him. "There are too many other imperative matters at hand to waste one more moment." Everyone in the chamber stopped their bickering and turned to regard their king with various looks of understanding. He looked tired as he rose to his feet and said, "I have decided to put this matter aside for now. I will review this issue further in private and will give you my final answer when we meet again."

As the council slowly departed, they continued bickering among themselves, and the only fact upon which all could agree was that they all disagreed. Surprisingly, the distressed deputation was not over new politics, commonwealth, or constitutional tradition. The clash had been over who should sit where at the King's

Council Table. This single factor was at the root of all the tension that seemed to be brewing throughout every department of the Halls of Law. So mighty was the fuss over this trivial matter that the king knew he would have to give this issue more in depth consideration. Sometimes the king felt as if he was dealing with a brood of spoiled children, rather than the intellectual class of the kingdom.

That evening, in frustration, the king retired to his palace chambers. He ate very little, even though the most delicious food surrounded him. The tables were spread with serving dishes of bread, meat, cheese, and the most costly candied delicacies. His appetite was lost. Still disturbed by the troublesome scene of intense arguments, the king wondered which council member should be seated where at the long Council Table. The ends of the table were considered positions of dignity and were most heatedly argued over by the most powerful lords. The proximity to the king's throne was also a subject of considerable controversy. That day, the quarrels had been so vigorous that matters of the highest importance went unresolved and were piling up. The king sought counsel with those closest to him. But no one seemed to have an answer for the king, not his wise men, not his advisers, not even his beloved queen, Zahra.

That same night, the king spent a sleepless dusk to dawn night, tossing and turning from one side to the other, wondering over who should sit where at the long table. If he sat the kings and aristocrats at the ends of the table, he would never hear the end of it from the royals and the nobles, and vice versa. Then there were the councilors, advisors, magistrates, scholars, judges, and patriarchs. He knew by the power of his crown who should be seated where, but he knew as well that the human heart was full of pride and vanity and no matter who sat where there would be trouble.

Six

The Meeting

Izz worked hard in his new shop allowing his new life to carry him along in its wake. The sun rose and the sunset, and so the days turned into weeks. Izz had fallen into step with the well trodden groove of everyday life, none the worse for it. He had come for one reason and stayed for another. It was a new stream of life, a new lease of existence, and somehow he knew this was where he was meant to be. The shop had been in his family for generations, and Izz took his place to be the next in line. In short order, his popularity and his acceptance grew by leaps and bounds, and soon to his uncle's honor, Izz was earning the reputation of being the most exceptional carpenter in the entire kingdom. Life as a carpenter was Izz's new reality, and all else had all but vanished. It seemed that the hand of fate had stretched forth and laid a firm hold of him, and set him irrevocably on a path he was so determined to avoid.

One day, as fate would have it, while Izz was working diligently on a dining table set for a wealthy merchant, a strange, peculiar character cast his shadow at the entrance of his shop. Izz gazed up at the unusual visitor trying to puzzle out his identity, but there was nothing recognizable about him. He did not know then that that very day would transform his life completely. The unfamiliar figure was stricken with age and moved with a slight rigidity in his steps as he leaned on a twisted staff, unmistakably a shell of his former self. He was astoundingly aged, an old fortress, still strong and sturdy, in the decline of a diverse and honorable life not yet fallen into ruin. So ancient was he that he could probably nearly recall when the moons of Zia were suspended in the heavens. His fine, thinning hair was almost silver white and was groomed straight back from his receding hairline down well passed his squared shoulders. Despite his long lapse of mortal life, his shoulders were still straight, his head erect, and his demeanor remarkably dignified. His face was drawn and networked with wrinkles of unquestionable kindness, honor, and compassion. His expression was unreadable. His seasoned face was covered with profound lines that read like a well worn map of the exceptional paths he had trodden in lands yet unknown. Each line was a measurement of a voyage into incredible discoveries few others had ever experienced, in places found only in dreams of wishes.

He had a sharp nose with deep blue-gray eyes that appeared hooded with weighty laden folds of baggy skin and peculiar, spiky, white eyebrows. His eyes seemed to have withered over the ages, surrounded by creases and lines, half latent under bags of withered skin. Izz searched out the old man's eyes, seeking the light therein. Providing that there was the power of outward light still within, expecting to find only the senility of waning age. Izz looked past the tufts of white eyebrows to see they accented a pair of heavy lidded, profoundly deep eyes. They seemed not to be optical orbs, but deep seas reflecting a keen, clear mind that seemed to burn with the fire of human genius and full life of experience. His mind seemed alight with thoughts, and the closer Izz penetrated its inwards substance, the sounder the old man's mind appeared. Without exception, the old man's indomitable spirit emanated more energy and confidence than a man half his age, radiating with more power and wisdom than anyone Izz had ever encountered.

When the old man first caught sight of Izz in the dimly lit shop, he cocked a quizzical eye at him, as if an uncanny feeling had come upon him. Izz looked back expectantly, waiting for the aged old man to speak, but the elder only stared intently, his gaze seemingly taking Izz's measure. As if something had stirred and deepened in him, something he felt driven to study more completely, searching out not only his characteristics but his inner essence, his wishes, his dreams. The seer eyed Izz knowingly as if he recognized who Izz was. Izz smiled uncomfortably at the scrutiny as he wiped his sawdust covered hands over the upper part of his carpenter's apron. Ammiz continued to stare expressionlessly; he moved closer as if to study Izz's face. An all seeing visualization seemed to spread over the gray bread's face. *This one was born to be fully alive,* he thought to himself then without thinking, the strange little old man spoke for the first time.

"It is written...a spiritual war has begun over your soul between the angelic beings of light and darkness." The seer had spoken the words he had not intended to disclose. He strained as he tightened down on the affixed words burning to come out. His succeeding words became just noise, as the seer unrelenting gaped at Izz, incessantly for the longest, uncomfortable time until Izz broke eye contact. The old man continued to stare and recognized Lott's characteristics stamped like a brand upon Izz's face.

The seer moved in close, so close that Izz could feel the force of his commanding presence. In the course of his approach, nothing seemed to escape the seer's careful attention. Ammiz tensed his jaw as if he were weighing in the balance the words he was about to speak. Then, at long last, the sound he was muttering turned back into words again, expressed in a courteous, soft tone anyone might trust.

"Where might I find your instructor, master carpenter Lott?" he asked as he unremittingly sustained his gaze over Izz. "Tell him his old friend Ammiz is here to see him." As he continued his thorough close up and down examination of Izz, he said, "Tell Master Lott, I have another special project for him." His voice was wise and exceedingly cultured.

Izz stopped his work to listen to what the stranger would tell. He took a shop rage from a nearby worktable and finished wiping his hands and brushed the wood chips from his carpenter's apron. "Master Lott has retired. I am his nephew, Izz of Zollerzon."

Ammiz seemed awestruck at what he had heard. A strange visible transformation of astonishment lit up the old man's face like the sun coming up in his thoughts. Like something outside of the ordinary self, almost like an insight into some other world.

"Izz...of the Southern Isles of Zollerzon...Yes..." His look became keener and most penetrative. He narrowed his eyes as they fixed on Izz and glistened with perceptive intelligence. "I have longed to meet you to see if all that I have read...Ahhh have heard"—he paused, choosing his words more carefully before he continued —"many exalted stories about you, of great feats of athleticism and selfless acts of generosity, and your masterful skill of hand. No man should ever live idle in the world. Yes, yes, indeed, it would seem that you are a very, very special young man. More than you could ever imagine." His final words were soberly spoken as he walked around Izz, examining him from every angle.

Almost overwhelmed by Ammiz's presence and intensity, Izz wondered if he somehow knew the odd old man as he searched every inch of his face.

"I am known as Ammiz the Seer, a healer, and the keeper of the empire's ancient chronicles." Ammiz extended his hand, and Izz noticed his hand was wrinkled and spotted with age as the gray beard clasped Izz's in a hearty handshake. As their fingertips made physical contact, two of the world's sturdiest spirits collided. The seer met the seeker, and the seer wondered if this could be the southern islander he had anticipated in this moon cycle. Izz's mind shifted into an action filled, brain seeking mode, searching the hundreds of avenues of his memory storing mechanism. But the old man sparked no hint of recognition in his eyes. At best, the old man who called himself Ammiz the Seer did not even seem vaguely familiar. Then why did he speak as if he knew who he was? And why was this stranger looking at him as a proud man might when welcoming back a long lost son?

"Out of the isles of the South, he shall come..." The old man's voice abated into unintelligible mumbling again. Then Ammiz's face suddenly became very solemn. His next words were said in a deep whisper. "Born of sorrow...of the southern isles...favored by fortune, more than most...through dreams, he shall be counseled." The gray bread quoted from his memory of the ancient prophesies written in the Great Book of Foretelling. His voice again tapered off, his words scarcely audible. Ammiz was astounded though he showed little sign of it.

"Out of everyday life, one never knows when the Great Creator will put those that are destined to meet on the same path. Truly, you are most fortunate," the seer voiced his thoughts. "You are foreknown. You are the one?" The old man discerned out loud to himself of a sudden realization. That statement surprised both of them. With his hand still firmly clasped around Izz's Ammiz positioned himself into an eye to eye posture in front of Izz. His ancient eyes seemed to be searching within. Izz took in the seer's intense look. He stared deep into the old man's eyes. He wanted to detect deception, but he saw none. With the hand to hand contact, the seer had unwittingly opened a window into Izz's soul. In one single moment, a parade of curious impressions flashed across the gray beard's illuminated mind. The seer continued as if he could not help himself. "Before you were born, you were appointed, predestined, and consecrated."

Izz broke contact and took a step back, sucked a deep breath, and then sighed it out slowly as an expression of unbelieving, he could not contain swept over him. What the old man was saying seemed more and more ludicrous, yet there was an incredible, curious intelligence in his features. A spark of something exceptional shone in his eyes, as of a person who had so cultured a mindset that could not fail. Ammiz stood suspended before Izz, deep in all consuming contemplation. As if his mind was flipping through the pages of a book inside his head. It was a strange situation. Izz did not understand what the seer was saying, nor did he want to hear anymore, and yet he wanted to hear everything. Who was this scholarly, gentle old man with his polite, understanding eyes? Izz instantly sensed a deep kind of connection with this unknown visitor. He felt as if he knew him from somewhere, somehow. And even though he was held spellbound against his own will, he felt immediately at ease in the presence of this man who had introduced himself as Ammiz the Seer, healer, keeper of the empire's ancient chronicles.

Izz had no clue of what Ammiz was referring to, but he had lived long enough to know not to interrupt or question too quickly, that if he only patiently listened the whole story would unfold. Ammiz's look intensified, becoming more animated and penetrative as his narrowing blue-gray eyes pierced right through Izz's eyes, straight through to his soul and into his heart. His intuition was telling him that he had found the final piece to the puzzle.

The seer broke his prolonged silence. In a gentle, quiet voice, he asked, "Shall we speak plainly, with actualities, rather than sentiments?" Those words were no sooner spoken when the gray beard abruptly looked over his right shoulder then his left as if what he was about to say might be overheard by the wrong ears.

Wide eyed Izz looked about as he nodded without knowing why.

"Do you believe in fate?" His voice was sure and firm.

Something about the way he asked it and the way he was staring at him set Izz's nerves on edge. As he absorbed every word, he became transfixed by the message.

"There is a divine destiny in you. I can see it shining like a beacon in your eyes. You are the one. Chosen from the time before you were formed in your mother's womb."

Izz was surprised by what the seer kept repeated, but his surprise was just beginning. Although the account rather pleased him, he was starting to think the old man was not all there. Either this odd character was very *wise* beyond measure or very *crazy*, and he wanted to find out which one applied. With one eye on the long ago and one eye on the impending future, the guardian of the Great Book of Foretelling continued, "I can see in your life the pain and the beauty of your journey. Your story may not have had a happy beginning, but I see in you, and my soul knows right well, that the rest of the story is who you were always, from the foundations, meant to be." The seer spoke with no trace of a shred of doubt in his voice.

The seer's declarations astonished Izz even more. It was as if his whole life was unreeling, and the seer was watching the best and worst parts of his life. Izz looked at the old man, quizzically. "Do you know who I am?" Izz had to ask finally.

"More true to the question would be, do you know who you are?" The seer's question was spoken so pointedly that it seemed that an answer was mandatory.

Izz was having trouble putting his thoughts into words. But finally, he blurted out, "I am Izz. I am a carpenter. I do not know how I could be anyone else."

"I deduce there are a lot of things you do not know. Most men are slaves to their doubts. How very little we understand about those mysteries that glow within us." Without a change in the solemn expression on Ammiz's face, he rose to his full height. "I am not sure if you are prepared to hear what I must say to you now."

Izz looked dazed and confused as he again unknowingly nodded. "There is a spiritual battle brewing in the sacred realm, and you will be swept away into its heart and shall be a deciding factor. When the proper time comes, all mysteries shall be revealed. Then you will learn and know why the Highest has sent you here in such a time as now." But the words died in his throat for the second time. The seer's faint smile suddenly ran away from his face and was replaced by a frown as if he knew he had revealed too much, too soon. The old man grew pensive for an instance, knowing that his declaration had drawn nothing from Izz but a blank stare, which quickly turned into a baffled and a forlorn expression of puzzlement. Ammiz hesitated for several minutes before speaking again, "I see you have much to learn, and I caution you not to jump to judgment too hastily. We must all play out the cards that destiny has dealt us, and we must all take part according to the rules set before us." His voice tapped off sharper than he had intended.

With a rattled look on his face, Izz slowly nodded yet again, still not knowing why.

"All is not always what it seems to be. Every step you have taken up to this moment has led you to where you were meant to be. Whatever you have thought, your purpose in life was, is inconsequential. Very soon, destiny will sweep you into its current, and in spite of the approaching passage that will lead you face to face with death's darkest nightmare, miracles and supernatural powers will surround and protect you."

So far, everything that Izz had heard sounded like craziness, but at least it was starting to sound like interesting craziness. There was something about the way the old man spoke as if there could be no doubt to the truth of what he was saying, that made Izz all the more curious.

"All the powers of pure evil will gather their forces against you, and you must overcome." As Ammiz spoke his latest revelation, an inner light shone out from within, causing the crinkled folds and the waxen dimness of his age to transform into an almost radiant guise of his formative years. "You will one day become a king."

Slowly the ultimate meaning of Ammiz's words gradually penetrated through the barrier of Izz's astonished mind. It all seemed so absurd. Izz gave the old man an odd look heavy with doubt but said nothing at first. When the full impact finally sunk in, Izz suddenly realized what he had heard. Befuddled, he puffed out a snorted laugh as if he had just listened to a funny joke and asked, "Who are you talking about?"

The old man got in Izz's face and said in a matter-of-fact tone, "A very extraordinary person, you!"

For a moment in silence, Ammiz studied Izz's face, staring deep into his eyes and saw the disbelief, but how could he be surprised. For just a fraction of a second, a tinkling of frustration flashed across the old man's self restrained expression. The seer closed his eyes as if praying for patience. With a scornful twist of his lips, he gave the young carpenter a corrective look. He wanted to force Izz to understand somehow. However, he knew that sometimes, faith needed a helping hand. His thick, bushy white eyebrows merged into a knot on his forehead.

"I see that doubt dulls your mind. I know it sounds absurd, but sooner or later, you will wake up to see it for yourself. You, Izz of Zollerzon, immensely underestimate your deeper purpose. I would have thought by now that you would have realized that what runs through your veins and springs up from the pool of your dreams could not help but tell you the truth within the truth. There is a lot you seem not to know, is there not? What you think to be a reality in your small little world is merely a fleeting shadow on a clouded day. Perhaps such things as these as of yet are too deep for you. There is much more to your life than sawdust or winning a few trinkets for the ability to outrun a jackrabbit."

Taking into account the intent, serious look on Ammiz's face, and the sharpness of his tone, Izz's ridiculing smile faded abruptly into a quizzical expression again. His head suddenly spun with the grandiosity of what he was being told, and he had to take another awkward step back, trying to help his mind process everything, anything, but only lost himself deeper in confusion. Finally, almost involuntarily, he asked, "Why...do you tell me... these things?"

"I see that I have said too much as it is. Some things are best kept unknown until their time has come." His voice had a sting in it this time.

Izz's perplexed expression did not ease from his face, yet something about the gray bread made Izz realize this was not a story haphazardly told. Sensing that Izz was attempting to give him the benefit of the doubt, he immediately dismissed his stern disposition, aware that harvest comes in due time, not when it is demanded.

"You are completely right to be skeptical. And since every unearthly anonymity tends to tell its own story at the most opportune time, you will undoubtedly see what I have said, all in due time. You seem to be a resourceful, self sufficient soul. I am sure very soon it will all fall together for you. When that time comes, you will feel the irresistible pull of your destiny as never before. And just as the fabric of fixed laws must obey the mechanic fluctuation of the coming celestial conjunction, you will then clearly know who you are and why you were born to be." Again the old man spoke these things as though there could be no question of their truth.

And even though that was not the end of Ammiz's foretelling, the old man abruptly ended his revelation. "My visit here today was not intended to follow this course. My purpose here," Ammiz said as he reached into this inner pocket and pulled out a scroll, "was to commission Master Lott to make this instrument for me." Then he spoke as if to himself, "I seemed to have misplaced one of my long eyes." For a moment, he paused to ponder some puzzling conundrum seemingly. Finally, he spoke again, "But since Master Lott has deemed you worthy..." He placed the parchment in Izz's hand. "I too, shall place my trust in you. I, therefore, requisition you to create this long eye for me."

Izz took the sheet of skin, unrolled it, and studied it intensely. Izz remained quiet. There was an unusual, intently, penetrating expression about him, a strange searching gleam that seemed to hint at an acute hidden complexity. Izz was turning various notions over in his head as he studied the drafted design, detail by methodical detail, trying to visualize it from different perspectives. Ammiz studied his face and saw a remarkable concentration in his eyes. The seer continued to stare, waiting patiently, allowing Izz to work it all out in his head. Looking curiously at the big question, Izz became deeply absorbed for what seemed like the longest time. But the young carpenter could not get his mind through it, under it, over it, or around it. Finally, his mind stumbled and drew a blank. Izz took in a deep breath through his mouth, held it for a few seconds, grimaced, and then released it through his nose. He took another moment before he felt confident enough to reply with assurance. In frustration, he shook his head and shrugged his shoulders.

Izz held the diagram out and shook his head. "This would be a tough knot to untie, and as much as I would like to say I understand it, the truth is it is much too complicated. I cannot make anything this intricate," Izz said as he handed the diagram back to the old man.

"I only ask what I know you can accomplish. It is very simple, as most things are. Trust your impulse, your intuition." With infinite patience, the seer maintained an expectant smile, as if the measurements and diagrams of his idea were real and tangible things, only waiting for its parts to be modeled into its physical self. But when Izz did not rise to the challenge, the seer responded sternly, "So I see you are choosing to give up even before you have begun. I am afflicted to hear you say the word, cannot. It is such a lifeless petty word. Perhaps you meant, I will not." As the old man frowned, he had to make a concerted effort to control his exasperation. "Perhaps it is quite beyond your comprehension, or maybe you are merely allowing your mind to get in the way."

Izz remained head bowed, like a chastised child. Without waiting for a response, Ammiz turned to walk away. "The most important thing that I have learned in life is that imagination is the gateway to our limitless power, making nothing impossible, not if you want it bad enough." The next few words would change everything. "For example, the new love of your dreams..." Ammiz spoke as one that knew what was in the heart of men's dreams. He then turned his head slowly for an instant and carefully watched for the reaction on the young man's face. Ammiz found that apparently, his remark had found its mark. He saw, with discernment, the deep emotions swelling up in Izz's eyes. Knowing the meaning within the meaning, the old man's eyes glinted beneath his bushy brows.

With an exclamation pasted on his face, Izz reasoned, thinking to himself, *It had only been a dream. A pleasant dream, that was all.* But the words spoken by the seer cast their mysterious spell over Izz all over again. Izz felt a shiver quake over him and course down his spine. Who was this peculiar man who knew things no man could know? He needed to know more.

"If you try and fail, then you are faultless. But if you do not make an effort, then you are defeated, then the fault will be all yours."

Izz nodded even though he did not have the slightest clue what the old man had meant by what he had just said. He only responded with a confused, questioning look. Ammiz looked as if he had the answers to Izz's probing questions about the dream and the identity of the girl in it. Ammiz considered Izz with an appraising gaze.

"I see you have already been conquered."

A slow, almost imperceptible nod was Izz's only other response. What he had just heard had touched something deep within. And Izz wondered, *Is it that obvious?* And then asked without thinking, "Who is this girl? Could it be...?" Izz fell silent and did not even notice that he had stopped talking in mid-sentence when he suddenly found himself lost in his mind where the memory of Princess Zuree drew him under its tow and availed him no escape. Izz's expression was accented with that of surprise and intrigue. Puzzlement flickered across his face like a man who did not even know the questions to the answers he sought.

"The larger picture obviously eludes you."

"How can I know?"

"You will know."

"You are not telling me everything you know, are you?"

"You will know when the time comes."

"How? When?" Izz maintained his appeal, hoping for a better answer.

The old man was about to answer but then hesitated, giving the matter a little more thought, at length, he said, "If *it is* of the Creator, He will bless your revelation. I can only say, as strange as it may sound to you, I believe you can achieve anything, and probably will. You will be who you choose to be, but the future will not happen until you make it come to pass. Pursue the dream, never compromise, and it will lead you to her. Savor the journey rather than racing for the finish. Sometimes that which you seek the most is the one thing that you cannot see. However, if your dream is profound enough, you have no other choice than to find it out, or it will find you out. The moment you look deep into her eyes and feel their power to the tips of your toes, you will know who she is. Cherish her, and she will exalt you."

For a moment, the old man seemed to lapse into a profound sequence of thoughts. Was that a tear glistening in the corner of his eye? Then as if returning from afar, far away place, he continued with a slight tremble in his voice. "When you find that love, it matters, not whoever it may be. Do not run away from nor chase after it. Only believe with all your heart and be patient, and you shall have her when you least expect it. Love is something you cannot hound after or lay a snare for, it reaches its destination on its own terms while you are paying attention to other things." Ammiz handed the parchment back to Izz. "Wise knowledge is life's ultimate aim, hence seek it out diligently. Though it cost you everything you have, seek wisdom. Of course, ultimately, you must follow your conscience."

A glimmer of momentary remembrance leaped from the old man's treasured memories of love, and for a moment, it shone brightly through his eyes then faded into dimness that seemed too painful to remember. Then the old soul composed himself and continued, "Yes, it would seem that destiny has called you to Edawn for a purpose, much deeper than you could ever imagine. It is time for you to awaken, to open the eye of your heart, and know the power you were meant to wield."

Izz opened his mouth to say something, but Ammiz waved him off. "It is a long story, with many changeable angles and varying parallels, and this is not the time to tell it. Nor is this the place for the lengthy account I have searched out in the Great Book of Foretelling. I have told you all that I can. Let that be enough for now. I will check with you at a later time to see how you are coming along with your task. As always, you will be paid in gold.'" Ammiz then turned to make his departure, and then hesitated, and turning only his head; he instructed, "I prefer that no further mention of this be made to anyone, not even your uncle, Lott. Say nothing to anyone about our discussion here. Many around these parts consider me possessed as it is."

Again, Izz opened his mouth to speak as Ammiz reached for the front door but was again cut short by the old man's raised hand. The seer clutched the brass handle and, without turning, yet again spoke, "Let me give you some priceless advice: believe one thing if you believe nothing else. Always give everything to your dreams. Believe in what you trust, withholding nothing, and your faith will never fail you. Peace be with you." With that, Ammiz disappeared through the door as suddenly as he had appeared.

And the question Izz wanted so much to utter remained unspoken, unanswered. There could have been a thousand answers; perhaps the question had no answer. Izz was left fixed, where he stood staring at the door looking more and more like a man who was expecting to wake up any moment. At long last, he turned his attention to the diagram of several sketches covered with a combination of complex measurements and instructions.

Izz picked up the parchment and gave it a blank look. It was something he could not, as of yet, absorb, could not grasp, its application unknowable, seemingly enigmatic, and beyond understanding. He continued to stare, vacantly at the diagram. He had never known anyone like this man who called himself Ammiz the Seer. Who was this enigma wrapped within a riddle? He did not know who or what he was, but somehow, he knew that he needed to know. Perhaps he, better than anyone else, could explain to him the meaning of life and just might be able to explain the true nature of his perplexing dream. Many of the strange things the old man had spoken were somehow beginning to fall into their place somewhere in his mind, but he ignored the more profound, mystifying total in favor of his fairytale dream. Izz did not like brain twisters and would have been more than happy to avoid the perplexity of this one. But he knew that he could never resist the curiosity that twisted in his mind, nor could he ever escape the pondering riddle the strange little old man seemed to foreknow. He looked at the diagram again. Utility rather than a whim dictated the design. After a long while, a light, little by little, began to dawn in Izz's eyes. With so many questions still lingering, every waking moment was cursed with a curiosity that led him on a wild hunt into the late hours of that night.

The next morning, the sun was rising to a brand new day that promised to be particularly pleasant and sunny. The sky was a brilliant tapestry of turquoise and crimson colors. The morning air was fresh and crisp, filled with the familiar clattering and clamoring of morning sounds and streams of smells that filled the air. The bakery across the street where Izz usually ate his first meal was already buzzing like a busy beehive. Just thinking about their mouthwatering sweetbread made him hungry. The familiar sweet aroma of honey bread from its ovens swirled around him like a soft cloud so thick that Izz could have reached his tongue out and licked its sweetness right out of the air. Izz found his way to the bakery's eatery, sat, and was waiting for his meal of honey bread and fresh milk cooled in the morning air. There was the sound of breakfast and the buzz of talking and laughter going on all around him. He smiled and nodded at other patrons lured in by the delicious odors of bread and pastries. In the open kitchen, the cook was pulling hand sized rolls of dark bread out of the large stone oven. Zophie, the meal attendant, greeted him enchantingly as she passed his table, bearing an armful of precariously stacked dishes.

"Just bring me that special sweetbread that could make the dead walk yet again among the living," Izz called out to Zophie as she scurried on passed him.

"You have become the talk of the kingdom," Zophie uttered in passing. Zophie was a fine looking girl, kind, and witty. And it was not as if the opportunity had not ever presented itself, yet Izz remained well mannered and detached. Good cheer lit his suntanned face, and all seemed right with the world. That is until he jerked with a quizzical expression as he noticed for the first time what took him a moment to realize, just over the edge of his table, two big eyes staring up at him.

"Uh!" Izz was unable to mask the astonishment of suddenly gazing down, and seeing the unexpected appearance of the round cheeked face of a beautiful child came up into view from just beneath the table's edge. The unsettling stare in those big, soulful, rounded eyes bore the guise of a lost, vulnerable kitten. The little girl was looking over the stranger with childish curiosity. Finding his voice, Izz asked finally, "Now, what do we have here? Come out from under there so I can have a look at you."

The little urchin brought her face forward obediently as she rose on her tiptoes. Izz looked down, and there before him stood a small child looking back up at him with a big, curious stare pasted on her face. She was a jewel. She wore a worn but clean white pinafore and worn black shoes that made her look like a downy chick too small to be out of its egg. Her curly amber hair spiraled around her innocent, smooth skinned face, making her look like a little gem of an angel that could not have been more than four or five harvest moons old. One could easily see an indication of the beauty she would someday grow up to be.

Izz offered her a warm smile and asked, "Hey, where did you come from?" Izz should have known better. If he did not wish to know the answer, he should not have asked the question. He seemed to have an uncanny knack for never missing an opportunity to attract stray puppies and children. *It is a fatal flaw, the one serious fault in my character;* he almost thought out loud. He supposed it was due to his endless, softhearted good nature.

The child seemed to know at once that Izz was someone she could trust. The young tot pointed east and said, "I live over there."

If there ever were a dog-eat-dog part of Edawn, it would have to be its eastern fringes. Still bewildered, Izz asked, "How did you get here?"

"I walked," she said with a giggle as a mischievous brightness danced her eyes. Her voice had a childish intonation, but the child's dark brown eyes held a clear intelligence that contradicted her age.

No, really, I thought you might have flown here, little bird, Izz thought to himself.

As Zophie waited for the next meal to come out of the kitchen, she took a cautious sip from her hot tea, and upon seeing Izz with the little girl, gulped in surprise, burning her mouth. She walked to Izz's table and laid Izz's hot honey roll, a clay jar of creamed honey, and a tin of milk before him and declared, "I did not know you had children!"

Embarrassed, Izz turned a noticeable shade of red. As he stretched his finger toward the child, he looked up at the young server whom he favored, recovered his voice, and exclaimed, "No, no, no!"

Zophie gave him a weary look and said, "Yes, yes, yes. It looks like a child. Tickle it and see if it will laugh."

"No, I mean, this does not belong to me. This is the first time I have laid eyes on the little butterfly." Izz turned to the little girl who was now staring at his honey roll and licking her lips and asked: "Where are your parents?"

She wrinkled her little nose and thought for a moment, trying to figure out how she should answer. "My mother and father are gone."

Izz recognized a familiar pain in her expression.

The little one stuck her lower lip out and said, "I have no parents I know of. I live with my Nana in the orphanage." Her words were childishly infectious, but the little girl's big, deep unending eyes sparked an ability to understand her fate that contradicted her young age. Izz asked her to sit down. She quickly pulled a chair out and slumped back against its broad, wooden back. Izz slid the sweet honey roll that the little runaway could not take her eyes off toward her as his heart filled with compassion. The sweet roll was still too warm to eat but was quickly cooling under the delicious cream, plentiful blackberry, and honey topping poured over it.

"For me?" She hesitated, unsure of herself. Her stomach rumbled. "Tis this for me, truly?" the child asked again.

"Yes, yes, all for you, little sprout," Izz agreed indulgently.

Her broad smile revealed she had a missing front tooth. Then her smile faded, and she stuck out her lower lip again, and said, "We have to have hard bread and butter for breakfast every day." With a quick word of thanks, she drew the roll to her and gave it an exploratory sniff. Izz pushed the milk toward her. She captivated him with her grateful smile.

As Izz wondered what he was going to do with the little urchin, he picked up a roll of cream filled dark bread and broke a wedge from it. While he was intensely preoccupied with lathering it with blackberry jam and pondering a solution, the sweet roll he had given the little girl vanished with a loud sucking noise and three huge cramming bites. When Izz looked up, he saw that the sweet roll was gone. He looked the tabletop over and then took a quick look under it, wondering if it had fallen to the floor. The lass was chewing on a mouthful and brushing tiny crumbs from her fingers as she blinked with surprise at its creamy, rich, sweet, fruity tastiness. She took a big gulp of milk to wash the roll down. As she swallowed, the luscious flavor left a satisfying sensation in her stomach.

Izz asked, "How did you eat that so fast?"

While the little girl was licking her fingers, she said, "It was easy."

She wiped milk froth from her mouth with the back of her hand. She then picked a large crumb from the empty plate and popped the last morsel of sweet roll into her mouth. "Want me to show you again?"

Izz smiled with amusement as he pushed a second sweet roll over to her with an impulse of kindness as his heart went out to her. "Another one...for me?" She laughed a sound like the chime of pleasant sounding bells that gushed forth from her little pure heart.

"Sure, little one, all for you," Izz said as a smile filled with tenderness lengthened his face.

With an appreciative sniff, the little one plucked the cake from the wooden plate, clearly not intending to share it. The little tyke held it to her bosom so that the mouthwatering aroma it was emitting would rise in the tot's face where she inhaled the fresh honeyed smell. Her tongue sank deep inside the creamy center. Buzu let out a little moan of pleasure as its flavor sparkled against her tongue. She took the first joyous big mouth filling bite of the second richly sweetened roll. The bite she took was so big, Izz thought for a moment that she might gag on it. She noticed Izz's distress. She continued to eat eagerly, but slower, savoring every bite. It was such sweetness. She thought it the sweetest thing she had ever tasted. Her eyes sparkled with delight. With her little hands and deep preoccupation, she tore one small piece after another, holding it up to her nose, smelling it, and then popping it in her mouth, eating it morsel by morsel. She smiled up at Izz, wide eyed in wonder as Izz stared with compassion. Her joyful smile was beyond price. She blissfully continued eating her sweetbread. She had never tasted anything so delicious. Izz was amused to see such delight through such refreshing innocence.

When she had finished, Izz rose to pay. Zophie put her broomstick in its place beside the counter and turned as Izz pulled some coins from his leather pouch and said, "Thank you, kind lady." He paid with a considerably higher amount than was due as he always did, and Zophie received it gratefully. Izz then turned to ask the little angel, "Now, you must show me where you live."

"Could I not stay with you?" the child asked with bits of cake clinging to her mouth.

"No, no, no! You will be a lot better off at the orphanage with your friends and Nana."

"Awww," the child moaned.

Izz took the child's hand in his own as a father would hold the hand of his child and looked into her big brown eyes with tremendous kindness and compassion and asked, "What are you called?"

"My name is Keira." She motioned with her little finger for Izz to come closer. Then she stretched up on tiptoes and whispered into Izz's ears, "But no one calls me that. Everyone calls me Buzu."

"Why?" Izz asked as she pulled away.

"I do not know, but that is what they call me. You can call me Buzu. Tis an easier mouthful."

"Well, Buzu, it is. Let us see if we can find where you call home," Izz said reluctantly.

Buzu instantly trusted Izz, and they walked down the street hand in hand. Buzu's eyes beamed like two dark amber gems, and her pupils twinkled like two black pears as she smiled inside. Buzu held on to Izz's hand with her full grasp, stumbling along at the pace of two footsteps to every one of Izz's. They walked along a backstreet Izz had never ventured into, an area he was unfamiliar with. It was an old street and was the oldest residual section of the kingdom. It was a more worldly part of the kingdom. As far as he could see, every house looked occupied. The bark of a dog came from somewhere in the background. Children were playing along the stone pathway of the lower end of the social scale. Buzu picked up the pace as they reached the end of the street. Tugging on Izz's hand, they turned the corner.

"There!" she said excitedly. "There is where I live."

Izz saw before him a tall stonewall with expanded wrought iron gates. Behind the gated walls as far as Izz's gaze could reach, he observed a spacious conservatory. The scene berthed a fractured memory. The ghosts of his early childhood appear as Izz was reminded of his schoolmaster. He had been the most valued companion in his youth. He was the teacher who taught him all the lessons a father was meant to teach his son. Why he took a particular interest in Izz, he would never know. He remembered how, as the strength of his body and mind grew, his schoolmaster spent more and more time with him, and his lessons grew longer and longer. He recalled his brain's capacity seemed to stretch and enlarge as his teachings lengthened. Besides the necessary academic skills that one would need in life, Izz was taught that the most essential thing in life was to do what was right. He could never understand how anyone could ever want to do otherwise.

When they reached the gates of the orphanage, they were met by several caretakers. As Izz stood outside the gates, he stared in amazement at the number of children going about, here and there, like great flocks of herded geese. They were different children from different lands, and they all looked well fed and clothed.

"Where have you been?" the attending caretaker asked in an unmistakably worried tone as she was unlatching the gate.

Izz surrendered the child to an attendant, neatly dressed in a head cover and clean blue uniform, neatly patched in several places. The first attendant having, thrown the gate open, stretched both hands toward Buzu and scooped her into her arms sympathetically. She wrapped her arms around the little runaway, hugging her like a doll, with love and compassion. She held her tight and kissed her for the longest time so hard that it brought tears to Buzu's eyes. So overjoyed was she that she swung her around in her enthusiasm. When she put her down, she looked at her at arm's length and said, "You must not ever do this again. We were all at our wits end with fret over you."

Several other caretakers, all wearing the same blue long dress uniform, came rushing to the gate. Childish voices mingled with the uproar of Buzu's return. Hearing the commotion, the orphanage proctor came forward from the main building's foyer. Her first thoughts were for the wellness of the little renegade as she approached; she asked the wayward child, "We have all been worried sick!" Where have you been little one? People are searching everywhere for you." No matter how much she scolded, the mistress seemed to find it hard to judge the child too harshly. She hugged her tight. It was good to feel her warmth again. She reached forward and kissed Buzu on the cheek and said, "I am so happy to see you are safe, the one true love of my life." She stroked her hair then transferred the child back into the outstretched arms of the attending caretaker.

The mistress was a short older woman. She wore a long white robe, a white turban, and a concerned look that was etched on a face that was fatigued but kind and expressive with large intense eyes, seemingly the pillar everyone leaned on. Assured that Buzu was safe, she turned to Izz, who had a faint, nervous smile tugging at his lips. "And where did you find our pernicious little Buzu?" the mistress asked.

"Well, madam, you might say she found me. My name is Izz of Zollerzon. I am the nephew of Lott, the Carpenter."

"Your reputation precedes you. You are the young carpenter from down the street, the champion runner."

"You heard about that?" Izz asked.

"Who in all of Edawn has not? The kingdom is on fire with talk of Izz, the fastest man in Zia, and your carpentry work is spoken of very highly in this sector."

Izz just knew he was going to like this gentlewoman. "I was fortunate to win...on both accounts," Izz said modestly.

"My name is Mistress Aria. I am the headmistress here," she said, graciously smiling as she extended a friendly hand. "And these are the children I have always wanted, and I am the mother they never had and have come to need so desperately."

"They seem very well cared for," Izz commented.

"You seem to be a fine young man, and what you have done for our Buzu was very kind of you," she added as they stood together at the gateway. Her eyes were set deep and revealed that they had clearly seen too much. And her lined face told a story of an arduous life filled with the hard labor of love, doing the work that never got done. "That one never sits still. Buzu, as we affectionately call her, has been in and out of mischief from the very day she discovered she could walk. She is the very fastest little whirlwind that ever danced upon the face of Zia." As she spoke, her eyes dominated her whole face. "Well, it would appear that we are in your debt. You will always be welcome here."

And Izz liked the mistress the more for her kindness. "Just knowing that you will keep a more watchful eye on this little angel in the future will be payment enough for me."

"I do not see any point in worrying about many things. Buzu is simply a high spirited soul being a child. An innocent needy heart called out by the voice of curiosity and adventure." A faint smile sparked in her eyes as if remembering her own mischievous childhood, wondering how she had survived the crazy things she had dreamed up.

"I can understand," Izz said. "I myself was raised as an orphan searching for somewhere to belong."

"Our children here never go to bed hungry, but what they truly hunger is love. They needed love so much, and it would seem they have received so little." Her voice dragged out, and she had to choke back her empathy.

As they stood talking at the courtyard gate, Izz spotted a person cloaked from head to toe, diligently flocking a large brood of the youngest children. Each child was obediently focused on the stranger that walked with a womanly, energetic stride, moving as if to meet any challenge with resolute determination. For some inexplicable reason, Izz was overwhelmingly compelled to ask, "Who is that?"

"That is one of our volunteer teachers. She comes every day for a few hours and teaches the children to read and write. She works with those that are less fortunate, especially the most disadvantaged. She has managed to turn many of our most troubled children's lives around, mostly those that still feel like social rejects. She truly loves them all, everyone, just as they are, even the most unlovable among them."

Izz's expression suddenly changed as a remembrance poked up into his consciousness. He was reminded of the kindly orphanage schoolmaster that had taken him under his wing when no one else could reach him. Finally, Izz came back to reality and said, "This world needs more people like you." With no other common ground and with nothing left to say, the two exchanged warm smiles as Izz dismissed himself, turned, and walked away.

"Please come back and visit us when you can," the mistress called out.

"Yes, I think I would very much like that," Izz called back as he disappeared into the crowded street, and with that, he was gone.

Seven

The Rift

ime went by, and the quarter moon past into a full moon. And on this day, as the twilight shadows lengthened, Izz had finally completed the final details on the strange tubular gizmo the seer had challenged him to put together. Izz held the contraption at arm's length and wondered just to what end this device he had produced would be put to use. He attempted to rationalize a logical answer, but it made no sense to him. He looked in through one end and out the other and whispered to himself, "What could this possibly be for," as he analyzed it carefully in his mind.

He extended the three sliding tubes to their most extended length then rotated it, viewing it from its different angles, but only drew an empty blank. He collapsed the tubular pieces into their shortest position, turned it, and again considered it from every perspective. Once more, he was clueless to the purpose of what he had so meticulously fashioned. Whatever it was, early the next day, he would deliver it to the seer in person. That night, while most of the citizens of Edawn slept, Izz lay wide awake, staring up at a crack in the ceiling. As the full moon shone like a giant gem on its silvery dance across the night sky, its luminous rays spewing through his window, his mind was tumbling with thoughts, and sleep was as distant as the moon. He thought about what the seer had told him, *And you do not even know who you are. I know who you are you are more than you think you have become. He had never imagined thoughts like this. Could that be? Was there an answer?* "There must be an explanation," he told himself. Deep inside, he had always harbored a feeling that he was born for some great purpose. He did not yet understand.

While the wheels of recollection spun in his head, the memory of Ammiz's persuading voice continued to hammer his mind. *You are the one...spiritual battle deciding factor...face of death powers of darkness through dreams, he shall be counseled.* He played and replayed each mental scene from his unique encounter with the seer. Like a repeating theatrical enactment reproduced in every detail, each word, body gesture, and facial expression unwound in his head again and again. Late into the night, still wide awake, Izz slowly nudged out, drained, and weeded out his thoughts, narrowing his concentration down to one signal moment. His mind wrapped around the words he had pondered since the bearded one spoke them. *Your new love I see you have already been conquered. You shall have her. You have only to believe it with all your heart.* This part was an exceedingly strange coincidence, too deliberate to be coincidental. The words rang in his ears, haunting and taunting him as if they had just been spoken.

"You shall have her. You have only to believe it with all your heart," Izz repeated the words in a whisper to himself but could not understand the force of their meaning. *Could the seer have possibly meant the café maiden, Zophie? No!* The only one that had truly smitten him was the princess Zuree, the mirror image of his dream angel. His heartbeat out yes, yes, yes, she is the one, but how could that be, his mind reasoned. She was the daughter of the king of Edawn, the emperor of the world of Zia, and he was a parentless, little more than a peasant, nobody.

Izz fell into a rare melancholy mood of depression. His heart sank. He wanted nothing more than to stop thinking, to fall asleep, and to escape his torment. But sleep would not come. He lay on his back, his side, his other side, put his head under his pillow, over his pillow; he grabbed it and pounded on it, but it was still too lumpy. What afflicted him was not something a comfortable pillow could ease. He tossed from one end of his bed to the other as his mind continued to ponder and ponder in redundant orbits. Still, the seer's words loomed maddening in his mind, vexing his soul. Despite all of his attempts to untangle the mystery of his dream, his muddled mind only reeled that much the more.

And so the myriad of thoughts and worries persisted well past the midnight hour, and for his own life's blood, he could not conceive its meaning. The only thing Izz had managed to do was to turn the riddle that perplexed him so, into a more profound mystery than it had been before he first sought its answer. Nevertheless, there was something about the matter-of-fact way the seer spoke those words that pierced straight to the core of his heart. If it was true, even partly true, then Izz had to know everything wherever the lots might fall. In the dead of night, waning on the twilight of consciousness, lost somewhere between whispers and dreams, Izz tossed and turned, falling in and out of shallow slumber. His heart would not let his brain rest, and his brain would not let his body sleep. There were too many things that would not stop jumping around inside his mind. It would have been easier to uproot a giant oak than to rip out the words the old man had sown in his head. He asked himself, " Who am I? What am I? Why am I?" And he sought to resolve an explanation.

The next morning before dawn, Izz woke from his drowsy nod, filled with eagerness and curiosity that continued to eat away at him like a ravaging wolf. He sat up in bed, chasing scarps of lingering imaginings from his subconscious. He brought his hands to his face, branched his elbows out, and stretched back slowly till all the vertebras in his backbone crackled. He then jumped out of bed, splashed some cold water on his face, dressed hastily, and was gliding down the stairs and out the door with the mysterious gadget in hand and a multitude of unanswered questions bubbling in his head. As dawning shadows shortened, Izz threaded his way through the streets of Edawn. Guided along his way by the instructions he gathered from passersby, he finally reached Ammiz's home. Izz made his way up the wide, white flagstone steps that ascended to an enormous white interlocking block wall of stone. Two huge carved pillars at each side marked the entrance of Ammiz's abode. Izz stood in front of an intricately carved metal and wooden doorway studded with iron bolts. The two massive doors were heavily timbered with course oak panels resting on four heavily forged brass hinges. Each door panel was as wide as a man and twice as tall. Izz took a deep breath and banged on the door with the flat of his hand, waiting for what the encounter might bring.

On the other side of the door, Ammiz was at his desk where he had been all night for many nights in a row. He was elbow deep in his painstaking studies. He was painstaking, committing to memory large portions of what he read. The guardian of the Great Book of Foretelling was so caught up with his studies that he did not notice the deadened sound of persistent knocking at his front door. Encompassed by old, dusty books, piles of strewn parchments, and scattered, half written notes of compiled information. Surrounded by the familiar smells, he loved the musty odor of old paper. Directly in front of him, he held a large open, ancient book written by the hands of the greatest thinkers of ancient times. Nearly illegible with age, he held the book to a brighter light as he painstakingly turned the page over and over and over as though he hoped to find an answer to the many unanswerable questions. Deep thought was a bridge way across life's most profound realities. He knew that to unlock the future, he had first to find the key of the past.

The guardian of the treasures of truth flipped through the pages. He read the passages carefully before reading them aloud to himself. The past leaped from its pages of faded writing from authors long dead and all but forgotten. It was a leather bound, iron clasped copy of compiled keys to the earliest clay tablet scripts. It was the richest deposit of wisdom left by previous generations. It was a book of secrets within a secret, a kind of roadmap of predated things to come, supernaturally foreknown. It was the Great Book of Foretelling. Ammiz had spent many years studying the code of the Ancient Truths. He had read and read and reread the prophecies and could not be quenched until he had memorized every word. Well studied heaps of books, hundreds and hundreds of years old, were strewn everywhere never left to gather dust. Containing most of the accumulated wisdom and knowledge that had ever existed, that ever would endure. His thirst for knowledge had become a cursed ritual of solitude. He had taken a solemn vow to study the ancient writings that molded him into who he was.

Day after day, Ammiz had pored over their pages. They stretched his mind, honed his insight, and seasoned his discernment. Within their pages, the seer had found a lesson to all humankind, a truth more valuable, and of infinitely greater meaning than any theories taught by the so called philosophers of higher learning. As the seer leafed through the stiff, yellowing pages, and despite the warmth radiating from the blazing hearth, the honorable old man's hands shivered with fatigue, and his knees throbbed with weariness. The letters of the words before him were starting to blur in front of his aging watery eyes. Suddenly, Ammiz felt older, weaker than he ever had before, and his stiffened structure slumped. There was no denying his well stricken age of nearly one hundred seasons that had by now made him a prisoner of his own body. His head ached, his mouth and throat were dry, and there was a foul ache pounding in his chest. His eyesight was now strained by the dim flickering candlelight that cast its meager ring of light. Age, it seemed, had caught up with him. Every inch of his body protested the strain he put on it, as he often did when struggling to decipher life's greatest paradoxes. He ran his finger over the document, and as the ancient parchment crackled, his eyes slowly traverse the page intently. He searched for the truth as for hidden treasure, sounding every word's depth, balancing one passage with the other, seeking for understanding by consistent and earnest meditation. The seer now seeker pulled the book closer, his brow was furrowed in thought as he read quietly to himself from the handwritten text. "When the Great Conjunction of the seven mother worlds appears in the eastern sky, there will begin a fierce struggle for the souls of men between the light and the darkness."

Ammiz then leafed forward through the pages until he came to the page he sought. He read in a whisper, "He who was spoken of, from before time...shall come from the Southern Isles, in a way not foreseen by men." He then forwarded a few pages. "The one that is to come will walk among celestial guardians... he will be a light in a dark place...carry the destiny of all. Evil will consume all but the pure in heart—when the seven mother worlds reach exact alignment, a rift in time and space will briefly appear. If he fails, all will come to darkness." Ammiz anxiously turned the pages over and over and over as though he hoped to find a more obvious explanation buried somewhere. He again read the verses slowly and prayerfully, and then he turned and sifted through the piles of his most personal notes, papers, and documents. When he found no decisive answers, he shut the book in front of him. The book slipped from his overburden hands. The thick book covers separated as its pages flipped randomly, coming to rest, open to a page Ammiz knew by heart. He rubbed his chin, deep in thought.

Outside, Izz knocked again and patiently waited for Ammiz to answer his door to no avail. A few men passed, and suspiciously glanced at him. Seeing a weighty, pockmarked brass door knocker at eye level, in the middle of the door, Izz reached and grabbed it and wondered why he had not seen it before as he banged it on its brass counterpart, the solid oak and iron front door echoed with a loud metallic clang.

Inside, Ammiz was running his finger over the familiar passage, perusing it with some care as if he was reading it for the first time. He sounded the words as if hoping to learn some extra hidden meaning between the lines. "From the Isles of Zollerzon, he shall come." Those very words jumped off the page just as the continues clanging sound waves slapped up against his eardrums. With a start, the patriarch cocked his head toward his front door. Ammiz stood stiffly and slowly came toward the entrance, encouraging his rigid joints with the assistance of his ivory handled walking rod.

Izz waited a few seconds and then knocked again. This time, he heard footsteps accompanied by a third thumping sound, shuffling toward the door. Locks rattled, bolts slid and scraped. A latch lifted, and the massive carved door opened a crack just wide enough to fit one eye that peered out warily from side to side and up and down. Then, as the door opened wider, a pair of deep set, piercing eyes under bushy brows appeared. Ammiz was surprised to see Izz standing there as he was unaccustomed to entertaining visitors outside his inner circle of most trusted servants. As his face broke into a broad, warm smile, the scholar's eyes beamed like two sky-blue sapphire lights, beckoning a welcoming gaze of recognition. The door swung open with a long, soft, oiled, sliding whisper. Ammiz looked about quickly, making sure that Izz was alone, as if spies may be lurking in the streets, and then pulled Izz inside.

"Come in. Come in," Ammiz said as he opened the heavy door all the way. He then bowed down with a cheerful combination of dignity and polite kindliness as he swept his extended arm in a graceful gesture of invitation. Izz had no sooner entered when Ammiz closed and fastened up all the bolts on the door behind him, shutting out the outside world. Carefully replacing the last latch in place, Ammiz then turned to Izz as his long white robe swirled at his feet.

"I was just thinking about you. It would seem we are of the same mind," the seer exclaimed as he pondered the sequence and the timing of events that had just unfolded. "There are no coincidences, only fate. I welcome you to my humble abode," Ammiz continued.

As he entered, Izz was as nervous as Ammiz was composed. The open waiting room led into a large corridor. The room was barely lit by the fluttering of the single candle placed strategically at the center of the seer's desk. The air was heavy with the scents of herbs and aromatic incense smoke. The shades were drawn to filter out the glaring light, interferences, and any other obstructions. The old man quickly walked around the room and enthusiastically lit several more wicks, covering each flame with a crystal cylinder. The crystal's reflective characteristics cast a luminous light around the room with a brilliance Izz had never seen before. As Izz came into the front quarters, he immediately noticed the walls of the space he had entered were aligned with books. There were hundreds of them, overflowing from shelves and bookcases that extended from floor to ceiling. Every corner was crammed with books piled up in systematic stakes as tall as the walls. Woven reed baskets were filled with priceless scrolls, stores of information passed down through the ages from hand to hand. Ammiz offered Izz a comfortable seat and said, "Please make yourself at ease. I will put some tea on the boil," and no sooner said than he disappeared into the next room.

Izz, obliging, sat down. And as he waited, his eyes continued their casual inventory of what the seer called home, drifting about the room trying to formulate an image of the man that lived in it. The dwelling was pleasant, old fashioned, homey, moderately furnished, functional, but not at all extravagant. The atmosphere was quiet, warm, and comfortable, exemplary of a humble, solitary way of life. Izz surveyed the cluttered desktop, noticing ink quill and well, rolls of parchment, manuscript sheets, writing tools, and the large book Ammiz had been studying, face down, on the desktop. The messy desktop had become a stormy sea of piled paperwork, which otherwise looked like an experiment gone wrong. Laid out on the floor were what appeared like reference books and stacks of handwritten notes. In the room to the right were more floor to ceiling shelves, which were lined with glass containers of all shapes and sizes filled with liquids of varying shades and colors. In the room to the left were yet more shelves filled with contraptions he had never seen before and could not even begin to imagine for what they were used. On the far wall were shelves upon shelf crammed with clay jars, bulbous bottles, tins, and bags full of exotic herbs and spices. By the window, there stood a lone three legged stool.

In the back, a doorway, past the first room, caught Izz's roving gaze. The thick tapestry that covered the entrance to the room was slightly pushed aside. He could see through the opening what looked like astronomical, schematic of spheres, and surrounding globes. Irresistibly drawn, he rose and, without thinking, started for the doorway of the next room. He paused to look around the gadget packed room. What he saw amazed him. The entire room beyond him was covered from wall to wall with maps sketched with perplexing intricacy of diagrams, graphs, and charts. Izz saw landmasses and islands that he did not even know existed. In the back of the room, along the wall, there were tables full of all sorts of instruments that had the look of being mechanical measuring devices. There were also several barrels, piled one upon another, containing bundles of more astronomical charts. The poor, aged fellow, had dwelt too long alone.

But what caught Izz's eyes next would forever remain seared in his mind. Suspended from the ceiling, he saw an unbelievable model mobile hanging before him. Huge marble like glass globes of different sizes and colors, dangled by thin wires from above. The display seemed to be a representation of the wall diagrams behind them. Izz wondered how anyone could have dreamed all this up. Awe quivered inside of him as all of a sudden reality hit him, and he realized that the placement of the globes was strangely familiar to the dream from his imaginary journey among the stars. The model opened up the many hidden wonders of a solar system previously hidden from him. As if in a trance, Izz stared in awe. As the multicolored spheres slowly turned, they cast dazzling reflections of shifting colors and changing patterns of light that danced across their surfaces. On the opposite wall behind the globes, occupying most of the entire wall, were more plots and maps. Marks on the charts were it appeared to be added to track the movements of the bodies. Other markings gave some indication of where they were going and seemingly predicted their projected positions. Incomprehensible mathematics, notes, and figures, explaining the workings and the relationship between parts of the whole, were scribbled throughout the chart. And at the bottom, an intricate, well designed illustration had been ruled in pencil, a union of seven globes. Izz began to lean forward to look at the image closer slowly. Beneath the aligned orbs was scrawled out, "The Great Conjunction."

When Ammiz finally returned to the front room, he carried a tray bearing a steaming round copper pot of tea and two huge heavy cups. Alarmed, he laid the tray on his desk, quickly walked across the room to where Izz was, and hastily re-alined the cloth curtain and tapestry tacked back over the door. Apparently, the contents of the room were for his eyes only. He then politely, but firmly, redirected his preoccupied visitor back to his seat.

"There are some things that are best kept unknown. It is dangerous to expose views that most cannot conceive, and it is much too dangerous to speak publicly about such things. My observations paint a different picture of our world than that of the flat world heads. The 'we evolved from nothing' society. These maps are strictly forbidden by those dismal, naive skywatchers who believe that the stars disappear when they shut their eyes."

"I have often wondered, as of late, if the world was in fact round as I saw it in a dream," Izz said as he slowly returned to his seat. Still deep in all consuming wonderment to realize that it might all be exactly as he had seen it in his dream, including the maiden.

Ammiz cautioned, "You must keep this a secret from these nitwits, so called Learned Ones, who think themselves sharp witted just because their heads are pointy. As far as I am concerned, Zia can stay flat for another thousand years until it is discovered otherwise. Unfortunately, the intellectual establishment is greatly influenced by Baddlock, who explains that the heavens flashed into being, but cannot explain what caused that to happen. His only explanation was that he did not require an explanation of his explanation. They make the laws of this land and could have anyone that merely speaks of Zia being other than flat, reproved very severely. I risk all by holding fast to my beliefs. As it is, I am being shunned by the self professed Learned Ones. But no matter what, I vow to live in truth."

The diviner of secrets suddenly became profoundly quiet for no apparent reason. His eyes seemed to look off to a great distance as if he had lapsed into a vague state of mind where one finds themselves following the dusty footprint of ghostly reminders. As Ammiz drifted, he remembered back to a time in his life when he was loyal only about discovering the truth. In his insatiable desire for knowledge, he sought after any facet of understanding his mind could grasp. He was indeed a man ahead of his time. He stood foremost in the inception of intellectual genius. To all young Ammiz was noted for his advanced intelligence, his abstract concepts were heard everywhere: in the institutions of higher education, in the citadels of the nobles, and palaces of kings. He was visited by royalty, barons, princes, seers, and seekers alike. He had significantly contributed to shattering the shackles of ignorance and superstitions. The power of his brilliance commanded the respect of both friends and rivals. At first, the seer's revolutionary ideas were received with great enthusiasm. But jealousy soon arose among the teachers of the day when they witnessed the vast crowds of scholars that were rallying around Ammiz. They knew that many people were hailing him, the most brilliant among the leading minds of the empire. Ammiz had students breathlessly gasping at his radical insights. Many traditional ideas about truth had to be realigned.

It was a time when Baddlock, one of the greatest of the seers, and Ammiz were the closest of friends. Baddlock had been a leader of men, a believer of goodness and truth. He was once a lover of humanity and an advocator of ideals. But that all changed when they fell in love with the same girl. Eventually, the haunting memories that disrupted his thoughts locked into place. The old man followed the train of thought that led him back in time and filled his mind with the remembrance of his first and only love. He seemed to be dreaming with his eyes open.

Against his willpower, his thoughts drifted. Feelings of depression, regret, and emptiness came bubbling up. He began to draw and expel deepening breaths. Suddenly, a painful memory formed a tear at the corner of one eye but refused to spill and roll down his cheek.

Izz asked, "Was there something—"

The old man abruptly raised a hand and said, "It is a very long story, and it would take me almost as long to tell you as it has taken me to live through it. Nonetheless, that was in another time."

The old man regained his footing, the recollection gradually faded, and Ammiz returned to the present. He had lost some of his optimism, but his boundless drive and radiant intellect were still there.

Ammiz abruptly cleared his throat and went on, "Sharp disappointment, overshadowed our friendship from the day I won the young girl's heart. Jealousy and obsession opened the door to the spirit of hatred. From that day, Baddlock seemed to go about more and more with a black look in his eyes and a grimace on his face. In due course, through clever maneuvering and witty deception, Baddlock managed to reach one of the highest offices of power within the Edawnian Kingdom. After a time, opposition and animosity arose between us, and it was not long before Baddlock set himself to hinder my work and rebuke my teachings. The empire's leaders began to fear me because of my nonconformist teachings. Baddlock managed to convince the ruling class that, inevitably, I would become a serious threat to their authority. My views on a round Zia was very unpopular. Anyone smarter than a box full of rocks can see that Zia curves when one looks out over its horizon." Ammiz explained, "When Zia casts its shadow on the moon, you can see that the outline of Zia upon the moon is round. The moon is round. The sun is round, why not our world? If our alleged lawgivers led by that beguiled soul Baddlock, would only have open their eyes, they would have seen the ignorance and the arrogance of their ridiculous declarations. It is not wise to discuss this with anyone, not even your uncle. We will never speak of our round planet again." The seer gave Izz a stern look. "Flatlands adrift in space on four elephants supported by a tortoise no less! Imbecile fools! Can they not feel the land beneath their feet as it turns?" Ammiz had to control his exasperation.

Izz reflected for a few moments on his state of bewilderment then asked, "If the world is round, what keeps us from falling off ?"

Ammiz smiled and shook his head, amused by such a probing question. "I once thought that the rotation of Zia created an inward pull to its center in much the same way you can spin a bucket of water over your head without spilling it. But more and more, I am beginning to think that everything has a magnetic attraction to the core of our planet."

"From where did the stars come? What is holding everything up? What is making it turn so perfectly?" Izz wondered to himself.

"The Creator of All Things spoke them into being," Ammiz answered as surely as if he had heard Izz's thoughts.

The Creator of All Things Who? What?

"Cast the stars upon the deep. Holds everything up and makes it all turn so perfectly," Ammiz said with a knowing gaze as if he had read Izz's thoughts.

Ammiz returned to his desk, where he began to rearrange the piles of papers, books, and moldy scrolls to accommodate the tea tray better. "You have begun to unlock the mystery. Someday, perhaps, I could explain it to you more clearly. But first, I must explain it to myself," he said with a little chuckle as he poured steaming, herbal tea into a cup and offered it to Izz, then sat back down and poured himself one.

A vapor of sweet smelling steam rose from his cup and swirled in the air. Ammiz raised the steaming mug to his lips and took a long, slow sip to remoisten his dry throat. And then as he looked up from his teacup, somber self control took hold of him. For several moments there was absolute silence, neither said a word. The solemn moment broke when Ammiz witnessed out loud as if of his particular account, "When a man reaches his most profound point of bleak darkness, in his last desperate attempt, he will turn to seek the light, and there he shall find his Maker."

Izz picked up his cup, blew on the tea, and tried a sip. He blinked when its heat wafted into his eyes. Izz reasoned *The One, the Source the Creator...whatever one what's to call it. Some Existence created us? Could we have come around by chance? Everything had to come from somewhere.*

Suddenly, Izz felt a strange, penetrating force like tiny electric impulse as the old man gave his unexpected guest a long, searching glance. The look was that of one who was primarily given to looking inward, one who deemed external substance of insignificant value. The seer's heavily hooded light gray eyes were so profound that they seemed for a moment to be deep cosmic oceans, radiating with insight and power. The old man finally asked, "How is your tea?"

As Izz's mind came swimming back up, he remembered his purpose for being there, and it suddenly dawned on him that the old man probably also was wondering why he was there. The seer's revelations had amazed him so much that he had almost forgotten the reason for his visit. Izz put his tea down and spoke, "I have been longing to speak with you, and yet I did not want to disturb you. And…oh, yes." He pulled the mysterious contraption from his inside vest and handed it to Ammiz. "I have completed your commissioned devise. I hope it meets with your approval."

Ammiz took the object and examined the completed project carefully, studying it from every possible point of view. "It does not surprise me that you were able to figure out it's completion."

"While it was exceedingly profound, it was at the same time exceedingly uncomplicated," Izz acknowledged.

As Ammiz continued his inspection, his hopes were not disappointed. He reached into a drawer in his desk and pulled out two leather pouches. He spilled out two glass lenses out of one, and the other he left on the desktop. Ammiz gathered the two glass pieces he had hand shaped and painstakingly polished. He took the bigger of the two lenses and fit it to the larger end of the sliding tubes. He carefully wedged the glass piece into place, impressed that Izz was so able to achieve the exact measurements. He secured it with a metal ring and examined the results.

Meanwhile, Izz sipped on his tea thoughtfully. Then the seer took the smaller glass and repeated the same process on the shorter end. He quickly looked over the assembled gadget, while Izz nervously sipped on his tea then sipped some more then sipped yet again. The seeker then took several even paces across the floor to the nearest window and pulled back the curtain. He held the smaller end up to one eye and adjusted the length of the tubes.

Ammiz admired the fine craftsmanship of the instrument. It functioned as if a master craftsman had assembled it. A very pleased expression washed over his face, finding himself admiring this skillful young man more than ever. Without removing the contraption from his eye, he motioned Izz to come to him. When Izz approached, Ammiz handed him the tube and instructed, "Look through this end," and pointed to the distant mountains.

Izz took the tube and looked through it in the direction of the distant mountains as instructed. The faraway mountains miraculously snapped into close focus. Stunned by the sudden enlargement and clarity of the remote mountainside, Izz stumbled backward by the shock of unexpectedly seeing it closer than it was. Unable to believe what he was seeing, he gradually lowered the telescope as if to assure himself that the mountain had not somehow shifted forward. He quickly returned his eye to the eyepiece repeatedly, startled at the suddenness of such a discovery, he asked excitedly, "How does it do that?"

Ammiz explained, "The combination of curved lenses placed at the correct distance from one another magnifies the image of a distant object to make it appear closer." Pointing to the larger end, Ammiz continued, "This lens collects light and reflects it down the tube to a focal point. The small lens then refocuses the image for the eye." A silent, awkward moment followed.

Izz stared, wide eyed, with an unknowing gaze into mid space. He had never heard of such things. Then Izz slowly nodded and shook his head at the same time, proclaiming his complete bewilderment.

"Well,...the most important thing is that you understand that by moving the tubs in or out makes the image clearer, now come, sit, our tea is getting cold."

Once seated, Ammiz slid the pouch still lying on his desk toward Izz. "This is for you. Your uncle Lott made it for me years ago. It has served in my studies to no end."

Izz assumed it was his payment and did not question the old man. The two men sat and sipped from their cups of tea. Ammiz glanced down at the Great Book of Foretelling that he had been studying and gave it a long, thoughtful look. He looked at the long eye for a moment, then turned to Izz and focused on Izz's eyes as if to capture some glimpse of his essence. "It would seem that you are an amazing young man."

His searching eyes continued to look for seemingly something within Izz's very soul. All the time was wondering to himself if this could be the one that the ancient's foretelling spoke of. The seer downed his cup of tea, smacked his lips, and went on with his usual confidence. The old man took a deep breath and then spoke very slowly, "Very few people know what I am about to tell you. I am going to reveal to you a tale that, at first, will appear impossible. However, the deeper we go down the labyrinth, the saner it will appear." His expression became weighty. "There is a present battle raging in the realm of the unseen. The Keepers of the Light and the dwellers of darkness stand on the edge of tomorrow, preparing for war over the glorification of man's soul."

Challenged by the seer's echoed tidings, Izz searched for a clue to the understanding of what the old man could mean. To that point, the old man's answers did very little to quench his queries. Izz disclosed, "I am not sure what you mean by all this...chosen one...Light and darkness..."

Ammiz stared back with a knowing smile. It was not the look of a crazed man; it was the look of the soundness of someone who knew that he knew what he knew. "It is all written in the stars. The flawless universe makes known its secrets to those who seek them out. The universe will respond with the same zest that we emanate toward it. The universe is absolute, and it proclaims the perfect fortunes of all. It is we who are impaired. And if my interpretation is correct, the stars have inscribed your name. Izz of the Southern Isles of Zollerzon, you have been preordained from the beginning, since time out of mind, to bring down the pillars of the dark underworld."

Izz studied the seer's eyes as they filled with passion and sparkled with youth as he declared his revelation. He studied Ammiz's expression as he spoke. Though the old man was a shadow of the brilliance he once was, he held his presence with authority and power.

With a raised hand, Ammiz cast a spellbinding hold on Izz's attempt to express his skepticism. "Forget everything you know or think you know. You have only to listen with your whole heart. Here, within these walls are contained the greatest and most complete records of mysteries, history, inventions, and the greatest monumental events of our time. It is the most sacred accumulation of the deepest knowledge in all the libraries in Xylenia. In these scrolls are written the account of our existence as it had been since the beginning of time. They have pointed me in directions I would have never looked at on my own."

Izz fell silent as if he suddenly realized in every fiber of his being that Ammiz was speaking the truth. Izz realized that he was staring widemouthed at Ammiz and looked away. His eyes rested on the stack of books and scrolls stacked everywhere, while he continued to listen intently.

"Some of these books contain forbidden knowledge. This knowledge, if it fell into the wrong hands, could be hazardous." The old man's eyes were inadvertently drawn to a bookshelf at the far end of the room where the spines of cryptic, coded, and epic book lined up on the shelves. The guardian of the treasures of truth took a long troubled look at the distressing gap that reminded him of the missing black book of dark secrets that once rested there. That particular book contained forbidden knowledge that he should have destroyed long ago. The seer redirected his thoughts. "They are in my care because I have managed to live far longer than any of the other so called seers, and I suppose that King Ozzdon deems me the most trustworthy. I believe he considers me harmless because, like most, he probably thinks me crazed. Well, maybe I am a little. It keeps me sane."

Izz was staring soberly at Ammiz. He finally managed to speak. "You have learned many profound and wondrous truths in your lifetime. There is no one like you in the whole of Zia," he said in a tone of complete conviction.

"I have indeed learned many things throughout my life, but my story is your story, only a piece of the story of all men. In reality, I know hardly anything at all. Only what I have managed to glean bit by bit from all these ancient writings. And it is little that I have been able to gather in my short lifespan by reason and by precept. Unfortunately, when I think I understand one facet of my in-depth studies. Just when I think I have figured it all out, new twists crop up to remind me how unpredictable reality is. Sometimes knowledge seems to be just one more burden to carry around. The truth is that the more I know, the less I understand. It just so happens that I know more about these matters than most, which is once again, almost nothing. Unfortunately, I know much too much to be cheerful."

Izz hesitated for a moment, and then he blurted out, "You seem to know everything about everything."

"It is true, age has revealed many things, and the most valuable has been wisdom. I have not sought satisfaction in honor, power, or riches. I have found that every self indulgent endeavor is fleeting vanity. Instead, I have sought to become the emperor of my innermost mind. But all I have learned is that there is much left to be discovered. Now I seemed to have reached the point in life when life stops giving and starts taking. I am old, and my days are numbered. I suppose I will go on toiling daily to learn something new until the day age puts me into the ground." Ammiz got very quiet for a few moments, and then a serious look came over his face. From across another time and place, out of the grave, trudged unbidden reminiscences into his thoughts.

The old man once again seemed to gaze beyond into some past shadow where his spirit stirred the same haunting recollection. He could not bear to remember, but could not forget memories of a young maiden that danced in his heart. The old man began to smile involuntarily, his eyes filled with tenderness. He unexpectedly frowned. A hard expression suddenly spread over his wrinkles as if he had suddenly felt a momentary pang of remorse. His gray eyes, under his white eyebrows, stared at something in his past that had scattered his beautiful memories and smeared them with unbearable pain.

"Enjoy the power of your youth while you can, and never waste an opportunity you have been given to truly be who you were born to be. You must look beyond what you think you see. For a man can run out of things to live for. Fix your expectations, follow your dreams, heart, and soul. And do not be anxious about failing, because there is no better way to gain that which you seek most."

Ammiz poured a second round of tea from the copper urn, steam from the hot brew whirled, and rose from the two freshly poured cups. Izz was trying to take in all that he heard, trying to think a little harder. The information he was soaking up was stirring his curiosity as never before. And a multitude of unanswered questions began to swarm to the surface of his mind. For one thing, he wondered what difference his life could make against what Ammiz referred to as the world of darkness.

Again, the man with the seemingly unfathomable soul spoke as if he had read Izz's thoughts. "It will all come to you at the time that you need to know it most. Always keep your inner light burning, and you will find your way."

Izz's mind seemed to be chewing over a familiar puzzle. He was learning more than he had ever anticipated as the old man seemly opened countless buried channels in his mind. He had to know more, had to know everything. "Where did the so called dark underworld that you speak of come from?" Izz interjected. "Why is there evil, suffering, and why is there death?"

Ammiz leaned back in his chair, making its joints creak. He paused for a moment as if to collect his thoughts as he stroked his long, white beard. He gave Izz a measuring look and saw not what he was, but what he was meant to become. He raised his pointer finger.

"The full truth of the future is linked to the past before time. To unlock it, one must first find the key in the present. It is all there, yet I must confess I know only the merest fraction. But I do have a fair notion as certain conclusions are unfolding and becoming self evident." Then he opened his hand, signaling for Izz to wait. Ammiz pushed his chair back from his desk. He then rose and walked into the next room.

Izz could almost hear the squeaking joints of Ammiz's stiffened knees as he made his way across the room. Through the open doorway, Izz could see Ammiz standing before a shrouded cupboard. Behind it was a tall strongbox, mottled and notched with time. From around his neck, the seer pulled what Izz imagined to be a key. Ammiz inserted the thin tool and twisted it. And it looked as if he had to toil with a lock that was not going to give up easily. Ammiz wiggled the key until, at length, the locking mechanism clicked open, and the door came unlocked. He turned the brass knob, and with an aged, prolonged metallic creak, opened the door of the strongbox.

When the old man returned to Izz, his eyes seemed to be brightened with a rekindled spark. Ammiz cradled in his hands a heavy ancient book with an unusual tooled binding. He held the leather bound volume as if it was a coveted, precious treasure trove.

"This book is a collection of secret chronicles, translated statements of facts recorded from ancient stone, clay tablets, and scrolls that reach back from past recorded time." As he sat at his desk, he continued, "There are very few that have been given the honor to look upon, much less study these writings. This book is written in a writing system of one of many ancient languages that have yet to be completely deciphered. As far as I have been able to figure out, the writings tell of the creation, the wicked fallen, and of a final judgment. Wherein awaits unimaginable eternal rewards, as well as unspeakable possible horrors. Its words are a timely coffer, a window into the days of eternity and the world beyond. It is a key into the deepest realm of accumulated human understanding. I have been intently studying and unwrapping their secrets hidden within their writings ever since they have come into my hands, which is longer than I care to remember. If the secrets of this wisdom were to fall into the wrong hands, the information in their possession could give them dark supernatural powers. Days ago, I discovered that one of these manuscripts has gone missing. The writing that I cannot account for is a collection of discoveries that would have been better left undiscovered. I am going to do my best to reveal what I have discovered within these text fragments because I believe that you are intricately intertwined within its pages. I will try my best to explain in the simplest terms as possible. You must listen carefully and with an open mind."

Sensing that he was standing at the threshold of a new reality, Izz wanted more than anything to understand. But he knew in his heart that, in all probability, he would not have the capacity to comprehend it in its entirety. Izz hoped that what was about to be unveiled would shed some light on the connection between him and the beautiful princess of Edawn.

The seer opened the book painstakingly sewn into the binding. As he flipped through the pages, almost illegible with age, he spoke, "This writing reveals the highest levels of realization that I have ever read. I have learned that heaven's purpose is grander than our own and that death is a part of eternal life." When the seer found the bookmark, he searched out. He ran his finger over the fragile pages as he continued, "According to these sacred writings, long, long ago, there was a great cosmic war. It was the most awesome confrontation anywhere from forever to forever. The very foundations of the universe were shaken to their very core. The existence of darkness is the result of a cataclysmic tear in the fabric of creation."

Izz listened intensely with a blank look on his face as the seer translated from the ancient inscriptions.

"This disorder was caused by the twisted, jealous desire of a trusted servant to rule over his own Master. It was in the time of eternal presence when the universe was one, and darkness was unknown. There was a free willed servant known as the Son of the Dawn, who was anointed and placed in the highest position of trust. He was given authority over the whole universe. Slowly, thought by thought, he ultimately allowed the love of his bestowed power to consume him thoroughly. Eventually, he fell victim to his own willful self deception. In his heart, he exalted himself above the mind of his Creator. His appointment allowed him to secretly convince a multitude of supernatural beings through lust, greed, and selfishness to worship him as their master. The wayward servant believed that he had become self intelligent, all powerful, and undefeatable. He was permitted by the Creator of All Things to hatch out his plot, so the flaw that was given birth could be fully disclosed. And that the corrupted should reveal to all the real character of their wickedness."

"The wicked servant schemed to slay his Master and take His throne by betrayal. The self defiled servant entered the presence of his Master, thinking that he had veiled his intended crime. He was entirely, unaware that his every move was being watched and recorded. The corrupted servant approached his Master, pretending to reinforce his dedication of loyalty, obedience, and love. Even then, the Creator was willing to cast his transgression into the farthest realm if only the servant would relent. To the very end, the Master hoped that the delusional servant would feel regret for what he was about to do. He desired more than anything that the wayward servant would divert from his intended abominable deed."

The seer shook his head, the weary lines under the old man's eyes stiffened, and a not entirely here expression came over his face. His voice crackled with age as he continued his story, "The Giver of all life knew that the stab to His heart would not be nearly as painful as the agony of betrayal. Knowing that someone He had loved unconditionally, one He had given everything and withheld nothing would be willing to murder for gain. His heart began to bleed, yet before the mortal wound had been inflicted, it bled because it broke from knowing that He was about to be betrayed by His most beloved servant. The fallen one embraced his

Master in a moment that should have been filled with trust and love. Instead of devotion, without hesitation, the corrupt minion plunged his concealed dagger deep into the pure heart that yet held compassion for His lost creation. The Master hoped with an expectation to the very point in time that He felt the dagger's razor honed blade pierce the chambers of His broken heart. But the dawning star would not repent of his lust for power as he plunged to the hilt and twisted his blade. The self seeking servant reared his head and jeered with delight, thinking that he had won. But instead, the Sons of Righteousness stepped forward and drove him through with their Swords of Light. The defeated foe fell to his knees, clutching his chest as darkness spewed from his wounds, mouth, nose, eyes, and ears. Light and darkness collided, clashed, and repelled itself so violently that in one timeless moment, the perfect cosmic sphere of oneness burst forth in sudden catastrophic upheaval. The state of singularity was sent pulverizing into celestial dust, hurtling in all directions to the remotest reaches of the fracturing universe. As the altered heavens dissolved into chaos, it became devoid of form and light."

Izz could almost picture the vivid scene Ammiz was weaving through the apocalyptic words he read.

"With the swiftness of a twinkling thought, the Master instantaneously reawakened from His self imposed state of suspended animation. In that instance, He was no longer One, but Two, both a separate Spirit Personage and the exacting Personage He was before. The boundaries of the expansive cosmos were shattered, but within the firmaments, their substance was used to knit together the fabric of a new creation. In one-millionth of an instant, in an imperceptible fraction of time, His Spiritual Self projected forth across the quantum face of the mega cosmos, all at once, in every trajectory and filled the heavens. The heavens were destroyed and reborn all in the same instant. Everywhere, His Spirit saturated, a new universe spread out in every direction, and the blackness of the void exploded with light. Stardust came together to form into perfect globular masses of all sizes and different elements. Suns simultaneously ignited as the Creator gathered all under His control. Within this realm, His voice went forth, and life sprang up on planets everywhere. He laid down perfect laws imposing perfect functions of His physical creation. With each passing moment, with each word spoken, the gravity of complications increased."

It took the farthest reaches of Izz's mind to grasp the vaguest concept of what he was hearing. He opened his mouth to speak only to find his thoughts had fallen into a paralyzed stupor. And Izz silently criticized his inability to give his perceptions speech. His silence was profound.

"From that moment," Ammiz continued, "the Sons of darkness, lead by their fallen lord refused to repent, calling good, evil, and evil good, choosing darkness rather than the light. The Sons of Light went forth and hunted down the rebels who had become hideous demons of the deep that hid in the darkest corners of the universe. Every single conspirator was captured and brought in chains before the great Source of all and executed. Only their spirits were kept alive to be imprisoned in the center of our world and other worlds. Here the prince of darkness was cast down along with his fallen to become demons, the rulers of the underworld of Zia. Their negative spirits to remain loosened, pending their final judgment until the universal clock set in motion winds down. At which time, the fallen, doomed to self destruction, will be cast into the void prepared for them, never to be seen or heard of for eternity."

Ammiz was glad Izz did not ask why their spirits were allowed to live because he was unsure he could give him an answer. But just as Ammiz feared, his hopes were short lived. He could sense the silent unanswerable thoughts brewing wildly and forming behind Izz's eyes. But everything Izz had wanted to say, and all the questions that wanted to flood out, all suddenly went blank, all vanishing into a pit of despondency. Then, as if rising from the murky depths, in desperation, he said the first thing that came to mind, asking, "How can you be sure that anything found in your book can be true, it is so old. The language is almost unknown. There is too much room left for interpretation."

"From what I have been able to gather over the years, the book is accurate. For longer than I can remember, I have been following a succession of events that have precisely unfurled as foretold. The odds of this happening by chance are impossible even by the widest margins. The book must be true to its word."

Izz was trying to absorb it all, but it was too much for him. "But if the Creator of all things has in-fact regained control of everything, then why is evil suffering and disease still allowed to continue? What is the reason for the poison injecting fanged snakes, for the great meat eating cats and sharks? What good are bloodsucking insects and poisonous spiders? And I do not understand why innocent people, especially children, have to suffer, and why must everything die?"

"These questions have obsessed seekers and seers alike for millennia and have echoed down throughout the ages. And these are questions we have all asked ourselves at one time or another. Perhaps these questions are too profound and impossible for the human mind to conceive fully. No matter what puny humans think, the Creator will fulfill what He has determined is fitting. I am certainly not intelligent enough to know the mind of the Creator. In reality, I know nearly nothing of such matters, which is more than most. But as far as I can figure out, we are in some trial period for our benefit, to discover for ourselves the penalties of the original rebellion. The writings hint toward the conclusion that the lovers of evil should be allowed to flourish to the full, so they may, beyond a shadow of a doubt, be destroyed utterly and forever and evermore. Suffering seems to be a purification process that perfects our character. Life in many ways is like an endurance race in which our courage, fortitude, spirit, and temperament are tested, measured, and rewarded for our efforts to endure. What I have been able to glean from the ancient writings, and what I have been able to fill in by reason, is that we are immortal beings encased within mortal shells. And when death comes, the spell of mortality will be broken forever, and perhaps we may learn that there is no such thing as death, only the eternal cycles of life. Mortality is a mere dream, a fleeting shadow on a cloudy day. No one knows how much time we are allotted from birth's first cry to death's last breath. We are given the exact time we need to accomplish all the things we are meant to do. No matter if it is the smallest moment or a hundred years, both are but a twinkling of an eye, in the eternal scale of time, the thinnest sliver between two opposing eternities. And so those that put all their hope in this life are destined for regret."

The subject of death seemed to have again touched upon a tender nerve. The old man's speech suddenly sounded slurred and tired. Tears that never spilled formed at the corners of his eyes. As if he once again recalled a long buried remembrance of a bad dream forgotten. The ghosts which haunted his nights forcing him to drift through remembered flashes that made him tremble at their recollection as if the unbearable pain they bore would find him out in the daylight.

He spoke suddenly, "As of yet, I have not completely been able to decipher death's riddle. Perhaps death itself is the only question that holds within it, its own answer." Ammiz's words continued slowly and burdened. "Have you never stopped to wonder whether the end of this life was the beginning of an adventure exceedingly greater than birth's first breath? We are like seeds that must be put into the ground to die so that we can spring forth in abundant rebirth to join with those that have gone before us." A single tear slipped and finally found its way down his cheek. "And now await us in a place where tears never fall, and beautiful flowers never die. "The seer set aside the residue of his final cup of tea.

The old seer seemed suddenly overcome by fatigue, leaned his head back and closed his eyes, withdrawn from the moment, apparently lost in thought. His eyes appeared to disappear, fallen between the wrinkles and folds, lost, or disengaged all together. Ammiz drifted off into a deep sleep there where he sat, suddenly seeming very old and exhausted, like a rag that had been wrung out once too many times. And at that moment, Izz could not bring himself to believe that Ammiz had once been young. Izz took the blanket that covered the seat he sat in and draped it over the aged man's shoulders. He took the pouch that still lay on Ammiz's desk and poured its content onto the desktop. The first thing Izz noticed was an object that resembled the instrument he had made for the seer, except that it was smaller and shorter. He extended and collapsed the looking glass, still trying to help his mind understand how it worked. From the desk, he picked up three golden coins that had spilled from the same pouch. It was much more than Izz had expected. He took the three coins and laid them back on Ammiz's desk as he whispered, "Good works are their own reward."

He concluded that the looking glass was more than enough payment for his services. Izz quietly walked to the door. At the door, he turned, looked at the old man, and whispered, "Thank you for your hospitality, words of wisdom, and the tea, my old friend." He unlatched the door and let himself out and pulled the self locking door shut behind him.

Eight

The Commission

Izz was determined to make the best woodwork in all the kingdom of Edawn and as Izz's carpentry skills became more widely known, he found himself often venturing into the Ebony Forest to gather wood for his growing business. He loved the forest with its smell of pine and wildflowers. He loved all the small creatures that seemed to appear and greet him every time he passed them by on his way to the clearing where he collected his wood. And every time Izz ventured there, he always longingly looked toward the Giants, standing like sleepy sentries in the middle of the forest, wondering how it might feel to stand in among the Ring of the Giants.

One day while gathering wood, as one might have guessed, overcome by enduring curiosity, his inquisitiveness finally got the better of him. Izz could no more oppose the temptation than make his mind up not to breathe. His wandering soul needed to know, to fulfill its never ending search for meaning and reason, and so Izz decided to take a closer look at the tallest trees in the world of Zia. Driven by reckless curiosity, he dropped the wood he was carrying as if the mysterious trees had cast a spell on him. Consumed with the irresistible urge to know, he started his long walk toward the Ring of Giants, enticed to see for himself just what was what. As he approached the dead oak, he saw the warning nailed to its base. The notice, he was told, read, "AHEAD EVIL LIES DO NOT ENTER." Izz paused for a moment as a shiver from an unknown chill ran through him. He had to remind himself that he feared no evil. He shook the feeling away as he whispered, "Silly fables, old women tell to their grandchildren on a moonless night to make them behave."

The forest became thicker and thicker as Izz stepped through an unexplored wilderness that still held creature no one had ever named. It was like entering an enchanted world that could only be found in a storyteller's dream. Its remarkable beauty was hauntingly beautiful and beautifully haunting. The closer he got, the more forcefully the biggest, tallest trees in Zia seemed to beacon out to him, come forth if you dare. And suddenly, he felt alive with the thrill of his forbidden calling as the pull of the unknown drew him onward. The majestic trees could be seen for miles around looming above all the other trees in the Ebony Forest, towering giants that dwarfed even the tallest trees around them. As he walked along, every other tree in the forest seemed to point toward the Ring of Giants. Izz homed in on the landmark that pulled him in like a signpost from which he oriented himself. But, after zealously blazing a trail for many, many miles, Izz did not seem to be getting any closer. Undeterred, he trekked deeper and deeper into the ever darkening forest. Anticipation quickened his senses, and his desire to know more than he knew swept him along. Eager to discover the absolutely, most fascinating sight that was sure to await him there, he hurried on his determined way. At long length, he drew nearer and nearer to the biggest and tallest trees that he could have ever imagined.

At long last, Izz stood trembling with excitement in the massive shadow that the giant trees cast across the forest and stared up in spellbinding awe. The only thing more remarkable than the tree's massive girth was their height. Along the base of the forested grove, Izz found a terrace of sparkling pools of water, glimmering in the mystic fog they created, ensuring the forest kings always received their share of water. Their loftiness guaranteed they never had to fight for blue sky, fresh air, or the light of the sun. Izz walked up to the tallest of the tallest trees on Zia and looked directly up. A sense of awe filled Izz as he stood next to the oldest living thing on Zia, having survived thousands of years, ever inching up higher and higher every year. In amazed wonderment, he saw the spiraling trunk ascend beyond the forest canopy, beyond the surrounding giants to its most glorious dizzying heights, which was its crowning top. It's woody bark overlapped like fish scales as they stretched to heights that pointed to the firmament of the heavens, testing the boundaries of his sight. He extended his arms around the massive tree, leaned up against, and embraced the bulk of the gigantic tree. It would have easily taken thirty-five men or more, hand to hand, to encircle the enormous trunk. He closed his eyes and could feel the slow rotation of Zia.

"You must be hundreds, maybe thousands of years old," Izz spoke to the tree as if it was a conscious living thing. There was no way of telling, but one thing was for sure, its top climbed into the sky further than any other living thing in Zia. Mystified by the grandeur of the tree Izz got the craziest urge to climb the towering monarch. He needed a release from the accelerating energetic excitement bursting from within him. In spite of his fear, the titillation brewing in his veins made him believe it was worth the risk. Ascending the tree was what fate had planned for him. Izz was the type of person that would instead do something than just think and talk about it. He took a pull from his water pouch while he examined the tree's incline. A wide crack ran up its barked face, and he knew that that would be the best route to scale. Izz was a skilled climber, having climbed many rock faces just for the thrill of it, yet he had never climbed a tree, not of this magnitude.

He felt his heartbeat quicken as he took hold of one of the many knobs that dotted the tree's trunk and started up the face of the tree, climbing into the unknown. He soon learned by heart how to maneuver from one very awkward position to the next. With high steps and long reaches, he pulled himself up. The bark was covered with holes, hooks, and so many natural holds that it made it possible to climb the base of the tree with ease. It seemed to come as naturally to him as breathing. Izz climbed ever higher, up, up, and up beyond his earthbound world, he went. The higher he went, the more he became aware that the consequence of making a single mistake would mean certain death. He carefully pressed the pads of his fingertips tightly against each handgrip on the bark and kept reminding himself to make sure his grip was secure and that he had a firm footing before taking each new step. There were very slippery areas dripping with sap, and he had to climb slowly with extra care, but his course remained direct with no deviations. He needed to see what was at the top. Moment by moment, bit by bit, the scenery changed at every step up along his climb. He could see the vast wilderness of the valley below and could now see the backs of the surrounding mountaintops. Izz was about one-third of the way up the tree when he started to think that climbing up the tree had been a terrible idea. One false step would send him tumbling to the ground to become a broken, bloody heap. He wondered why he would risk life and limb only to say that he had stood on the top of the world of Zia. The top of the world!

At that moment, the temptation to keep climbing proved too great, so upward he went, suddenly energetic, alert, and eager to go on. The ever expanding scene around him took his mind off the long, long upward climb. The further Izz climbed, the more serious his undertaking became; no longer was it the pleasure jaunt he envisioned. His pace slowed as the heaviness in his arms and legs steadily increased. He reached a large branch just above him ,where he thought he could rest awhile and catch his breath again. As he reached to pull himself up and over, suddenly, without warning, he heard a horrifying, blood curdling, earsplitting shrill. Every hair on Izz's neck and back stood on end as he felt something frantically flapping and slapping at the flesh across his arms and face. To escape the onslaught, Izz had no other choice but to let go of his grip on the branch. His eyes widened, and every muscle in his body strained with tension. As he fell back, he caught a glimpse of his assailant. It was a giant White Crested Eagle. It's raised crest showed that she was not at all happy with the sudden intrusion. The very angry mother eagle lashed out at Izz as it clutched two eaglet eggs under her vast wingspread and screeched wildly. In the thinnest slice of time before plunging, Izz and the eagle's eyes met and locked for what seemed like an eternity. Within a twinkling of an eye, Izz was in between the firm death grasp of gravity, and the razor sharp barbs of the eagle's talons. He felt his heart leap against his ribs from inside. He worked his mind frantically to keep panic from engulfing him. His face froze with fear as he tumbled back and downward. Caught in the grip of breathless terror, somehow, Izz managed to pivot at the last moment as he dropped to what he thought was certain death. But instead, unexpectedly, he landed with a terrible thud among an outcrop of thick branches just out of the eagle's reach. He lay there face down in a sprawling heap, saved by his celestial guardians. The unexpected impact knocked the wind out of him. He felt his head start to spin as dizziness closed in on him. Everything turned misty and transparent and then went completely black as he faded from consciousness.

When Izz finally came to with a gasp, he found himself reaching for the small ax he carried at his side as he precariously lay across the branch that saved him, as if impaled, suspended above what seemed like an infinite drop. Instinctively, he clung to the thick bark of the branch for dear life, digging his fingers in hard. It was just short of a miracle that he had not gone tumbling headlong to his death. He knew in his heart of hearts that he had narrowly ended up as a bloody spot at the bottom of the forest floor. Izz was trembling half to death with fright, his heart thundered as he tried frantically to brush those thoughts away. He struggled to focus on something, anything. He clenched his fists till his knuckles were white as he bit down hard on his lower lip. He drew slow, deep breaths until finally, his panic fell away, down onto the forest floor beneath him. The fall had rattled the root of his confidence, but Izz was the kind that did not give up easily. He lifted himself upright and felt that his cooling limbs had stiffened, and a terrible leaden heaviness had set into his legs. Still woozy, he struck his legs with his fists, trying to regain some feeling back into them. Then he massaged his muscles until he was able to return some agility into them. The pain diminished, and he convinced himself that he was going to be okay. He spoke these encouraging words to himself. "I have never given up or turned back in my life, and I shall not do so today."

After a long while, Izz regained his courage, resilience, and equilibrium. He closed his eyes and drew a deep breath into his lungs, and decided that he had gone too far to turn around now. He reminded himself that a faint heart never accomplished a thing of any significance. Like someone resurrected from the dead, he gathered his courage and picked himself up. He cleared everything from his mind, and with the fearlessness of youth, he carefully continued his long scramble up. He climbed a few stiff steps aloft until full strength came back into his arms and legs. Izz took great lengths to avoid the eagle's nest and eggs. With every move, he reminded himself to tread carefully. He trudged forward and up-ward, determined to make it to the top, regardless of what obsta-cles might get in the way. He climbed and climbed and climbed, and still, Izz could not see the top above. He distracted himself with thoughts of gallows humor. You cannot rise if you will not risk a fall. Besides, it is never the fall that kills. It is the sudden stop at the end.

After an agonizing climb that seemed to take hours, finally, the top looked to be in reach, but that was only an optical illusion, a distorted perception that told him he had a short way to go. Izz looked up, and then down, with hundreds of paces below him and hundreds of paces above him; he realized he had reached the mid-point of no return. He did some rough figuring in his head and grimaced as he calculated the towering top's height. *It is impossi-ble to quit now that the top is in sight,* he kept telling himself. At that point, every step he took was ever so carefully and plodding, requiring every ounce of will he had left. The challenge of the climb had proven to be more than he had anticipated. His heart thundered in his chest, trying frantically to keep up with the exer-tion of his muscles. Exhausted by gravity, it would have been easy to make a critical mistake here. His face was bathed in sweat de-spite the coolness of the breeze wafting down from the northern mountains. Izz switched his hand grip to his left hand long enough to wipe away the sweat. Still, he went on and on. He had to be sure to find good anchors for his hands and feet at each step as he climbed the stairway into the heavens. Sweating from head to toe, Izz knew he would have to stop soon, stop to rest, and catch his breath. Weariness once again crept in, and he became so exhausted that he could barely feel the deadness in his legs. He had pushed himself so hard that he almost did not have the strength to put together a coherent thought.

Izz reached a good branch to rest upon. He sat there perilously suspended above an infinite abyss, feeling the ache of fatigue in all his being. He looked out into the vast expansion before him in all directions as far as his eyes could see. The panoramic view that stretched out before him was breathtaking. At this point, he dare not stop his accent to what seemed the top of the world. Izz took air deep down into his burning lungs, and once again, his strength began to return. With an effort that was greater than any he had ever made before in his life, Izz hauled himself up and continued his climb above the clouds. His curiosity would get him there. It exhilarated him, and he intensified his efforts, increasing his pace. An occasional glance toward the summit kept his goal in perspective. Even though many beautiful scenes were there to be observed from each new vantage point, he did not wait.

When Izz finally reached the top, he felt exhausted yet triumphant. Soaked in sweat, Izz's shirt clung to his back, and perspiration trickled from his brow. He raised himself the last few cubits without resistance, climbing to the roof of the great unknown. He had reached a height where not even eagles dared to fly. He felt a triumphant sense of accomplishment, but he was too tired, too sore, and too woozy to find the energy to celebrate. He stood on the uppermost branch, facing toward the southern horizon, his shirt clinging to him soaked with sweat. He wrapped his arms around the circular contour of the treetop behind him and interlocked his fingers. He whistled softly in awe, and then his jaw slackened with amazement. Izz's face was filled with exhilaration and wonder as he looked out over the edge of heavens rooftop like a dumbstruck bird, peering its fuzzy head out of its shell for the first time. The spectacular scene seemed in its enormity to be endless. Izz sensed his insignificance as he felt the turning of Zia beneath him. He towered over the world of Zia like a conqueror over a defeated opponent. The giddying height was a dizzying and wondrous sensation revealed only to those who dared. Izz felt weightless, suspended above an infinite space between heaven and Zia.

Simultaneously pangs of excitement and foreboding rippled through him as the treetop genially swayed, and the winds whispered across the roof of the world. His wildest imagination could not have prepared him for what he saw. The sky was a clear, brilliant tapestry of blues, azures, and turquoise colors. Before him lay the full panoramic view of Zia, farther than the eye could see beyond the southern coast of Xylenia, across the vast southern sea, and to the other side of the point of no return. Izz saw beyond the beyond, across the skies with eyes like a falcon far to the South-East, the East, and the West. A labyrinth surrounded him as vast and infinite as the deep blue sky above him. It was like peeking into an enchanted world. He had never seen anything so beautiful. It was beyond belief. Izz was looking at a view that no one alive had ever seen before. He was so high in the thin air that he felt he was soaring in the upper reaches of Zia's atmosphere. He saw for miles and miles and miles. He could see everything at a glance: valleys, groves, hills, fields, woods, and steep mountains. His eyes bounced wildly from one thing to another as he wanted to take in everything, all together, in one ravenous instance.

Izz could not help feeling small and insignificant in an immense. The full brilliance of the sunbathed him in a cheerful glow as he began to catch his breath finally. Elation began to fill him as if he was breathing magical air. He looked out across range after range of lands that searched as far as the end of the globe. And he could see the circular curvature of the horizon. The world had to be round. He caught a glimpse of his dream and saw the bustling complex network of the immense universe in his inner mind. He felt Zia slowly rotating beneath him as it hurled at an unimaginable speed around its sun among the stars. He felt a oneness with the eternal rhythmic heartbeat of the universe. It was a surreal world of celestial scenery, and Izz absorbed the full magnificence of it all. In his third eye, Zia seemed like a tiny mote floating in the endless expansiveness of the universe. His awareness seemed to be expanding, deepening, and stretching itself beyond its worldly limitations. It was all there, and it was all so real. All at once, he understood. *It is my destiny to be here,* Izz thought to himself as he saw farther than he could see.

Between meshing clouds below, Izz caught the view of the realm of Edawn. The kingdom seemed a miniature plaything of itself, with neat rows of toy model ships lined up in its bay. The vast Wazoo Valley came into view, shrunken into clusters of tiny farmhouses, lost in the center of a vast, squared patterned field of farmlands and orchards. The lofty hillsides that sheltered the kingdom looked to him now like mere anthills. The boundless sea south of the kingdom, half hidden by the swirls of puffy clustered clouds, was no more than a wind tossed pond. To the West lay the endless flatlands that stretched away toward the horizon. Beyond the forest, the bogs stretched out endlessly. Beyond the marshes as far as the eye could see, the lands turned into the Wastelands of Woe. Here the surface of Zia appeared as if it had been cut clean by some unknown force.

Far off over the marshland, Izz's keen eyes spotted a White-Crested Eagle, soaring, circling, wings moving gracefully in the usual steady breeze from the North. The magnificent creature must have been the mated partner of the nesting eagle, scouting out the land. Izz watched with great interest as the magnificent creature effortlessly flowed through the air, patrolling, searching for its unsuspecting prey. In that instant, Izz wondered what it would be like to fly, to feel the onrushing wind across his face, to sail through the air. The thin air and his heightened exhilaration were intoxicating, making him feel like he was one with the sky. So fascinated by the moment was he that he felt as if he could take flight by merely leaping out into the depths of infinity to soar among the clouds. So powerful was its alluring force that it could have easily distorted his better judgment with bewildered imagination. Fear entered Izz; the fright that protects all men from self destruction was the counterweight to his foolish courage, which urged him over the edge. The spellbinding hold was broken when out of the corner of his eye, Izz noticed something odd. Where the sky seemed to touch the mountain, desolate wastelands of the Noragore Rim, along the skyline where long shadows were already starting to crawl along its southernmost horizon, he saw what looked like puffs of smoke rising from the face of a cliff in the distant mountainous peaks.

That is odd, he thought, *how can smoke be coming out of stone?* Unclasping his hands and shading his eyes against the glare of the bright sun, he saw that the dark cloud was growing and whirling through the air. Izz stepped around the top of the tree, wrapped one arm around the tree's pinnacle, and pulled his long eye out. He focused his lens, and to his amazement, he saw millions of bats.

"Vampire bats," he thought out loud. He squinted his eyes, attempting to focus his lens and eyes enough to see from where the bats were coming out. What captured his imagination was the eroded craggy mountain on top of the notorious Noragore Rim. He saw what looked like a megalithic human skull, or was it just a shadowy freak of nature playing tricks on his eyes. Izz marveled at how sometimes natural landscapes could look so much like real lifelike things. He could barely make out what seemed like the crumbling entrance of an old and forgotten ancient ruin. Forgotten because it could not be seen from any other place but the vantage point he was standing upon. He had heard of this lost, forbidden kingdom, but always thought it did not exist. He had heard many tales of such a place from the older sailors on his many voyages. Izz stared intently as his heart thundered. *Could it be the fabled kingdom, the lost Forbidden Kingdom of Skullsdoom?* He wondered to himself.

An undetermined number of moments later, Izz noticed that the sun had started its dip toward the western horizon. So great was his preoccupation with taking it all in, to absorb, and to memorize every astonishing detail, that he had not realized that the day was rapidly rushing to its end. Time had slipped away faster than he had expected, and he had remained longer than he intended. Darkness could easily trap him high on the tree. Far below, the forest floor beckoned, so he quickly readied himself for the long trip back down. He would have to push himself hard to make it back down before dark. Still riding the euphoria of having made it to the tree-top, he was amazed that he was feeling so strong. The descent was faster and easier, yet he knew full well that he could not make any costly mistakes that could send him plummeting to his end. When he reached the midway point, he took great care to avoid the eagle's nest.

When Izz was safely on the ground, he dropped to his hands and knees and dug his fingers into the forest floor. He touched his face to the ground and kissed it in recognition of his small insignificance when compared to the grandeur of Zia's creations. For a moment, Izz thought about how arrogant he had been, believing he had seen all there was to see. The world of Zia was just a grain of sand in the immensity of the universe. As he brushed dry leaves and bark fragments from his clothes, the impact of the celestial world he had just left was still sinking in, burning itself into his brain. The knowledge of his epic ascent struck him with such force that any notion of ever forgetting this experience was unthinkable. In no way would he ever be able to see his world or his life in it as he had before. There was an entirely brand new world all around him. Izz felt wholly alive; the human need for adventure satisfied. And as he took his handkerchief to wipe his face, he thought, *No matter what comes to pass from this day on, I have truly lived.*

As the twilight shadows lengthened, the waxing moon rose above the eastern horizon, echoing its beams across the moonlit forest as he walked quickly along the path that led to the clearing where he had left his wood cart and donkey. Izz could hear the night sounds of the forest all around him, the call of nocturnal birds, and the trill of insects chirping relentlessly in the woods. This section of the forest was peculiarly eerie in the moonlit night. Retracing his steps, he found himself through the twisted wooded trail as the wind whistles an eerie tune through the treetops. Soon he was halfway there, and by now, the moon was straight overhead, highlighting the dirt path like a silvery ribbon. As Izz neared the border of the forbidden forest, unexpectedly, his acute sense of awareness detected something amiss up ahead where the brush virtually enveloped the trial. Izz had an uncanny ability to sense things that went completely unnoticed by others. A noise arrested his attention. There, in the near distance, he heard the crackling sound of steps muffled on the graveled path. Just ahead, his keen eyes caught a slight, shadowy motion and heard a faint rustling of leaves. Izz stopped dead in his tracks and held his breath. Suddenly, the beauty of the moonlit forest was transformed into a dark, threatening place of unpredictable dangers. And the shadows of the night triggered his imagination.

Could it be some wild forest creature lurking out there somewhere, getting ready to strike? In the condensing winds brawling in from the Northwest, Izz heard his uncle's voice echo in his mind, *Do not venture past the clearing, people have been known to vanish, never to be seen again.* Could it be robbers, or a hungry wild beast stalking him? Izz put his hand on the small dagger; he carried at his side and unclipped its retainer. He cautiously moved ahead, ever so carefully listening and scanning the trail before him. The trail was spongy and kept his foot footsteps quiet and muffled. Izz spotted an unusually high bustle of tracks crisscrossing along the path ahead. Suddenly, there fell an unsettling, ghostly stillness that seeped deep into Izz's bones. Because of the thickness of the forest, Izz found that going around was not an option. Besides, facing a threat would be better than being hunted. As he moved along the trail, he spotted a long branch like a staff. He gathered the stick and hastily sharpened its end with his small ax.

There was something absurd and prehistoric, but very reassuring about the stick he carried. His orphanage schoolmaster had taught him that a long stick could be a formidable weapon in the right hands, especially against a wild beast, or worse. Stealth as a cat, Izz crept forward along the curve of the trail. There ahead, he saw something move again and then heard something scurry away. Izz's tense nerves slightly eased as he continued along the path, stick in hand, and his dagger only inches away. His pace quickened as he hastened to get passed the high entanglement of foliage. Then suddenly, his extraordinary skilled eyes caught a glimpsed glimmer of movement out of the edged corner of his vision, and at once, he snapped to attention, stopped, and whirled about with a sidelong glance.

There in the dense shrubbery, agitation caused Izz to freeze. Yes, most definitely, something moved. Izz heard a low, throaty growl and saw sharp teeth flash in the darkness. There was something there, holding its breath, watching. Izz stumbled back through the thick brush. With his free hand, he slowly drew his dagger; its metallic hiss whispered out its warning. He crept to where he thought he had seen the movement, preferring to face the danger than risk being attacked from the rear. His heart pounded, his breath came in short bursts as he carefully reached out and drew back the twisted growth. In the pale full moon, amid the tangles of the wilderness, on the adjoining trail, he saw that the bushes hid a darkened obscurity among them that would have gone unseen by an untrained eye. But his eyes were too shrouded by the dusk to reckon whether it was a hedgehog or a bear. He adjusted his eyes to the dim light, and his great surprise, he found himself looking down on a colossal wolverine, half as big as a bear, weak and grieving. It was caught in a most unusual twist, a grotesque trap of some kind, set by some cruel person.

Baddlock, the Wicked Warlock Wizard was the first thought that popped into his mind. Izz remembered seeing the very same traps hanging from the wizard's street vending stand. The trap was the kind that was set along the path and, when sprung, delivered a sharp spike into its unsuspecting victim. As the animal struggles to get away, several other traps subsequently seize its feet. Once fast in the snare, the unfortunate victim was assuredly doomed, condemned to die a slow, agonizing death. Izz considered life to be sacred, and killing for the sake of killing was evil. He instantly grew to hate these metal traps, vowing to destroy every trap he came upon thenceforth. As he stooped toward the pitiful sight, the fur around the carnivore's neck bristled, its ears pricked toward him as it began a growl from the depth of its bowels. At that moment, he could have sworn he heard the wolverine say, "Come one step closer, and I will tear you limb from limb. Izz hesitated for a moment and wondered if he had honestly heard what he thought he heard.

Izz felt the beast draw a deep breath, seemingly reserving its last fury to be vented on closing its jaws on his hand. Izz just knew trouble was waiting for him, but he could not bring himself to turn away. Very soon, the warning snarl turned into a strange, rasping, strangled whimper. He wondered how anyone could be heartless enough to set such a cruel trap. To mutilate and to kill without need was a wrong against universal intelligence. He looked compassionately down at the helpless animal, all four of its paws were caught in clawed traps, and there was the wicked metal spike buried deep into its back. Izz's heart ached with a mixture of pity and wrath as he looked into the wolverine's dull and spiritless eyes. It would have doubtlessly gnawed its limbs off to escape if it could have gotten its teeth to them. The wolverine stared back at him with unseeing eyes as it continued to make strange gurgling sounds. He took note of the plants growing all around him; some had curative properties. Izz hastily gathered some herbs and their roots. He put the mixture into his mouth and chewed them into a meshed ball with his teeth to produce a healing juice, while he tore strips from his shirt. The creature's incisors were bared in a hushed snarl. As Izz neared, the wolverine shot him a warning stare.

Izz genially spoke, "I am here to help if you will allow me." He continued his soothing words until the beast grew calm.

Izz watched the wolverine for a moment as the awkward rising and falling of its chest told him it had little time left to it. By now the unresponsive beast seemed to care little whether Izz was there to help or end its misery. For a moment, Izz wondered if now was a good time to add to the beast's burden.

Izz carefully and firmly placed one hand against the wolverine's broad back, felt the creature take in a deep breath, and then with one smooth, quick stroke, withdrew the impaled spike with the other hand. The beast's head lifted, swayed, and its eyes opened wide. Izz saw small tears flow from the corners of the wolverine's overgrazed eyes. Izz quickly did his best to clean away enough of the bloody gore to insert the herb plug into the wound. The wound was perilously close to the creature's heart. He took his time to bandage the injury. He tightened and tied off the dressing so that it would stop the bleeding. He could barely feel the vibration of the wolverine's growl as it bore its fangs. Even though Izz tried to comfort the wolverine, he held out little hope for its survival.

Izz spoke again, "I am going to free your feet now; please do not attack me." Izz could have almost sworn that he saw the creature nod in agreement. Slowly, Izz freed the mortally injured wolverine's feet. They did not seem broken. He made a makeshift nest of woven grass in a hidden place, gave the wolverine the rest of some bread, honey, and nuts he had brought for his trip. He found himself staring into the dim, haunted eyes as if the wolverine was solely waiting for death to ease its soul. Izz covered the wolverine with leaves to keep it warm.

He assured the beast, "There, now you will be fine." Izz took a wooden bowl he carried in his satchel, pressed it into the ground, and filled it with water. The wolverine just lay there, scarcely breathing, its tongue dangling out of its mouth. Izz paused for a sad moment. He gave the wolverine a long suffering glance of pity as the declining moon signaled that the moment of parting had come. As he walked away, he wondered if it would not have been more kindhearted if he had ended the beast's misery. As he quickly put distance between him and the wolverine, he thought he heard water lapping sounds.

By the time Izz came out of the dark, dismal forest and reached his wagon and donkey, the full moon had gone down beyond the horizon. It was fortunate for Izz that the power of innumerable bright stars lighted the night and that the donkey was familiar with its way home where it knew oats waited.

Within the Inner Circle, the bickering over whom should sit where continued in such disarray that it continued to take precedence over the administration of the Edawnian Kingdom. Men of learning, men of noble birth, upright men honored for their integrity and wisdom, squabbled using lopsided logic like drunken sailor brawling over a tavern stool. They became more and more concerned with where they sat than the administration of the kingdom. On this particular day, the heated dispute among the Council of Nobles was so violent that, at first, the king only shook his head and even laughed, giving vent to his nerves. But it was the end of the day, and nothing of any value had been accomplished as it turned out. The king wondered how such a trifle thing could overpower the mind of men. Finally, his mouth tightened in annoyance, and the king's fist came down hard on the armrest of his throne. He shuddered in disgust and stormed out of the Halls of Law.

Nine

The Conundrum

That night, King Ozzdon laid awake tossing and turning, unable to fall asleep for thinking about a possible solution to this insignificant issue that was quickly becoming an impossible dilemma. At wit's end, anxious for an answer, a thought came to his mind. He thought of Baddlock, the wise wizard; now there was a man who seemed to know everything about anything. His night was sleepless. He rose at dawn the next morning and at once sent for his head squire and ordered him to summon the wizard to his chambers as soon as possible. It was midmorning by the time Baddlock showed up, escorted by the royal guard. And just as expected, Tigbone followed along, clumsily as a wayward puppy, looking much like a big toad, complete with rangy legs, slumping shoulders, and spiny arms.

"You sent for me, my lord?" Baddlock asked as he bowed, tilted his head forward, and extended his humblest expression.

"Yes," replied King Ozzdon. "It is an insignificant matter, yet it would seem of the gravest importance."

"I have only your best interest at heart, Your Highness. Whatever you wish, it is my command, Your Majesty," Baddlock said as he bowed again, this time even lower.

King Ozzdon explained how the senseless bickering of his Inner Council cabinet over where each should sit at his long table was hindering the administration of the empire. Quarrels over position and rank, concerning who should have precedence, were so heated that it was becoming the central issue of each meeting.

"What is your advice on this matter, honorable Wizard Baddlock?" the king finally asked.

Baddlock was silent for the longest time, lost in thought. At length, he spoke, "It is quite simple, my lord. What you need is a round table in which all that sit are equal, and no one can boast that his seat is more favored over any of his fellow men."

"That is brilliant, admirable Wizard Baddlock. You, my good man, are a genius, and you will be well rewarded," exclaimed the king, sending Baddlock on his way with a heavy pouch of gold as a token of his appreciation.

By this time, Izz's reputation as one of the most skilled carpenters in the kingdom had become legendary. And so it was no surprise to anyone, but Izz, when King Ozzdon showed up at his woodshop. On that fateful day, Izz was busily working on a cabinet for a wealthy merchant when he heard the shop bell announce that someone had come through the front door of his shop. The oddest premonition came over him, disrupting his inner peace. Izz slowly looked up to see the king standing there. He was so shocked at this abrupt onset that it almost made his knees buckle underneath him. For an awkward moment, Izz just stood there and stared. The king stood there bigger than life dressed in his royal blue silk tunic, trimmed with ermine. Over his tunic, he wore a fur hem and neck lined mantle of scarlet satin with embroidered long sleeves that widened at the elbows and were adorned with contrasting bands of colors at their edges. His shoes were bright blue, studded with jewels, and tipped with pointed, curled toes. Two royal guards flanked the king. It was the armed guards that concerned Izz. The guards were not needed as such, but King Ozzdon was so admired and dearly loved that, everywhere he went, his subjects wished a moment of his attention; however, those moments quickly multiplied. If the guards had not surrounded him, he would never have gotten anywhere with such a heavy schedule.

When Izz regained his composure, he immediately bowed to his king and said, "I am ever your faithful servant, my lord, how may I serve you...Your Majesty?"

The king regarded Izz with a measured glance as his gaze flicked for a moment over his face as he offered his hand. Izz took his hand and shook it firmly and said his name, "Izz of Zollerzon…Ahhh, of Edawn, now. That is the city of my birth is Zoller-zon. I am from here now." Izz tried to receive his unexpected guest in a statesmanlike fashion.

"Word has reached my attention that you are a craftsman worthy of his hire. Yes, yes, Izz, you seem to be making quite a name for yourself, not to mention your monumental victories in our recent games." The king said, shaking Izz's hand warmly as his face eased into a smile.

"It is an honor, my lord," Izz returned as he smiled his most pleasant smile.

Then the king's smile faded as he turned to business. "Please, Izz, be at ease," the king said. "I am personally here because I find that it is good business, in matters of great importance, to deal with a man face to face."

Izz tried to poise himself mentally, but despite the king's reassurance, Izz still felt nervous, awed by the momentous possibilities this unexpected opportunity might represent.

"The purpose of my visit this day is because I have a serious commission proposal."

Izz dared not refuse the king anything. The king turned and took a few steps seemingly as if inspecting the shop as he spoke, "What I need is a table...but not just any table. It must be a grand round table for my royal court."

Izz was amazed that the Emperor-King of Xylenia would entrust him with a commission that he seemed to deemed of such importance. He gave the king his undivided attention.

Izz was about to lose his heart; he just did not know it yet. It was as if destiny had wanted to meet fate face to face; well, it was about to happen. Accompanying King Ozzdon on his visit was his beautiful daughter, Zuree. Zuree often went along with her father on his ventures about the kingdom and had ever since she was a child. The royal responsibilities of the kingdom kept her from having much fun, so she often sought out diversions, a kind of amusement to break the monotony of royal life behind the palace walls.

Izz of Zia

As the king moved away, there between the royal guards Izz caught sight of Princess Zuree standing before him. When Izz laid eyes upon her, up close for the first time, he was awestruck like a blind man whose sight had all at once been miraculously recovered. His heart made an odd noise. Instantly, the conversation he was having with the king grew undetectable. Izz heard only silence as he stared directly at Zuree in amazement. He knew in an instant that he had never seen true beauty before that moment. His unbridled gaze played over her as long as he had the courage not to look away. Their eyes met for a fraction of an instance. It was the longest instant Izz had ever lived before. Long lashes framed the most beautiful blue-green eyes, more beautiful than words could describe! Izz's eyes twinkled with a glimmer of recognition. Up close, he recognized those eyes more vividly than ever from his dream. The resemblance to the maiden in his beautiful planet dream and the girl in the looking stone dream was uncanny, too uncanny. Izz felt his heart miss a beat. His dreams had collided headlong into reality. The coincidence was too much to endure without being overwhelmed.

Zuree stared back as long as she dared. Izz's glance shifted away quickly, convinced his eyes and heart were playing of trick on him. However, to have seen her standing there in front of him, this close for the first time, was to love her forever. Izz could not tell whether she was more flattered or annoyed by his odd stare. *What on Zia am I thinking,* his mind reeled, almost out loud? In an amused surprise, Zuree turned to look at him again? The glance stirred an unfamiliar but far from an unpleasant impression within her. She noticed that there was a definite spark of recognition in his eyes. She did not understand why he was looking at her as if he knew her.

Zuree briefly made eye contact, and Izz heard her speak to him in his mind as her lips moved soundlessly, as her face dawned quizzical expression. *Do you know me?* Then the second slewing glance came, that finished melting Izz's heart, plunging him further over the edge of no return. When Izz's and Zuree's eyes met for the second time, their mutual interests were drawn like magnets. Their eyes interlocked, and some unexplained infusion discharged through their bond. An unexpected moment of fondness ensued as each seemed to know what the other was feeling. Zuree's gaze fixed on the handsome young carpenter. Her eyes and mouth arched, bringing her high cheekbones into robust prominence, granting him the warmest and most welcoming of smiles that almost knocked him down, showing the whitest, pearly teeth he had ever seen on a mortal's face. Forces that could not be seen or touched, only felt, mounted all at once. Izz could see nothing but her and did not hear a word the king continued to say. Izz's eyes held Zuree's spellbound for an ever lengthening moment. She seemed to be searching his tan toned face as if its strong features were somehow familiar. She seemed to be trying to remember some forgotten memory somewhere on the edge of her mind just beyond her recollection from a far off, misty, distant dream.

Neither she nor he could quit staring at the other. They stared and studied each other in silence for what seemed like a prolonged split second in time, unable to tear their eyes away, surrounded by forces of involuntary attractions, raising themselves to a peak at the speed of a mere heartbeat. Her eyes flickered nervously to take in the rest of him. His face was tanned, and his raven black hair was thick, wild, and unkempt. As far as physical appearances, he was strikingly handsome in a powerfully masculine way. He wore coarse, work stained garments that had seen better days and a pair of boots that noticeably had some severe mileage on them. As she returned Izz's stare, her thoughts descended every corridor of her mind, searching her memory for an association but found none. Feeling a shiver of magnetism, Zuree tore her eyes away at once with difficulty, wondering why she had taken so much time to notice his intriguing features. It was simply beyond her understanding. Suddenly she felt annoyed at herself for staring so. She turned and fixed her eyes on her father as he went on and on about the table he wanted. She could feel Izz's intense, unbridled eyes playing over her, just as surely as if he was reaching out to touch her, but she kept her own eyes fastened on her father. Zuree tried to act indifferent, trying to regroup her splintered attention. Yet she could not help feel something mutual with the carpenter.

Izz's wide eyed stare was unwavering. She was exquisite. Like a drunker, he drank in her intoxicating beauty. Her bone structure was ideally balanced, her skin flawless. Her nose was wonderfully straight and narrow, her cheekbones high, her mouth was full and rosy, plus her square jaw outlined her face beautifully. Her sparkling eyes were the most mesmerizing shade of blue with a touch of green that immediately drew and held one's attention. Her brilliant eyes were crowned with velvety lashes and outlined with the softest light brown eyebrows superbly sculptured into gentle arches. She had the longest eyelashes that nature could have bestowed on any woman. She was as flawless as any physical embodiment could be. She was the most exceptional example of health, looking as if she had never missed a square meal in her life. This was a woman that, without any doubt, led a blessed life and was accustomed to the choicest things it had to offer. Her clothes were of the most excellent tailor made quality. She wore a taffeta tunic dyed bright red, fastened together at the shoulder with a golden clasp. The flowing garment hugged and accentuated every curve of her womanly body. Her long golden hair was plaited and covered with a silken fabric, decorated with intricate embroidery and embellished with gold and silver that cloaked the contour of her sleek frame down to her feet. On her neck, Izz's attention was drawn to the most elegant necklaces, studded with the most exquisite cobalt blue stone. The stone refracted the most unusual and intense fluorescent light.

Indeed, the work of the most skilled artisan. However, if life had taught Izz anything, it was that beauty was only skin deep. Yet in the young princess, there was much more than met the eye. Izz saw right to the heart of the fair maiden's soul. There was depth, richness, and fullness of life so vibrant that it seeped through her skin to set her aglow. Not even in his wildest of wild dreams he had ever dreamt, had he ever imagined that anyone could be as beautiful as she was. But it was her dazzling, deep shade of blue-green eyes that captivated Izz most of all. It was the way the light of keen intelligence and complexity burned brightly in the windows of the purest soul that he had ever seen before. Of all the beauties he had ever met, never had he seen a woman so perfect in every way.

All the while, the king's entourage, with their faces split and corners curved into the broadest of grins, were giving each other knowing sidelong glances. They were aware that anyone that had ever gazed upon the face of the fairest maiden in all the land, near and far, compelled most to take a longer, closer look.

Aware of Izz's unyielding examination of her, Zuree awkwardly gave him a nervous sideways glimpse. The king noticed her uneasy shift. Sensing the intensity in the air, he glanced toward the two. He saw how Zuree's eyes were constantly drawn to the carpenter and noticed the blush on her cheeks. Then he turned to see the strange expression on Izz's face. At first, he could not understand the reason behind it. He turned and raised an eyebrow to the carpenter, who seemed to be looking into some other universe. Gradually, he realized by the look in Izz's eyes that he had fallen into a deep, all consuming state that had to be overwhelming his head, heart, and all his senses simultaneously. For a moment, he paused to consider what it might all mean. He recognized that it was, in fact, his precious daughter, that was the reason for the carpenter's crazed condition. It was as if the air between them was intensely oscillating to some primeval music no other could hear but they. For the first time, it would seem that the king saw his daughter through renewed eyes. He should have known his little princess would someday be all grown up. And that day, seemingly, was this day. She was a woman now, an intelligent one, and one of unusual beauty. He turned his attention back to the carpenter.

"Izz...Izz, Carpenter Izz!" called the king in an increasingly louder voice. "Have you heard anything I have said, young man?"

Izz abruptly returned from wherever he seemed to have been. The king smiled as he shook his head. "Have you met my daughter, the princess of Edawn?"

Izz involuntary started slowly nodding his head and started to say yes, but then abruptly paused for a moment as if in some deep, private thought, trying to get a grip on the situation. He pressed down into his heart, the knowledge of his dreams as if they would somehow be found out, hiding them within, like a coveted treasure. "No, no, I have not had the pleasure, my lord."

"This is Zuree, princess of Edawn, my daughter," the king proudly announced.

"Zuree," Izz said slowly, rolling the name over the top of his tongue like the sweetest of tastes as the letters of her name dripped like honey from his lips. His smile moved into his voice. "What a charming name." The genuineness in his voice felt like a gentle caress to Zuree.

There was something very likable about the carpenter that had drawn Zuree to him. She faced Izz; her gaze was direct and steadfast. She was not timid, nor did she seem as spoiled as she might have been, given the status of her privileged life. With her eyes fixed on the handsome young man, she offered him her hand.

"I am pleased to meet you." Her voice was pleasant and smooth as gentle as a summer breeze, warm and sweet, as luscious as candied honey dripping from a flower petal. She smiled, sweetly exposing her perfect teeth again, encouraging his self assurance. Izz somewhat clumsily brushed his hands against his trousers, making sure his hand was clean enough, and then extended it.

"Izz of Zoller...Edawn. He bowed low with the reverence due to an angel. "It is good...a pleasure to meet you, milady... Princess Zuree."

A smile slowly curved her lips in response to his politeness. Sparks flew from their fingertips as they touched. Izz warmly took her hand in his. The princess's hand was as soft as the most elegant satin, if not more so. Lord, she was lovely. Zuree found her hand enclosed in his. In some magical, mystical way, the sensual sensation from Izz's hand managed to spread and enfold itself affectionately around her, embracing her in his strength. With that first touch, their spirits leaped and cast themselves deep within the other, setting off a million tiny jubilant bells tinkling one with another. The electrifying touch caught them so suddenly off guard that they both flinched inwardly. As they briefly held each other's hand, the air around them seemed to tingle with an aura of intensely focused energy.

That touch of wonder spoke it all. Izz felt an abrupt, overwhelming undertow, drawing him into the depth beyond the beautiful pigment and hue of those eyes. Zuree suddenly felt as if a vast swarm of butterflies was fluttering around inside of her, trying to escape against the barrier of her ribs. A seed had been planted in the mind and heart of each. Zuree's shuddering indrawn breath told Izz that she was as moved by the contact as he was. Zuree flickered a thin momentarily smile across her face as she felt strange vibrations ripple down to a sensitive area at the core of her soul. That thin thread of caution Zuree had felt earlier began to unravel in her heart. Their eyes synchronized and locked. Starbursts of unseen forces soared between their hearts like shooting stars racing in every direction at once, vibrating throughout their minds like stringed instruments simultaneously playing an opulent trill with each tremulous string struck. The air around them seemed to fill with a million brilliant lights, and they imagined that everything was slowly inwardly turning as if all that existed was created only to bring them together. They both sensed that something extraordinary must be happening. At that moment, a light breeze could have knocked either one of them head over heels. Each saw a soul that radiated volumes of emotional messages to their own. These were feelings neither had ever experienced before. They regarded each other with mounting curiosity and wondered again and again why they had the oddest feeling that they knew each other intimately. It was a relentless, matter-of-fact feeling that they knew that they knew, they had known each other before, or shared some mutual experience in the distant past. As they broke contact, Zuree withdrew her hand up and held it in the other. While she shuddered slightly, she wondered, *How did he do that?*

Suddenly, they both looked away nervously, each wondering what the other was thinking. The king shook his head in exasperation as his brow furrowed in curiosity. Unable to disguise his concern, he interrupted when he saw his betrothed daughter staring at the carpenter in that searching way that women use when they are unmistakably attracted to a man. Fixing his penetrating stare upon the carpenter, the king loudly cleared his throat before he spoke, "I want this to be the finest table ever created, or will ever be created." The king intruded on Izz's reactivated, all too vivid waking dream of memories and sensations Izz had no idea from whence they came.

King Ozzdon walked up to and handed Izz the design of the table he wanted. Izz stepped out of his trance and said, "Yes. Yes," as he took the parchment and glanced at the diagrams he was given. The one thing Izz noted was its massive dimensions. "Of course, it will be the most superb table ever seen by anyone, anywhere," he said as he glanced back to Zuree for a moment that seemed to last forever.

In an attempt to make an impression on the king and especially the princess, Izz waved his hand before him as though he was magically producing what he saw in his mind's eye. Zuree watched as Izz's enthusiasm spilled out over him and found such sudden confidence exhilarating.

Izz continued, "I see it all now, it will be the most magnificent table in Edawn, in all of Zia. It will be made of one piece of wood. Four mammoth yakoxen facing north, south, east, and west will support the massive tabletop. The yakoxen sculptures will be surrounded by the greatest exploits of Zia's greatest kings." Izz paused to gauged Zuree's response from the corner of his eye. On the opposite side, the king was frozen, not daring to move, breathe, or speak, afraid that the magnificent vision Izz was painting would be lost. Zuree purely smiled as she gave Izz a long enchanting look. There was something irresistible about this man that she beheld.

His enthusiasm and charismatic personality immediately struck the king. "Yes, yes, I can almost see it." The king's eyes sparkled as he smiled broadly and stared into space at the table Izz was creating as he spoke.

Izz continued to pull away the veil, little by little, from his imagined masterpiece with every word. "The rim of the tabletop will be covered with the intricate carvings of the most exotic animals known and the design of every flower in the forest. The flowers will be created with inlaid stones of every color."

The king was swept off with the vision Izz was spinning. It was as if the table were standing before him as he added, excitedly, "The table surface should be etched with the history of Edawn's accomplishments, heroes, and champions."

"Yes, of course, it should be made with one piece of the finest wood in the kingdom," Izz added.

"One piece of wood you say?" the King questioned. "It must accommodate my entire court. It would have to be an unbelievably gigantic tree."

"I know of such a tree, my lord," Izz proclaimed in a triumphant tone. "It is growing in the middle of the Ebony forest, in the middle of the Ring of Giants. It is the perfect tree for the perfect table."

"I know of this tree you speak of."

"Bring me this tree's base, and I will build you your table," Izz promised.

The king was ecstatic at the proposal; he turned to Izz. "I must make haste. I must make arrangements at once. I will bring to you the trunk of the tree you speak of, and you will make for me the table just as you have described."

And with this, the king excused himself. Zuree gave Izz a long parting glance, and the king, the princess, and their entourage were all gone as suddenly as they had arrived.

On the carriage ride back to the palace, Zuree thought of the young carpenter with a whim of idle inquisitiveness that fluttered among her deepest thoughts. The one thought that struck out was that uncanny feeling that she somehow knew she was meant to meet this young carpenter. She did not know what her feelings meant, but she knew there had to be a reason they seemed to have shared the same vision. At that moment, the king turned to Zuree and said, "Well, at least you look as if you have your tiptoes back on the ground." Then he asked, "What was your impression of the young carpenter?"

She chose her words carefully as she took control of her runaway emotions. "There was something extraordinary beneath the carpenter's rough outward appearance, an unusual intelligence that was an integral part of Izz's intriguing personality. Other than that, he was just a well mannered carpenter."

"You seemed to have been taken in by the well mannered carpenter."

"I think he is interesting."

"When you say interesting, what exactly do you mean?"

"I mean, I think he could be an interesting acquaintance."

"Acquaintance, you say?"

"Yes, very special acquaintance," Zuree teased as she laughed her most lighthearted laugh.

"Purge yourself of the notion. Need I remind you that your hand has been promised to Rizan from the day of your birth? And it is he who you will save your interest for."

"It is my heart, and I should have the right to surrender it to whom I wish to surrender it to." She defiantly said as she found herself caught between her resolve and her obedience to her ancestral obligations.

"I am your father and your king, and you will marry whom I say you will marry!" he said in an irritated tone. The king felt a slight pang of uneasiness, but he suppressed the urge to be indignant as he continued. "A king's oath cannot be broken!" He said more genially this time.

Zuree felt annoyed at the forceful reaction her father embraced when it concerned her right to make her own decisions in the matter of her love and marriage. But she could not let it show, or it would only make the controversy worse. Besides, she was content enough to give her heart to Rizan. After all, he was one of the richest, most powerful men in the empire. He was a champion. He came from one of Xylenia's oldest and most respected families. And in addition to all that, her father, the king, and her mother, the queen, adored him without end.

Attempting to relieve her father's concerns, Zuree said, "Do not worry yourself, Father." She laughed, her whispered laugh again. Convinced that it had all been just a fleeting, impulsive flirtation, she dismissed the whole matter. Implausible as it might have been, uneasy as it might have made her feel, she was in some way irresistibly attracted to the young carpenter.

For the rest of the carriage ride back to the palace, the princess lapped into silence. She folded her hands and leaned way back in the thick, cushioned seat. Her train of thought once again led her back to the encounter with the carpenter. His memory still burned brightly in her mind. She thought about the profound look he had given her and the way it had made her feel. She thought about his straightforwardness, even the uncivil way he had studied her, almost as if he could not help himself. He was certainly a contrast to the high minded, calculating, power chasing affluent types within the castle walls, who gathered about her like bees around honey. Of course, he was beneath her nobility, that she did not have to be told.

And yet, she could not characterize what it was that made her admire him more than she cared to admit because she had never come across an experience like that before. It was all so ridiculous. Everything about him was the opposite of what she was. He came from a rough hewn, earthly breed. His line of work, his uncultured characteristics, and the hand sewn clothes he wore, and even the unrefined way he spoke. He was all too crude, unpolished, and of common ancestry. And yet, in spite of everything, in truth, she realized that she had more in common with the carpenter than she was willing to admit. There was something about this carpenter Izz that had succeeded in gaining her admiration. On the one hand, he was very handsome, physically vigorous, tall, and utterly lovable, there was no question of that.

On the other hand, they were from two different worlds. The young carpenter's entire character was an image of an ordinary, underprivileged, drifting vagabond, who was likely to drift soon wherever his feet would take him. But what did any of that matter? He was unquestionably intelligent, talented, and seemed to ripple with the liveliness and vitality of someone who had the forceful energy to pursue whatever he might desire after. She could appreciate that in any man.

At that moment, she wondered if the carpenter might be thinking of her as she was of him. The thought of his mutual enchantment opened the door to her heart. She saw in her mind's eye the smile that had warmed her soul. Her lips formed Izz's name; she mouthed it softly as she stared inwardly. An impulse of a kiss flashed in her mind. As the thought crystallized, she tried to imagine what that might feel like. Her heart pounded as her voluptuous smile and dreamy stare into space gave her away. The king gave her a suspicious sideward glance and puzzled over what could be whirling in that spirited head of hers. Two opposing dispositions seemed to be struggling within her mind. He asked, "What are you thinking?"

As she tried to banish the ridiculous image from her head, Zuree recomposed herself, shifted to meet her father's alert eyes, and answered, "Oh, nothing."

"Well, that nothing of yours is making me wonder."

The thought had been too ludicrous. The princess rebuked herself for having considered something so outrageous. How could she have imagined becoming so quickly fond of someone she did not even know so soon? She shrugged her thoughts of him away, but they just came bouncing right back to her, and she did not know why. She squeezed her eyes shut, trying to blot out the images of his eyes. But each time, her thoughts returned to Izz. He did not measure up to royalty. However, in some way, it was more charming to think of him as an enchanted prince in a brilliant disguise, perchance a wealthy monarch of a dreamy kingdom from far, far away. Her heart swelled with sweetness, something she had never felt for anyone before. It was a feeling she had never had before in her life, not even for Rizan. Suddenly, a pang of overwhelming guilt tugged at her. She was betrothed. And that reality would remain beyond love, beyond reason, and nothing could change that beyond the end of life itself. She silently criticized the wisdom of her wild and flirtatious imaginations. Then she dismissed the carpenter from her thoughts. She tried to focus on Rizan, and solitude touched an empty place deep within her. She wrapped herself securely in a haze of apathetic detachment, erasing all her jumbled impressions and shutting out her cluttered emotions.

At that exact moment, Izz was having thoughts of Zuree as well. He somehow found it hard to think of anything else. His eyes still sparkled with the memory of the beautiful face he could not get out of his mind. He could still feel the impression of her fingers on his hand. He touched his fingers to his lips. The sweet scent of her skin still lingered upon his hand. He was sure that their souls had touched and that their hearts were yet beating as one.

He mouthed her name, Zuree; he whispered it softly, "Zuree." Then he tested the sound of it out loud, "Zuree, Zuree, Zuree." Like a beautiful musical recital, he sounded each syllable of her name like notes sung instead of spoken. Every beautiful sound in Zia could be heard in one word. She had a name as beautiful as her soul. The scene of their encounter played over and over in his mind. The memory of her hummed in his heart, and he knew it would be an everlasting recollection, to be cherished throughout all of his life. She was the embodiment of his vivid dream coming true. A priceless diamond would not have been a more significant gift. He could not explain it to himself, but he somehow knew that from that day forth, he would never be the same. At that moment, he would have given anything—an eye, the rib closest to his heart, even his life, to hold her and whisper in her ear, "I love you. I always have and always will." Odd as that thought was, it cheered him considerably. After all, the possibilities were endless. Had not the seer said, "Believing, made it so." Meeting her, hearing her voice, feeling the touch of her hand had made his life a heaven on Zia during the short time they had spent in each other's presence.

But then, suddenly, out of nowhere, an onslaught doubt and anxiety pierced his heart. His heart abruptly collapsed, and a change came over his soul, darkening it with an ominous, burdensome gloom. Reality like a villain reminded him that all he had to offer was nothing but a fistful of sawdust, adoration, and dreams that only made sense in his sleep. His thoughts just crumbled. Izz felt his heart plummet. He lived in a removed realm, separated from her by birth as far as the East was from the West.

Moreover, worst of all, the heavenly smile that had brightened up his day was meant for someone else. Izz thought frantically. Who did he think he was, anyway? Life had played a cruel joke on him. His bitter disappointment brought on a tight chest. Gone was the musical resonance in his heart; only the throbbing ache of pain that would never heal remained. But again and again, his dream came floating up from the deep cistern of his mind to provoke him. Continuing to believe in his dreams, which could never possibly come true, would only be flirting with beguilement that could only lead to heartbreak.

It was not the first time he had rebuked himself for daring to dream, and he was almost sure it would not be the last. He forced himself to suppress the insuppressible. "Foolish heart," he said grievingly. "See what you have gotten me into? What am I even still doing in Edawn anyway?" Izz thought wildly to himself as his heart argued against his fears, denying the doubts that pressed upon it from all sides.

Ten

The Treasure Trove

On that very day, the king issued a decree throughout the empire. There would be no delay, and no cost spared. The king offered a priceless fortune to anyone that could bring the mighty giant down. The reward to the person or persons who toppled the colossal tree was a large chest filled to the top with pure gold and precious gems. There were dazzling diamonds, sparkling red rubies, genuine white opals, and green emeralds. It was the most brilliant treasure any command man had ever seen. It was more riches than a man could ever hope to gain in a lifetime of hard toil, and sure of transforming any life forever. Messengers journeyed to the farthest reaches of the empire, and the word spread like a wildfire to every corner of the habited globe.

THE KING OF EDAWN EMPEROR OF ZIA OFFERS TO ANY
A FABULOUS TREASURE TROVE TO ANYONE THAT CAN
BRING DOWN THE TREE THAT STANDS IN THE MIDDLE
OF THE RING OF GIANTS

Almost overnight, a procession of men and beast of burden, moving slowly under the weight of their heavy packs, made their trek from the farthest corners of the empire toward the highly prized tree. Loggers, foresters, and common men of all trades alike descended on the tree from every region of the empire that they might be the ones to claim the great reward. Campfires lit the mountainside with their golden glow as the assault on the tree went on nonstop. Hundreds tried day and night, night and day, driven by hope and desperation to topple the massive tree. Axes, saws, and every chopping tool with a blade mounted on a handle were used relentlessly without success. Either the tools broke or quickly became dull and ineffective against the impenetrable surface that seemed to heal itself with a hardening self sealing resin tougher than iron as soon as a cut was made. In vain, the best engineers attempted to improvise their ingenious strategies to topple the ominous tree. But the tree would not even burn. As one ground crew yielded to the tree, another crew scurried to take its place at the tree's massive trunk. One by one, man and beast of burden, thwarted in every attempt, fell with exhaustion without doing significant damage to the mighty tree. The tree proved too strong and the roots too deep to be conquered by mere mortal men.

In distress and disappointment, the king called the hierarchy of the Inner Council to assemble. As usual, the most renowned members of the kingdom started to fill the seats of about one hundred. Scribes at the ends of the table opened their book of common records, inked their quills, and began to write, noting the date, members in attendance, the matter at hand, and other so deemed consequential details. And as usual, the highest ranking members resumed their squabbling about who should sit where. Finally, more out of frustration than anything else, with a loud voice that echoed throughout the great dome, the king ordered with an oath for everyone to sit down where they stood.

"Enlightened men of Edawn, let us work together to find a way to bring this invincible giant down if we expect to have our magnificent round table and put an end to all this strife."

They all regarded him with various looks of understanding.

"Who in the entire assembly can offer us a solution?"

When the meeting of the minds finally came to order, many decision makers offered various options, and several of their suggestions were weighed as far as they were understood. And soon, it became evident that they were getting nowhere. The king stood before the gathered court and again inquired of the best minds in Zia.

"Does anyone else have a suggestion as to how we should proceed?" His eyes moved quickly from one face to another as he looked for a response.

A highborn elder stood and suggested they consult Ammiz, but most considered his wisdom unreliable. One of the eldest of the Inner Council members stood and openly addressed the noble assembly.

"Fellow citizens of Edawn, why do we not consult Baddlock, the grand wizard? He seems to think he knows everything about everything."

Baddlock was not a member of the official deliberation, but lucky enough—or ruthless enough—he gained prosperity and influence in the King's Court. And thus, he was hailed to be one of the wisest among the kingdom, and so they were quite willing to include him.

"Yes, the wizard, of course." The king looked at the elder, ironically. "Why did I not think of that?" the king asked himself.

Immediately, the wizard was sought out, but could not be found anywhere. He was a recluse, continually changing his whereabouts, and no one seemed to know exactly where he spent most of his time. He was thought to dwell alone with his assistant in strict seclusion just beyond the kingdom's walls. Couriers were dispatched everywhere, but as often happened, Baddlock just seemed to have dropped off the edge of Zia. The wildest rumors were circulated that the wizard had been seen crossing into the deepest parts of the notoriously forbidden Ebony Forest, where he always seemed to vanish into thin air.

In Izz's spare time, he went to visit Ammiz as often as his work allowed. He considered his wisdom the greatest he had ever come upon. Under the old man's tutelage, Izz learned things he had never even dreamed. Izz felt privileged to be taken into the seer's confidence, treasuring his most weighty beliefs, and his frequent visits were the highlight of his week. Their friendship rapidly ripened into a bond of great mutual favor. Izz and Ammiz spent more and more of their spare time in each other's company, and soon, Izz was visiting Ammiz almost every day. Each cultivated their blossoming friendship, and it had been intellectually inspiring for both.

Izz asked many thought provoking questions. All geared towards the mysterious unknown side of life. Ammiz had his hands full and answered as best he could. Izz sat at the seer's feet, listening with enthralled attention and never interrupted. The seer taught to his classroom of one, never seem to be at a loss for words, pleased that Izz always listened so intently. The old man spoke of things few men lived to tell. The seeker and the seer were like two windows into one mind, each mirroring the other's thoughts. Ammiz taught Izz eagerly, and eagerly Izz learned. Soon Izz's mind was percolating with not only innovative thoughts but complete new categories of ideas he had never thought.

Each time they met, they buried themselves in study. Izz was an honest and patient listener, and Ammiz was happy to feed his unquenchable curiosity. Ammiz poured himself out, and Izz's razor sharp wit soaked it all up, like water into a dry sponge. Ammiz fitted together, piece by piece, an ominous puzzle of realities Izz had never conceived. Izz expanded and ripened his range of understanding. The seer created an immeasurable mosaic of oddities, and the seeker was propelled into visions of unfolding mysteries. Questions about his dreams and the maiden were seldom, if ever, spoken of, as it seemed Izz had pushed them out of his head or to the farthest corners at least.

As old as the seer was, his logical discipline, retentive recall, and activity of mind were sharper than that of a man half his age. And thus, Ammiz had become the young carpenter's adopted teacher, his comrade. Izz, who was usually by nature, a quiet spirit, had never talked so much in his life. Suddenly, everything he had held inside erupted from within him, and he longed to tell Ammiz everything he felt and everything he thought. He spewed out all to this man who appeared aware of so much. Without realizing it, Izz had become the son that Ammiz never had, and Ammiz had become the father Izz had been denied.

Matters of death, which seemed to stir some tragic memory that Ammiz had long ago pushed into the background of his mind, were never discussed again. However, Izz asked many other profound questions, and Ammiz endeavored to find simple descriptive language that was easy to grasp and explain. The patriarch spoke more and more about the coming of the Great Conjunction, the transitioning of the cosmos, and the great conflict between good and evil. The seer never pretended to know everything, but what he seemed to know was that the universe was moving into a preset position. In this alignment, it would instantly reset itself back into its perfect, pre-interrupted state before the celestial rebellion when time and space did not exist.

"As of yet, the ripples of disobedience still echoes its dregs throughout the universe. The fallen ones know there is little time left to them. Therefore, soon, they will play out their last attempt to fully pervert the Creator's most precious creation, humankind." The seer spoke as if there was something he was sure of, and this was it.

Izz did not know if he understood much of what he heard, but he was eager to know. Although, for the most part, he was convinced that Ammiz did not know where mythology departed from reality. Therefore, Izz regarded Ammiz's revelations with a grain of skepticism. More than likely, ancient superstitions had steeped into his mind for so long that they now embodied themselves in his heart as truths. It could be nothing more than made up reasoning to fill in the missing pieces, a result of gazing up at the stars for far too long. Tales that had most likely passed from writing to writing in such varied repetition, that fables had become myths, and myths turned into parables, Parables turned into legends and legends had finally become historically recorded truth. Ammiz's keenness of perception allowed him to note Izz's uncertainty. But the seer knew that the reality of these truths would soon slap him up the side of his head. And so he tried his best to prepare Izz for the great tribulations he would soon have to face.   Nonetheless, despite his misgivings, Izz considered everything and continued to the next question of an endless list of unanswered inquiries that came bubbling up out of his mind. Of all the myriad of perplexing inquiries, there was one particular issue that had again begun burning a hole through the back of his mind. He was just about to ask the question that had long confounded him but thought better at the last possible moment, and so he asked somewhat of a less bewildering question.

"I want to know everything. Tell me why it seems that I can understand what people and sometimes animals are thinking, and they seem to be able to understand what I am thinking, especially animals?" Izz inquired wonderingly.

The old man whispered something to himself in a hushed tone: "Sanctified in his powers to make animals obey his will. Well, well, this is a truly rare and extraordinary gift indeed."

This time, the old man spoke at full volume, "We are all part of an outside reality that is not always clearly understood. Words were invented to help us organize and record the wisdom of our past and dreams of our future. Since the dawn of thought, there has always existed something known as the universal consciousness. It is a web of energy that occurs in all living things. And to some degree in nonliving things as well. In every grain of sand is recorded the history of our world. And in every drop of water, there is an ocean within an ocean. Because of our collective consciousness, every thought, even our dreams, are interconnected and guided by the Omnipresent Mastermind of the universe. In the cycle of nature, all conscious beings have a body and soul, and all awareness is one vast, interconnected, and mutually dependent union. You have, in all likelihood been able to tap into a higher level of awareness, and the creatures you have interacted with have responded in kind. Knowledge and instinct are intertwined. Your knowledge and instinct have managed to intertwine. This interlacing occurs in everyday life to a certain degree in all of us. But very few can or bother to tune into it. Our minds are the greatest creation ever, a universe within a universe, as inwardly deep as the heavens are wide. And it is capable of doing the most astonishing things for us; it's masters. Even so, the greater part of us continues along our daily rut, totally oblivious of our amazing potential, no better than the most simple of animals seeking to satisfy only our most mundane needs."

For an instant, Izz envisioned reality breaking through, and then an unfocused look came over Izz's eyes, like that of someone who had suddenly stepped out of the bright sunlight into complete darkness. The only thing he managed to understand was that, somehow, all those in Zia, along with all of nature, and all its forces were in one way or another intertwined into one giant interconnecting web. Ammiz was bemused to notice that Izz had, at that moment, reached the limits of his perception and said, "Let that be enough for now. Let us stop and enjoy a soothing cup of tea; we can continue this discussion very soon."

As they sipped on their piping hot tea, Izz finally asked the question that he had been dying to ask from the beginning, and now he could not control himself any longer. The single inquiry that had burdened his thoughts for the longest time suddenly came tumbling out.

"The two dreams I had...that seemed so real...I could not tell if I was awake or not. Tell me," he implored, "about the maiden that I have dreamed of, a maiden that bares Princess Zuree's unique image! Tell me everything. I beg you. Tell me no more half answers or riddles."

Izz insatiably hungered to unearth all there was to be discovered. The seer discerned he could not remain silent about this matter any longer. It was now time to disclose what he knew or thought he knew, he knew.

"Dreams are harbingers filled with mystery and wonder, sometimes they confirm, and sometimes they contradict. Many times I have made major decisions based on visions and dreams. Some dreams are adventures yet to take place. I believe your dreams are truths, a great treasure trove of the heart. Lock them away deep within. Do not let these special dreams die. Nourish and protect them with all that you are. And they will come true. If it were not possible, life would not have provoked them upon you."

Izz listened, as faith was kindled in his soul. By some divine supernatural power, he envisioned his dream appearing before him. He saw, heard, smelled, and tasted its vivid colors. He felt his heart swelling with expectation until he listened to the oracle say, "Everything will be revealed in its own time, and only you can solve the riddle of your dream." The seer concluded sternly. With each vague answer the seer gave, new questions came into sharper focus, and although frustrated, Izz did not persist out of respect. He realized that this could not be a story randomly told. With a deep sigh, he smiled a lopsided smile. He was content in knowing that Ammiz would, in due time, make any new revelation known. And thus, in this manner, two minds melted together. The seer took the seeker under his wing and saturated and filled his soul with wisdom until his mind felt as if it would burst of it. Together the unlikely pair formed a special bond, and together they explored a fantastic spectrum of wisdom and discipline. They spent more and more time adrift in thought, investigating and discussing many hidden secrets of the ancient writings. Izz intently listened as Ammiz voiced his thoughts. He was eager to learn everything about everything and anything that ever was, is, and even of what was to come. Izz's eyes were opened to unseen things, changing his understanding of life, and the role he played in it. His thoughts took on turns and byways in new directions that he had never expected. And so Ammiz lectured to his sole student on astronomy, mathematics, history, science, politics, religion, and nature as if Izz would someday fill his shoes. These were among the subjects that Ammiz implemented to distract Izz from the details of his destiny as it pertained to the ancient prophecies, hidden knowledge that Izz could not yet face. The seeker entreated the seer, "Enlighten me with everything that you know."

Word finally reached the king of Baddlock's return, and that same day, he was brought before the Supreme Inner Council. And as usual, Tigbone was stuck to the wizard like a barnacle. Baddlock swayed an awe inspiring presence as he moved bold and haughty across the inner court of the empire. He clinked and clacked the heels of his high black button boots with every step. Within the chambers, a lane was at once opened through the crowd of curious spectators that had gathered. They stared as Baddlock, a man of prominent force and authority, made his way to the front of the assembly. Great applause greeted his appearance as if each regarded him as the scholar among scholars. Dandork, the senior magistrate, addressed Baddlock as the king looked on with intense anticipation.

"It is so gracious of you to accept our invitation. On behalf of the Royal Inner Council, I bid you welcome." Little did the king know that his reception of Baddlock was the same as accommodating a thief by unlocking for him the treasury stronghold.

"Honorable Wizard, can you offer this distinguished council the solution it seeks. What we beseech of you is the key to bringing down the giant tree that grows among giants in the northern range of the Emory Forest."

Baddlock swelled with self importance as he stepped slowly to the raised platform with his hands firmly clasped behind his back. His hood shrouded his face, casting a shadow over his eyes to hide the venomous lies he was about to spew. Baddlock grabbed the podium with hands that bore rings on every finger and two on each thumb. The wizard faced the assembly. Before him, row upon row of seats built in steadily rising levels toward the back of the room was filled to overflowing.

"Esteemed members of the Royal Inner Council, I, myself, cannot tell you how to bring the tree which you speak of down."

A deflated gasp sucked the enthusiasm out of the room, and the crowd began to murmur but were quickly silenced when Baddlock continued in his authoritative tone.

"However..." He paused for effect, and then pure evil emptied out of his mouth. "There is one among us that I have heard boast that he can conquer the tree single handedly, no less." He let the words dangle in the mounting silence. The flock of listeners seemed to melt like butter in his hands, believing without question every falsehood he began to spew. Baddlock thought to himself as he thrust his nose haughtily into the air, *This is my opportunity to be rid of that thorn in my side.* "It grieves me to no end," he continued as he shook his head back and forth somberly. Baddlock somberly placed his hand over his heart for emphasis, "To have to tell you that this culprit is no other than our own beloved carpenter Izz, who has come to us from the Isles of Zollerzon."

Many assailed him with scorn and sneers. A grimace of disapproval flickered across the king's face. "Impossible!" The King stood as he drew a deep breath, and after a moment, added, "Many experienced men have tried and failed to bring down this ancient monument of time. How could anyone man possibly believe that he alone could bring this tree down?"

Baddlock straightened his crooked self up, narrowed his eyes, and said, "I cannot say how, all I can say is what I have heard with my own ears." The wizard scratched at his grizzly beard for a moment. Then his outward appearance suddenly changed to a pained expression. With profane boldness almost beyond belief, he continued his charade, "I know how unbelievable that might sound, but I have not even come to the most grievous part of this woebegone affair." Baddlock lowered his head as if in sorrow, his sense of right and wrong barely shuddered at the twisting of lies. "This young carpenter that we have all taken in as one of our own dared to say that he was amazed that...I can barely bring myself to repeat it." Again, Baddlock paused for maximum effect, considering whether he should force a tear. "He said that he was amazed that such a bungling old dolt such as our beloved king could rule over such a great empire. And that a dimwitted donkey could rule better." Baddlock stated these words as though there could be no question of their truth.

The account given of the carpenter both surprised and angered the king. A scowl of condemnation flickered across his face. The watchdogs of the law gasped almost in unison and began to talk among themselves in grumbled whispers. Being a practitioner of law, a legal zealot of the highest order, and knowing the rules of its application, Baddlock's strategy was half truths, and bald face lies.

"You all know as well as I, that one of the laws adopted early in our empire requires that if anyone proclaims a falsehood against the king...and if that person be found guilty of such a transgression, that person is subject to the rule of law unto its fullest extent."

Suddenly, a deathly hush fell over the crowded hall. The king was as unprepared for Baddlock's accusation as anyone else in the room, but it seemed to ring to the force of law. The king looked at the wizard with narrow calculating eyes, frowned in thought, and then motioned the chief law keeper to show him the law Baddlock had quoted. An oversized book was brought forth and opened before him. The principal law keeper's finger traveled over the face of the Eternal Book of the Laws, where the law Baddlock referenced to was written.

"Oh yes, by all means, if I have made an error in any of these points of the law, I will most humbly submit myself unto your correction, my lord," the Wicked Warlock Wizard said with a disdainful sniff.

The chief law keeper gave the king a solemn nod. The king motioned that the book is turned toward him that he might weigh the vagueness or inconsistency of Baddlock's allegation in the balance of truth. The wizard's accusation had the force of law behind it. The king finally spoke.

"This edict is older than the hills...nonetheless, it is still in effect," he concluded disparagingly. "However, the accusation you allege is your own and does not carry the weight of the law." He laced his hands before him and made eye contact with the wizard. "The accused has the right to face and challenge his accuser." *There has to be a rational explanation;* the king reasoned to himself.

"Oh, most assuredly, Your Majesty! Allow the lad an opportunity to explain himself. If he fails, he is a liar, and should be dealt with according to our laws." The wizard knew fully well that the penalty for lying to the Inner Council was, without a doubt, death. "By all means, send for the carpenter at once," the wizard implored, convinced that Izz was doomed.

Everyone in the great hall raised their voices in agreement.

The Master of Arms, Dandork, accompanied by two armed court guards, arrived at Izz's carpenter shop unannounced. The ruthless unrelenting pounding from without rattled the shop door on its hinges. Izz stopped what he was doing, opened the door, and marveled at the strange intrusion. He smiled broadly. No one else reacted in kind. Dandork pulled a scroll from his leather satchel and proceeded to read the warrant out loud.

"By order of our Noble King Ozzdon, it is hereby commanded that you present yourself before the king in the Halls of Law at once."

Izz's faint smile faded into a quizzical expression. He put his tools down, took his apron off, and brushed the sawdust off himself. He asked in a controlled voice, "And why, may I ask, am I being summoned?" Izz looked blankly at Dandork, who only gave him back an unfriendly, probing stare out of the corner of his eye.

Izz inwardly cringed. The one way conversation had taken a worsening turn. Izz could feel the stiffening of spines all around him, giving him an uneasy feeling. He tried to read what was happening on the faces of his onlookers, as he felt a knot twisting in his stomach. His eyes widened and shifted from side to side, but without a word and utterly confused, he complied.

The armed contingent made its way as quickly as the crowded streets would allow. As Dandork cried out, "Open a passage. Make way, in the name of the king."

In the crowd, scoffers peered at Izz along the way as the guards led him where trial and persecution waited. Izz did not know what to think. He had a strange, foreboding warning that something was amiss, but could not imagine what it could be. He was amazed at the corresponding hush that fell over the great hall following his entrance.

It must be worse than I ever imagined, Izz thought to himself with an air of caution. He knew next to nothing about what to expect. It was like being invited to take part in a game where the rules would not be disclosed until after the player had made a mistake. He appeared frustrated, intimidated, and confused. He wanted to believe that this was all some joke, but no one was laughing. Izz was directed to a polished cherry wood table just behind the center podium. As he approached the table occupied by several junior magistrates, they glared up at him from their law books with suspicious eyes.

Izz sat silent and alone at the defense table, ill at ease in the hard wooden chair where he had been directed to sit. As Izz glanced around, he noticed some of the judges were spearing him with dirty looks. Izz's eyes darted around the room before spotting Baddlock seated at the head of the next table, carrying on an insidious low voiced discussion with a group of shady looking men. He had an eerie feeling that Baddlock and Dandork were behind this action, but to what end. Izz noticed the sardonic smile twisted on their faces and how pleased they seemed to be with themselves. They gave him menacing glances as they continued to mumble, deliberate, and jot notes to each other on their parchments. Izz knew for sure it could not be good. He could sense their shared disdain for him, and at that very moment, he would have eagerly boarded any ship going anywhere. Tigbone sat next to Baddlock with his lopsided head and puzzled, squinty eyes staring at the cut of paper before him as he scrolled out scribbles over its surface in amazement. Izz took his place at the table, sensing something terrible was about to happen. He could not see beyond the somber expressions floating on the surface of the crowd. Nor could he know the corruption boiling beneath Baddlock's self assured appearance.

***

A court page faithful to Ammiz, the Seer came to his home secretly and informed his master of Izz's unfolding fate. The fermenting contempt Ammiz held for Baddlock at the lowermost cistern of his soul was kept well under control. He thanked his servant and dismissed him with a copper piece. Before the page walked out the door, he turned and informed the seer, "The penalty is death."

Ammiz's solemn nod went almost unnoticed as the page let himself out. The seer retreated to his study, sat at his desk, and slumped back grimly in his chair as a frown crawled over his shadowed face. Ammiz whispered to no one there, "So it all begins. The ancient evil that once was has been reborn in the heart of men."

He always knew the darkness would return in an attempt to finalize what it had started. He also knew he could not intervene, knowing that this would be only one of Izz's many tribulations, readying him for the ultimate destiny he was born to fulfill. He swiveled his head toward his celestial model and plotting charts.

"Eternal Providence has begun its work. The seven sister planets have now entered into a new cycle that will bring them into their astronomical alignment, which will usher in the Great Conjunction. Izz must now be tested in preparation for his greatest trial. It all depends now on the strength of his heart, whether Zia enters into unspeakable horror or unimaginable harmony." Ammiz had long known that Baddlock would be a key player in the upcoming conflict between good and evil. And now, he had made his first move on the universal game board. What his next step would be, only time would tell. Ammiz felt the crushing weight of questions that kept multiplying, while their answers only retreated.

"The villain is capable of exuding any foolish plot to destroy Zia's only hope." Ammiz's mouth curled as he had a sinking feeling at the thought of Izz's footing. He knew that from this day forth, Izz's life would irrevocably forever be changed to an unimaginable extent without measure. The seer marveled at what length one man could so vastly influence a change in the course of history.

<hr>

This situation was more severe than Izz could have ever imagined. And yet he could not think, for the life of him, what he could have done. He tried to ignore the chill running up and down his spine as the council administrator moved to the podium. Izz had never appeared in the presence of a more imposing assembly than this before. The accusations were restated: "Izz of Zollerzon, serious charges have been brought up against you. It has been alleged that you have made some outrageous claims of possessing the power to bring down Ebony Forest's monumental tree. Furthermore, you have been accused of making treasonous statements against your king. How do you plead against these charges brought against you?"

Izz swallowed hard, shocked, and hopelessly confused by these ridiculous allegations. With a puzzled look on his face, Izz had to hold on to the table to steady himself, trying to absorb what he had just been told as he searched out the king's eyes. The king gave him a clueless, unanticipated quizzical look and shifted his eyes to Baddlock as he pointed to him with his chin. Izz did not feel like laughing, but he smiled weakly nonetheless. He felt wholly inadequate, ill prepared, but the grave situation demanded it. Izz stood his ground, ready to plead his case, that truth might be judged. Little did he realize that life and death would hinge on his every word.

"What! I have done no such thing. I do not know who you have talked to, but these are bald faced lies."

"How do you plead?" the council administrator insisted.

"My plea is, of course, that I utterly deny the charges! I have not done anything wrong." His voice trembled as he searched the faces around the table of judges. Their unchanging expressions did not tell him a thing.

"LIES!" Baddlock challenged from where he was sitting with a sneer before Izz's words were hardly out of his mouth. The wizard leaped to his feet. His chair shuffled back as he faced Izz and asked, "Did you or did you not tell me, on my last visit to your shop, that you could bring down the mighty Ebony Forest giant whenever you wished?" All the while, court scribes were taking down every word spoken.

Izz straightened his backbone, faced Baddlock, and choosing his words carefully; he stated, "For one thing, up to this day, you have never stepped foot in my shop, and for another, everything you say is an outright fabrication." In the background, Izz could hear the measured voices around him, the broken cadence of whispers, and the words that were being said out loud.

"Do you think that I would make such claims if I did not have proof?" Baddlock boasted.

Izz sat back, vaguely stunned, and fell silent with astonishment. Baddlock rushed in to fill the gap. "Why humiliate yourself? You would do well to take my advice. Admit to your wrong, that this honorable court may have mercy upon you."

A murmuring of mixed contradictions filled the room. Izz flexed the muscles in his jaw. As his heart drew integrity, he stood to his feet, found his voice, and said, "You, Sir Baddlock, the wizard, whatever you want to call yourself, are a liar and a perpetrator of wickedness. You should be known as Baddlock, the Wicked Warlock Wizard! Your lawlessness reaches beyond despicable, have you no shame?"

At that moment, it seemed that some powerful force had sucked the breath out of everyone in the room, as tension as thick as fog filled the air. No one had ever dared to speak to the grand wizard in this manner. Exchanges between the judges resumed between them in whispered tones. Some of the cabinet members were outraged. No two reactions were the same. Baddlock's lips pulled back in a mocking grin as he traded an anxious glance with Dandork. He gazed up at the committee of elders. His eyes grazed from one face to the other. Some returned his scrutiny with expressions of expectation others with suspicion, and he knew he was on the verge of losing credibility among most of them. In that instance, Baddlock's hatred for Izz was magnified. He shot him a venomous evil eye that could have killed. He stared at Izz as if he would like nothing more than to skin him alive, right where he stood, and have his skin hammered to the wall of the great hall. He saw his chances of removing this impotent defiant little churl from his life slipping away. His face became woefully pathetic, and for that moment, he was silent, as if wounded. Desperately, he fumbled for a new angle of attack. Agile in the debate, he quickly polished his acting skills, as he again addressed the assembly.

"Now, now, there is no need to be uncivilized." His voice was silky smooth and placid. "We are all after the same end here, which is to uncover what you did or did not say. Our aim is not name calling or personal insults. As I see it, we are all only interested in the truth. You would do well to keep that in mind." Enchanted or bewitched, the assembly's sway fell deeper under the wizard's deception as he took full advantage of his high respectability and political influence. None could see his motive, or find any reason that he should lie. "My fellow Edawnians, we are all men of principle and intellectual depth, men of honor, and moral strength. Be not deceived by this newcomer. This innocent looking young man has brought dishonor upon us all, and according to our noble code of conduct, must pay the penalty!"

Izz sat in stunned silence, watching Baddlock's persuasive performance and the multiplying, frowning stares from around the room that were growing with animosity. The king sat on his throne, having heard from both sides of the issue at hand. His face remained impassive, his emotions mixed. He knew Baddlock to be a shrewd man, yet his clever display of polite weakness made it hard to discredit his motives. There was no reason that he should lie. He waved one hand in the air as if he were directing an organized group of musicians as he motioned the proceeding to continue. Turning to his captive audience, Baddlock proceeded where he left off.

"Defenders of virtue, champions of order, protectors of the law," Baddlock addressed the judges, "from the beginning of our civilization; the law has been the glue that has held our empire together." He pointed his long, gnarled finger at Izz, and with a sharp faultfinding tone, spoke, hurling his every word as if pronouncing a sentence over Izz. "You have no idea how much trouble you have gotten yourself in with your careless remarks." A spark of evil showed in the wizard's beady eyes as they darted back and forth in their sunken sockets. He felt he had scored a critical blow, and his case against the carpenter had become conclusive. Then in a hushed voice, he said, "I do not know how things are done in Zollerzon, but here in Edawn, we obey the law of the people." There was a rumbling murmur of agreement from the crowd. "The statutes of our law books make clear that the callous lies you have stated and the careless claims you have made against our beloved king are capital offenses punishable by death. You ought to be ashamed of yourself, not standing there, arrogantly acting as if you have done nothing wrong."

"I have done nothing wrong! These are all fabricated lies," Izz said in a blameless voice. Unable to control his frustration, Izz's eyes filled with outrage. Why was it that he was the only one who could see through Baddlock's preposterous made up story?

Noting Izz's increasing agitation, the wizard shot Izz an ominous look. Then, without warning, his voice lashed out like a whip. Baddlock flung his next accusation, "How dare you accuse me before the eyes and ears of this noble assembly of being a liar? Listen well and heed my words. There are others present in this room that have heard your blasphemous claims."

"This charlatan is a venomous viper bent on my demise. For some mysterious reason, I know not why. Everything he has sworn to is a blatant lie." Izz fearlessly maintained his innocence, refuting every wrongful falsehood and repelling every accusation as the sparring words escalated.

"You, carpenter profess to be a person of honor. If that is true, in order so that this court may be merciful, we are ready to hear both your confession and your offering of remorse. You do know how to apologize, do you not?"

"I have nothing to apologize for," Izz replied without hesitation as he glanced around in disbelief. He was hoping it would all turn out to be some foul prank, half expecting someone to start laughing. But the evil delight in Baddlock's eyes told him it was no jest. Sensing that he was getting outtalked by Baddlock, Izz took a moment to take a deep, calming breath, striving to break the momentum of the mounting confrontation against him. As Izz looked around at the bleak, glaring faces, he was determined to keep his temper in check. He knew that he could not afford to let his anger get the best of him, even though his rage was intensifying in his heart. Even so, Izz conserved a composed appearance as he spoke without a guilty conscience, "Is there any among you that cannot see that this windbag is trying to make fools of us all with his slanderous ranting and wailing."

Baddlock had been waiting, calculating the precise moment to put into action the final stage of his diabolical plot. He was convinced that Izz was as good as banished if he ran, and better yet executed if he did not. Now was the moment to put the next nail in his coffin. Baddlock called upon Dandork, the senior magistrate, Pongo, and one other witness, who no one seemed to recognize, to the platform. Izz felt suddenly cautious, sensing a trap being set. Dandork had long thought he had been looked over for advancement. Baddlock had offered him power, riches, and authority. The lure of power had been much too tempting, and Baddlock had been much too persuasive to resist. But in the end, it was Baddlock's promises of gold that had turned him against the king. Dandork had betrayed his king, joining Baddlock on the dark side, to become Baddlock's pone regardless of his pledge.

Baddlock questioned the three in a loud voice, "Tell this honorable assembly if what I said to be true or not."

Considered the most reliable witness to a man's honesty, the magistrate was called to the witness stand first. Dandork swaggered forward, giving his master a sly look as he approached the podium.

The statement Dandork swore to be the truth, and nothing but the truth began with one lie after another. His thin lips twitched as he spoke without assertion as if he knew the barrenness of his words. "It is true, honorable wizard, every word as you have said," Dandork accused in concealed annoyance.

The king discerned that there was something a little too tight and thin lipped about Dandork's response. Izz did not know precisely how to react; it took all he could do to keep his astonishment in check. He would not lose his composure. He was not sightless to the threat that endangered him, but he gave no ground in his stance as he maintained a courageous attitude. The other two, Pongo and someone introduced as Mossca, both unscrupulous scoundrels from the northernmost outposts of the realm, voiced their agreement in support more from fear of the wizard than loyalty. All three men gave Baddlock conspiratorial nods, which he returned in kind. Izz could feel his eyes getting big. He could also hear, from the elder council members behind him, hushed declarations of disdain. He shook his head at the injustice of it all, trying to build a defense in his mind. He desperately sought the right words to clarify his innocence, wondering how anyone could make such ridiculous allegations.

The council administrator asked Izz, "How do you respond to these witnesses?"

Izz could feel his lips and tongue moving, but he could not hear himself saying anything. His mind was utterly shocked, too stunned to think of anything to answer. Baddlock's eyes snapped and blazed with sudden contempt.

"Let his silence be his condemnation. By his silence, he admits louder than words that my account is true." Baddlock said with a tone of sarcastic contempt creeping into his voice.

Throughout the charade, Izz sat in total shock. His entire rebuttal had had no discernible effect. Izz felt a lump forming in his windpipe, and he could not speak. He swallowed against a dry throat. Before Izz could regain his self confidence, he reasoned against the carefully sprung trap, *Anything I say seems only to worsen my situation, saying nothing makes it even worse.* Still vexed with shock, he found his voice, and his intonation rose in fear and anger, trembling as he spoke, "I am innocent!"

Eager to win Baddlock's favor, Tigbone jumped from his low wooden seat, and as if just on the edge of laughter, chimed in,

"Carpenter Izz, he tells to me he have magic. He say he can bring big tree down by self."

"Do you see? What could be more honest than a simpleton?" Baddlock asserted with a hint of a triumphant smirk fixed on his face.

The crowd burst into laughter with nodding, jeering, and mocking. Tigbone gave a humorless laugh, thinking his stammering like a joker had made a laughingstock out of him. Baddlock waited until the laughter subsided. Then he stepped forward, the look in his eyes dared anyone to speak out against Tigbone, and no one spoke. Not even Izz.

Baddlock rubbed his hands together, congratulating himself for his brilliant performance. "My friends and fellow citizens," he said in a voice that carried to the farthest corners of the chambers. "These are crimes against the king, the kingdom, against the empire. The law is clear. The carpenter must prove under penalty of death that what he stated is true. If we allow one person to step out of the boundaries of our tried and trusted law, then the very foundations of justice will be threatened." He glanced over his shoulder at Izz and grinned a malicious grin. Izz was feeling more and more overwhelmed with every passing moment, as he struggled to comprehend the weight of what was happening. He could scarcely begin to understand the motive for Baddlock to falsely accuse him. He wondered what demons could have possessed his mind. Conflicting turmoil unraveled within him. Was this a punishment for having dared to dream bold and impossible dreams? He felt a premonition of forewarning, like a noose tightening around his neck. Izz began to feel like a cornered animal. He sensed the spirit of demon wolves closing in for the kill and evil vultures circling for the feast. Suspended in disbelief, Izz thought he heard an intimidating, far off thought call to him out of nowhere and said mockingly, *I will send you back to wherever you came from, minus your head.*

The council administrator addressed Izz again, "Izz of Zollerzon, do you have any witnesses you wish to bring forth at this time?"

Izz's eyes darted around the crowded public sector in search of a friendly face among the sea of scowled expressions, ready to clutch at any hand that might reach out to him. His uncle Lott had not been notified, but where was Ammiz. He, of all people, should at least be there, yet he was nowhere to be found. Then, sensing Izz's thoughts, Baddlock spouted, "Cannot everyone see for themselves that not even his teacher, the great seer, is here to defend this rogue. Ammiz has evidently withdrawn his loyalty." He turned to Izz and addressed him directly, "That alone, more than words, proves your guilt. Obviously, he is so ashamed of the disgrace you have brought to him that he has, without question, decided it would be better to stay away. No doubt grieved by what he is inclined to imagine that we must think of him for being duped into trusting you." There was a rolling rumble of agreement among those judges in attendance.

Dandork, the master at arms, made his way to the podium. Dandork was a dauntless man with a stern face with a fixed, discontented pout. He paused for a moment and gave Izz a long displeased look. With a deadly serious expression pressed on his face, he shuffled the papers in his hands. *Not a single breath was drawn while Dandork spoke, "Although it would please the court to be merciful, we are not in a disposition to tolerate boastful and scandalous untruths.* Justice must be served. We are all obligated to obey the laws of the land and the people. It is written that if three or more witnesses agree, the account will be established as reliable."

Izz struggled to speak several times, but with each attempt, he only managed to stammer with incoherent emotion. Izz was too overwhelmed to say anything as the verdict enveloped itself around his heart and began to brutally strangle the life from it. Izz could only sit there, numb, his mind jarred with disbelief waiting for something to happen, but what that was he could not imagine. Izz stood rigid with apprehension, and finally, his words escaped him.

"Why can I not make anyone believe me?" He turned to the council, holding his hand out to them imploringly, his eyes wide and questioning. "Can you not see it? I am guiltless of these ridicules charges." His voice tapered to a whimper. Izz could speak no more. So overpowered was he by all that was unfolding all at once.

Dandork looked up from the document he had signed and announced, "We need no further comments from the condemned." Izz's eyes slid in Baddlock's direction for the briefest of moments. "Either this assembly is crazy, or I am!" His voice sounded like that of a child that was about to be unjustly punished. Humiliated by the exhibition he had become, bewilderment washed over his mind.

Like a slap to the face, Dandork ordered, "Silence!" As if Izz had been granted all the time he deserved. "What need do we have for any more statements? We have the firsthand account of the honorable Baddlock, who has been a member in good standing as long as most any noble elder." There was a mumble of agreement from the crowd. "I heard the carpenter's loud mouthed talk with my own ears. What further confirmation does anyone require?" Dandork concluded.

Izz carefully glanced at all the grim faces around him, and again in vain, he searched for a single sympathetic look. Izz realized that it was pointless to argue and had to restrain himself forcibly. The trap had been sprung, and he was helplessly caught in the web of Baddlock's deception. Izz felt helplessly impaled by the crowd's denouncing glares. It was as though the game was coming to its end, and even though Izz had the most to lose, he was not going to be allowed to make any more moves.

Dandork gave Izz an unhurried, torturous up and down glare. When he was fully convinced that Izz had turned a satisfying, deeper shade of pale, the Master of Arms read the judgment, "If the tree does not fall by tomorrow at sunset, the one called Izz of Zollerzon shall be taken to the public square and beheaded."

Silence engulfed the room like a surge of icy water splashed over the crowd. There had not been an execution in Edawn in anyone's lifetime. The stillness that followed was like a death sentence that held no chance of reprieve. For a short eternity, the room was seemingly darkened, cold, and void of empathy. Izz had become their sacrificial scapegoat for their frustrating inability to bring the tree down.

Suddenly, suspiciously, the king's expressionless face twisted into a frown. There was something fundamentally wrong at the heart of this matter. The king heard himself protesting weakly and started to say something, opening his mouth to speak, but closed it and said nothing. He was caught between a rock and a hard place, put in a problematic position upon to balance, between his fondness for the young carpenter, the letter of the law, and the discretion of the royal judges. Even though something did not entirely seem all that was true and just, he connected dots that were not there until he had reached a foregone conclusion. The lawful lines had been drawn and could not be altered.

On the other hand, something did not entirely pass the smell test. Baddlock, who had been watching with stern eyes, sensed a silent question of doubt forming in the king's mind. Baddlock quickly faced him, made a low bow, and in a deep, resonating tone, proclaimed, "This is a law written not only on tablets of stone but on the hearts of all the kindred of Zia, which never can be broken. It must stand fast as a faithful witness to all that dare to bear false witness against all that is true and just. Without law and order, and those unwilling to enforce rule over, their citizens will cease to be civilized. I am only grateful that I have been able to serve you in weeding out this tyrant, my lord. I will forever be your faithful and humble servant." That would prove to be the biggest lie that Baddlock would utter that day.

Wordlessly, Dandork looked to the king for the final decision. Silence greeted his questioning expression. The king seemed to jerk a little at the questioning glance, as his gaze remained on Izz's puzzled eyes. Nothing, but his word would be the final decree. His ultimate decision was a sensitive matter for him to make. The furrow in his brow deepened. He lifted his voice, "Is there anyone who doubts or disagrees with the wizard's account or the conclusions of the Master of Arms, or any of the witnesses?"

The king drummed his fingers while he waited for a response, but everyone held their tongue. He called to him his most trusted advisers; the consensus was that the law was clear regarding the matter. The king steadied his heart as his gaze swept over the stern faced judges, their conclusion by this time finalized. He waited for someone to say something, before he pronounced, sorely against his will, his final judgment. This moment would not be the ideal time to revoke any part of the law. Caught in the cobwebs as set forth by the ancient letter of the law, destiny would not stay the unjust fist, nor free the innocent's shackles. Finally, yielding to the wrong conciliation, too proud to object, King Ozzdon whispered under his breath.

"The law is the law, and all must obey it." Then, with reluctance, he stated for all to hear, "So be it as it must be." While he was yet speaking, his crown seemed to cause his head to ache as if in protest. He looked to the judges; all had reached a mutual agreement. Contrary to both reason and revelation, they all harkened to the old traditions of the law. And the king murmured to himself, "I have no other choice."

There were a few gasps from the crowd. Izz could not help but flinch as if stung, as he stared back at the king blankly. Despite fearlessly maintaining his innocence and denying every accusation hurled at him by his persecutors, the truth did not prevail. Men of integrity, men of an intellectual ideal, the king himself allowed the most blasphemous and dishonorable travesty to befall an innocent man. Everything Izz believed in was suddenly shattered. Never in his wildest dreams would Izz have thought that so much could go so wrong so fast. Members of the Inner Council sat in the section that occupied the front row, babbling in private, deciding the details of Izz's fate in muted whispers. The decree was finally written as if in stone and could not be changed, not even by the king him-self, even if he wanted to.

Dandork walked to the podium with the judgment of the court in his hand. Izz knew by the firm look pasted on his face that he was dead serious. All sat mute as sweat beaded on Izz's brow. In a faultfinding tone, Dandork announced, "This court determines that the accused be given one day, from sunup to sunset, to bring the tree down. As he has stated, he could, or final judgment will be executed as prescribed by law." He read each word with a harsh, incriminating tone that could have chilled one's blood. Dandork punctuated his proclamation with a ridged finger pointed at him. The finality of his sentence wiped out any lingering doubts that all this might be some terrible mistake.

Izz stiffened. He could only stand there with his mouth open. Izz could hardly believe the silence that ensued. Surely one of those present would speak up for him. Why had not Ammiz come to his defense? Up until that moment, he had not fully real-ized how much danger his life was actually in. He suddenly felt a seizure of dread like a hard kick to the pit of his gut. Izz shook his head in disbelief as he struggled to recapture the breath that had just been knocked out from the blow he had just suffered. Izz was so utterly stunned, and his heart sank so low that all he could man-age to utter was, "Is that not a little extreme." His voice trembled with disbelief. Anger followed quickly, and he cried out, "But it is not fair!"

The whole event had started and ended so quickly that everyone who knew Izz could not fully believe they had witnessed what they had witnessed. The king thought maybe he was permit-ting too harsh a sentence too soon. Had he made a dreadful mis-take? He trusted Baddlock's wisdom. Besides, who was this com-moner who threatened to come between Zuree and Rizan? The young carpenter had made a fool of his trust and bewitched his daughter. What was done was done and could not be undone.

Baddlock's lips were curved, showing his teeth in a wolfish grin, busy trying to contain his amusement as if he was just on the verge of laughter. Izz felt a rare agony in his spirit as the council began to dissolve. And while he was still struggling to understand the gravity of what had just happened, the keeper of the chronicles closed the book of records. The scribes closed their ledgers, and the resolution was posted throughout the kingdom. *As two court guards roughly led Izz out of the Halls of Law, Baddlock jeered inwardly with glee and could scarcely resist laughing in Izz's face as he passed.* The Wicked Warlock Wizard turned to Dandork and said with finality, "The carpenter will not be around long enough to figure out what happened to him."

At that moment, aware of the devilish laughter glinting in his eyes, Dandork saw a darker power sealed within. Hatred was like an intoxicating wine that would birth only death and destruction. Baddlock rubbed his hands together, sure that he had seen the last of the lowly carpenter who had become a thorn in his mind.

The judgment that day was so far away from the inception of wisdom that it was the inception of senselessness. Good men permitted wickedness to come full circle. Thus a mighty blow was struck against truth and justice that day.

Eleven

The Ring of Giants

hen details of Izz's ill fate reacched the princess; she was devastated beyond which she thought she could ever be. She immediately sought to confront her father. As she entered his presence, the king instantly sensed that she had something very urgent on her mind. Her determination was firmly in place, and she did not look happy. Her face was defiant, her shoulders squared, and her spine as straight as a rod. He had encountered this manner before and was well acquainted with the signs. Nonetheless, he gave an indulgent nod of the head. She did nothing to hide her displeasure.

"How could you let this happen?" Were the first words that came out of Zuree's mouth. "This is all wrong. You must do what is right and abolish this decree! What were you thinking?" The tone of her words came out more biting than she had intended. But the words had been spoken, and they could never be taken back as if drawn from her lips by divine intervention against her own will.

The judiciary proceeding had left him at odds and had not left him in an agreeable frame of mind. And now, confronted by his daughter's sudden outburst, the king blurted out in his defense, "He has broken our laws and must now face the consequences. No one is above the law, in spite of who they are. The carpenter has been charged as a lawbreaker. I had no alternative but to carry out my responsibility as the chief administrator of the law. The carpenter is no exception. Not even I am above the law of the land. Therefore, I cannot undo what has been lawfully done."

Zuree spoke more cautiously, "You cannot, or will not! Is it truly the law or just a matter of course? You are the king. You can do as you will." Zuree turned an imploring gaze on her father as she placed her hands on her hips.

A flicker of annoyance flashed across the king's face as he looked at Zuree in exasperation. He was not at all sure he wanted to deal with her new assertiveness at that particular moment. But he knew from the determined look on Zuree's face; she would not let up until she had said her peace. Trying to choke back his temper, he snapped, "Do not talk to me in that tone. I do not like what I am hearing, nor do I like what I think I see. It is the people's will that inevitably creates the laws we must all live by. I did not like it, but I saw myself as having no choice. Baddlock—" The king started to say when the princess cut him off, not giving him time to finish.

"Baddlock!" Zuree's jaw muscles went rigid when she said the name. "Just the thought of him makes me feel as if something dirty is creeping over my skin. Only a dunce would place any trust in him." She tried to say under her breath. She became disheartened by her own conduct, immediately regretting her words, but she had not been able to help or stop herself.

The king was stunned by her spontaneous reaction. His forehead slowly wrinkled into a frown of concern, notably annoyed because he was not used to having his rule questioned, especially not by his own daughter. His disdainful groan made it obvious how displeased he was.

Zuree wanted to yield, but some willful streak within her would not let her give in, just yet. "I should have known!" Zuree continued. "I have never had much esteem for the likes of him. He makes me ill every time he comes near me. There is something amiss about him. There is something about his eyes when he looks at me, the way he talks. I do not exactly know what it is, but I know he is not an honorable man. I know it in my heart of hearts, and you should have known better than to listen to him. He has played you for a fool!" She cut short her remark an instant too late as she recognized what an insult she had let loose. She lowered her head and raised her shoulders in frustration. She had to do something about her slack tongue.

King Ozzdon's frown deepened as his eyebrows knotted. He looked more surprised than angry over her poor choice of words. He had never seen this particular side of his daughter before. Caught by her pleading eyes, he allowed her to vent, since she was so vividly upset. Zuree pressed on as if she was trying to negotiate terms for a deal.

"My heart tells me that Izz is a virtuous soul and would never have said the outrageous things he has been accused of." Her voice hesitated. "I do not know how I know it. I just know it." Zuree realized she was wringing her hands and, at once, folded them in front of her, trying to look self assured.

"You know all this about this carpenter after meeting him only once? What you know of this carpenter is less than nothing. Nonetheless, you have taken his side over the word of the honorable wizard. You have come forward in defense of a man that clearly cannot be trusted. You have been blinded as we all have, by the charm of an uncultured immigrant." His words were measured, but there was no mistaking his tone.

Zuree stared at her father, resenting the picture he was painting of a man he clearly did not know, but she knew that if she was to sustain her integrity, she had to maintain her dignity. To hide her building anger, she forcefully kept herself from raising her voice, as she struggled to put her concerns into words. "Izz is a good and kind soul. He is innocent of these contemptible charges. My heart declares it to me."

The king clasped his hands behind his back. "And what do you know about the matters of the heart?" he asked in an injuring tone. "What I see is that this common carpenter of uncertain parentage has managed to drive a wedge between you and your own father and turned you against your people." His lips pressed tightly together as if to hold back the anger that was beginning to boil within. "Put him out of your head. He is a teller of tall tales and cannot be trusted."

Matching his tone and finding the resolve to meet his icy glare with her own, Zuree responded in retaliation, "You and my people have condemned a good man for a phony crime."

"You should listen more to reason and less to your heart. The law has been written to protect us from charlatans like this vagabond. Baddlock has been a loyal and valuable subject as long as I can remember. Consider that for a moment, and until he proves otherwise, I must trust him and his insight. And you, young lady, will remember your place." His tone was condescending. "You are in my realm, and I alone have the right to raise my voice within its borders. You would be better served to focus your attention on Rizan, the rightful owner of your heart."

"So you keep reminding me." Her voice was a sign that she was more troubled than honored. Her chin rose up in a spontaneous act of defiance. "I am no longer a child, but a full grown woman, and I should have the right to follow my own heart as I please," she said with a fleeting moment of resentment. "Why should I be subjugated to ancient oral traditions and outdated customs?" she asked defensively. Her chin went up another notch as she added, "My life is mine to live as I choose and to surrender my heart to whom I will."

The king self consciously wondered, *Who is this rebellious, harsh stranger with whom I, for so long, have shared a roof and the blood that runs in my veins?* The king raised his voice with every word that followed. "Has it not occurred to you? These are sacred traditions that have been passed down from generation to generation from the beginning of recorded time. They cannot be changed, and you, young lady, have been pledged to Rizan," he reprimanded.

Zuree did not like the abrasive impact of her father's statement. Her frown intensified. She wrinkled her nose and rolled her eyes as she realized she was about to hear the whole worn out historical betrothal story to its last detail.

"Listen well and heed my words. My word is well known to all among the hierarchy to be good as gold, and once spoken is an oath that cannot be broken. That is a fact of life. From your birth, you were promised to Rizan when he was little more than a boy." He pointed to a different finger on the opposite hand each time he stated a fact. "I have sworn by my word and oath. That is the way of things. Your mother herself was betrothed, as was her mother and her mother before her. Your mother, the queen, and I have taken great care in ensuring that you marry the perfect man for you in all of Zia. Rizan is that man. He is the youngest king in the empire. He reigns over Ziyontopia, the most enchanted kingdom in Zia, and he comes from one of the most affluent families in Xylenia. He possesses extremely honorable qualities. He is handsome, strong, good hearted, and brave, very brave. On top of all that, he is the greatest athlete in the world. I do not think you have thought this through. We are bound by deep rooted tradition, and that is more important than your childish infatuations for a carpenter who you do not even know."

Zuree bowed her head so her father could not see the hurt she was feeling inside. He was her father, her king, and even though she thought he was being ruthlessly unjust, she could not bring herself to disobey him. She had to surrender to what was best. Yet beneath her poised restraint was still that flicker of unbridled fervor, and she could not keep herself from speaking out. "Be that as it may, a life without true love is a price too high to pay for a time worn tradition." The noticeable tinge of defiance in her voice began to rise again and threatened to escalate at any moment.

He had brought her up with love and taught her the best values he could. These defiant traits had to have come to her through her mother's blood. The king abruptly held up his hand to interrupt her. His scowled expression was not kind. Trying to control the tone of his voice, just barely containing his irritation, he made an earnest attempt not to seem as angered as he was becoming. Zuree's whole body tensed in anticipation of what he might say next. The king's posture grew rigid as if he were waging a losing battle against what he wanted to say and the words he should say.

"Since you insist that you are an adult now, daughter, I will speak frankly. I had hoped that you would have outgrown that rebellious spirit that seethes within you. Your defiance threatens to upset a noble ritual of the highest order, one that has been in place for eons. There is more to a royal marriage than a commitment of love."

"You mean merger, not marriage. That is what you are asking for." She met the fixation in his eyes defiantly.

"It is about strengthening our bloodline, our kingdoms, and our empire. I wonder where your loyalties might lie!" His voice took on a harder and harder edge as he continued to chastise his daughter. The words he spoke next hurt even before he forced himself to say them. "You have only one choice. As long as I am breathing, you will do as I wish. I am commanding you as your father and king to obey me." His expression took on a harshness that Zuree had never seen before. His words struck her like blows. His tone cut her like the sting of a whip. They both stared at each other without warmth. The force of his words made her shudder. Zuree looked as if she might burst into a rush of weeping at his blunt outburst. How could he talk to her this way? He had hurt her deeply, more deeply than she had ever known she could be hurt, and worst of all, she felt betrayed. She felt helpless. Zuree wanted to cry, wanted to implore her father to be merciful, to see things from her standpoint. She rebuked the tears gathering behind her eyes, as she stiffened defensively, refusing to let her emotions control her. The exchange was not going very well at all. And the hurt look in Zuree's eyes made him ache all over. It was madness how his love for his only child kept coming out like malice, laced with contempt, and condemnation. What he wanted to sound like fatherly wisdom became a slap in the face.

Before her words could get all balled up in her throat, Zuree spoke in the heat of the moment, "You have condemned an innocent man to death, and you know it. And now you want to force me into a marriage I may live to regret. How can I marry for any other reason than true love, whether it is noble or otherwise?"

"Because I say it will be so!" An ache constricted in the king's heart when he saw the overwhelmingly hurt feelings erupting in Zuree's eyes. There was a sudden warning in the king's spirit. His fortified armor cracked as it became clear that the dictatorial approach had taken a turn for the worst. He forced his anger back down into the seething cauldron within him and decided to try reason. His voice softened.

"Why must you complicate everything? You must understand that it is noble blood you carry, and that means you can only marry those in your regal bearing." He added a mortified expression for good measure, "You must remember you are a princess, born of royalty, and someday you will be a queen. I cannot tell you it will be true love, but I truly think Rizan will suit you much better than you deem. So we have nothing further to discuss."

He had not heard a thing she had said. He was not listening to her, not now, perhaps never. Or if he had, he had chosen to ignore it all. A stormy response formed in her mind, but her thoughts were forcibly subdued when she caught the increasingly troubled expression on her father's face. Her vocal objection collapsed. Zuree now found herself caught up in two battles at two levels: in her heart and her head. She loved her father more than anyone else in Zia, even more than herself. Zuree hesitated a long moment. She clasped her hands in front of her to keep them from shaking and finally decided that she would have to put her pride aside, saying, "Do not fret yourself. I will fulfill my end of your bargain as you wish." Her words came from her head and not her heart. She turned her full lower lip in a pout. "Your happiness is all that is important to me."

The king took her hand; his touch was warm and gentle. Zuree laid her head against his shoulder as though if she just closed her eyes for a moment, all this would somehow go away. The king thought that women could be such irrational creatures, then when one least expects it, they reconsider on a whim.

Meanwhile, Zuree waited, wishing, hoping, so urgently needing to hear the words she yearned to hear, but the words she longed to hear did not come. Anxious by what might be conceivably true, scorned by what Zuree had said, the king decided to put the matter to rest. He started with, "I have always been proud of your intelligence. It gladdens me to see you have finally come to your senses. You have been my pride, joy, and my world since the day you were born. I only want what is best for you. Your misgiving this day is my fault and only proves that I have waited too long. I have taken it entirely for granted that the time was not yet right. But you are all grown up now, and it is clear to me at present that you should have been long wed by this time. Rizan and I will be gone for a short time on a trading voyage to the northwestern coast. If he is to follow in my bloodline, he must know how an emperor conducts business. You and Rizan will be wed immediately upon our return," the king said, then gave Zuree a quick kiss on the cheek. After that, he turned his back on her in an attempt to give her a notice of dismissal. He quickly walked away before the polite veneer might wear away before words that they would both regret were exchanged.

But Zuree was not ready to be dismissed. Zuree knew once her father had made a decision, he would not change his mind. Her shoulders slumped as she tried to say, "But I just need a little more time to..." Her breath released in exasperation. Nevertheless, the conversation was over, ending as abruptly as it began. For an awful moment, Zuree felt her hopes for Izz drain out of her, despair taking their place. "And what about the carpenter?" she asked as she caught a glimpse of her father turning halfway around the corner, and suddenly, she found herself talking to the king's receding shadow.

That night, the king could not sleep. It was an unthinkable thought, but something felt wrong. There was a feeling in the pit of his guts that ate at him like a hungry parasite. It was a feeling so foreseeable and overpowering that it had the force of doom. He kept repeating in his mind, *I had no choice. What is done is done what is done is done.* "And cannot be undone." The king said to himself in a whisper so quiet that he had hardly heard it himself.

Resigned to his fate, Izz gathered every conceivable cutting tool he possessed. He dreaded the impossible task ahead of him, for he felt wholly hopeless. He carried out a last minute equipment check of everything, and then he loaded it all onto his cart. He hitched up his donkey and headed for the Ring of Giants. The sun was setting when Izz set out because he wanted to be within the Circle of the Giants when first light broke over the horizon. Keeping to the backstreets where most of the lights were out, he made his way northward. He glanced in both directions along the street from time to time as he thought of how his uncle Lott had offered to hide him.

How he had told him he would rather be dead than to bring shame to their family name. He also did not want to give anyone reason to accuse him of being cowardly. Nor did he want to be a fugitive and a vagabond for the rest of his life. He wondered what the princess must think of him now. Had Ammiz actually too ashamed to come to advise him, console him, something, anything? He thought of how believing he could somehow bring the tree down evaded common sense, but Izz had to try and die trying if he must. But he knew in his heart of hearts that it was no use. What other choice did he have? He hastily made his way to the northern outskirts of the kingdom. He passed the two men at arms at the northern gate. He looked up momentarily only to see the gate guards spit on the ground as he passed. Outside the kingdom walls, Izz drove his cart along the never ending winding road that led out over the valley and toward the infamous Forbidden Ebony Forest. Grim faced, he entered and made his way through the woods. With a gloomy countenance and a troubled heart, he rode over a tortuous, crude trampled path as far as he could pass the main trail. When he could go no further, he unloaded his cart and packed his tools onto his beast of burden. He got the bulky backpack, strapped it to his back, and led his donkey toward the Ring of Giants. His resentment grew as he trudged up the precarious path, listening to the night sounds of the forest with his donkey in tow.

Tom Icon

By the time he reached the trees, the sun was falling. He made camp under the tree that rose majestically up into the sky to dominate the forest. With the little light that remained, he quickly gathered some firewood and hastily built a small campfire in the diminishing light. He slumped back against the giant he had come to fall. He sat there in silence. With the darkening of the night came a feeling of foreboding that refused to let Izz unwind. He sat there enfolded in the solace of the wilderness, wide awake, looking up at the night sky, and feeling perplexed. He did not know what set of moral principles to believe anymore. Nothing made any sense. It was as if he was trapped in some cruel dream that he would sooner or later, somehow, wake from. The absence of sound was interrupted by the occasional hooting sound of an owl and the faint crackling sounds of the fire.

Eventually, even these noises, at last, subsided as the fire died down, and darkness fell all around him. All he could hear now was an intermittent cricket. A refreshingly cool mountain breeze blew in, chilling his skin. It was still hours till dawn, but he knew tomorrow would be today too soon. He reached for his bedding and stretched out over it. Above him, there was nothing but stars and distance. Gradually, the constellations appeared. So clear was the night that Izz felt as if he could see every celestial constellation in the cosmos. A spectacular array of summer stars twinkled brightly to tell stories that were as old as time itself. Star arrangements that marked the velvet sky shifted in Izz's mind from random clusters to suggestions of meaning. He saw what appeared to be outlines that formed entities and riddles and impressions of strange creatures. Other groups of stars seemed to be representations of people and faces. From the East, he suddenly saw a luminous flock of shooting stars that raced across the heavens. He watched as they fell from the sky. The head of each was an oblong ignited mass followed by a long luminous tail. As they blazed like torches across the night sky, for an instance, Izz imagined he saw himself with Zuree in their patterned trek, hand in hand, dancing across the face of the celestial heavens, and disappeared. Thousands of threads twined throughout his mental vistas. Why was she always popping into his mind? Had she spun a spell over him? He stared into the searing void of the dark skies beyond the stars. He wished he could just shut his brain off and go to sleep. He pulled his cloak around his shoulders and huddled up against himself. He tried to turn his mind to a faraway thought, but every reflection returned to her. He tried shutting her memory out, but after less than a few moments, he saw nothing but Zuree's smiling face in his waking dreams. It all seemed so irrational. He found himself drawing a line and kept it there with all his concentration, locking all thoughts, but sleep out of his mind. Just before closing his eyes, he saw a solitary shooting star dance across the roof of the night sky, vanishing almost immediately. He shut his eyes for a moment and thought of how life was that way. How for a short while we burn so brightly, dim, then we are gone. As the faraway stars seemed to be looking down on him without pity, he was filled with grief and overwhelmed with uncertainties.

The night grew quiet. The only sound was the lonely waft of the whispering wind, sweeping across the giant treetops. Izz spent the rest of his waking hours trying to erase the recurring memory of Zuree. With open eyes, he finally drifted off into a half conscious slumber, interrupted by fits and starts. Nightmarish wisps of wind that would not go away woke him again and again during the elongating night, seemingly calling out to him. "I am death, and I alone am your only escape."

Many times through the endless night, he was not sure if he was awake or only dreaming. The reality, recall, and imagination were so interlaced, and his dreams so disturbing that, that night became the longest night of his entire life. At long last, dreamless slumber released him from his scourge, coming in such an unexpected manner that he did not realize he was asleep until he came around tossing, turning, and trembling in a cold sweat the next morning. He had slept poorly; in fact, he had barely slept at all. The worst thing about waking up in the twilight hour was the dreadful despair of realizing that what he hoped had been all just a bad dream was, in fact, a painful reality. Izz resigned himself to his foredoomed fate and decided he was not going down without a fight. He was not going to simply wait around for the end to come. He thought of what his old schoolmaster would always say when things looked hopeless. The most significant loss in life is not to fail but to sit down by your failure and give up hope. A sense of urgency suddenly seized him. He sat up and shook the last remnants of sleep from his mind. With his eyes still blurry from the lack of sleep, Izz rubbed the crust from the corners of his eyes and took a swig from his water pouch.

The brilliant morning starlight began to break over that horizon in flashes of dazzling, flickering bursts against the rose-tinted sky. As Izz prepared his tools in the dusk of the rising sun, the royal timekeeper in the palace readied himself to set the glass timer that would measure off the hours from sunup to sunset. The hourglass was set, and the sand began to slowly slip through the glass timer as the faint glow of dawn came sweeping down the mountainside's spine. Early sunrise brought Izz to the part he was not going to like. Izz stood at the foot of the giant sentinel that reared up from the forest floor, rising to dominate the morning skies. He took a moment to consider the many ways he might bring the tree down, but every solution seemed to create a hundred new problems. Izz studied the base of the tree for a sign of weakness and found none. He hugged the tree to decide which way the tree was leaning to determine the lay in which the tree was likely to fall. He cleared a workspace and started chopping with the ax he had honed razor sharp. First, he would attempt a horizontal cut in the direction of the fall of the tree, and then he would start the wedge cut. It was all a matter of tact; he convinced himself. Izz took his first mighty swing. The ax head struck the tree and sent vibration up and down his spine. It was not long before the ax became dull, and pieces of its edge started breaking off. It was said that the magical tree bore particular awareness and cried when they were cut into. Izz examined the tree. The small slivers he had managed to whittle off bled out a sticky resin that quickly hardened into an iron like substance. But the young challenger was not deterred from his work. He whetted his ax until it was razor sharp once again, minus a few chips. He took a long guzzle of water and continued his assault. As he chopped, he listened for an indication of a hollow or weakness, but he heard none. Finally, when the ax was so damaged that it was useless, he brought out his saw and continued his hopeless assault on the base of the invincible tree.

Midday had come way too soon. The sun was high in the sky when Izz stopped to rest for the first time. He was wet with sweat and getting wetter. His hands were both blistered across the palms from gripping the ax handle too tight. Izz sat down on the shaded side of the tree, exhausted and disillusioned. His heart sank. Attempting to cut down the giant was all so pointless. He brought his water jug up to his parched lips and took long sips of water. He eagerly reached into his pouch, pulled out a morsel of bread, tore off a mouthful, and chewed off a little end of the dry meat he had packed. In a voracious fit of appetite, he hungrily rushed through his meal. Between gulps of water and mouthfuls of bread, he rested, still determined not to crack or quit. When he had finished, his stomach was thankful, but it growled for more. He stared up from where he sat and looked at the inconsequential scratch he managed to make in half a day of backbreaking work and cracked. The miniature interlacing of green veins had bled their hardening iron resin and made it impossible to make any significant progress. Why should he keep going? He had to conclude that it would be insane to go on finally. In his hopelessness, from time to time, he glanced up at the sky to check the position of the sun.

The sun had gone past its meridian. His time was quickly running out. His heart begged the question, *What have I done to deserve this? What was the use?* His life was slipping away like the granules of sand in the palace hourglass. Fatigued and weakened, sweating from head to toe, Izz felt all hope leaking out of his spirit through the fatal crack in his will. With the last ounce of strength he had left, he threw himself upon the tree and cried with a loud, desperate voice, "What have I ever done to deserve this?"

He slid back to the ground, crumpling into a small heap of despair, and he curled up in despondence against himself at the base of the tree. For what seemed like the longest time, he lay in numb silence, staring into mid space. He could hear fate laughing at him. He tried to cast it off, he wanted to reject it, but it was too real. He thought of the things he had not done, would never do, and the children that he would not leave behind. After what had only been a few minutes but seemed like ages, he unexpectedly felt courage suddenly rise in him halfheartedly. He heard a voice from the depths of his heart speak, *The greatest catastrophe in life is not to fall, the greatest tragedy in life is to fall down and not get back up.*

Out of nowhere, Izz heard himself say, "Stand to your feet or stay fallen forever."

Izz staggered to his feet, put both hands on the tree, and dug his fingers into its bark. And then half crazed, he pushed with every ounce of strength he had left and shouted, "I need to bring this tree down!" His voice reverberated across the valley. Half a dozen birds flew out of the nearby trees and took flight, screeching across the valley as though some tormenting demon hawk from the pit of hell was hot on their trail.

He looked toward the kingdom and caught a glimpse of the king's guards coming on horseback from the kingdom's northern gate. He wanted to run. *No, no, my name and that of my family will be disgraced throughout Zia, forever.* Izz whipped out his spyglass and watched the approaching horsemen, followed by a small donkey drawn cart. Perhaps it was Ammiz the Seer coming to tell him it had all been a dreadful mistake. He focused his eyepiece. "NO! NO! NO!" Izz thought aloud. What was this? Izz could not believe his eyes. It was unmistakable; he would have recognized that pointy, red hat anywhere. To his shocking disgust, it was Baddlock, the Wicked Warlock Wizard. He felt numb, jolted, shattered. He had never had such a feeling of total and utter anguish. He could feel his guts wrenching in terror 1 he had never felt before. What would his family say when they heard of his execution? What would Zuree say? In his mind, he saw flashes of himself ascending the steps to meet the executioner's ax. He put his hand up to his throat; he could almost feel his head rolling. His lower lip trembled. He seldom cried, and even though he was alone, he did not want to cry now. Izz felt a lump in his throat growing as he uttered, "I am going to die!" His dread soared as he heard out of his own mouth the sentence of death pronounced upon himself. Almost eager for death to end his torment, he felt like saving the gravedigger the trouble by digging a deep hole as far as he could and pulling the dirt in behind him. He closed his eyes and slipped into a weary, dreamlike state of mind. His thoughts turned to his family. He wondered how it would make them feel when he was dragged out before the public and decapitated. The last thing he wanted was to be beheaded in front of Zuree like a helpless chicken on the chopping block. He wondered what happened to his secure world, where it was safe and warm. Where was the world of order ruled by love, kindness, and justice, where bad things were never allowed to happen to the blameless? Where was Ammiz's great Creator? Most likely, He was just as big an illusion as his uncle's forest's spooks. He looked toward the kingdom again. There he saw the long arm of the law, seemingly inching their way toward him, and the Wicked Warlock Wizard had come for the satisfaction of watching him being slapped in chains and taken into custody. Why could anyone not see that he had falsely accused him? He felt a swift jab of sympathy for himself. Tears swelled in his eyes. He quickly wiped them away with the back of his hand. Izz had shed few tears in life, tears of sadness, tears of joy, but he never dreamed that he would live to see the day that he would shed tears of empathy for himself. All the resentment welled up inside of him as he started to lose all composure. He threw back his head and let out one final dreadful shout of resistance.

"NO! NO! NO! It is not fair! This is not happening! It could not be happening! WAKE UP, WAKE UP!" In that instant, he thought he had only one option: face the executioner's ax or run. He decided death would be less painful.

Tom Icon

He withered to the forest floor in anguish. From his knees, he screamed, "I curse the day I ever set foot on Edawnian soil." Meaninglessness was his only reply. At that exact moment, he would have instead been anyone else, even Tigbone.

When he came out of his crazed state and rose slowly to his feet, he felt different. He felt calm and somehow peaceful. The thought of death, in some way, no longer terrified him. By some means, he accepted the fact that the end of his life was at hand. Beheading, even though it seemed somewhat horrible, had to be one of the quickest and least agonizing ways to die, if the executioner was practiced and his blade sharp, and he held himself perfectly still. For whatever it was worth, for whatever few hours he had left, he was going to face his fate with as much courage and dignity as he could humanly manage. He was trying his best to prepare his heart for the inevitable when suddenly out of nowhere, his acute hearing picked up a faint snapping of twigs and rustling of leaves just behind him. He felt the hairs on the back of his neck stand on end. Something or someone was closing in on him from behind. He listened to the soft sound of steps at his heels. He reached for his dagger tied at his hip and unfastened its keep. His palms were slick with sweat as he tightened his fingers around the hilt of his blade and waited for the intruder to come closer. A million thoughts raced through his mind. He remembered his uncle's warning: The main rule of survival in these woods is this, you must never allow yourself to get so caught up with anything that you neglect to notice the out of the ordinary sneak up on you. Something was breathing; something was moving. Could it be the two strange goons that testified against him, coming to ambush him?

Wondering why the scoundrel had not struck yet, he preferred to die now rather than be beheaded before a jeering audience; before his family, Zophie, Buzu: before Zuree! Carefully, in one single flow, smooth and swift, he withdrew his blade from its sheath, ready to deliver its deadly sentence. He stood tall, held his razor sharp dagger, blade point down, and at the ready. He felt the body warmth of something almost against his legs. He tilted his head down, and through the blur of his tears, made out the silhouette of a figure. He clenched his dagger's butt tighter over the hilt. It was cold and damp against his already sweaty palm. He turned set to deliver the deadly blow and froze with his blade held over his head at the ready. He swiped away the tears with the palm of his free hand and focused his eyes. He immediately recognized the wolverine that he had rescued from the wicked trap. He knew the wolverine by the vicious scare it bore on its back. Izz no longer feeling threatened, fell to his knees, and extended his hand toward the wolverine. It sniffed his hand and licked it.

Izz was so excited to see the wolverine he thought most likely dead with very vigorous life in it that he almost cried out. It was as if a familiar friend had come to pay him a final visit and share his troubles. As he resheathed his blade, it slid home with a firm grating click, Izz grabbed the wolverine by its head and said with a joyful voice, "You made it. It is so good to see you are alive and well." He gently ran his fingertips along the length of the scar. The bond that brought them together was strong. "I am sorry for what you have suffered," he whispered.

For a moment, there seemed to be some unspoken language between them, an unexplainable communication they both somehow understood. A joining of mental images and word impressions took place. For a while, Izz had forgotten his plight, but then all too soon, the whole horror of his nightmare came back to him with a vengeance once again, and he asked, "Have you come to see me off, my furry friend? You see those armed soldiers?" He pointed with his dagger toward the distant detachment. "They are coming to take me to my death." He informed the wolverine in hushed tones. Then anger overtook him. He stood, turning to pound his fists against the base of the tree. "And it is all because I was falsely accused of being able to bring this cursed tree down." Izz caught himself and held insanity at bay, realizing that losing his head was not going to help. He slid himself back down to the forest floor.

The wolverine sniffed the air with its long toothy snout and bobbed its head repeatedly. Without hesitating farther, the wolverine turned quickly and scurried off into the thick forest. *Perhaps it sensed the approaching danger,* Izz thought.

Izz called out, "I do not blame you. Fare ye well, my furry friend, and live long. I should have the sense to run too. Turn tail and run? Risk being remembered forever as gutless and unmanly? No! I will not disgrace my name. If I must face the reaper's blade, I will face it like a man." His mind was made up. "I would rather die with honor than live with dishonor." In the receding evening light, he slumped back down against the tree that would not fall, and he waited to be taken to his execution. He felt weak as he tried to prepare his heart to meet death.

Suddenly he felt a peculiar vibration in the ground beneath him. In the same instance, he heard a rushing noise, like the faint rumbling sound of a faraway thunderstorm. Then out of nowhere, the whole slopping side of the forest seemed to be caving down on him as an enveloping wall of dust filled the air with a fine powdery cloud of leaves and dust. Within the billowing obscurity, Izz saw a horde of what seemed like hundreds of wolverines descending on him like an avalanche of fur. Izz was having a hard time believing what he was seeing. He did not know what to think about what was happening. All he knew for sure was that he was powerless to stop it. The stampeding wolverines converged around the giant tree, each wolverine picking a spot. Then, as though a silent command had been given and heard by all but Izz, all at the same time, they began to burrow around the tree's deep root system. Izz saw what was happening and was unbelievably amazed.

The arresting patrol was in no particular hurry as they made their way toward the Ring of Giants. Baddlock, sitting importantly on his small cart, came along to witness the arrest, cursing and complaining because his overburdened donkey was having trouble keeping up with the stallions on the steep grade. He did not seem very smart, not even for a donkey.

With his majesty's execution orders in hand, he was ready to escort Izz to the executioner's block personally. Tigbone brought up the rear, trudging along at the back of the procession, dragging his feet wearily over the dirt path. He was too tired to care about the situation that was unfolding around him.

The captain of the guard turned to his first lieutenant and said, "It is unfortunate about the young carpenter. He seemed like such a pleasant fellow. We have not executed anyone in hundreds of years. I, for one, am not looking forward to this distasteful task."

Suddenly one of the lower ranking officers pointed toward the ridge where the Ring of the Giants was well in sight and asked, "What is that up ahead, smoke?" "Perhaps the young carpenter is trying to burn the tree down, poor unfortunate soul."

The hour is late, much too late, the Wicked Warlock Wizard thought to himself. Ridding myself of that insolent vagabond will be one of the most memorable days of my life. He could hardly wait to see the look in the eyes of the condemned carpenter. Baddlock impatiently tapped his foot on the cart's floorboard as he hurled insults at the donkey as it staggered along.

Tigbone sluggishly followed with a sore limp, gibbering something unintelligible to himself. Finally speaking out, he asked, "Can I ride wit you, Muster?" Whimpering and mewing like a wounded kitten as he reached for the donkey drawn cart.

With his anger smoldering, Baddlock barked, "Back away, you silly sausage." As he put the heel of his boot on Tigbone's shoulder and shoved him backward with all his might, sending poor Tigbone sprawling rearward, somersaulting, end over end, down the forest's slopping floor without a trace of empathy. Baddlock gripped the reins and snapped them forcefully, urging his struggling donkey on with a harsh command. He looked back only long enough to say, "Keep up, or I will have you flogged, you graceless bumbling sloth!"

All the while at the base of the invincible tree, the legion of wolverines continued their assault on the deep rooted giant. Down they tunnel toward the tree's root system with their mighty claws, each one sending towering plumes of dust, rocks, and dirt into the air behind them. When the tree began to tremble, Izz heard a loud screech from above. The wolverines stopped digging for a moment, looked up, and sniffed the air then went on burrowing as fervently as ever. Izz shaded his eyes against the glare of the rapidly setting sun. He looked up to where he had heard the screeching sound come from and saw the giant White Crested Eagle leave her nest. Izz remembered the eagle's eggs. A concerned look swept across his face. In a fit of compassion and without stopping to think, he grabbed his blanket. He emptied its content and strapped it around his shoulder as he ran to the tree and started up. Beneath him, growing mounds of dirt began to pile up at each hole as the army of wolverines dug down and around the tree's complex root structure. Not knowing how much time he had left, Izz moved as quickly as he could. Up and up he went, as agile as a cat he ascended. He was only halfway to the nest when the tree began to sway. He quickened his pace, concentrating intensely on his every move.

Suddenly when he was about to reach the nest, the mother eagle came shrieking as it dove toward him in an attempt to pluck him from the tree with her razor sharp talons. She was huge with a wingspread so vast that they blocked out the setting sun, and the turbulence they created almost knocked him off the swaying tree. Izz moved around the tree just in time to evade the sharp, knife like talons of the protective mother eagle. Without losing a beat, knowing he was almost out of time, Izz returned to the nest as the mother eagle soared, circling to make another pass at him. He hesitated for a moment, knowing that if he touched the eggs, the mother would never take them back. The tree began to wobble. As Izz reached for the eggs, he felt something move inside. The eggs were huge and hard to handle, but somehow Izz managed to tie them to his back with his blanket. He was hoping that he would not drop them or that they would not prove to be too heavy and bring him crashing to the ground below. But he did not have time to think. The tree was tipping, and he had to move—now! He centered the eggs on his back and started back down as fast as he possibly could. As he climbed down at breakneck speed, he could see down below the dust and debris continued to bellow from around the base of the tree. The mother eagle made another sweep. Izz again maneuvered around the tree in the nick of time, almost losing his grip. He was midway down from the nest when the tree began to teeter. Suddenly all digging came to a halt, every wolverine rushed out of the burrow it had hollowed, and backed away slowly.

All at once, the tree began to shake violently. The tree wobbled, swayed, teetered, and then passed its tipping point. Sensing that he only had moments before the tree toppled, Izz began to recklessly slide down against the taper of the tree with his feet wedged inward and his arms wrapped around the tree as best he could. Izz rode the gradually increasing thickness of the tree down, gaining speed as he dropped. When he was about ten body lengths from the forest floor, the tree tottered past the point of no return and began its descent to the forest floor. Under its massive weight, the taproot all at once snapped, slapping Izz back, and as he leaped backward, his arms shot out to balance him. As Izz fell, he tucked the eggs in front of him, while the ground below him seemed to leap up all around him. He somehow managed to land feet first on the soft rooty ground. Then pulling off a maneuver that looked virtually impossible, Izz flipped back to front, stumbling, somersaulting head over heels, and came to a shuddering halt on an overgrown mossy patch. Izz let out a whooping, "YEEAAA!" at the thrill of leaping back instinctively and almost not making it as the tall woody giant fell. Limbs shattered thunderously, crackling and creaking as the patriarch of all trees fell all the way down to the forest floor.

The mounted guard, to their great astonishment, had seen the tree falling straight toward them just in the nick of time. Without time to think, they dug their sharp spurs into the sides of their riding beasts, causing them to rear, neigh, shrill, and bolt, all at the same time. They scattered like scared rabbits hunted by ravenous wolves into the dense growth of underbrush at the last ditch moment.

Just moments earlier, Baddlock had been whipping his donkey mercilessly, doing all he could to get more speed out of the worn out beast. He was thinking, *My greatest wish is coming true, sooner than I thought.* His broadening grin was suddenly erased as his hollowed eyes and mouth quickly widened in shock. Immediately upon realizing that the tree was coming directly toward him, he jumped like a bolting rat at the very last possible instant. He windmilled as he tumbled down and landed in a twisted heap on a thicket of thorny poison oak. Within that same moment, there was the loud smashing, splintering sound that echoed throughout the forest. The Wicked Warlock Wizard's fear filled screams were all but swallowed up by the landing temblor of the tree as his wagon was flattened into a thousand pieces. Numerous birds and other forest creatures scrambled for their lives as the mighty giant settled with a final rumbling and reverberating crash. Zia groaned and trembled and quaked as the falling of the giant of giants belched a monstrous dust storm into the surrounding air. In the obscuring dust cloud, the Wicked Warlock Wizard could barely be heard as he tried to scream, "Someone, help, me!" But instead, the scream of alarm ended in a strangled whisper of gasps and sputters that poured from his lips in a torrent of babbling curse words.

Izz was scratched in a hundred places, cut in a few more, and was not sure how injured he was, but with little concern for himself, he quickly untied the blanket and miraculously found the two eggs intact. His attention was abruptly drawn to his hands. They were badly splintered and burning from the friction of his hurried descent. He rubbed his hands together until the ache went away. He knew from the nasty, and throbbing pangs felt that he would bear many black and blue bruises before this night was over. He held one egg up, then the other against the setting sun, and examined each egg for cracks or any damage. He was relieved to discover that neither egg was broken. A cloudy spot inside revealed that each egg contained a growing embryo.

When Baddlock finally came to rest, he found himself held tight in the grip of hundreds of barbed thorns that riddled his wrinkled hide. His head just kept jerking from side to side as he looked around to see every eye around him fixed upon him. He could sense that Tigbone was doing everything he could to choke back his bellowing laughter, restrained only by the slightest thread. The donkey, by some divine intervention, survived by the minutest of margins. It had to be cut away from the cart, which lay under the tree as flat as a pancake.

When Izz gathered himself up, he turned and was surprised not to see hide or hair of the wolverine pack. It was almost as if they had vanished off the face of Zia. He then turned his attention to the enormous writhe of tree roots before him. The ancient monarch of the forest was slain, never to rise again. The statuesque marvel of the forest's skyline was no more. Izz was saddened to think that the oldest living thing whose ancient history had stretched back hundreds of generations before the founding of Edawn, before the Great War, even before the rise and fall of the Old Empire, now lay dying on the ground. The only thing Izz was glad of was that he had been saved from the executioner's ax.

"Why do you stand there, gawking? Get me out of here, you fools!" Baddlock scorned. Baddlock had to be pried from the fish hook throned like barbs of the thorned poison oak, cursing and swearing at the top of his lungs one terrible oath after another.

Tigbone helped pull and tug on his grimacing rat faced master. Every time Baddlock screamed in pain, Tigbone would say, "I sorry, I too, too, so sorry, Mazter."

Try as he may, Tigbone found it impossible to restrain what would have been a toothy grin, if he had had a full set of teeth, which threatened to erupt into uncontrolled laughter at the slightest provocation.

Finally freed, Baddlock just stood there looking like a poorly plucked turkey, gawking at the fallen tree. The fall had shaken the foundations of the kingdom and sent small, expanding ripples across the bay. Everyone in the kingdom saw the enormous cloud of dust and debris billowing up to the heavens, and everyone knew, to their surprise, that the tree had fallen. The ancient giant had hit the forest floor as the sun kissed the western horizon, and just as the last grain of sand had fallen through the glass timer.

Twelve

The Jubilation

By the time, word of Izz's conquest spread throughout the kingdom, the sun had long fallen, but that did not keep the jubilation and excitement from erupting everywhere all over Edawn. The execution guard had become the messengers that first brought the tale of Izz's triumph over the giant of giants. Pandemonium poured out of homes, shops, taverns, and into the streets. Torches and bonfires were lit high and low, inside and outside the kingdom. Trumpet brigades made such a commotion that they could have woken the dead. Bells rang out from every ivory tower, spire, and steeple. The anticipation of Izz's arrival began to draw a crowd as citizens of Edawn assembled by the thousands and started dancing in the streets, singing and chanting in one voice. "IZZ HAS CONQUERED THE MIGHTY TREE."

Citizens who lived along the road lit their oil lantern and set them on their window ledges. The crowd continued to swell, and the royal wineries were opened by order of the king. Soon every man and woman in the kingdom was toasting to Izz's triumph. He had conquered the unconquerable giant of giants. Immediately his fame spread throughout the neighboring villages like a wildfire driven before a headwind. A monument was guaranteed to be erected to commemorate the occasion. People flocked in great numbers to see the would-be arresting contingent, escorting Izz on his cart along the approach to Edawn, not in chains, but as an honored hero. He rode into the kingdom a conqueror, the excitement of his triumph went before him. Torch bearing villagers were all waiting. Over a thousand of them gathered at the edge of the kingdom in masses, lined up along the highway and byways to greet Izz with friendly waves and warm smiles. Many revered him, and everyone stared at him as if he had just returned from the presence of the gods and esteemed him by virtue of his powers. Izz greeted all graciously, bearing a triumphant smile as he gazed out into the sea of well wishers. Izz was amazed that Edawn could produce such a vast, teeming crowd in such short notice, especially after sunset. Plus, they were all there for him, and it lifted his spirit, making him feel like a conquering king. Children pointed at him in awe and amazement, and young maidens waved at him endearingly and became animated when he smiled back. Their hearty cheers resounded to the heavens and shined back like a deluge of glory, a drenching that covered Izz with the recognition he did not feel he deserved. As Izz passed, the congested procession rushed along the roadside, guiding their small children by the hand, chanting his name, "IZZ, IZZ, IZZ!" He was indeed one of them now. He had won their love and respect, and soon everyone in Edawn would know his name. No longer did he feel like a foreigner. Edawn was now indeed his home where he belonged.

When Izz entered the kingdom's gate, he stepped out of his cart and walked into the midst of the suffocating crowds and found himself immediately caught up in the people's wholehearted adoration. All stared at him as if he had suddenly grown ten feet tall. Izz had never imagined himself as a hero and was astonished at all the attention. The king himself was there opulently attired, as usual, in deep blue velvet. Accompanying him was his royal guard, Zandor, and his twin, Kondor, to welcome Izz's victorious return. It was a momentous occasion, and the whole kingdom was eager to see this remarkable man called Izz of Zollerzon. The crowd of well wishers pressed in from every side, eager to hear Izz's story. But no matter how many times Izz told the story of the wild wolverines, no one seemed to believe him. If Izz had not lived through that event, he would not have thought it possible either. They were all convinced that Izz possessed some kind of mystical powers, powers beyond the mortal world, greater than that of Baddlock.

"THOU ART MIGHTY!" They all echoed. Everybody just wanted to express their admiration and wanted to hear how he had managed to bring the legendary tree down. But Izz was tired, dirty, and was not used to being the center of attention. Besides, he had two eaglet eggs that needed his immediate attention. While Izz made his apologies and excuses, the princess watched unseen from high atop her balcony window, relieved that the young carpenter was safe. She was looking out of her window at the crowds that had gathered, down in the street below. Just then, her chambermaid came bursting through Zuree's bedroom door and proclaimed excitedly, "The carpenter has fallen the tree, my lady, and there is the talk of a grand parade and celebration to memorialize his name."

Somewhere during the passing days, Zuree had been forced to be honest with someone, and that someone would have to be Atta, her chambermaid. Atta was a sweet, plump, heavily jawed, mid aged lady who had divine brown eyes that twinkled with warmth. The heavyset woman with wide hips had taken care of Zuree since her childhood. Atta was more than a servant; she was part of the family. Thus the only soul in the kingdom Zuree had confided her fondness for the young carpenter had been her chambermaid.

By now, in the streets below, there was laughter laced with the exciting conversation of Izz's triumph. Zuree stepped to the hearth pretending, to warm her hands, but she did not need the fire's warmth for her heart was aglow. The blood in her veins was oddly aroused, and the rosiness in her cheeks was not a result of the heat of the fire. Zuree smiled to herself and wondered pleasantly, *Who is this enigma called Izz?*

While the kingdom's rejoicing reached its peak of merriment, Baddlock was spending the night in his nearby cottage just beyond the kingdom walls. He stood against the wall of his bedchamber. All the while, Tigbone forcefully removed countless thorns, one by one, from Baddlock's skinny sack of bones. The humiliation was almost more than Baddlock could bear. His temper exploded.

"He should be dead! I will kill him. I will kill him with my bare hands!" He kept repeating. As Tigbone worked on a particularly deep thorn stuck in the Wicked Warlock Wizard's rump, Baddlock dug his nails into the wall and winced, saying, "I can feel you smiling, you natural born simpleton!"

Tigbone's smirk collapsed. "Oh no, no, my mazter."

On top of his painful moans, Baddlock could hear the sound of merriment, blasts of trumpets in the distance, and was eaten up with jealousy and frustration. "How could he possibly still be alive when he should be dead?" He gnashed his teeth, hungry for blood. "Instead, he is being celebrated, hailed as a hero, and has become as wealthy as a prince. Nothing just happens, He must truly be the one."

"The one?" Tigbone asked with a dumbfounded expression pasted on his flat face.

"Yes, the one. Shall I explain it to you alphabetically, or shall I simply draw you a picture? The one!"

"I like pictures!"

"The one spoken of in the Great Book of Foretelling, you dolt."

Tigbone's eyes shifted back and forth as if something had not connected.

Baddlock vowed over and over, each time with an oath. "I will kill that lowly carpenter!" His eyes filled with savage hate as foam bubbled at the corners of his mouth. "I will kill him with my own bare hands if I have to!"

Every time Tigbone pulled on a particularly stubborn barbed thorn, the servant winced and instinctively shut his eyes tightly in anticipation of a blow in retribution for the pain he was inflicting. "I am too, too, so, so sorry, mazter," Tigbone said as he cowered back. Finally, the last thorn was pulled, and the wound it left was dressed. Baddlock hobbled to his bed, and Tigbone rushed to his side with a cushion for him to sit on. His only reward was to receive a sharp slap that rattled the few remaining teeth in his head for his troubles.

"You have done quite enough for one day," Baddlock snapped. "Get out of my sight!" He yelled as Tigbone cringed back and opened the tall, imposing bedroom door. Baddlock gingerly sailed across the room toward the door as Tigbone crossed the threshold just in time before Baddlock, in an outburst of fury, slammed the door so forcefully that it clattered on its hinges.

That night with Izz gone, the festivities soon came to an end. Lamps were doused, and the well wisher had all gone home. When Izz finally made it home, it was late. The entire bustle in the courtyard had slowly dwindled and come to an end. But Izz was not quite ready to sprawl out on his bed and get a well deserved night of sleep. The first thing he had to do was build a makeshift nest structured from sticks, twigs, and line it with sawdust and moss. When he finished, he gently laid the two eggs on the soft materials. Izz worried that the shop was too cold for his new wards, so he placed lit candles around the eagle's eggs to keep them warm as they continued to incubate. Izz held one of the eggs up and could see a shadow moving within. It was hard to believe that this small form would someday be a mighty White Crested Eagle, the biggest bird on the planet when fully grown. These giants were very rare and could only be found in the very highest upper corners of the world. An adult could weigh as much as ten grown men and have a wingspan the length of seven men from head to toe.

It came as no surprise when the council called an emergency meeting at the midnight hour. Every member in attendance threw themselves into a frenzy of preparation for the honorable celebration to come with the new raising of the sun over Edawn. No great deed went uncelebrated, and the falling of the tree of trees would not be the exception. They worked all through the night, endeavoring to surpass any previous flamboyant commemoration of occasions. There would be none more extraordinary. The nobles loved nothing better than a royal procession in which they and their women could array themselves in their elegant attire, and brightly colored silks and satins. Edawn was well known for their eccentric parades, and there was a splendid spectacle for nearly every event or celebration, and this was undoubtedly a momentous occasion for a grand procession. The capital of the empire was associated with the trappings of festive feasting and merrymaking, and it was sure to be an event that would not be soon forgotten. The final details were completed, and that very night, invitations went out throughout the land to every one of all ranks and walks of life.

As the sun rose, a new day of celebrating had already begun. By high noon, it seemed that the whole kingdom had lined the streets to cheer and hail Izz, the latest hero of the people. Crowds flocked to the event. Thousands assembled. Not only the main avenue, but the side streets and back roads were thronged with people of every class and station, hoping to get a glimpse of Izz. Mounted upon a horse magnificently adorned at the head of the gathering procession was Izz, in the saddle right next to the king himself. Izz was not the kind to hold a grudge, so he had dismissed his misgivings concerning the king entirely.

To the left rode Rizan. Behind them followed the royal court, their golden carriage drawn by seven of the most elegant white stallions in the empire. Among the royals were Queen Zahra and Princess Zuree in their multicolored robes and jewels. Behind them was an impressive assortment of nobles, proceeded by trumpeters and followed by aristocrats and magnates all in dazzling array. Then came the royal guard in full uniform, carrying their banners and wearing their swords and armor. And they, in turn, were followed by a royal protocol of everyone that was anyone. All around the procession was spread out in a gala of minstrels playing their flutes, drums, and harps. There were jugglers, acrobats, dancers, fire eaters, bear handlers, and exotic beasts, and their trainers. There were also masked jesters in brightly colored costumes and wild hats, circling around and around. Drink and candy vendors added to the flamboyantly contained bedlam. Every avenue was crowded with spectators eager to look upon their newest champion. Along the streets, the fronts of taverns, shops, and alleys were jam packed with encompassing droves vibrating with excitement.

Izz was undoubtedly the center of attention and the object of admiration to all. Dressed in his finest, he rode upon Lightning, the king's favorite horse, named for his lightning speed. Lightning was decked out with gilt, ribbons, and tassels in his braided mane right down to his particularly long silky tail, groomed to a lustrous white shine, without one single dust mote on its hide anywhere. Lightning strutted along impressively as Izz sat there smiling triumphantly, starting to enjoy his own pretentious glory, drinking it all up in big enormous gulps. If he was just a little too thrilled, a little too lost in his personal exaltation, in which case they would just have to forgive him because he had just come back from the gates of an imminent death sentence. Izz spotted his uncle Lott and family along the way, beaming with brazen faced pride as he passed by. Izz gave them a distinguishing glance and smiled to let them know they were regarded individually. His cousins cheered and boastfully called out his name.

As the column moved along the main avenue, at every corner, Izz was welcomed with great applause, shouts of admiration, and his name was exaltations above all names. Flowers showered down on him, and streamers drifted down around him as the celebratory procession made its way toward the royal palace, the soul of the city. The throngs crowded forward that at least Izz's shadow might fall upon them by his passing. The fortune and fame he had dreamed of since childhood had arrived. At that moment, Izz would not have changed places with anyone, not even the king of Zia himself.

Buzu, who was amid the grand splendor of the riotous capacity crowd, broke away from the mistress and ran toward Izz with a bouquet of wildflowers clasped in her hands. Izz stooped down to take the flowers as his mouth arched in sheer delight, a smile dancing in his eyes. Buzu smiled back with her prominent joyous expression full of love for Izz. Zuree, who had tried desperately to keep her eyes unglued to Izz, took notice and could not help but be touched by Izz's obvious love of children. Her heart melted like a wedge of sugar dropped in a cup of hot tea.

The greatest cavalcade spectacle by any standard ended in front of the King's Palace, where a tremendous mouthwatering feast awaited. Citizens of every status and class were invited to attend. The grand banquet hall soon filled with hundreds of nobles, statesmen, merchants, artisans, and their ladies, attired in their most luxurious robes, dressed in their most spectacular and fancy garments, glittering with jewels, indicators of their wealth. Men were attired in embroidered garments of gold and silver cloth, colored in stripes, circles, checkers, and dots of every hue of the rainbow.

The privileged guest sat in the places assigned to them. Izz was, of course, the guest of honor. He had never seen, let alone eaten in a place like this, decked with fine table linen, polished silverware, and faultless crystal. He was not particularly keen on the extravagant reception. Inside, Izz sat next to the king, who sat next to the queen, who would be seated next to the princess who had not arrived. Rizan was sitting in the next chair. Rizan raised his wine goblet in recognition of Izz, who nodded in response. Next to them sat the royal members of the court and their wives, according to their rank and status. Their privacy was interrupted only by the soft footed serving men and cupbearers bearing fresh appetizers of food and drink. The two twins sat at the far end of the hall, among the Royal Guard.

Izz looked around and smiled, pretending not to notice that he was the center of everyone's attention. The gigantic hall was filled and poured out into the streets. Flames too numerous to count flickered from tall white candles in their lustrous golden keepers. Enormous, long, trestle tables, covered with richly embroidered, starched, white cloth, which reached the floor on all sides, fill the room. Crystal goblets filled with the most excellent wines lined the centers of every tabletop. Giant bouquets of fresh flowers of every color graced every table and high backed chairs like thrones bordered each table from end to end. Rows of priceless, decorative, green jadeite plates set with lustrous silverware filled with enough food to supply an army, and this was not even the main course. The fragrant delicacies of venison, mutton, turkey, chicken, partridges, pudding, pies, and cake unmatched by any other banquet in memory filled the air. The aroma was sweet, and everything sparkled brilliantly. At the door, Mozlow, the king's head servant, greeted every new arrival. Cupbearers carrying white cloths on their shoulders poured wine for everyone, while other servants continued to set dishes and silverware for the swelling guests. Izz had never seen so many unusual ceramic bowls, casserole, platters, plates, pots, pitchers, cup, and utensils. Magnificent rugs covered the floor, and richly woven and embroidered tapestries hung on the walls.

As Izz was greeting one dignitary after another who wished to pay him tribute, suddenly, there was a communal gasp that seemed to suck the very air out of the room. Zuree had stepped into the hall, and the moment she did, she was noticed by all as she filled the room with her presence. Everyone, including the king, turned to watch her walk in. She was a beauty adorned with the face of a flawless angel. When Izz's eyes fell upon her, his breath got caught in his throat at the beautiful sight of her. The room about him and everyone in it faded as all his senses suddenly centered on Zuree. She was looking as radiant as ever as she drew sharp breaths from the crowd. Her crown glittered radiantly on her golden head, and the most elegant, white gown she wore seemed to glow. It was a magnificent dress of smooth white silk fabric, sewn with seeded pearls that sparkled like liquefied white light. Silver tassels on her sleeves dangled one after another, loosely against her sleek bare arms. Zuree's body looked like that of a goddess, perfectly sculptured with soft round curves and angles. Knotted on her elegant throat was her dazzling blue diamond coming of age stone pendant given to her on her thirteenth cycle of the sun. It hung from her neck on a gold chain. It was the rarest of all gems, encased in its golden filigree; it split the candlelight like silken threads that sparkled as she walked. The light it was reflecting seemed at times much brighter than anything else in the room, except for Zuree's hypnotizing blue-green eyes. Alone with the pendant where a strand of diamonds and pearls were thrown in for good measure.

Zuree's long beautiful blond hair brushed to a luminous sheen, swayed gently at her waist with every regal step she took. She was indeed the most gorgeous woman in a room abounding with beautiful women. She was so stunning that no other woman in the banquet room could hold a candle to her. Zuree's gaze moved over the crowd of faces until she found Izz. Her eyes sparkled as they met Izz's. They glimpsed directly at each other for the slightest moment, a fleeting glance that spoke volumes, captivated in an eternal sliver of time. The yearning look behind Izz's eyes made her heart shudder. Neither one spoke a word. There was no need for words. A light fragrance of jasmine caught Izz's attention as Zuree walked behind him to sit by Rizan's side, who had for the moment gone unnoticed by Izz until then.

They appeared to be the perfect match. Rizan was tall, handsome, and a perfectly mannered gentleman. Izz's heart collapsed, and his spirit imploded as he caught Rizan's eye. Without showing it, he swallowed his dispirited pride and lifted his crystal wine goblet as a show of courtesy. Rizan, in turn, raised his wine glass and saluted and motioned a congratulation.

Izz took a hurried sip from his wine glass. Perhaps later, when he was alone, he might be reduced to a heartbreak overkill. But this was the highest point of his life, and he was not going to let anything dishearten him. He thoroughly persuaded himself to relish over the higher immanence he had won. And everyone knew he deserved every momentous moment meant for him, but was he just kidding himself. The queen interrupted Izz's thoughts, to assure him of how relieved and proud everyone in the palace was that he was well. She insisted that Izz tell her the whole story at the next opportune time. Zuree's awkward preoccupation went unnoticed by everyone, including Rizan, as she picked at her food and seemed to wish she was somewhere else suddenly. All around, there was laughter and good cheer in the air as the best wines in the kingdom ran freely. There were merriment and music, and the kingdom was gathered to enjoy, enjoy, enjoy. It had been far too long, so everyone imagined since the kingdom had shared this much festive energy.

Again and again, cheers and applause shook the room. The king stood and held his hand up for silence, and a hush immediately fell over the lively festivities. He lifted his golden wine goblet in salute to his queen. She was making those eyes and smiling that smile. She was still the stunning beauty who had taken his breath away the first time he had laid eyes on her. Then he turned to the crowd and announced, "As everyone knows, our very own special carpenter Izz has done what a hundred men could not. He has single handedly brought down the seemingly invincible giant of Emory Forest. And in doing so, he has earned the promised reward. How it was done is not exactly clear. However, the fact is that it is now possible to create our magnificent round table."

The assembled cheered enthusiastically. The king clapped his hands loudly, and four men with broad shoulders came into the hall, bearing the fabulous treasure so many had tried to win and failed. And with that, Izz instantly became a rich man. The king raised his golden cup and proposed a toast to Izz.

"I drink to you in the name of all here. Health and long life to you, Izz. May the sun always shine upon your face, may there always be work for your hands to do, may you always be rich in blessings, and may your fondest of dreams come true." All along the hall, fingers curved around flagons or wine chalices. Everyone lifted their drinks and toasted to Izz.

Izz glanced toward Zuree as if he were casually glancing around the room in acknowledgment of well wishers and lifted his cup into the air. Loud cheers and applause broke out in tribute to Izz until the hall was in a loud uproar. Izz lifted his cup to his lips and muttered into his glass of wine, "...Fondest of dreams...How ironic," then drank long and deep.

Once again, cheers and applause quaked the room, and this time the thunderous uproar threatened to lift the roof. Dandork, who was sitting in the farthest corner, was picking bits of meat from between his teeth as he stared at Izz with a seething glare.

Blotting his lips with his handkerchief, King Ozzdon again held his hand up and lifted his goblet with the other, suggesting another toast. After a long while, the clamor died down, and the king spoke again, "I have sent our top emissaries to the leaders of the Norticlan tribes. Darkon himself has led a dispatch of negotiates for our proposal of trade. The Noragore Mountains hold vast and largely unexploited resources that would benefit our empire. I have decided to negotiate the details of this trade agreement personally. Rizan, my right hand, will accompany me."

Before the crowd had a chance to express their approval, he raised a hand. "I have one more joyous announcement to make. As you are all aware, my lovely daughter, Princess Zuree, has for some time now been betrothed to our honorable King Rizan of Ziyontopia." Izz immediately raised two eyebrows as his forehead knotted. "Upon my return from our trading voyage to the northern territories, Princess Zuree will wed King Rizan and will soon be known as Queen Zuree of Ziyontopia." His voice boomed out above the escalating cheers in the long banquet hall as the crowd erupted in a resounding ovation of congratulations that shook the walls. The king then commanded, "Honored guests, eat, laugh, take pleasure, and be joyful!"

Izz's heart froze in mid beat. He felt it twisting inside out as if it had been suddenly hung, drawn, and quartered. His soul gave way like sinking sand, and his dancing heart's joy turned into sorrow. He just sat there with a ridiculous grin contorted on his face. Izz hung his head, whether, in lament or relief, he could not be sure. He felt a numbing ache in the middle of his chest as his heart thudded an especially mournful sound. Everything he had secretly hoped and yearned for fizzled out of him like air from a leaking wine bag. For the first time in his life, he had fallen in love with someone who could not love him back. But how could he keep his heart still, mute, unfeeling?

Izz's gaze found Zuree's immediately. The announcement seemed to have left her fumbling the silverware next to her plate with panicky fingers. Izz wanted to lock his eyes on her eyes, but he knew that would be inappropriate. Besides, Rizan might catch on and come over and break his face like he did Pongo's. Izz struggled to get a fresh grip on his heart, mind, and soul. He consciously resisted the overwhelming anxiety and the look of mortification threatening to overpower him. He reached for his refilled crystal wine goblet. With his hand shaking, he brought it to his trembling lips and emptied it, swallowing with difficulty for the lump in his throat. He signaled the server to refill his glass once again. The servant, who had just filled it, raised an eyebrow but said nothing and did as he was bid. Izz quickly drained his second glass and lowered it to the table with controlled forcefulness. Izz refused anything but the painkilling sedative of wine. And even though Izz was not given to indulgence, he drank yet another glass with one gulp. He was afraid that the pain too deep for words would make him imprudently break down and virtually wreck everything for everyone. He should never have allowed his heart to eclipse his mind with the impossible fantasy he should have never permitted to escape his foolish heart. Fortunately for Izz, the consoling effect of the wine took effect before anyone could notice that he was not quite himself. Finally, Izz managed to cast his feeling down into the depths, a dungeon where he kept every remembrance that ever grieved him or made him cry out. And although he concealed his secret feelings well, he grew pale as his pain struggled to wreath out through the breaks in his heart, like a venomous serpent from its burrow.

Izz instantly felt some relief when everyone's attention turned to Queen Zahra as she signaled Mozlow to begin serving the food fare. And almost immediately, a succession of severing vassals began their orchestrated affair as they came streaming out of the kitchen's double doors. Members of the serving staff began presenting the food in an abundance that astonished Izz as if any change could somehow ease the pain of the moment. Mozlow ushered in the imposing procession of servants that came out carrying the main course. Big silver platters bearing peacocks, pheasants, and quails that had been baked then stuffed back into their cured plumage were served. A course of duck, geese, fish, and lobster was brought to the king's table first. The next wave of servers carried silver trays crammed with roasted boars, stuffed with roosters, which were stuffed with fish and other delicacies. The procession of dishes continued with stag, beef, sheep, and rabbit. Meats were flavored with thick gooey sauces heavily seasoned with ginger, raisins, pine nuts, cloves, cinnamon, and honey. Side dishes of fruits and vegetables of every kind were served alongside the main meal in an excess that astounded everyone.

Outside, there was yakox and basted pork roasted whole with a continual progression of covered dishes and drinks of everything being served in the banquet hall. Food was presented on large rectangular pieces of flatbread, and everyone ate with their fingers. Even the mountain and hill clan who rarely came into the kingdom attended so that they might know the face of the man who slew the giant of the forest. Jokesters, jugglers, dancing bears, and other fascinating characters romped around for children who had never ventured beyond the outskirts of their villages. Crowds cheered as musicians played lively tunes. Buzu and the other orphans darted from one exhibit to the other. The name Izz was on everyone's lips as everyone seemed to be talking at once, telling stories of Izz's conquest, which grew with every telling.

Inside, King Ozzdon swayed by drink once again, raised his golden goblet of ale high, and went on offering one toast after another. So thrilled was he that now he would finally have his table that King Ozzdon did not stop offering acknowledgment to everyone in Edawn until he had bestowed salutations on all including the street sweepers.

Guests cheered, and the brewmasters ensured that the ale, cider, wine, and brandy continued to flow nonstop, and there was merriment among the inhabitants of Edawn. Temporarily distracted by the sight of all the exotic foods and tipsy from the wine, Izz reasoned, *I have only been fooling myself.* He took a contemplative drink of wine, *I am not some naïve boy that could fall in love at first sight.* He took another deep swallow. *After all, it was only a dream, fog and haze and smoke, something elusive that could never come true,* and he took yet another drink. He knew all along that his obsession would come to nothing. He had only been averting the foreseeable revaluation that was only inevitable. After sorting it all out, Izz's look of remorse faded as he looked forward to the rest of the evening with a twinge of hope. As Izz's mind returned to the present, he discovered he had been chasing a pickled olive around his plate with a silver spoon. By then, Izz had found his appetite. He took a deep sniff of the plate of fried meat pie before him, breathing in its aromatic vapors, and Izz suddenly realized how hungry he really was. He took a taste and found it surprisingly delicious. He did not know anything about dining;,only eating. Izz took a moment to consider which appropriate utensils to use and then finally choose just to use his fingers, and the pie disappeared. And then he ate several turnovers filled with chicken, fish, and cheeses.

Izz found that, in fact, he was so hungry that he began to eat like a starved man. He then emptied bowls of vegetables and soups, drinking heartily after every bite. Servers hurried about with large urns and filled each chalice with dark wine. Each time Izz emptied his goblet, it was again filled to the rim. One course followed another in rapid succession as servers moved silently back and forth among the tables, keeping the plates and glasses full. Izz had hardly finished one mouthful before something else was pushed or poured in front of him, and Izz ate and was filled to the full as never before. In contrast, Zuree ate mechanically; the food had lost its savor. She stared at her serving dish with distaste, taken away from her desire for food; she drank her pomegranate drink to wash its taste away.

When the great feast neared its end, an ornamental desert of pastries, candied fruits, and cakes decorated with different colored puddings was doled out. Plump date, fig, and nut filled tarts smothered in honey were also served. Everyone ate and drank to their fill. Then, hands were washed from golden basins filled with scented rose water and dried on soft white serviettes. Zuree was quietly braiding her fingers through her thick blond hair and had only picked at her food and seemed preoccupied in deep thought. After the final course, the king clapped his hands together, and the entertainment began. Musicians performed followed by jesters that told jokes, storytellers that recounted historical tales and poets that recited epic poems of love, and heroes, and conquests. The twin warriors, Zandor and Kondor, especially ravenous, were still chewing on mouthfuls of wild duck long after the rest of the guests had finished. They only momentarily paused to laugh at the antics of the jesters and then went back to eating. Children listened to legions and fables of the pioneers that had brought power, peace, and wealth to the land.

King Ozzdon and Rizan were busy discussing their upcoming voyage. It was during this time that Zuree approached Izz, who was once again explaining how the tree had been taken down. As he told his story, his listeners stared at him intensely, filled with awe and astonishment, as if Izz had suddenly grown a third eye. Silence fell over the group surrounding Izz when they saw the princess approach. Izz felt a mysterious feeling of warmth and excitement as Zuree's eyes came upon his. He wanted to gaze into those beautiful blue-green eyes that were one in a million until he died. But at the same time, he felt a great uneasiness that made him want to run and hide. He had called himself a fool a hundred times for having loved her. Loved her! What was he thinking? He dismissed the thought almost immediately. At least he had not thought of her for at least—well, at the very least, he had not called out her name in desperation. Izz grew nervous. After all, she was a princess. Even though he was rich now, she was royalty, and he was a commoner. And although loved by many, he would always be just an orphan, a lowly carpenter, in his innermost mind.

"This is what I am and what I am is all I can be," he reasoned mutely. He thought he was going to be sick. At that very moment, Izz was in desperate need of a little walk to clear his mind of all the wine he had whirling in his head.

Zuree spoke first. "I could not retire without congratulating you on your amazing conquest." She seemed fascinated by him as she looked at him under some newly discovered light. "You are not the man I expected you to be. You seem to be the kind of person who has the uncanny ability to rise to any occasion, to triumphant under the most extreme circumstances. By what strange and miraculous means would any man dare, let alone even attempt the impossible, against overwhelming odds and yet triumph. You must be no ordinary man." She let out a little laugh as she reached out her hand.

Her acknowledgment gave Izz a sense of deep, intense delight. When their hands touched, Izz's spirit became buoyant as if he was once again soaring atop the loftiest pillar of the forest. After a moment of uneasy hesitation, Izz finally choked back his feelings of inadequacies. The wine did little to help as he stammered, "Thank you, Your Highness. If there is ever anything I can do for you, I am at your command." He had been truthful in giving her that pledge.

Zuree smiled warmly. "I may take you up on that offer someday."

Something abruptly and without warning leaped into Izz's heart with such sudden force that he was almost rendered senseless. His heart ached within and beat so hard against his ribs that it was almost painful. Izz carefully studied the expressions that crossed Zuree's face and was filled with curiosity over what thoughts might be going through her mind. Zuree tightened her expression suddenly as if to keep from disclosing some deeply personal emotion that was making its way to the surface. She glanced away to hide the feelings of admiration her heart was conveying through her eyes. She looked down at the marble floor, feeling exposed. After a long, lingering pause of awkward silence, the princess excused herself, and in a moment, she was out of sight.

Izz could no longer deny he had fallen in love with her. And all he was left with was nothing but heartbreak to show for it.

As blissfully overfed, guests began to excuse themselves. The king approached Izz as he remained standing there in stunned awkwardness. The king put his arm around Izz's shoulder, then he drew him closer and asked, "Now, how was it that you truly brought that tree down?"

Thirteen

The Bonding

Izz started, "There was this pack of wolverines—" The king interrupted, "Oh, yes, the wolverines. I have heard that one." In an attempt to change the subject, the king turned and began to introduce Izz to those around them. The king spared no pains to make sure Izz met everyone in his Inter Court. Izz greeted each person courteously with a bow and a smile and shook each hand extended to him. He mentally repeated each name, committing it to his memory as he strove to remember each face. The parents introduced their lovely highborn daughters. And as they eyed Izz over from head to toe, their glowing faces beamed with flirtatious smiles as their laughter reverberated off the high ceilings. Izz, still feeling lightheaded from the wine, had never been curtsied to by so many eligible and very charming maidens who stepped forward to be introduced, who becomingly blushed as they displayed their most bewitching smiles. All seemingly assuring Izz that at any moment, he could have easily had the pick of any of the most beautiful of beautiful women in the kingdom. But Izz shied away, unbalanced by something he could not quite unknot. He was sure he would do better to save his smiles for grandmothers and the unworldly sisters of the orphanage.

As the grand celebration drew to its end, the king once again puts his arm around Izz's shoulder. Already woozy from the wine, he spoke freely and said in a respectful tone, "You are such a lucky young man. You are at the threshold of your life, and your whole life is ahead of you. When I was your age, if you can imagine me ever being young once, I was quite the ladies man." The King paused for a reflective moment "I have slowly grown old...man is allotted a certain span of life. Your allotted span has not been spent. Life is short, son, and who knows what tomorrow will bring. It may not always be the celebration we look forward to, but while we are alive, we should make merry and dance. Laugh without restraint. Break the rules now and then. Love profoundly and truly. Be quick to forgive and slow to anger. Kiss deep and never lament anything that ever gave you joy. But above all that, dream your dreams and, no matter what it takes, make them come true. To settle for anything less would be unacceptable."

If only you knew, Izz almost thought out loud.

"Dream as though you could live without end. Live as if you may perhaps die tomorrow, for when our memories outshine our dreams, you have grown older than you think."

"You have nothing to be concerned about. You wear your years extremely well," Izz interrupted.

"I like this young man," the king said to Rizan, who was shadowing the king's every move, standing close enough to Izz so that he could feel his size and strength. There was not one single frail bone in him. "Always keep your dreams alive, Izz. Listen and always be true to your heart," the king admonished Izz, then he ordered four of his castle guards to carry Izz's treasure trove to a waiting cart and donkey. The overloaded chest noticeably weighted the small cart down. The palace guards escorted Izz home and unloaded the treasure and carried it upstairs for him. It was the perfect finish to a perfect celebration, and so it seemed to everyone but the two hearts that beat as one.

That night in Izz's upstairs bedroom, where the treasure lay next to the window, Izz finally stumbled to bed. Izz tossed away his clothes, swaying slightly with wine that still swirled in his head as he undressed. He kicked off his boots, snuffed out the flame of his bedroom's single candle, and lay there with his hands behind his head. He was interested in no more than in resting his weary bones, only to lay there sleepless in the darkness with his eyes wide open, reviewing the night's events. Izz took in a deep breath. He could see the brilliance in Princess Zuree's haunting blue-green eyes flickering in and out of his mind. Exactly the same eyes he had seen in his dreams. Why did he have to think of her this night?

The angelic being had proclaimed that this would be his love. And Ammiz had said all he had to do is believe with all his heart. Even the king himself had unwittingly told him more than once to pursue his dreams. How could this be? There were just too many unanswered questions.

Well, it was very simple; his dreams had played a very cruel trick on him, and Ammiz, the great seer, was as crazed as everyone thought he was after all. But that did not change the fact that he loved the princess as though he forever had loved her. It was as if his love could somehow undo something that had already happened and drifted into the past. Izz struggled to disconnect his mind from his feelings, but his clutching heart kept managing to get in his way. The more he reasoned, and the more he thought, the more obscured were his conclusions. His thoughts were stained. The covenant between him and his heart was broken while her life overflowed with promise. Izz was pained by what was going on inside of him. Drained from the events of the past few days, he needed rest, not recollection, not regret. He pushed the intrusive memories that Zuree had stirred away again and again—finally long enough to drift into a deep, dreamless emptiness where fear and sorrow and uncertainties warred with his heart.

The very next morning, Izz woke at first light. He slid his eyes over to where the large wooden treasure chest was sitting by the window. Its lid held fast by its metal clasp. He slipped out of bed and walked over to the window where the treasure waited patiently. He unfastened the clasp and opened its top. The vision that leaped out at him took his breath away. The velvet lined chest was filled to the brim with exquisite gemstones: diamonds, rubies, emeralds, sapphires, jaspers, agates, and topaz. There were hoards of pure gold and silver; coins, pendants, vessels, ornaments, medallions, rings, necklaces, and adornments. Spectacular jewelry perfectly made, richly decorated, set with pearls and inlaid with precious stones, and much, much more. Izz moved closer as his eyes sparkled. It was a just reward, and at that moment, all things seemed possible. He had seen trinkets here and there, but this was beyond the other side of his wildest imaginations. He stared in awe; his dazzled eyes glistened among the gems as the treasure trove glimmered in the sunshine flooding in through the window. He dropped to his knees before the vast fortune and stuck his two hands, elbow deep into the pile of gold and jewels. He brought his hands up slowly and watched as the great source of wealth cascaded, sparkled, and cast brilliant prisms of color throughout the room. It was good to be alive, after all. Not to mention rich and in the king's favor. He reached in again as his over exhilarated thoughts and feelings rushed excitedly through his senses. His fingers raked through his prized possession as if of their own volition. Suddenly, he came across something that made his fingertips tingle. With the tips of his fingers, he searched out its source.

He felt something solid, something smooth with intricate patterns, an extruding knob of metal. He gripped the object, and he knew at once what it was. He pulled it out and held it up to the bright light. Izz's eyes narrowed on the white jeweled, embellished hilt and sheath, which appeared to be inlaid with solid gold. It was a handsome dagger with a two headed eagle handle of the most exceptional workmanship he had ever seen. He drew the dagger to him to examine it more closely. He turned it slowly in his hands, and it flashed bright as a fire in response. This dagger was old—so old—that he wondered who or by what means it had been made. It was perfect, as perfect as the day it was created. His eyes were drawn to the makings worked into the flat, shiny surface of the sheath. These were older—much older—than any writing he had ever seen. He slipped the tip of his fingers along the etched grooves along the smooth surface of the metal, the glimmering intricate scrollwork created by the hands of someone who could easily rival the craftsmanship of the most skilled master metal worker. The dagger's sheath was made of gold similar to that of the king's jeweled crown, and its markings were identical as well. The grip of the hilt was sure and seemed to be formed, especially for his hand. He watched with rising excitement as he pulled on the gleaming blade, freeing it from its sheath. The blade slid out with a whisper as sleek as silk as Izz ran his eyes along the silvery length of the excellent twin edged shank.

It was the very best refined metal he had ever seen. The symbols mottled on the long blade were not merely etched; they were forged into it in such a way that it made the weapon appear far thicker and heavier than it was. As the blade cleared the sheath, it flashed a brief metallic glint of firelight that seemed to surge through his hand and course up his arm. Izz wondered what magic he held in his hands. The blade felt true and perfect in his grasp; its smooth feel was like that of forged glass. Izz swung the dagger in the air, testing its counterweight. The deadly sharp dagger was straight and perfectly balanced. He traced his eyes and fingers along the length of the cold, beautifully imprinted blade, and his hand trembled with the beauty of it as his captivated eyes fixed on the dagger, and he knew instantly that this could be no common weapon.

After a few days had slipped into the past, Izz's life returned to normal. During this time, Izz saw less and less of Ammiz as the seer sequestered himself among his books. Izz worked hard and tried to keep his mind on his work. Meanwhile, the gigantic tree continued to cure. It had been discovered, from branches that had been broken off during Edawn's many storms, that once the invincible tree died, its hardwood crystallized and became workable. While Izz worked diligently in his shop and patiently waited for the tree's trunk to be brought down off the foot of the mountain, Izz took a moment every day to make sure the candles surrounding his eagle's eggs remained lit. It was especially important during the long, cool nights. He methodically turned each egg at least three times a day to ensure the chicks grew normally. Every so often, he held them up to the sun and could see their little hearts beating. One day while enthusiastically working on a table for a wealthy local merchant, Izz's attention was drawn to the nest as he looked up from his work to notice that one of the eggs was wobbling around. Izz eyeballed the eggs curiously and then turned back to his work. Izz put his tools down and stared at the odd sight as the wobbling increased. He shook the sawdust from his hands as he walked toward the eggs. He heard a faint picking sound against the shell as the egg rocked back and forth.

When he reached the eggs, he noticed a small hole beginning to appear from the inside out. As the hole got bigger, Izz could see the eaglet moving inside. He saw little wet feathers through the hole as the eaglet continued to break away at the shell. It paused for a moment and then once again continued to peck the eggshell apart. After that, there was a jagged crack. Finally, a sharp snapping beak appeared, forcing its way through the opening. The tapping sound stopped abruptly. Eventually, the chick had strength enough to push its head out as its little clawed feet kicked aggressively. The smooth surface of the egg suddenly splits from end to end, and the eggshell divided into two halves. The eaglet gawked into a murky new world out of its unfocused yellow slashed eyes. It looked very weak, wet, and sticky as it finally escaped from its cramped enclosure. Its head wobbled back and forth as its eyes were opened wide with curiosity. Its egg mate also started to rock and roll about, driven by an innate magical power. It chipped away at its shell as well, and after a brief struggle, it too was free, floundering about with legs and wings thrashing, and its head bobbing about. And there, writhing in front of Izz, snapping their beaks, yawning and stretching their wings, were two perfect gleaming baby eaglets, with eyes blinking in the bright daylight. They were two feathered riddles, mysteries hatched out of an egg each, with its funny little crowned tuft on its head.

Izz stared at the tiny beasts in awe. The newborn eaglets bonded with the first moving object they saw. And so they both doddered toward Izz and snuggled up against his outstretched hand. He looked down, and gave the firstborn a long, thoughtful look and somehow knew it was the male and the other a female. Then at long last, Izz's face slowly broke into a big smile and said, "Bolo! That is it; your name is Bolo." Then he turned to the second born, and after a while, he said, "And your name will be...will be...Fina! Bolo and Fina." he repeated their names thoughtfully several times just to hear how they sounded. It was a perfect fit, and that was that. Izz proudly looked at the pair. He looked at one and then the other, and gladly, Izz took the two baby eaglets under his care and into his heart.

And so it was that Izz became the proud father of two newly hatched baby eagles. Their feathers dried quickly, and soon they were looking like two very large fluffy balls of cotton. Their baled heads were all gaping eyes and yawning beaks, and whenever they caught sight of Izz, they stretched out their wings. They reached their scraggly necks upward, and their wings quivered with frenzied motions in anticipation of whatever their new surrogate keeper was going to feed them. Every single day, Izz would go to the local meat market and purchase fresh meat scraps for them. He would hold the bits of meat above their snapping heads, and the birds would sweep a second set of eyelids over their eyes and lurch up, ripping the flesh from Izz's flattened fingers to keep them out of harm's way, narrowly avoiding their snapping beaks only by the slightest of margins. With jerking head motions, they gulped the scrapes down whole and immediately began begging for the next offering. The newborn pair grew fast and seemed always to be hungry, snapping at everything and anything, including each other. Soon the thriving eagle fledglings lost their puffy eaglet down, and soft gray feathers began to sprout as their wings filled with flying feathers. Every time Izz came into the shop, he would hear Bolo's and Fina's cries, sounding notoriously hungry, with their feathery wings stretched out and flapping, with their claws clattering noisily across the floor.

One day, Izz carved out a whistle that produced a unique, sharp sound that the eaglets seemed to respond to immediately. When it was feeding time, Izz would blow his whistle, and the eaglets would react excitedly and knew it was time to eat. Most of their feathers had turned from a peculiar speckled of plumage to a darkening black of new growth feathers. Both birds were very alert to what was going on around the shop and were getting stronger every day. Soon they were hopping, stretching, and flapping their wings all over the place. Izz knew that the day would come when it would be time to take them out and somehow teach them how to fly, hunt, and fend for themselves. Over time, Izz had gotten quite attached to the eagles and was not looking forward to that day. But he knew in his heart that, that would be the right thing to do. So every time he went out to collect wood, he would carry them with him. His donkey was not too happy about that at all, but she grudgingly complied. Izz would place a hood over the juvenile eagle's heads.

Each time Bolo would squawk in protest, as Izz slipped the covering over his head but would always obey, quieting instantly, calmed by the soothing darkness that all of a sudden cocooned his eyes. And each time Bolo braced his feet to keep Izz from lifting him, and Izz always struggled to put Bolo in the wood cart. Fina was more accommodating. And so it was that with increasing difficulty, Izz would lift and shove them unceremoniously into his cart. Izz thought it best to keep the pair out of sight under the cart's canopy when he would carry them out into the county. When he came across a suitable hill, he would unload the pair at the top. Izz would then remove their hoods, then run down the hill and blow his whistle. At first, the pair tried hoping and running down the hill but soon learned that it was safer and a lot quicker to spread their wings and glide down to Izz, where he waited with a pork treat. After several trial runs, Izz's eaglets began gliding to the rhythm of Izz's long gentle stride, farther and farther each time they went out. During this time, Izz had kept himself so busy that Zuree hardly ever crossed his mind—hardly ever.

One beautiful morning out of the blue, Izz decided to visit the orphanage. He rose at the crack of dawn, and after washing up, he took a leather pouch, filled it with gems and gold coins, and tied the pouch to his belt. He had a leap in his walk as he bounced down the stairs and out the back of the shop into the stable where he harnessed his donkey to its cart. He drove his cart down the alley and out into the bustling street he went. The first stop was at the already busy eatery across the street from his shop.

He gave Zophie a great big warm smile. He laid a gem on the counter and pushed it across to her and said, "This is for you."

Zophie picked up the precious stone with mouth wide open and asked, "What is the occasion?" When she realized its value, she danced across the bakery, proclaiming, "It is beautiful!"

"It is to show my appreciation for your kindness. Now, I need my usual breakfast. I have a busy day ahead of me."

"What are you up to?" Zophie asked, her eyes still gleaming as she secured the stone down the top of her dress next to her bosom.

"Oh, this and that, nothing really," Izz replied.

After breakfast, Izz searched the kingdom over for every tailor shop and cobbler shop he could find. Before long, his cart was filled, overflowing with new children's clothes and shoes for every orphan in the orphanage and then some. Then he stopped at every bakery on the way and bought every loaf of sweetbread he could find. At long last, Izz was on his way down the street toward the orphanage. He had been longing to see the sparkle in Buzu's eyes and hear the sound of her laughter. When Izz finally pulled in front of the orphanage gate, he was greeted promptly by one of the attendants. He drove his cart through the gate, and as soon as Izz was spotted from the backyard, chaos erupted, breaking the mundane everyday life of the orphanage. Children came running like a flock of stampeding wild geese from every direction. He was a hero, and by now, everyone in the orphanage, of course, was aware of his noble feat. The orphans surrounded Izz and his cart and stood with inquisitive wide eyed wonder. Izz's heart went out to them, and he cared for them as his own. Their great joy was his greatest reward.

From behind the cluster of excited children came a cry. "Izz, Izz, Izz." It was Buzu. She was Izz's clear favorite, and it reflected in his sparkling eyes. He gathered Buzu into his arms. Joyous giggles erupted as he encircled her in one big hug. She reached forward and kissed Izz's cheek.

"I love you, Izz," she said as her huge eyes adoringly stared into his. Her light brown eyes were as round and vulnerable as a fawn's eyes.

Izz set her down and turned to his cart. "Brand new clothes and shoes for everyone," he announced as he dropped to one knee to tie a beautiful rainbow colored scarf around Buzu's delicate neck.

The headmistress came from the main foyer, wearing a welcoming smile. "Izz, how wonderful it is to see you." She turned to the cart and asked, "And what do we have here?"

"Oh, it is just a little something for the children." Izz extended his hand for a warm handshake.

"You are an unusually generous young man, and I am sure that the Giver of all things will someday shower your fondest dreams with His blessings."

"You too!" Izz whispered under his breath.

"I have just put some tea on. I would be honored if you would join me." She was soft spoken, and very polite.

"Yes, that would be very nice." Izz obliged her with the broadest of smiles.

They entered the main corridor of the orphanage; it was surprisingly clean and well organized. At the end of the hall, Izz saw a long room that was filled with roll after roll of beds where one orphan after another slept. The hallway was alive with the sweet fragrance of summer flowers. As he continued to look down the hall, he once again saw the mysterious hooded teacher enter the hallway from one of the many side doors. The shrouded figure turned to look at Izz for a moment, then turned and walked away. Izz could not see the concealed face but could tell from the delicate curves of her hips that it was a young woman. Perhaps the same girl he had seen before. The headmistress led Izz into her office, where a pot of tea was already brewing. Outside, the air was filled with the festive sounds of laughter and play as the attendants joyfully distributed the shoes, clothes, and sweetbread. The mistress offered Izz a chair and turned to close her office door as Izz glanced around the room. Everything seemed to be in its place.

"You run a pretty tight ship around here," Izz complimented.

"At the moment, the children are enjoying a period of free time. The days start early here. We wake up when the first rooster crows followed by breakfast."

Hard bread and cheese, Izz remembered what Buzu had said and smiled to himself.

"A half hour of playtime or rest follows breakfast," the mistress continued. "The children then go to our school and return to the orphanage's dining hall for lunch. In the afternoon, there are two hours of extra study, followed by free time. At sunset, the children complete their chores and schoolwork, and then it is bedtime. And that is the extent of daily life here at our humble orphanage. The children do not complain about all the studying or the food or much else. Upon first arriving, they think me stern with them, but early on, they discover how soft my heart really is."

The kettle suddenly announced that it was on the boil, and the mistress excused herself. She reappeared with a silver tray and placed it on the table, and then she set the table with cups and goodies. Izz let her pour him a cup of tea, and then he took a piece of pastry and spread it with jam. He inhaled the rich aroma with gratitude before tasting a cautious sip from his cup of tea as the mistress carried the conversation.

"We run a unique orphanage here that serves the entire empire. We only accept thermally ill children. They are essentially sent here to die." Her voice trailed off and had to choke down the emotions that were making it difficult for her to speak.

Those words cut deep into Izz's heart. "What about Buzu?" he stammered and blinked back the pain as a sudden childhood memory had shifted in the back of his head.

"Keira, Buzu, as we affectionately call her, is a very special spirit and is very dear to all of us here. Her mind and heart are filled with great wonder and curiosity. Therefore, she tends to venture off. Her outward appearance is that of a normal child, but inwardly, she is afflicted with an extremely rare disorder. It is not known if she will live from one year to the next, so we tend to be very lenient with her. I refuse to chain or bar the windows and doors. This is a hospital for orphans, not a prison. If a child like Buzu is determined to wander off, that is a chance we have to take. For this, I offer no apology, but I assure you that we have kept a closer eye on her. We try to make every child as comfortable and as happy as we are able."

"What happened to Buzu's parents?" Izz asked.

"They were lost at sea. When Baddlock's concoctions only seemed to make Buzu worst, they went off seeking a cure. Their ship went down in a terrible storm. There were no survivors."

Izz shifted uncomfortably as refections from a dark corner of his youth stirred. Thoughts from a darker world that he seldom thought of had shuffled among the forgotten things he wished to leave behind him.

"The whole thing is such a tragedy. Keira is such a beautiful child," Izz said sorrowfully, and in his heart, he loved Buzu the more. "She is very special as all our children are. They are beautiful flowers that have been trampled on the ground by their fate."

"I myself was orphaned. My mother died giving me life. I was left all alone in the world without even a memory of her and my father. They say, my father died of a broken heart in the middle of the following winter." Izz said sadly.

"I am sorry to hear that." Izz's account moved the mistress.

Izz looked off into the distance. The expression on his face became one of dispirited despondence. "Immediately after my father's death, I was placed in an orphanage, never to experience the loving embrace of a caring mother or the proud smile of a loving father. Fate had a different agenda. The orphanage was the only home I ever knew. I would often look out the window wishing for a better life and wondered what the world was like beyond the gates. I was sent off into the world with a crippled heart filled with torn dreams as soon as I reached an age that was deemed appropriate to fend for myself. I was drawn to the open sea, so I became a sailor for some reason I am still not sure why. I spent most of those early years in emotional turmoil, unable to understand why some must suffer so."

The mistress smiled at Izz with great affection. Her smile was etched with compassion. "Within these walls, I have seen a lot of sadness and pain too deep for words. These old eyes have seen far more suffering than perhaps they should have been allowed to." A lone tear slowly rolled down her cheek, and though her face was timeworn through hard work and grief, there was no brokenness of apathy in it, but instead, a commitment of faithful hope. She reached out and warmed up Izz's cup of tea and continued, "I have seen young lives end before they have had a chance to start. I have often wondered what kind of men and women they would have grown into and whose lives they might have touched. But once your heart has been broken, it grows back together bigger and stronger. That is if one confronts the heartbreak and sheds it so that it does not enslave them. And once your heart has been injured, it will change you. During these difficult times, you either get stronger in your relationship with your Creator, or you get weaker. But you never stay the same."

Izz gazed straight ahead, unfocused, as though suddenly seized by a question that had continued to perplex him ever since Ammiz had mentioned the subject and was eager to gain someone else's view. After giving the matter all the time it had required, Izz at last, spoke as he gave the mistress an unwavering look, somehow knowing that she wanted him to ask who the Creator was. So he did. "In your speaking, you have mentioned the Giver and Creator. Of whom or what were you speaking of ?"

The mistress paused for a moment and then continued, "When I speak of the Giver and Creator, I speak of the same. He never was, He never will be. He does not exist in the measure of time. He is—without beginning or end. And as the words imply, the Creator is the one who has created everything. The fingerprint of the Maker is on everything from the intricate geometric form of a snowflake to the vast expanse of the constellations and freely gives everything to us."

"I see that you are a student of Ammiz the Seer," Izz said teasingly. "You know, many think the edge of madness rules him."

"Ammiz is a profound thinker far advanced of his time, and for this, he is thought to be mad."

"If the Creator, Giver who you speak of in fact does exist, why can we not see him?"

"When one sees the created, one sees the Creator. The beauty of Zia cries out the glory of its Creator. How is it that we can so clearly recognize the orderly laws of nature and not identify the presence that whispers to us all?"

"Why does he not simply reveal himself?" Izz asked with a sigh.

"Oh, but He most certainly does. I have seen enough evidence. Creation itself points to the truth of the Creator's existence. His Spirit is unveiled to us in beautiful star filled nights. We need only to open our eyes, and we will realize that He is truly within us all. Their own narrow sightedness blinds those that refuse to see. I see the face of the Creator every time I look into the eyes of one of my children. Each in their special way, they are the most brilliant children in the world of Zia. I sense Him when I smell the fragrance of a flower. I hear Him distinctly in the whispered music of the smallest of birds as sure as I hear His voice in the loudness of His roaring thunder. I feel Him with the warmth of every rising sun. I have come to find out that the great Source of all wants to be known. He pursues us. He is persistently seeking us out. He created us with the specific purpose that we should know him."

Izz thought for a moment then stated, "Now that was an excellent classical answer." The conception of God had never rooted in his mind. He could not conceptualize a being that permitted pain and suffering, especially those that deserved it the least, which prompted him to say, "If he does exist, this Creator of yours, then he must be a very angry Creator."

"No, quite the opposite, He is the Author of true love."

"Was it true love that sent my parents to their graves at such a young age?" There was a tinge of bitterness in Izz's voice.

"Of course, I do not assume to know the magic answer to every perplexing question. I have confronted the same questions without being able to conclude a perfect answer. Many answers only raise further questions. Therefore, I must acknowledge that I do not know how I know what I know. It may be an unreachable answer. The only conclusion I can offer is that suffering is a result of our rejection, which has forced the Creator to distance Himself. When trials do come, it confirms that there is evil in the world, and that suffering is the ill fated wickedness, which testifies that whatever thing contrary to the Law Giver's will is bad, detrimental, painful, and leads to death. And just as it must rain on the good, the bad, and the noble, we must all endure the fleeting effects of a disrupted universe."

Izz suppressed a laugh. "You speak as if you expect me to believe in something I cannot see, hear, or touch. I can, however, see people who struggle under the impossible conditions of disease, pain, and sorrow. The belief in the existence of a Creator is not defended by convincing evidence, reason, or logic. Instead, in its place, people are expected to have blind faith. Faith, however, is an untrustworthy counselor to the truth or a reliable means for obtaining facts. The Creator was most likely created in the image of the believer."

Without responding, the mistress stood and walked over to a strange box and said, "This is a gift from Ammiz. It is a timekeeper to mark the passing hours of the day."

Izz joined the mistress and saw before him what looked like a mechanical contraption that consisted of two large water containers, one higher than the other. The water seemed to travel from the upper container to the lower container through a series of connecting tubes. The draining water drove a succession of moving interlocking gears that moved a needled pointer, which in turn moved along a path of markings on one of the containers, seemingly to show the level of the water.

The mistress pointed to the marks and said, "These symbols plot the passage of time. It is extremely accurate and helps us keep our demanding schedule on track. Now consider this, if I were to come upon this timekeeper for the first time unwittingly, I would need no proof that a skilled artisan created it. Therefore, if I look at the complex laws of unchanging nature and the precise movement of the sun and moon, I must conclude that a Divine Hand must have created and sustained it. If this does not prove through sound reasoning and good judgment that a deliberate Designer created it, then you may count me among the mad. You must ask yourself, how did we come to be here? Were we put here? Or did we simply come to be by some blind, random, meaningless process? Or were we fashioned with a reason? The question we should be asking is not why or how, but to what proposes. Ultimately, we must trust the one who sees the beginning from the end. In your heart, you must know this. We all struggle to find the reasons that we cry. For some reason, that is not easy to understand, but apparently, suffering is important to the great Giver of Life. Who are we to question the great Source of All? Did we create the animals, the world of Zia, the sun, time, or the eternal stars? Can a bug understand a human? Can an ant conceive reasoning, art, beauty, hope, or love? We are wrong to think our human minds should be able to demand an account of the Creator's action. We must accept that the Creator does not just allow suffering. He seems to want and even promote it! The fact of suffering is a mystery we do not understand and must be accepted upon faith."

"Blind faith, you mean?"

"The Holy of Holies does not force us to believe in him. Instead, He has offered adequate evidence of his existence for us to freely respond to Him. Before faith, there must first come reason. Reason helps us develop the understanding that convinces us that the Creator exists well beyond any reasonable doubt. In every life, there will be some suffering. For some, it will be minor. For others, it may be almost unbearable. Their souls overwhelmed with sorrow to the point of death! Perhaps how much suffering we must endure and how one reacts to it, influences and determines the reward we will receive while we live and then in the life to come after our death. I truly believe that the day is coming when pain, misery, sickness, and death will be no more than a faded, distant bygone dream in a minuscule fraction of an instant on the timeless scale of eternity."

Izz was less than convinced, yet out of respect, he did not challenge the mistress further. An attendant enters the office and informs the headmistress that the children were asking for her.

"I see that my duties call. Unfortunately, food and a warm place to sleep are simply not enough to gently calm the inner pain that an orphan feels. What an orphan needs most of all and can never get enough of is love. Love is as vital to the soul as blood is essential to the body. And these children need so much more than we have to give."

Izz finished his tea and said, "I too must be getting to my obligations as well."

As Mistress Aria rose to her feet, she declared, "Izz, we are having a little celebration in our garden in honor of the founding of our orphanage. It will be soon. Would you come? I know the children would love to have you, especially Buzu."

"How could I say no?" Izz replied.

"Come, I will walk you to the gate?" the mistress invited.

The cart and donkey were waiting for Izz, minus the new clothes, shoes, and sweetbread. Even the crumbs were gone. Izz climbed on his cart as the mistress held the gate open. The experience had had a profound effect on Izz, and for the longest time, he pondered the things the mistress had spoken of. The insight the mistress had gained from caring for the most vulnerable of souls was intriguing

Fourteen

The Gift

On his first visit with Ammiz after Baddlock's accusations and the falling of the tree, Ammiz was still working on the answer to the same farsighted riddle. Ammiz just smiled, shook his head, and almost laughed as he greeted Izz at his door. The first question Izz asked was, "Why did Baddlock attack me as he did, and where were you?"

"What does not destroy you will strengthen you. I have been through almost everything. You name it; whatever you could imagine, I have stepped in it. Baddlock has attacked you because he fears you because you were getting too close to something. I did not intercede because if you had not seen for yourself, you would not have fully understood the power of who you truly are. And soon, you will know what seeks you out. No one will have to tell you. From this point on, no matter where you go or what you do, you will not be able to escape your fate. You will have to discover for yourself. I cannot intervene. All I can do is point you in the right direction. There will come other days of testing, and there will always be a price to pay. The only thing of importance will be your response. I did not interfere because only your judgment will determine what your life will be, and you will make your choices, and your choices will make or break you. What we do in this present life will pass on to the next. Always remember the universe is perfect. It is we who are imperfect. Never forget, there are few things as odd as reality. It comes to us bearing many faces wearing many masks. What I know, you will know." And this was the spirit that pursued most of their proceeding encounters.

Over the next few days, Izz stayed busy, working on the many furniture orders that kept pouring in, mostly in part to his newly attained fame. Sure, he could have left his shop and lived off his riches, but working with his hands was in his blood. And what about Zuree? Why should he worry about things that were out of his control? Every morning Izz would jump out of bed, throw the window shutters open, and yell out, "Is there anyone on Zia, O sun, who can doubt your loyalty." There were thousands of things that needed to be done. The tree's resin would take at least another moon cycle to crystallize to the point where it could be worked. It would then take another moon cycle for the base of the tree to be cut and transported into the kingdom. He would need new tools, new instruments, and new equipment. There were so many things that needed to be done, but no matter how busy he got, Izz always seemed to have the time to make the many little dolls and spinning toys for the children in his district. He was so busy that he had almost no time to think about anything outside his work, and thus he thought even less and less often of Zuree. He did not even seem to notice that the small doll he was carving in his spare time looked exactly like the princess. He repeatedly tried to convince himself that the toy doll he was working on did not look like the princess at all. He managed to convince himself that he had all but forgotten about her. Any resemblance was surely entirely coincidental. And so life went on as it should, and all was well. That is until that faithful day when an unusual hooded stranger paid him a visit that was about to turn his world upside down.

While Izz busied himself outside, around the corner on a nearby avenue, the hooded stranger moved secretively along the street that led to Izz's woodshop. The cloaked one did not stop to talk to anyone. Great care was taken to blend in with the rest of the countless, nameless pedestrians that made this part of the kingdom their home. As the stranger inconspicuously neared the shop, amidst the citizens that were buzzing to and fro, the unknown wayfarer pulled the folds of the hooded cloak across a face that did not want to be recognized. Upon reaching the shop entrance, the stranger hesitated as if wondering if any part of the concealed disguise had been revealed. After a moment of reassurance, the faceless visitor casually entered Izz's shop, hoping to find him alone. Inside, Izz was hard at work, putting the finishing touches on a bookcase he had promised Ammiz. Suddenly an alarmed expression crossed his face. Izz got a funny feeling, and without thinking, he held his breath when the incomer walked inside the shop, divulging no features that could be determined. Izz was alarmed at the fact that his unexpected visitor was deliberately hiding their identity. It made him at once become particularly uncomfortable. The cloaked and hooded stranger's chin came up a notch. Confident that Izz was alone, the figure drew up into a pivotal posture. At first, Izz could not identify the mysterious person dressed in the long hooded robe because the hood was too deep and pulled well down over so that Izz could not see the unmistakable eyes within it. He had one eye on his jeweled dagger he kept close to the front door

"Hello. Can I help you?" With a vacant and somber face, Izz endeavored cautiously and then held a sharp breath. The indistinguishable intruder found the clasp that unfastened the disguising cloak that would soon reveal the stranger's face. Izz saw a glimpse of pale skin against the black hood of the cloak, and it occurred to Izz at last, to his great relief, that this was not the decrepit wizard. Could it be the mysterious stranger from the orphanage? Hair began to tumble out from under the hooded cloak as more clasps were undone. Izz pretended to turn back to his work, but then he paused and looked again with a slow smile of recognition. Izz stood there silently, thinking hard and questioning himself if what he was seeing could be real. The caller pulled off the shroud, and all her glorious blond mass of hair sprang free, tumbling down from the spiral on top of her head, spilling down to her waist.

Izz saw to his surprise that it was indeed Princess Zuree herself as she removed her hooded cloak. She had worn her disguise to conceal her identity from those she might pass along the street. Izz could only stare in amazement in that first instant of recognition as they faced one another at the door. The first few moments were the most awkward. As Izz stared into Zuree's fathomless eyes, the soft glow from the window light cast a golden beam over her face, and everything about her that he had tried so hard to forget came crashing in on him. Taken by surprise, Izz's confounded expression dissolved into a nervous smile as he fully realized it was the princess, which he was utterly unprepared to see. Izz desperately tried to act nonchalant. He drew his stomach in and broadened his chest. Zuree pulled her hair back into some balance of order and smoothed her white dress down.

"I had not thought to have the pleasure of seeing you again... so soon." His thoughts suddenly became buoyant as he took a deep breath and exhaled blissfully.

Zuree's eyes, which were browsing over Izz's wood and sawdust cluttered shop, settled on Izz. His chest was exposed, and his sleeves were rolled up, revealing his muscular forearms. She refocused her eyes on Izz's as she smiled with just the right amount of charm and said, "I see you are never idle. I hope that I am not intruding on the business of your day." She delivered her words in a matter-of-fact rhythm with an apologetic tone. Not knowing how to respond, Izz struggled to come up with the right words that he hoped were not too obviously anxious.

For a while, he was speechless, caught in a moment of uncertainty, hoping that somehow the princess could not see how much she meant to him. However, before the confrontation had even been set in motion, his stunned mind fumbled, groping for the words that dangled at the end of his tongue. Finally, finding the words, he let them stumble out, "No, no, not at all. You honor me with your visit."

The conversation between them was tongue tied at best. Izz did his best to gauge her response, wondering where she was going with her informal intro. She, on the one hand, had readied herself well for this encounter. On the other hand, Izz was caught totally off guard at every twist of this unexpected visit. The first few moments for Izz were most awkward. His every expression was so refreshingly earnest and transparent. It was abundantly evident to Zuree that she had the upper hand, and she was using it to her full advantage and enjoying the pleasure of every moment. As she continued to scan Izz's shop, she commented, "You have so many interesting things in here."

"I see no point in throwing useful things away," was the first thing that popped into his mind.

"Is that why your shop is overflowing of useful things?" she teased. The turned down corners of her mouth made her look as if she was suppressing a smile. Izz laughed awkwardly, which surprised him as much as it surprised her. *Do not get too thrilled;* he kept telling himself.

Zuree acutely angled a beautifully arched eyebrow at him and said, "I am looking for something special, something unique." Then she gave Izz an elongating, memorizing up and down look, tilting her jaw as if she was ready to weigh his response in the balance.

Izz only heard the sound of her voice playing like soft music in his ears and not the words. The spell was cast, and once again, he was hopelessly lost in it. She was indescribably beautiful beyond words, beyond thoughts. Izz tried not to stare, but it seemed impossible to tear his gaze away. She looked even more strikingly beautiful than when they last met. Was it conceivably possible for such a lovely creature to come to be more beautiful with the eclipsing of each passing day? Izz felt a sudden wave of weakness ebb over him, settling in shakiness, deep in the pit of his being. Izz shook his head hastily as if trying to clear it. Zuree roamed through the shop with a gliding motion as her keen and probing eyes scanned over all the wonderful things the young carpenter had made. She was amazed by his work, mind numbing as it seemed. She suddenly turned to Izz with an expectant look. As the echo of what she had said last registered in his mind, he struggled to wipe off what he was sure was an absurd look of admiration. This time when he spoke, he weighed his words more carefully, "Yes, of course, if there is anything at all I can do to help you. You have only to ask."

Zuree turned back to taking stock of what Izz had made and was making and said, "You certainly are clever with your hands." Izz felt the shakiness inside again as he could not stop staring at her as she moved from one crafted wooden thing to the other. As Izz observed the princess moving gracefully about, he felt in his bones that there was something beyond the bounds of very special about her. And he wondered why nature sometimes played favorites in the matters of physical beauty, which went way more profound than the depth of the skin. Could this be the physical representation, embracing the beautiful soul, which had whispered into his dreams? She was truly a bundle of loveliness, and there she was standing in front of him more wondrous than the most vivid of dreams. Izz yearned with all his mind, heart, and soul to say something that would be significant and meaningful to her without making a complete fool of himself. He started to say something, wanting to tell her about his dreams, but yet somehow thought better of it, so he restrained the words that he wanted to pour out of his heart. He clenched his lips shut, and his eyebrows rose, seemingly painful as his face twisted in a half smile. In his mind, he carefully tried out precisely what he was going to say next, and even precisely how he was going to say it—the pitch, volume, and tone of voice. His lips parted even as he kept adjusting his thoughts, but instead, Zuree spoke first.

"Rumor has it that you make the most lovely jewelry boxes. I am looking for something extraordinarily special, something different, and something that is a one of a kind."

Izz lost his train of thought there and then. His mind went blank. He opened his mouth to speak, but nothing came out. His breath caught abruptly in his throat as if there was a dry wad of cotton stuck in his windpipe. For one agonizing instant, Izz expected the princess to break out in laughter. Instead, she stood there patiently in anticipation of Izz's reply.

"Uh...oh, yes, yes, yes," was all Izz could manage to say as his thoughts seemed to stumble one over the other before reaching his tongue. Izz turned and reached up to a top shelf and brought down an elegant jewelry box he had recently completed. A glorious sight met her eyes. The fine, richly carved jewelry box was intricately linked together with seamless joints. Magnificent patterns marked the entire surface of the hard redwood that Izz hand polished until it was smooth and brilliantly glossy. He turned and put the box into Zuree's waiting hands. Their hands touched. It was the slightest brush, but the current in it sent quivers through both. Zuree looked down at the box as her mouth dropped open at her discovery, and a curious expression crossed her face. As she studied the box, her eyes lit up with delight, and her lips softly formed into an O of astonishment.

"It is better than special. I have never seen such a unique and fascinating work of art!" She caressed the surface design gently with the tips of her fingers. "It is magnificent. Izz, you have very clever fingers. A special gift that is truly rare." She looked at him, genuinely pleased.

Izz was so thrilled by her response that he felt as if someone had reached in and tickled his heart. Zuree opened the box, and there inside, sitting in one of the compartments, she spotted the doll Izz had been working on with such affectionate skill. Her eyes suddenly gleamed full and questioning, alive with amusement. A small smile showed at the edges of Izz's mouth. She reached in and picked up the doll and pulled it toward her, and held it dreamily.

"Awe," Zuree exclaimed, and she pouted cutely.

And as she was turning it around, again and again, Izz gritted his teeth and looked skyward as his face colored with embarrassment and then went pale. The resemblance in every detail, right down to the crown, was unmistakable. Zuree's mouth opened in a bigger oval of astonishment.

"What is this?" She asked.

Izz's face flushed from pale to a hundred deeper shades of red as he felt an ill feeling coarse through him. He cringed as if Zuree had levered open a guarded confession out of him. For an embarrassing moment, Izz's voice was hesitant. Finally, his heart retreated enough from his throat, where it had lodged itself.

"Oh, nothing," he said as he was filled with awkwardness; his voice fumbled and stammered.

Zuree started to take a closer look when Izz tried desperately to take the doll before she could recognize that it was an exact image of her. But Zuree was quicker than Izz anticipated; she managed to pull the toy doll away and out of Izz's reach, then hid the doll behind her, making Izz reach.

"Is this your dolly?" she teased as her lips quirked, and her eyes crinkled at the corners with amusement at his exasperated look. Her long lashes swept across her blue-green eyes, twinkling mischievously as a trace of flirtation danced across the bemused half smile playing about the corners of her mouth. She pouted and somehow tauntingly smiled triumphantly at the same time as she seemingly gave Izz that come-let-us-jest look. She had clearly spent a significant part of her young life, learning how to get what she wanted. It was a ploy that she had managed to perfection on her father, the king.

Izz had not seen this facial expression before, and he could not tell exactly what to expect, nor was sure what mood this signified. Desperately and acutely mortified, he again reached for the doll with his other hand as Zuree shifted her weight to the back, and Izz found that he was unexpectedly holding Zuree in his arms. The shock of the sudden unintentional contact caused them both to freeze, and neither could seem to stir a muscle to move away from the other. His hand was enclosing hers, hip to hip, heart to heart, nose to nose. Their lips close enough to kiss. It was a light, magical embrace that warmed them both to their toes. She was exquisitely formed, fully padded in all the proper places. Her bosom was full, her waist unbelievably narrow. Izz found himself pleasantly pillowed. She was so soft all over, and he was firm all over, and wherever they made contact, they experienced tingling trails of warmth.

Izz's eyes were suddenly drawn to Zuree's stone necklace to see a faint bluish glow that like misty flames, surged as if a mystic power from without had come within and illuminated all along its edges. An unexpected passion rushed through Zuree as a sudden blush colored her cheeks. Izz took a deep breath and exhaled blissfully. It was the most wonderful feeling that neither were prepared to experience. Izz's heart made a strange fluttering noise inside of him as a slow smile flickered crossed his face. For the longest moment, they both found themselves in an awkward position, in uncomfortable silence, with awkward emotions stirring like two stricken sparrows on the verge of plunging beak first from their perch, off the edge of a cliff. Their two hearts danged dangerously suspended like two leaves whirling in the wind held up by a single delicate strand. Time and space imploded into a million perspectives as they were involuntarily melted into each other by their closeness, like honey in a warming liquid.

Izz felt a fleeting instance of disquieting doubt, fearful he had stumbled over his bounds. Zuree experienced a sudden urge to pull away, but she found herself overpowered before she even realized it. And that small thread of warning they had both just felt began to untangle. He could not stir a muscle, and she could not seem to make herself pull away from him. She shuddered hot and cold all at the same time. The sensation grew from a pleasing glow into some magical heat that managed to extend, spread, and envelop warmly about her, embracing her into his essence. She never knew such sensations existed until that moment. For Izz, there was no room for reason in his mind. Zuree sucked in a ragged breath. Her tongue moistened her suddenly dry lips.

There was no sign of objection in Zuree's expression. Seeing the blend of desire, uncertainty, and surprise there, something in those blue-green windows betrayed her. The look in her eyes reflected the same warmth he was feeling in his heart. Zuree was an incredibly charming girl and getting more so by the second. The elegant features of her face only enhanced the intensity of her brilliant blue-green eyes. He could not stop the want of looking into the gripping, hypnotizing soul behind those emerald sapphire eyes. Passion intensely blazed in her incredible crystalline eyes, and then and there, he realized that her eyes could be as daunting as they were alluring. But above all else, now there could be no doubt, especially apparent at this proximity, she was indeed the angelic maiden of his dreams. Utterly captivated, Zuree stared right back, both curious and terrified, overcome with emotions and feelings that were so new and so unexpected. Both were having difficulty remembering how to breathe. Both trembled deep inside; their heartbeats quickened as they felt the earth beneath their curled toes shudder.

The air crackled, charged with energy as it is just moments before a violent lightning strike. The room was ready to go up in flames. The tinder was stacked, only needing the slightest spark to ignite, and pulsating sparks were flying all around a love that begged to be kindled. They were two souls lost in a whirlwind of feelings they did not understand as the tantalizing spirit of love filled them both. No sense, feeling, or emotion was left untouched. A profound stillness fell between them. They stood motionless as two statues lost in the infinity of each other's closeness. She was like fine wine coursing through his veins. Izz's heart was thundering so hard and loud he was certain Zuree could not help but hear and feel its pulse beating up against her everywhere they made contact. The moment was so absolute and genuine that it could not have been quickened by anything other than true love. Izz could barely stand the torment of having the mate of his soul so close. In the heat of his eagerness, he almost said, *I think I love you. You are everything that is right in my life. Tell her now how you feel,* his heart urged. Izz's tongue burned with the words that pleaded to be spoken, but his groping thoughts could not be forced passed his trembling lips. Communication it seemed was at some subconscious, coextending plane, holding them spellbound for an adulating moment that turned off time. Feelings were their language. An electrifying symphony of awareness pulsated in their mist, making words irrelevant. They stared into each other's inner eyes, exchanging unanswerable questions, and unknowable answers.

Izz's thick mane of black hair curled in tangles around his manly face. Zuree nibbled softly on the inside of her lip, trying to suppress a deep moan building in her throat as an accelerating little throb beat frantically in the hollow of her neck. Her heart was opening its petals as a warm knot inside her began to swell. By now, she could see her wanton reflection in the depth of his endless agate eyes, dark pewter pools that drew her in and pulled her under. Izz had, by an unexpected chance, found the vulnerable mark in her heart and poured his love into her. Her blood went to her feet, weakening her knees on its way down, and she knew then and there that she was at his mercy. The need for his lips on hers was all he could focus on before he went up in smoke. Her lips were parted as if poised and prepared to allow his kiss. Every vibrating nerve in her begged him to do what he was going to do quickly. Izz felt her tremble as she arched up in need to unite her fiery lips to his. When their deepest emotions had come full circle, there was only one of two things that could have possibly happened next—losing themselves in the inferno that was enveloping them, but instead, it was the other thing that happened.

Suddenly, the kiss he so longed to bestow upon her became somehow unexpectedly forbidden. And out of nowhere, from the back of Izz's mind, came the last thought he wanted to hear. *The princess's hand is pledged to another. She could never belong to you!* The reality of it all reminded him for the thousandth time, and with that, the magical spell was broken. Izz's toes uncurled, and his heart seemed as if it had stopped. Sensing the abrupt, stabbing change in Izz's beautiful soul, Zuree relaxed her grip slightly on the doll. And Izz was able to pry her slim fingers gently and managed to recover the doll from her hand.

She asked, "Did you find what you were looking for," as she turned her lower lip out in a pout.

She wasn't sure what Izz's mood shift signified. Then that small thread of warning she had felt earlier began to unravel in the pit of her stomach. And the answer to her question, she could almost read in his mind.

"Please forgive me," Izz said at once in a whisper. He took several agonizing, eternal moments more to draw himself away from Zuree slowly. He secretly wished with all his being that he could somehow drive all the feelings he had just felt back into his heart and quietly lock them away forever. His heart was still beating wildly as if he had just finished running a grueling race. A cold knot tightened and froze in Izz's guts as he desperately tried to pretend everything was normal. He opened his mouth and then choked back. He did not know what to say. What could he say without making a bigger fool of himself than he thought he had already? He cringed noticeably as his face screwed itself into a broken, apologetic smile.

Feeling somewhat responsible, Zuree searched for the words that lurked just past the tip of her tongue. She tried to say, "I am the only one at fault here," but her voice was too feeble and shaken. Both of them at once felt inept and withdrew from the other as if forbidden love had tainted their hearts. Even though neither felt any real guilt. An uneasy silence grew between them, and they did not speak or make eye contact for a lingering moment that seemed like an eternity stretching on forever.

Finally, Izz spoke without meeting Zuree's eyes, his words tripping all over themselves. "That was wholly unintended," he assured the princess. "I am truly sorry." His muttered apology was said in an apologetic tone and with an accountable, fractured, lop-sided smile.

A lock of hair dangled over her right eye. She tried to smile and tried to act nonchalant. She compassionately said, "There is nothing to be sorry about." As she brushed back her hair and adjusted her dress.

The expression Izz kept on his face seemed to be trying to offer solace for everything he had done and thought in his madness up to that day. He quickly brushed his feelings aside and recomposed himself. He asked in a jittery, thoroughly unsettled voice, "Should I have the box delivered, milady?"

Feeling just as awkward, Zuree stifled a nervous laugh and answered, "No...no, I'll take it with me." She let out a sigh. "How much do I owe you?" she asked as she drew a soft leather bag filled with gold pieces from her money belt.

Izz took a deep breath and then released it slowly. "Consider it a gift. A token of my loyalty," he finally said with a sobering face. "It is for you." He placed it into her hands.

She looked at him without understanding. Zuree laughed pleasantly and asked, "But why would you give me such a priceless piece of work?"

"It is my pleasure entirely to give it to you because you have seen beyond its cost and have been able to see its true worth." There was an astonishing sense of genuine generosity about the way he said it.

Zuree could not refuse his generosity. She thanked him profusely. "I will treasure it all my life," Zuree whispered as she nodded her gratitude and smiled warmly.

The pleasure in her voice warmed Izz with heartfelt gratification. "It would seem that I am in your debt. Perhaps then someday, I can return the favor," she said. Her tone was a soft promise. Then she turned away, grabbed her cloak from the table, and whirled it around her shoulders. She reached back and pulled the hood over her head. Her lovely face was once again framed in concealment by her hood. Adjusting her hair under her cloak, she pulled her hood further down to shadow her face. When she reached the door, she paused for several moments, emotions and sensations were still alive and boiling within her. As she hesitated, Izz was doing his best to gauge her disposition. She questioned if any of it could even possibly have been real as each questioning thought began to ache in her heart. Such thoughts were becoming immodest, and the moment was becoming a long, wordless farewell.

Then came a long and troubled silence. Groping for something to say, Izz felt a dull, throbbing pain all over, wanting nothing more than to prevent her from leaving, to reach out to her and ask her to stay, and in the heat of his agony, he almost said, "I love you." The words just hung suspended in his mind like an emptiness that could neither be fulfilled nor denied. He could not conceive saying such a thing and was ashamed that he had even considered doing so. But in spite of it all, he wanted so much to call out, but uncertainty arrested his tongue, and with all his will, he held himself back.

Zuree reached for the door latch, and without turning back, she said, "Till the next time we meet again...And I do hope there will be the next time." Her words were cut short. "For the time being, I bid you a good day and fare ye well." She suddenly realized that she had to get out of there before she could not resist turning and running back into Izz's arms. She opened the door, and just before she stepped out, she added in a whispered hush, "Truly I hope the day will come when we meet again," clutching the box to her bosom as she stepped through the doorway, leaving behind an emptiness in the wake of her departure.

I could visit you in my dreams, Izz wanted to cry out, but, he thought better and said instead, "I would like that very much." The few words they spoke between them were awkward at best, but they had already said so much by saying so little.

The experience had left both shaken to the core. Just outside, again, Zuree hesitated as if she wanted to say or hear something. She waited until it was painfully evident that her departure was stretching into the most prolonged farewell ever. She composed herself, trying to be casual so that she might blend with the other nameless faces. As she closed the door behind her, she felt the enchantment lose its luster, replaced now by an empty void deep within her. Izz watched her walk out, wishing for just one more moment with her. He reached out his hand toward her, rotating his outstretched fingers and then froze. His hand seemed to suddenly wither toward him as he felt an overwhelming urge to pound his fist into something solid. Why did her presence have to linger?

Zuree strolled back into a swiftly moving crowd; her feelings ebbed, leaving her a trifle weak, wondering what had taken possession of her, questioning how she could have suddenly felt so helpless against the raw power between them. She was not comfortable with the way her body had at once arched up toward Izz. It had been absurd! She had acted like an impulsive tart in heat. She had given herself so quickly, so wholly, submitted so easily. Even now, a wave of welcoming sensations he so quickly brought to life lingered over her. If they had waited any longer, they might have both so quickly lost control. She had no business being there unaccompanied. She had been in the wrong.

She stepped into the carriage, waiting for her around the corner and sat back. Mozlow, her trusted friend and servant, sensing from her a withering look of distress, asked, "Is all well, milady?" Zuree solemnly nodded, and Mozlow did not press on the matter. "Very well, milady." Mozlow punctuated with an apologetic expression.

Zuree's heart glowed for Izz as she clutched the precious gift that was very much a special part of him, and she was humbled by it. Encircled by familiar surroundings, she buried her inner feelings as deeply as they would go and wondered what on Zia she was thinking. The thoroughly rational part of her could not comprehend how she could feel what she was feeling, and yet she desperately clung on to the box as her mind and heart reeled, believing all sorts of crazy things were possible. She ached within as she sank back into the carriage seat as though she hoped it would somehow comfort her. Izz missed her, the instant she closed the door behind her, and wanted nothing more than to run after her. He wanted to beg her to run away with him, but he understood that she could never be released from her father's promise. Even if she broke it, she would still never be free. He promised himself that they would be best of friends; anything else he was sure would only lead to sorrow and disappointment for both of them. Their love could only ever live in the thoughts of his mind and the emotions of his heart. It had been at best, a torturing taunt. His hand coiled into a trembling fist, and taking it, he pounded it against his throbbing, troubled heart. Then with his other hand, he clasped over his fist as if to comfort it. Izz shut his eyes but could still not get Zuree out of his insight. The distinct scent of her stayed behind in the air. He felt the painful breaking of his heart. He sensed a tinge of loneliness overshadow him. Izz stood alone quietly for the longest time. Eventually, he pushed those feelings away; they faded and were replaced by thoughts more practical to the responsibilities of the familiar world around him. Once again, Izz stepped out of the path of his heart as if the whole thing had never happened. But a distinct fragrance lingered in the air, proclaiming she had actually been there. The encounter left an indelible wound that never would heal, an invisible scar that would remain with him for the longest time.

In the coming days, Izz preoccupied every waking moment with hard work, caring for his eagles, and filling every spare moment visiting with Ammiz. It seemed as if the eaglets were always eagerly calling for food and growing at an alarming rate. In less than three moon cycles, the birds had long outgrown their nest, and sooner than expected were getting too big for the shop. And Izz was struggling to keep up with their voracious appetites. At first, meat scraps were enough; but now, Izz found himself having to feed them whole buckets of fish and entire carcasses of goat and sheep. Whenever it was feeding time, Izz would blow his whistle, and the young eagles always eagerly responded to it immediately. Soon Fina and Bolo had grown so big that Izz could no longer keep them in the shop, especially when they spread their fully feathered wings and vigorously stretched and exercised them, filling the shop with the sound of beating wings. Before long, Izz was forced to move the pair of eagles out into the back stables. The presence of the two predators was making his horse and donkey very nervous. It was plain to see that the time had come for them to learn how to fend for themselves.

Early the next day, with a fish, Izz lured Fina and Bolo into the back of the biggest wooden cart he owned, while his donkey jittered back and forth, wide eyed, trying to look back past its eye blinds. The feathered pair nearly did not fit, and the cramped enclosure made them uneasy until Izz covered the birds' eyes with their hoods to keep them calm. When they had reached a spacious clearing at the forest's edge, Izz brought his exhausted donkey to a halt, gave it a share of oats, and unloaded the fledglings. Once on the ground with their hoods removed and happy to be free, they beat their wings in unison as they raised their head crests and ruffled their feathers, making themselves look twice their normal size. Almost instantly, both their eyes tilted and their heads rotated. Both birds zeroed in on the little forest creatures as they romped on the branches of a nearby tree beyond their reach. They both looked down at the ground around them, looking hungrily, and scratched in the dirt in search of any meager meal. Izz walked back and forth, wondering where to start, then he walked in a big circle around Fina and Bolo, trying to formulate a plan. As he walked, the fledglings rotated their heads while remaining stationary, turning their heads almost all the way around, never losing sight of Izz, obviously looking for a handout. Something on the ground caught Bolo's eyes. Izz turned to watch as Bolo struck like a viper, pecking and snatching a lizard with his beak. Fina instinctively reacted and ripped half of the lizard out of Bolo's beak. They both ate it hungrily, their first kill.

Both birds had already learned to run and glide downhill. Now it was time for them to learn how to launch themselves from where they stood. Out of nowhere, a thought occurred to Izz. He jumped up on an outcrop of rocks and started to flap his arms, looking very much like a moonstruck albatross. The fledgling at once started mimicking Izz with their ever expanding wings. At first, their movements in the gentle winds were awkward and uncoordinated, but in due time, as their wing strength increased, they began to catch the wind and lift themselves off the ground gradually. Soon they were launching themselves into the air with growing skill. Their wings billowed, producing blasts of wind that stirred and blew dust and leaves across the grassy hilltop.

Over time, one day, to Izz's surprise, his fine feathered friends simply lifted off the ground and continued to climb, their wings a blur. Izz watched anxiously as they both mounted into the air on the rising thermals, which carried them spiraling into the lofty sky. Up and up they went at a steady rise on great wings that pushed down against the air with a tireless strength, carrying them higher and higher above the windswept hills, beyond the tallest trees, until they were soaring among the clouds. Days passed, and each time the pair flew, higher, farther, and longer than before. They seemed delighted in soaring for long periods with little to no wing flapping, riding on the wings of the winds, while below, Izz gathered wood for his many projects. Izz occasionally looked up to admire the captivating beauty and utter elegance of these impressive creatures as they soared together information and circled overhead, gracing the sky with their presence. Over time, Fina and Bolo began performing spectacular aerial displays, playful teasing that included chases, dives, and mock attacks. From time to time, one would roll on its back and interlock talons with the other while in flight and tumble toward the ground, not separating until the last moments before reaching the ground, to Izz's heart stopping dismay. The pair had inherited the spacious skies as if they had belonged to them all along.

One particular day while Izz was making a final selection of some choice pieces of wood, Izz's keen eyes caught Bolo and Fina soaring high in the upper levels of the clear sky. They were floating across the roof of the heavens like celestial butterflies, taking in the panoramic view of the Zian landscape beneath them. Bolo suddenly seemed to be fixated on something below. The male's circling sweeps appeared to be getting tighter as it seemingly held to a target in the center of its circling flight pattern. Bolo's vision was so sharp he could have even spotted a small mouse on the ground from the highest distances overhead. Once a mature eagle finds a target, it is doomed, but Bolo was still a youngster, and Izz's anxiety mounted. As he raced in ever closing circles across the sky, all at once, he gracefully spread his winged canopy wide as his expansive tail feathers fanned out. Bolo gently undulated in the thermal winds, slowed to a hover, tucked his wings, and then bolted headlong into a spiraling, plunging dive downward. He folded his wings tightly behind his shoulders as he swooped down, dropping like a streaking falling star. Faster and faster, Bolo plummeted, cutting through the wispy layers of midday sky as the wind whistled past its stealth formation. Izz watched breathlessly as Bolo effortlessly sliced through the air earthward at mounting speeds, never moving so fast, exceeding Izz's realms of possibility. The speeding eagle's feathers quivered as the velocity transformed the giant black bird into a grayish blur, crashing toward Zia at an unbelievable rate of speed. Faster and faster, the wind shrieked as the distance between Bolo and the ground shrunk. His form was an obscured haze, slashing through the sky, as a blurred streak followed him reminiscent of the tail of a comet. Izz could almost hear the wind shrilling through the bird's feathers as it dove. Bolo's exceptional command of the skies made Izz's heart race with excitement, but Bolo was quickly running out of the distance between the rocky ground and himself, and Izz began to wonder if the inexperienced eagle had lost sight of its projected target. A twinkling of an eye before impact, Bolo unfurled and spread open his wings. They caught the air snapping full like yawning canvassed masts. Bolo extended his yellow feet forward, expanding his powerful razor sharp talons spread like deploying daggers that raked forth and would not quail. Then there was a sickening thud, and in the distance, there was a final turbulence of wings and dust. Bolo had slammed into something on the ground, rolling with it over and over.

Izz screamed, "Bolo!" and dropped everything. With his heart lodged in his throat, he bolted into a full speed dash toward the cloud of rising dust. At full stride, Izz could see the dust clearing. Fearing the worst, he strained to catch sight of Bolo. What he saw next unexpectedly seized him by complete surprise. There, Bolo was ruffled feathers and looking dazed. The great bird was perched upon a mature, wild, prong horned, bearded ovis. He was shrieking deafeningly as its terrible dagger like talons buried deep, closing like a vise, digging into its prey's thick hide, piercing the rib cage through to the wild buck's heart and lungs and squeezing the life out of it. Instinctively, Bolo's powerful beak began tearing savagely in search of the soft, pale underbelly. Fiercely and furiously stabbing at his victim repeatedly, ripping and renting its quarry to shreds with its curvy, powerful, razor sharp beak. The ovis's eyes were wide with shock as it wheezed, bellowed, and bayed in pain as it struggled in Bolo's grip. Fountains of blood streamed from the terrible wounds on the exposed underbelly. Izz watched in terrified suspense as Bolo tore the dying creature's heart out and swallowed it in two gulps. Bolo's hunting abilities were purely instinctive; he was a natural meat eater, a born killer, taking his rightful place as a primary predator of the food chain niche. Once its prey was subdued, and after a short rest, Bolo raised its head and looked toward Izz, then twisted up awkwardly into the air, taking flight as if the full grown ovis weighed nothing. The eagle flew toward Izz, beating its mighty wings through the air, dangling the limped corpse from his talons as blood streamed from its terrible wounds. Bolo finally came to perch on a nearby ledge, dropping the ovis at Izz's feet with its blood still dripping from its beak. Their eyes met with an acknowledging glare as Bolo seemingly offered Izz first choice of his kill.

Soon Fina arrived, and Bolo willingly shared his prize with her. She sliced the kill open along the spine, deboned it like a fish, and began to eat. It was an ovis this time, but full grown White Crowned Eagles had been known to bring down full grown yakoxen. Izz gathered his wood and tools as the pair gorged themselves, wolfing down huge portions of meat. When it was time to go home, apparently, Bolo disagreed. The two hunters refused to leave the kill, and at that moment. Izz realized that the inevitable had come upon them. It was time to surrender them to the wild, to live their lives freely and on their own as it was always meant to be. On the way home, as the sun dipped toward the horizon, Izz felt a rare emptiness that he had only experienced once before. In his solitude, Zuree once again had begun to ease herself right into his every thought, consuming him so that he could barely think. As his cart's wheels beat out a rhythm of time, he wondered what she could be doing right then and what thoughts might be going through her mind. He felt uncomfortable thinking of her and banished his inner feelings as far away as he could, but he knew they would return to haunt him again and again.

In the coming days, Izz saw less and less of his two feathered friends. Nonetheless, when Izz was in that area, gathering wood, he would pull out the whistle he always carried with him and called to them. And on that rare occasion when his whistle was heard, the pair would come sailing out of their secret havens to present themselves. Izz would joyously pet, hug, and throw them each a special pork treat that he carried with him just in case the occasion arose. When it was time to go, they would follow above his cart for a way like two kites on strings, but eventually, they would fly back into the wild where they were they now called home.

The latest news Izz had received from the engineers in charge of cutting and transporting the base of the fallen giant was that the tree was ready to move. After having dried enough to be worked on, and its iron like resin had finally crystallized. Three teams working around the clock had trimmed the tree of its root system, and the lower section had been separated from the main tree. The whole complicated plan was nearing its end, and arrangements had been made to transport the massive piece of wood. The gigantic tree stump had been slowly cut, trimmed, and maneuvered at a backbreaking snail's pace. Izz was there to see the giant tree trunk loaded onto the transporting wagon. First, the seasoned tree trunk had been rounded, and then long ringed iron screws were drilled on both sides of the trunk so that ropes and chains could turn and stabilize the towering bulk of solid wood. A long rigid frame was used to slowly roll the trunk down to the flatlands where a mighty twelve wheeled oversized wagon waited. A plank reinforced earthen ramp and tussled platform was constructed. A complex array of sleds, rails, ropes, pivoting blocks, and tilting stones were used to roll the massive tree trunk into position before the loading ramp. The massive log began to inch up the ramp as ropes, chains, and pulleys came taut, powered by large numbers of men and animals working in unison. Timbers creaked and cracked under the weight of the enormous slab as it surrendered to the bidding of man and beast. Large timber wedges were used to keep the trunk from rolling back. The massive form swayed slightly as control lines on either side tightened. The low flatbed wagon groaned as the enormous trunk was positioned onto its reinforced bed. Engineers worked energetically to perfectly center, balance, and block the bulky wooden giant. A force of at least a hundred giant yakoxen would be required to overcome the enormous weighty inertia of the truncated giant. Large thick planks cut from the upper part of the tree had to be laid on the dirt road to prevent the iron enforced wheels from sinking into the ground.

The signal was given. Yakoxen drivers flicked their reins against the backs of the yakoxen as drivers alongside encouraged the beast of burden with the long slender sticks they used as whips, and muscular yakoxen forelegs strained into life as they dug into the ground. With several jerking movements, the wagon rocked and swayed, rattled and creaked, clattered and clamored, as the tree trunk began its long journey to Edawn.

The next day, just before the first light, Ammiz stood on the highest tower of the kingdom's lookout. Strewed around him were bundles of folded papers, notes predicting the movement of the bodies in the heavens he had updated the night before. With a practiced eye and tireless vigilance, the seer scanned the horizon in the early morning sky with his new long eye, which he had attached to a tripod. He had strived to mathematically calculate the pattern and the exact time of the first planetary arrival, but its placement eluded him, perhaps because of insufficient figures, a miscalculation perchance.

"It should be somewhere there," he muttered to himself, "but where?" It should have been there, close enough to Zia to be seen in the early morning mist. Always alert for error, he rechecked his notes to be sure he could read what he had written about his reckoning. His notes read, "In the middle of the Spring Equinox, when the sun crosses the celestial equator and the length of the day and night is equal, the Great Conjunction will align with the rising sun and moon." The seer recounted.

He fine tuned his long eye yet saw nothing—no harbingers in the morning silence. Now was his best hope of spotting the first appearance of the Great Conjunction while the sky was uncluttered by thousands of dots of light overlapping on a vast, utterly black backdrop. He turned to his carefully calculated charts and studied their intricate patterns, predicting the movement of the bodies he was tracking in the heavens. He checked his star charts, triangulated the signposts of the sky. Possibly there was a flaw in them. But he reasoned that if he was to believe the Sacred Book to be a revelation from the Creator. He also had to believe that the facts written of the coming of the Great Conjunction had to be accurate. And therefore, the revelation of the young carpenter had to be true as well. Perhaps there was more than had been revealed. Something he missed in their telling. *How strange are the workings of the heavens,* he mused? Ammiz returned to his optical instrument and saw nothing of significance but waited there for a moment then continued to pursue his search expectantly and methodically. Then suddenly, he tore his eye from the long eye and rubbed his best eye with the back of his hand and blinked it clear. Sure enough, even with the naked eye, he could barely see them. There, where there should have been nothing, he saw the tiny smoldering fragments of dwindling light, only just the size of pinheads, so small it hardly registered in Ammiz's eye at all. It was not a meteor or a star. He precisely recognized what it was and what it preordained.

<hr>

Izz woke at the crack of dawn. The rays of a new sun filtered across on a beautiful day. It was the approach of the Summer Solstice, the day the annual garden banquet, commemorating the founding of the orphanage would be celebrated, and the day promised to be warm and bright. It was the day he had set aside to visit the children in which he would be one of the honored guests.

Izz felt an escalating surge of excitement and could not understand why he felt as joyful as he did that morning. It was as if something very unusual was about to happen to him, but for the life of him, he could not figure out what that could be. Izz had by now become quite attached to the children there. His days as an orphan created a special bond between the children and himself, a bond of understanding and compassion that only a parentless child could identify with. Izz especially had become very attached to Buzu. She had managed to conquer his heart completely. The fact that she did not have much more time to live stabbed him in his heart like a thorn. Izz was determined to make this day extra special. First, he would stop at the eatery and get Buzu's favorite sweetbread for everyone, and then he planned to stop at every sweet shop to pick up more sweet delicacies on his way. Written on his list were honey and almond pie, baked rice milk pudding, apple rolls, candied fruits, and molasses confections. The orphanage field day would surely be an occasion to remember. Izz washed and dressed, harnessed his faithful donkey to its cart, and he was off. It was a glorious day, and the sky was an extraordinary colored roof of bright blue bliss.

Moreover, the sun was a splash of shining light that glorified Zia below. Izz's first stop was the eatery where Zophie worked where his order was already waiting for him. Zophie's beautiful smile greeted Izz.

"The baker has been baking since midnight!" she exclaimed. She served Izz, a sweet roll, honey, butter, jam, and a flagon of warm milk. "Are you feeding an army?" Zophie asked with an air of admiration.

"You could say that." Izz returned the smile. He ate hastily as the bakers loaded his cart. And as always, he paid more than he owed and left Zophie a silver coin. As planned, Izz stopped at every sweet shop on his way to the orphanage. By the time he reached the gates, his cart was filled to overflowing with sweet treats.

The orphanage grounds were buzzing like a busy beehive at the peak of the honey season. They were all dressed up, looking much like multicolored birds, fine looking, orderly, bright eyed, all of them sporting brand new shoes. Every child was so different, total strangers who happened to share the same set of circumstances, brought together in one accord by worldly conditions beyond their power to control. Upon his arrival, the excitement was so thick one could have sliced it with a knife. Izz's arrival doubled the excitement, and the sight of the overgenerous pile of sweets atop of Izz's cart redoubled it. A young maiden of the order quickly opened the gates for Izz. In the distance, there was the sound of childish, boisterous laughter, and cries of delight. The pattering of feet resounded as the children all rushed over and crowded around Izz. An unexpected pang of empathy came over Izz, painfully aware that in the orphanage, life could be a very lonely world. They all looked up at Izz with hungry eyes bulging bright with curiosity, small heads straining up, with mouths wide open, looking like a flock of baby eaglets expecting to be fed.

Buzu broke away from Mistress Aria's skirt and came rushing over as she always did, calling out, "Izz! Izz! Izz!" She came to stand directly in front of Izz. Her love for him made his heartache. Izz gathered her up into his arms, kissed her cheek affectionately, and hoisted her upon his shoulders.

"How has my favorite person in the whole world been?"

"I have missed you, Izz. Why have you not come to see me?"

"I have been far too busy for my good."

Next, Izz was greeted by Mistress Aria as a caretaker led the donkey and cart away. "Izz, I am so happy you could come. It is always so wonderful to see you, welcome."

Izz and the mistress walked down a trail that led to one of the grandest sectors of the kingdom, the acclaimed gardens. As they made their way, Izz carried Buzu as the other children followed everywhere they went. They seemed starved for attention. They lined up to take turns holding Izz's free hand. He walked hand in hand with one and suddenly found another one came up behind him and slipping their hand into his palm, or taking hold of his elbow. They were all smiles, everything seemed to be as it should be, but Izz could see a deep sadness in their eyes that no one else seemed to recognize.

The afternoon was magic. The sun shimmered a bright golden glaze from above, bathing all in a cheerful glow, and the air chimed with a choir of birds pouring out their hearts with song. The gentle breeze carried the fragrance of blossoms that promised golden fruit.

"All has been made ready," the mistress stated. "The children have worked hard to prepare for this day. It is their favorite day of the year, and your presence, it seems, has made this day that much more special."

"I would have never missed it for all the treasure in Zia." As Izz spoke, a movement caught the corner of his eye, and he turned to see the hooded stranger approaching from a fork on the trail up ahead, and a chill ran down Izz's back.

When their paths crossed, the robed person removed her hood. Izz's eyes danced as they watched Zuree's hair rain down around her face, shoulders, and down to her waist like a cascade of golden fire in the morning sunlight. The unexpected surprise stole the breath right out from inside of him, yet by now, he knew that it had been Zuree all along. The princess had found a much needed purpose and passion in her life. At first, the king had refused to allow his only child to help in the orphanage. He insisted that any work, at all, was beneath the dignity of the royals and should be better left to the commoners. But in the end, he had finally conceded reluctantly to his strong willed daughter's insistence, knowing that she needed something to counterbalance her boundless energy. Izz put Buzu down, and she was happy to run off and join the other children in their playful games.

"Good morning, Izz. How fare you?" Zuree asked in her usual cheerful voice.

"I should have known it has been you all along," Izz whispered back after he caught his breath. "You are the mysterious benefactor."

"Yes, actually, it is my father, the king who supplies the orphanage with anything they may need."

"I am impressed," Izz said as he locked his eyes on hers. In the bright sunlight, Zuree's beauty was enchanting and becoming more radiant with every beat of Izz's throbbing heart, sending its blood bouncing excitedly from wall to wall, his passion reborn like a seed of love that was meant to bloom.

Zuree, too felt the familiar bewildering rush of mystifying sensations come over her. She was troubled that she seemed not to have the willpower to control the strange emotions that had suddenly possessed her, unable to comprehend how quickly she had once again been overcome. A flicker of a smile crossed the mistress's face as she paused to witness the unusual phenomenon that seemed to stretch beyond the boundaries of the normal. Finally, she interrupted, saying, "I see you have already met."

The two hastily regained their composure. Buzu's sweet giggle suddenly broke the uncomfortableness of the moment that Zuree and Izz had fallen under. "Hurry, Izz. We are all waiting for you and the princess!"

"Will you join us?" Izz asked Zuree.

"I would be honored." Zuree wanted to know more about Izz and to hear what he had to say, but she took care not to seem too eager. Zuree and Izz spoke as they walked toward the meadow ,escorted by their entourage.

"You are certainly full of surprises," Izz continued as he felt a strange floating sensation come over him.

"As you have proven to be."

"I would think that a princess's life would be crowded with things pertaining to royalty."

"There are few things that bring me more pleasure than the children of this orphanage."

"You inspire me," Izz said in an impressed voice.

"I have heard many noble things about you as well. Not only have your incredible achievements become legendary. I have also heard that you are kind, considerate, and very generous."

The two behaved as if they were casual friends that just happened to be sharing the same path. Somehow they managed to mingle offhandedly, each knowing each other's place, and the result was nonchalantly mutual and had seemed to have found its own peculiar equilibrium.

Before Ammiz left the high tower again, he looked through the lens fitted tube and finely tuned it. The powerful device showed the great galleons of space in the midmorning light. Ammiz whispered in a voice that was barely audible to himself, "Who but the Great Creator Himself can foretell events in the distant future?" Then he answered his own question, "Only One...the One who gives testimony of His existence and the trustworthiness of His written Utterance! The hand of the Maker will very soon strike the awaited hour."

Fifteen

The Garden

It was a rare summer day in the garden. Zuree and Izz continued down the path side by side, taking pleasure in the joy of walking in this bright, beautiful morning, breathing and smelling the clean, fresh air as the glorious sun kissed skies smiled down on them. Izz turned and flashed Zuree, the unique smile that never failed to fill her with warmth. Did he have any idea how appealing his smile was? She managed not to shudder under the long, intense stare from dark pearly eyes that seemed to see into the depth of her soul. Then suddenly, to her immense surprise, she almost heard herself saying, "I mainly came here looking for you." She dismissed the thoughts racing through her mind before they had a chance to take root. Along the path, flower covered vines flourished against the sunny garden wall. Tall evergreen hedges bordered with shrubbery lined the vista of the garden walk along their way. The walled sanctuary was mystically and wonderfully alive and beckoning. Early spring seemed to be vibrantly erupting around them everywhere as they walked.

With every step and every moment, the garden grew more and more flowery as it brought forth its bountiful abundance. The midmorning air was so pure and temperate that one could not seem to breathe it all in deep enough. There was a rich scent in the light whispering breeze, heavy and alive with sweet fragrant blooms of every color reaching skyward to be caressed by the early warmth of the sun. Songbirds filled with vitality were musically chirping mating calls to their companions in the branches above them. Izz's head seemed to be floating in the clouds as his feet walked on air along the well worn path. With a gentle pleasure gleaming over his face, Izz could not seem to quit smiling. The warmth, the sunshine, and the flowers were casting their spell all around him. And especially the mysterious feeling of Zuree's closeness was proving to be intoxicating. Suddenly, Izz was overpowered by a most uncanny sensation that he had been there before, but he knew full well that this was the first time he had ever ventured there. To him, it was a place visited only in dreams. He could feel the excitement building within him as he wondered where he had to draw the line. He knew full well that his feelings were foolish, but his heart seemed committed to a comforting course of denial. Inwardly, Zuree was hiding a beaming smile; outwardly, she was strolling calmly and confidently, but inside, she was desperately setting up barriers, fighting a losing battle to conceal her excitement building within her. They walked until they came to a light, brightened clearing where the garden opened far and wide and up unto the full height, ascending from Zia to the heavens. The beautiful grounds were a well groomed lawn surrounded by a world carpeted in wildflowers of a thousand vivacious colors, and their soft blossoming scent filled the air like a striking melody heavy with the sound and scent of an opulent spring paradise. Over the years, the mistress and her staff had managed to create a stunning garden oasis in the shadows of the kingdom. It was the one place in the kingdom that the children could play freely.

As they all walked down into the garden, the wind swirled and danced across the grass as birds chirped, squirrels scampered from tree to tree, and delicate butterflies gently sailed across the lush green meadow before them. Water sprang from natural fountains that playfully danced their way down into a calm mirror lake of dreams that reflected the surrounding trees on its shoreline. While just over the clear mirror surface, swarms of golden ladybugs joyfully danced in the brilliant sunlight, like clusters of sparkling miniature stars when the gentle breeze touched them. The orphanage staff was busily tending open fires on which meats of all kinds were roasting, and outdoor ovens were baking loaves of bread and rooted vegetables. The children trotted briskly down the path and poured into the clearing, craning their necks and pointing to things that suddenly seemed so amazing to them. And the hearts of every living creature under the beautiful sun seemed to be rejoicing the approach of the Summer Solstice.

Mistress Aria proudly announced, "The princess has contributed all of this" —she waved an extended finger out in front of her—"as she has faithfully continued to do every year." She ushered the children off to play as they gladly did. Then she took the princess's hand in her own as she spoke, "Even though our princess Zuree could be doing more prestige things with her time, instead she has chosen to dedicate herself to helping the less fortunate. Many troubled children owe her the deepest debt of gratitude for setting them back on the right pathway, or helping them off the mistaken one." She heaved a deep breath and wiped the wetness from her eyes. She took a moment to compose herself, then clapped her hands together and said, "I have many things to do to make ready for our little feast." She turned to Zuree and Izz. "You two do not worry yourself about a thing. Go on, find a nice shady spot, and enjoy yourselves."

Izz and Zuree walked with a lively spring in their steps, through a sea of rainbow colored flowers joyously baking in the sunlight. The two meandered over to a small hillside where the broad branches of a big oak tree cast shadow upon shadow that spread a canvas of shade across the flowery blanket. On the hillside floor, a carpet of new green growth was fresh, peaceful, and inviting. They both sat on a flowery blanket, pausing for a moment to drink in and enjoy the scenery, to relish the simplicity of being out in the crisp morning air. Izz was impressed with Zuree's noble bearing. There was such poise, such stateliness in her manner as she sat herself down. Before them, the beautiful fields were a visual feast of fragrant groves and gardens loaded with perfumed blossoms and golden fruits. Around them, birds filled the bristling trees, each bird singing its song seemingly just for them. Starlings made their smooth liquid sound warbling, whistling, chattering, and chirping. Songbirds that could not keep still chorused out their series of whispered, peaceful sounds. Parent birds were tweeting back to the peeps of their hungry baby chicks who strained their tiny heads toward them. The magic of spring was in the air, and every living thing seemed to be looking for their soul mates. As Izz watched the children play, a little smile lengthened across his lips as bright, joyful, and warm as the spring sun that was bathing them in its cheerful glow.

"What is it like in Zollerzon where you come from?" Zuree asked with reservation. Her words were spoken with hesitation, and she was careful about what she said. She twirled her fingers through her thick blond hair as she spoke. Her nervousness was contagious.

"Oh, it has its splendor too," Izz replied. "But nothing nearly measures up to the lands of Edawn. I guess you could say I am from Zollerzon, but I grew up all over the southern region of Zia. I lost my parents when I was but a baby." Izz guarded his feeling and also took care to keep his responses short and reserved.

Zuree noted the pain in his eyes, and unthinkingly said, "That is a long trip to take by one's self. The gulf between the two landmasses is vast. You must be good company for yourself."

"Life has demanded that I grow up fast." Izz paused momentarily, just long enough to formulate his thoughts before starting a conversation he believed would be more fitting to the occasion. He began with a few words that spread over a variety of topics, mostly small chitchat about simple pleasantries of inconsequential things of little or no significance. Regardless of his rugged outside appearance, he was a perfect gentleman in every way. He was as noble in his mannerisms and thoughts as any royal. "You have truly led a charmed life." Izz then asked, "What is it like to be a princess, having anything that anyone could ever want for?"

"Sometimes, I think it is more of a burden than a blessing. I often feel trapped between my longing to serve the less fortunate and the duties of being the royal Princess of Edawn. I find more fulfillment in the amazing transformation I see in many of the children here just from feeling a kindhearted human touch and hearing a few words of affection. The medical treatment they require does its part to relieve their pain, but it is compassion and love they so desperately need to treat their souls." Zuree replied as a calm, unusual smile played on her lips that appeared like a veil concealing the mounting pleasure she felt by the closeness of their companionship. *We have so much in common, why not be friends—yes, very close friends,* she almost heard herself say.

As the morning wore on, their conversation varied over an infinite number of subjects. And by and by, there was a disintegration of barriers as their two intricate minds meshed. Most of what Izz said paralleled Zuree's thoughts. They each forgot every self conscious thought. At that very moment, their conversation took a very personal turn. Izz kept the conversation lively by painting pictures in Zuree's mind, telling of his many assorted adventures at sea. She was captivated by the exciting accounts of life in far off places. She hung on every word of his accounts while trying to imagine what it might be like for her to be there.

At the same time, Zuree's words poured out more freely as she studied his reaction carefully. Gone was the restraint she had felt before as words from her heart rolled off her tongue into an increasingly natural, steady, and animated exchange. As he spoke, a marvelous change came to Zuree's eyes. Izz told her many intriguing things, and when he spoke, every word had its tale to tell. Zuree found everything he said was witty, charming, engaging, and made her think of things that had never entered her mind. She listened with an awed adoration that she had once reserved only for her father alone. Izz's eyes twinkled as he called into remembrance his most exciting adventures. She found in Izz a bristling vitality that made him seem so different and so alive.

"It is you that have truly lived a charmed life," Zuree injected and then picked up where Izz left off, continuing to seed her most profound thoughts into Izz's heart. Izz listened with ever increasing interest as if beautiful music wonderfully soothing to his soul tingled in his ears. She found herself talking at great length about everything under the sun. Izz found her highly intelligent and challenging in a reinvigorating sort of way. She spoke of her interests in music and then went on to literature and then the humanities. Before long, her conversation centered on her aspirations and beliefs and dreams of her vision of the world. They matched wits so naturally, and Izz enjoyed her ingenious attempts to outwit him. They grew together in self realization and of one accord as they measured each other's minds and discovered that there was now no doubt they were as much alike as they were different.

Feelings and thoughts intermingled into one another, and they found that they were equal in so many ways, connected at so many levels in many respects. They carried on and laughed together, drawn closer as though it was the most natural thing as if they had known each other forever. Deep in conversation, Zuree seemed to be able to perceive many of Izz's thoughts as effortlessly as he could hers. They were so like minded that, before long, they were finishing each other's sentences. And Izz very nearly knew what Zuree was thinking almost before she did. They were enjoying every moment, free of unnecessary thoughts. It became one of those days where time just flew by with incredible speed but seemed would never end. The pleasurable feeling of being so near the princess began to seep to the surface. Although Izz had taken so much care not to betray the feelings that steadily dislodged from his will and drew him under the princess' charming spell, suddenly, Izz had to pause to press his lips tightly over his resolve not to dare speak of the dream he had had of her. The more urgently he strived to hide his adoration, the more brilliantly and distinctly his exultation showed within him. They were about to find themselves.

The green grass and the light blue sky suddenly seemed to intensify the astonishing color of Zuree's eyes. Izz tried distracting himself by looking away to refocus. Zuree followed Izz's gaze to where two bushy tailed squirrels were affectionately chasing each other around the base of the next oak tree. They both spontaneously drew a shuddering breath at the same moment.

Then Zuree and Izz both turned at the same time to stare into each other's eyes for the longest time. Zuree had a pleasing, happy look upon her face as she bore another piece of her soul. And suddenly, Izz consciously realized that he was the reason her jubilant smile was there. Izz felt a surge of very strong affection welling up from the deepest part of him. *She feels for me what I feel for her. Great,* he thought to himself. It was arrogance, yes. He knew they were of two different breeds: she was a princess, and he was a modest man from a very different world, which she knew absolutely about nothing. Before inheriting the shop, the only land he had ever owned was the one caked to his boots. And yet, surely to let such beautiful fantasies dwell in his heart was a forgivable transgression. He had no better excuse for his lack of common sense than that.

They continued to engage in conversation with such enthusiasm that soon they were teasing and joking around. Zuree's sense of humor matched Izz's. And soon, they were laughing at the slightest jest, and it was almost as if they were laughing for the sake of laughing. And they laughed and laughed until tears filled their eyes.

All at once, Zuree realized that this was one of the few times in her life she had talked to someone genuinely interested in her opinions, her feelings, and her beliefs, and it seemed as if it had been forever since she had shared genuine laughter with anyone. Izz was different, unlike most other people who pretended to listen, while they concentrated on what they were going to say next and anticipating the first opportunity to turn the conversation back to themselves. He struck her as being well informed, even scholarly, although she could not for the life of her seem to imagine him ever opening and reading a book. Zuree had never met anyone like Izz, and there was still very little she actually knew about him. She scarcely knew anything about his past and nothing of what was in his heart. Why was she so concerned with such things, and why was she so attracted to him? She had heard of love at first sight. Could that be the result of what she was experiencing now in his presence? Izz saw the fracture in the defensive barrier Zuree had raised around her heart, and his heart had every intention of widening it.

But suddenly, everything changed in an instant, when out of nowhere a horde of children came running toward them. Their tinkling laughter and pattering feet followed with them, breaking the calm like a herd of wild mongooses. The orphans gathered, standing all around like a flock of baby ducklings. Their eyes gleamed with delight. They carried wreaths they had woven from beautiful wild white and orange marigolds and red and blueberries. Buzu came forward and placed a crown on Izz's head and another on Zuree's. Zuree allowed two elated youngsters to pull her to her feet and out onto the rolling green grass. At the same time, Buzu ran up to Izz, touched his head with a colorful sponge ball, and, with a gleeful shout, informed him, "You have been tagged Izz!" She then dropped the ball on to his lap as she scurried off, running behind the nearest tree. There was a scramble. Children, especially orphans, were used to making up games with what was on hand. It was a similar amusement Izz was familiar with, one he had learned as a child in his orphanage. The one tagged had to tap someone with the ball without throwing it to be freed. Teasing children engaged fully in the spirited game buzzed all around him like bees around a hive. The persistent giggling and calling out to him, punctuated by Zuree's merry mood and deep, ceaseless laughter, taunted Izz.

"All right!" Izz laughed out loud and set his mind to play. "If it is a frolic you want, a frolic you shall have!"

"Oh, yes!" they all shouted out with one accord.

The children were blissfully happy. Merry children found great pleasure in the game of lighthearted pursuit as they ran to and fro with bursts of laughter bubbling over the edge. Players raced fast and nimble from tree to tree in the wild game they had started. Chirping birds flew off in all directions, and squirrels scampered up nearby trees as Izz darted after Buzu. She knew the area well, and her nimbleness more than made up for her lack of speed. An outbreak of held back snickers gave away her hiding place. Izz cornered Buzu against the tree. There was no escape. Izz stooped down low in a hunch and pretended to be a wild bear. He began to growl and froth as he crept toward little Buzu. Between her screams and shrills, she resonated with chuckles and glee. She erupted in laughter when Izz swept her up into his arms and gathered her into a big bear hug. Izz nibbled at her cheeks, this turned into little kisses, causing Buzu to hold her head up high. Her eyes danced with delight as she expelled a long infectious giggle.

"You are still it Izz, because you cannot tag the person that tagged you!" Buzu triumphantly informed Izz. *Had she just made that up?* Izz wondered as Zuree threw her head back and gave a full, vigorous laugh filled with genuine amusement. Her laughter was sweet and pure as refreshing as the early morning dew. The sound of it was so delightful, almost lyrical. Izz put Buzu on the ground and turned his attention to Zuree, whose face was alive with laughter. His target was now Zuree. Without warning, he lunged after her, but even as she protested, she wanted him to chase her. Finally, at the last minute, before Izz reached her, she turned and bolted in the other direction, like a happy child, irresistibly cackling and bubbling over with joy. She was in the prime of her life and seemed to overflow with energy. She had easily been able to cleverly evade Izz's first attempt to tag her. She was the perfect example of womanly poise and intellect. There was a natural sway to her hips as she ran, an unpracticed grace that was innately appealing as she dashed behind a tree and gave Izz that catch me if you can look. Izz ran toward her, attempting to cut off her escape. When Izz closed in on her, Zuree was laughing so hard that she forgot to lift the fringes of her long dress. As she ran away, she tried to change directions. Her feet tangled in the flurry of her skirt, and she lost her balance as she turned.

Consequently and quite unexpectedly, they both lost their footing, and together they came stumbling down onto the soft cotton grass. They both exploded with laughter. Zuree turned to one side as she fell. She was laughing so hard that it sent jiggles through her flesh to the core of her soul. What an exhilarating feeling it was to laugh, so jovially that neither of them could catch their breath. Izz unintentionally landed over Zuree, pinning her hands above her head, immobilizing her under him. His legs sprawled over hers, coming as close as two hearts and souls could get. Zuree was instantly aware of the heat of his body. Izz found himself nestled intimately against Zuree with her breast crushed against his chest, and the juncture of her thighs against his. She was filled with a warmth that doubled the searing heat from Izz's body. Fiery feelings of prohibited passion infused profound feelings of awakening from her upper and lower body too. Zuree sucked in a breath and let out a nervous giggle that stopped halfway in her throat as she struggled to hold back a quickening rush of sensation far more profound than she had ever known possible. She plummeted fast into a state of confusion. Everything she felt was careening too swift and surprising for her. With their hearts entangled, Zuree permitted her body full contact with his. They both froze for a lengthening moment, and then another, and then another. Neither nether able to move.

His profound eyes fixed on her. She lifted her gaze to his for a moment, and Zuree's eyes told Izz he had her right where she longed to be. She had to stop staring into his agate, dark eyes so she could recapture her balance. But instead of finding her footing, her eyes locked into the depths of a great distance beyond Izz's jet black orb. And there was not much left unsaid between their souls. Suddenly, everything else around them seemed so irrelevant and unimportant. Each happily focused on the amplifying rhythm of each other's hearts as the feeling intensified with each passing moment. Zuree smiled up at Izz as her essence radiated as a jeweled rose in bloom. She was a striking beauty. Izz smiled back down at Zuree, and she felt the sudden warmth of his smile like a flame within her. Still, neither made any endeavor to move from under, or from above. Once again, they found themselves froze, eye to eye, nose to nose, and mouth to mouth. Their full length touching was like stoking a furnace. The gratification his touch gave amazed her. In the too vivid light of day, the sun caught the brightening profoundness of Zuree's eyes and, for a fleeting second, cast a distinct ray within their depths that illuminated each facet into a dazzling glow of such stunning beauty. Its twinkling sunbeams created soft, rich, creamy shadows beneath her high cheekbones and down the length of her delicate neck as smooth as the enticing silkiness of satin. Warm as the gentle kiss of the sun, Izz's winded breath stirred little wisps of golden hair that fell over her forehead and near her eyes that shimmered in the brilliant sunlight. Izz could feel the sweetness of Zuree's respiration soft against his face, becoming his with every breath. Her skin smelled of sweet frankincense. But just beyond her perfume, Izz sensed somewhere in his innermost perception no more than the slightest remnant of her feminine essence as she pleasantly smoldered beneath him. It was a fragrance more alluring than he had ever known and never to be forgotten. In each other's arms, sensations within flesh and blood were enslaved and could not be rebuked. Yet the moment had been untainted, flawless, abounding in innocent's purity, and guiltless love.

Their eyes remained fixed; neither spoke nor drew breath. Izz's eyes were dark, deepening ponds, and at once, Zuree knew that she could have been so quickly plunged adrift in their vastness. Zuree's heart heaved with a jerk, and she felt the blood flush to her face. Something startling seized Izz with the overwhelming power of what he felt for her. Zuree was frightened and marveled at the same time. She willed with all her common sense to hold off the breathtaking impressions rushing through the wide, unbolted door to her heart.

Somewhere within the deepest corners of her intelligence, she knew that permitting this to linger was inviting the most colossal of follies. But yet, at the same time, the tantalizing new sensations surged wave after wave, coursing across, over, and through her, jolting her with the delight it gave. With each throb of her heart, her senses swung back and forth like a pendulum from befitting and unfitting, from wrong to right, from yes to no. Suddenly, a note of caution sounded in Izz's mind as he paused to reconsider: this was the daughter of the king. But Izz could not have moved even if he had wanted to. His legs and arms felt weighted down as if he had drunk too much wine. As through his will, like a magnet to steel, had been drawn into the innermost depths of the heart of love. Zuree felt the emanation of Izz's manliness drowning her, filling every empty space, as her instincts rotated down a spiraling undertow of overwhelming, primitive, animal magnetism. Her flush deepened with such mixed feelings. This time the quivers rippled all the way to the tips of her toes. Izz could now feel Zuree's heart fluttering like the wings of a captured hummingbird in her beneath him.

He hopelessly tried to quell the intense rush of ecstasy, radiating and powerful, that felt as if his very soul was bursting inside out. He may as well have tried to change the direction of the sun. With every extending moment, tiny electric bolts sparked through both, bristling wherever they came together and touched, sending energy and warmth rippling in every direction across an endless sea of passion. Zuree had never been this close to a man, and Izz's lack of worldliness just barely allowed him to understand what was happening to him. Both were of age, and yet they were so like children in their virtue and inexperience. Nevertheless, it was a magical, eternal moment that existed somewhere in a perfect universe without end.

Izz watched the play of emotions crossing Zuree's face as she lifted a hand to brush the hair from her eyes. He sensed that something extraordinary must be happening, something bigger than both of them, so real and powerful that it could have realigned the planets. The lightning of true lovestruck, even though a kiss and the word *love* were their forbidden fruit. Zuree fought the urge to reach out and pull him down and crushing him to her. And once again, Izz wished with all his heart that he could utter the words that begged to be spoken. His soul ached, his heart throbbed, and his tongue smoldered with the words of his affection, he could not urge past his lips. He understood the truth, and it was hopeless to deny it.

Finally, the taunting of his restless dreams had, at last, eclipsed his waking world. He slowly lowered his head down, moistening his lips as his mind submerged into an odd kind of haze. Zuree's head was spinning. No one in her life, and in such a short time, had ever made her feel so alive and so carefree and so spontaneous. While the last grain of sense slipped past Zuree's self possession, she closed her eyes tightly and tried to keep them closed as she bore her heart in a way that was altogether new to her. But finally, she had to look up at him. As she looked up with an expression of anticipation and approval, she heard her heart whisper; *You will forever love this man. You will bare his children.* Her eyes sparkled like gems on her smiling face as she half wondered from where the voice had come. She wet her lips with a desire she barely knew existed.

The feel of the incredible length of her loveliness, the fragrance of her embodiment, the sweet nectar of her breath, and the strong honeyed musky scent of her essential nature, sent his bowels bristling up his loins. There it was again, the same smile that Izz had seen in his dream. The smile that made him believe anything was possible. Izz took a deep breath and closed his eyes. With the next heartbeat, he seemed to somehow slip out of himself. In his mind, he watched as his lips continued their descent. Souls were searching, hearts pounding, emotions colliding. The sun shimmered in a bright golden glaze above. Birds sang, and little woodland animals peeped out of their hiding to see what seemed to be electrifying the atmosphere. The sound of leaves in the breeze swept trees fluttering all around them. And as their lips came closer and closer, they listened to the pounding rhythm of their hearts slamming up against each other. Distant laughter of children, just barely audible, reached their hearing as children started coming out of their hiding places to stare and wonder if Izz and Zuree had been injured in the fall in some way.

Suddenly, out of nowhere, the beautiful, perfect, iridescent bubble that had engulfed both of them, burst with a snap into countless evaporating shades of blue and red and purple fragments by the sound of someone clearing their throat. The unexpected disruption abruptly snatched them away from their blissful spell. The intrusion was like a chilling splash of icy water waking them from their entrancing flight of abandonment. They both abruptly repositioned themselves back from the reality of the there and then to the appropriateness of moral order in the here and now.

Izz and Zuree froze. Each looked to the other and saw only their own personal stunned surprise mirrored in the other. Both were thoroughly lost in the other's attention up to the very moment when they had realized they were being watched. Gone were their childish giggles, their smiles disappeared, their happy glow faded. Even the bright sun seemed to have suddenly ducked behind a dark cloud. Izz tried to get up but only slumped back against Zuree. The astonished headmistress could not keep herself from grumbling. Finally, after what seemed like a thousand eternities, both leaped to their feet like recoiling springs. They brushed the grass and dry leaves from their hair and clothes, feeling as found out as two June bugs unearthed from under a stone. Both wishing a hole would open in the ground and swallow them up. Izz gave the mistress a nonchalant, guilty as charged grin and even had the grace to look slightly shamefaced. Zuree, who had jumped up just as quickly, stood there tangled up inside with the flowers of her makeshift crown falling around her head in cascading disarray. Her knees wobbled as she straightened up. Zuree wiped the hair out of her eyes as she let out a deep sigh of discomposure, feeling like a child caught misbehaving. She laughed nervously as her skin flushed with unmistakable embarrassment as she tried to hide her mortification behind a broken smile that fell into a lopsided grin. And she too looked just as guilty as the mistress's eye charged. The children had gathered all around. The echo of laughter was everywhere as they stared, winked, and pointed at what seemed suddenly whimsical to them.

It was amazing how an individual's condition of mind could alter the discernment of time. It had all been over in just a few moments but seemed to encompass a lifetime. Among the tiny slivers of the splintered moment lay the evidence of love too powerful and too real to be denied, and regardless of the appearance of inappropriateness, Zuree and Izz somehow understood that they had absolutely no reason to feel ashamed.

The mistress announced with a somber tone, "All is ready. Will you join us, or do you two have other plans?" Their compromising posture reflected their current state of mind as they both concurred, first nodding, and then quickly shaking their heads.

No words were said between the two. They both just looked straight ahead as they walked toward the feast, each surrounded by children who were still wondering why the two were looking so wounded even though they both seemed uninjured. Izz walked, looking into his empty head with a broken arrow of love embedded in his heart. The mood was shattered beyond recovery.

They sat at separate tables and ate quietly. Now and then, Izz gave Zuree a sideways glance to see if she was looking at him looking at her. And now and then, she cast a fleeting glance back at him with a half glimpse and then stared straight ahead. After a while, Izz was sure she was intentionally averting his eye contact. She seemed self conscious now as though Izz had somehow seen her unclothed, and now they could nevermore, by any means, go back to just being acquaintances again in the same way as before.

As the day wore on, a peculiar heaviness settled in their chests. For the longest time, neither dared look back at the other, not even when they felt the other's eyes longingly glancing their way. It was the end of something very beautiful. Something neither had ever felt before, even more intense than any earlier encounter between them. All that seemed so right kept going so wrong. Izz kept casting a remorseful glance at Zuree out of the corner of his eyes, hoping to see her looking back at him. They had shared an intimate moment, and an eternal bond had been entwined. That was what destiny had inadvertently given them, a gift so hallowed that even Izz could not be permitted to comprehend what it meant. But now that she was away from him, sitting there in effect alone, she felt uncertain. Zuree had no clear response to fall back on, not having any previous experience to compare. She had to think, to assess the situation, to sort out impulse from the facts. She had never been affected by anyone in this way, not even by Rizan. She had to ask herself if such a thing was even becoming of her. She had been a willing accomplice.

Where had her common sense taken flight? She had permitted her full body contact with his, a virtual stranger. Was she behaving like an imprudent lassie? Was she just a stop along his way, just another conquest? After all, he had been a sailor, and she had heard all those wild stories about sailors. Had it all only been a perfected trick? Zuree had no answer. She began to feel uncomfortable over her wanton reaction, vexed by the unfamiliar emotions that had so overwhelmingly conquered her. She was exasperated with herself, feeling more than a little foolish. It was too illogical for words. After all, she was a princess, not a gullible, naive girl. As well, I am betrothed to Rizan. She did not expect that confirmation to pain her so, although it suddenly did. Her heartfelt all at once wounded.

Meanwhile, Izz was having trouble taking the thrashing his heart was beating out. His thoughts turned inwardly. Had she lured him into an entanglement that would promise the undoing of his heart? He felt perplexed, unable to understand anything anymore. The conflict between head and heart, intellect, and nature were warring within. The rest of the day was a burr spent watching the children frolicking joyously in the sun as they engaged in their energetic games, singing scratchy phrases, and giggling between their songs. Zuree silently ate as she listened to the joyous glee and exclamations from the orphanage staff on how perfectly delicious everything was. The festivities wore on finally dissolved in closing laughter. Everyone bid one another their last farewells as they headed their separate ways. And everyone seemed refreshed with a renewed zest for life, except for the two that needed it most.

On Izz's way home, he wondered over every detail of what had happened and wondered if Zuree might, at that very moment, be thinking about him too. The memory of his stolen moments close to Zuree filled him with amazement. He could hardly regret the encounter. The meeting had been more precious to him than any reward in Zia. He could not, however, make sense of how this young maiden could have so effortlessly affected him so profoundly. All he knew for sure was how he felt when she smiled the way she had just a short time ago, precisely as she had in his dream. Yet it seemed all too whimsical to believe. But at the same time, somehow, it seemed to all be falling into its place. He shuddered, knowing no emotion in his heart had been left unstirred. Izz mounted his cart and all the way home; he felt that he had become trapped in an impossible situation.

At the same time on Zuree's coach ride back to the palace, she too was struggling to unravel what had come over her. She had been reminding herself for the thousandth time that what she thought she remembered as reality was simply a fluke. It had to have been an accidental mixture of circumstances that could never be duplicated in a million years. The sunshine, the fresh air, the laughter, the flowers, the birds, and the merriment all joined to make her for a time momentarily crazed. That had not been Princess Zuree pinned under the carpenter. It had been someone else, and she did not recognize that girl that wanted recklessly to melt her lips into the lips of a man she hardly even knew. But somewhere during the hour, she was forced to be honest. She turned her thoughts to Izz. Her feelings for him were, at best, a tangled mass of contradiction. Who could tell whether one particular moment of irresistible attraction would grow or fade away with the passing days? Zuree tried to think about Rizan, but the harder she tried, the more her thoughts were drawn back to Izz. Who was this man, who was so opposite of her, but could so quickly awaken her heart and unlock an intrinsic part of her she never knew existed? There were too many unanswered questions. Zuree shook her head in an attempt to loosen herself of the memory of Izz. Perhaps things would have been otherwise in another world, in another life, in another time, under different circumstances.

That night as Izz lay in bed, remembering everything, as a weak smile danced around his lips. He could not imagine it actually happened as he remembered the sound of her voice, the feel of her embodiment, the smell of her girlish skin. He allowed thoughts that had no words to flow on their own accord and just watched and listened to the shuffling and filing in his head as if a magical hand was stirring a basin of liqueur about in his brain. He could not put a name on the feelings he had experienced, but he knew they went much deeper than mere carnal longings. Izz knew that Zuree had bestowed upon him something very sacred, but even after much thought, Izz still could not penetrate the substance of it. He ran his fingers through his thick black hair, thinking of how he had never met anyone quite like her. He concluded Zuree was the living image of the girl in his dreams. The one he longed to be with. Wishful thinking, perhaps, but he found himself hoping it was so with all that he was.

Then, unexpectedly, he heard a laughing voice inside his head say, *You insignificant FOOL. In a very short time, the princess Zuree's hand will be given in marriage to King Rizan. She is merely toying with your doltish heart. The cruel joke is on you, you pathetic, imbecilic fool.* His thoughts clattered and shuddered in discord, sending tiny fissures throughout from top to bottom, inside and out. All at once, his heart broke! At that moment, he felt as if his heart were being hacked to pieces, and in the silence, he could feel his heart coming apart. Retched heart, what was the reason he could not stop thinking about her this night. In that instant, Izz saw the image of his disillusioned hopes and dreams suddenly shatter and fall away like tingling pieces of glass cascading onto the floor below. His dying dream lay on the ground among the dusty remnant of decay. In the next heartbeat, before those thoughts even had a chance to complete, in a fit of delirium, unable to relinquish his precious dream, he saw a thought thrust upon his mind of him dropping to his knees. He saw himself pursuing the pieces of his treasured dream with a mad passion. In his mind he scurried to gather the hemorrhaging shards like a blind vagabond who had suddenly heard the chime of golden coins jingling and rolling away cast on the walkway by a rich man.

With his mangled love recovered, the illusion vanished as his mind argued with the feelings in his heart. And even though his heart was shattered into a billion fragmented pieces, he was astonished that he still loved her with every broken piece. Izz knew that somehow, in some way, it was right. That is what he wanted to believe. With all his heart, he wanted to believe. And for what seemed like more than a fleeting eternity, Izz became frightened by the power of what he allowed himself to feel for Zuree. She is promised to another. The voice returned the fatal sound of his shattered dream. He agonized over the fact that Zuree could never return his affection. He had not wanted to fall in love, yet he had utterly opened his heart without hope of ever having anything to show for it. Heartbreak is the price he would have to pay for dreaming.

Why! O why, O why could he not learn from his mistakes. Why did he seem to have the knack of being more interested in what he could never have, instead of being satisfied with what he could have? Even if he had wanted to fall in love, and he was more than sure, he did not. One of any of the beautiful daughters presented to him at the banquet would undoubtedly accept him, not to mention Zophie, who he was actually quite fond of and she of him. At least they came from the same cut of fabric. Izz's thoughts just fell apart. His soul felt like an empty crater, and his heartfelt like a vacuumed space. After a while, his profound sense of pain was beginning to decrease, and finally, he was able to tune out the pangs altogether. He lay still, and soon, he fell asleep, and without his conscious mind to stand guard over his heart, his innermost mind allowed his heart to blaze brilliantly in the darkness, with love for Zuree, long into the dead of night.

At about the same hour, awakening from a restless sleep, Zuree felt a jarring jolt of disharmony rattle her to the depths of her soul. Zuree's heart trembled as her head fell back against her downy white pillow. She caught her breath as memories of Izz pour over her. Then she too was comforted by her heart and went back to sleep, smiling as she slept. Zuree woke early the next morning to the rays of the sun flooding in through the seams in the heavy blue draped satin that intertwined under curtained windows. Izz's memory lingered like a soft love song playing in her mind. It was unlike any song she had ever heard before. It was more like a pleasing succession of harmonious tones and arrangements of rhythmic sounds. Zuree rubbed the sleep from her eyes and climbed out of her white gold framed bed. She washed her face with refreshingly cool water and lavender scented soap. She dressed quickly and slipped her shoes on. She walked alone down the brightly lit hallway. Zuree hurried down through a maze of corridors into a high rise hall that extended through the depth of the palace that eventually led to the queen's bedchamber. Her purposeful footsteps clicked on the marble floor, echoing hollowly throughout the long high walled hallway. In the early morning hour, the entire length of passage was brightly lit by gold and silver, candled chandeliers, jeweled with multifaceted crystal. Each cast a glimmering deluge of luster that sent prisms of brilliant colors flashing over the white stone walls. On the panels that rose to arched vaults, high overhead, costly varicolored tapestries hung between glittering golden mosaics and rich velvet draperies. The marmoreal floors, inlaid with colored alabaster set in brilliant geometric designs, were so highly polished that it reflected Zuree's image before her as she neared the queen's chambers.

When Zuree reached her mother's door, she put one palm and her ear to the massive carved doors, hoping that her mother, the queen, was not busy. She stood quietly for a moment, nervously chewing her lower lip, trying to visualize the right questions that she needed an answer to, answers that would not dash her hopes or break her heart. With determination firmly in place, she reached for the brass handle and cracked the door open. She wanted to get this over with. It was only going to become more difficult the longer she put off. Zuree peered in to see the queen seated, surrounded by servants that were grooming her hair, manicuring her finger, and giving her toenails a pedicure. The air inside was heavy with the scents of beautiful flowers. Oil lamps cast rings of light that filled the room with a golden glow.

When Queen Zahra saw her daughter standing at the partly opened door, she called out, "Zuree!" She waved the servants away as she came to her feet and advanced with outreached arms to meet her beloved daughter.

The inner palace servants all submissively scattered to go about their other daily tasks. The queen received Zuree graciously with a warm embrace and said, "I am delighted to see you." And she meant it for she adored her only child with all her heart. "It seems that you have been much too busy lately, and I have missed you so." She then held Zuree out at arm's length and gave her a lingering look, her eyes soft with the light of love. She stared at Zuree as if for the first time and saw a younger imprint of herself. "Just look at you. You have come of proper age. You are no longer a child. When I first laid eyes on you, you were the prettiest little maiden with the prettiest golden hair in the entire world. And now, in the twinkling of an eye, it would seem that you have passed into womanhood. Where have the years gone?" How had her little princess possibly managed to grow up so fast? "My precious rosebud has suddenly bloomed into a beautiful flower."

"I am my mother's daughter," Zuree said proudly.

Queen Zahra fell into a deep silence for a fleeting moment, as if reminiscing a distant faded memory for the first time further back than she wished to remember. "When I was your age, I was already married, with you, already clinging to my skirt." That thought made her smile. She closed her eyes and smiled a long flamboyant smile. A while later, she said, "I was once reputed to be the most beautiful maiden in all the land to the four ends of Zia. Adored by countless champions and nobles, the most powerful men in Xylenia knelt before me and sought my hand, long ago, in my youth." Stunning eyes that had won her a court of suitors sparkled with remembrance. The queen moved and stood before a full length mirror, her hourglass figure had defied time, and her skin was still as smooth and unworried as a girl's.

"Mother, you are still the loveliest of lovely women," Zuree said very enthusiastically. "You have only deepened in beauty."

"Bless you, my child. I believe you speak in earnest. But I know all too well that I am getting older. I know that aging is the natural order of life."

"The years have been extremely kind to you, Mother."

"You are truly your mother's sainted daughter. Now, what has brought you to me this beautiful morning? I have noticed you have not quite been yourself these past few days. Even now, you look as if you carry a heavy load." The queen then took Zuree's hand, stepped over to her bed, and sat her next to her. She put her arm around her waist and gently pulled her against her. There was a time when there was nothing Zuree did not confide in her, but lately, she seldom shared what was on her mind. She had become silent and had kept to herself of late, and even though she had not asked, she wondered what was disturbing her. Finally, the queen asked pointedly, "Now, please tell me what is on your mind. What is wrong?"

"Nothing and everything," Zuree answered as her bright smile faded a degree. Everything that had been so clear in her mind just moments before suddenly became jumbled, as she leaped from one effort of laying the first thoughtful stone to another. One moment she exactly knew what she wanted to say, and the next moment she felt that part of her brain had all of a sudden gone gray as if a murky cloud had overshadowed it. Many thoughts raced and crowded into the forefront of her mind as she tried to figure out where to start. Zuree hesitated, carefully considering for a moment what she was about to say while she contemplated how her mother might react. She took a deep breath, laced up her slender fingers, and then spoke in a rush, "Well, I was just wondering." Zuree paused and started over again. "I know you were betrothed...that is promised to father by your father, and I was just curious as to how you felt about that." She held her breath as she waited for her mother's response.

The queen's eyes took on a dreamlike expression as the years rolled back in her mind for more years than she cared to remember. She recalled in every vivid detail the magical encounter with the king of her heart. "Your father was powerfully built with a long thick stock of black hair, and he came from the lineage of Xylen, the greatest king of all time. There was a presence about him that made other men mere shadows. Your father was more than handsome; he was magnificent. When I first saw him, I loved him almost at once, as I love him still." As she spoke, she ran her slender finger along the length of a strand of diamonds and pearls dangling from her elegant neck. "I remember as if it were yesterday. I was scarcely out of girlhood. I was so young, and there was so much I had yet to do with my life. At first, I felt like a frightened little girl, so afraid that I would regret our union. But the longer I knew your father, the deeper I fell in love with him. I wish for you from the depth of my heart, the same fate, for the only thing that can make the soul whole is true love."

"That is exactly why I have come to seek your wisdom, Mother."

"And what exactly would that be?"

"Love. True love, to be exact. For the first time…" Zuree bit down on her lip as the words tried to come out of her mouth.

The queen covered Zuree's hand with her own and drew her closer. "In the matters of the heart, love is a beautiful, fragile flower, endowed with irresistible attraction. It pulls like iron magnetized to the allure of its power. Only love can make a woman perfectly willing to surrender herself up, body and soul, without giving the future a second thought."

When the queen spoke, she presumed that Zuree was referring to her feelings for King Rizan, her betrothed. "Oh yes, you are so blessed indeed, child. I felt the same thing. Rizan comes from one of the finest families in all Zia. He is handsome beyond words, rich, powerful, and wiser than his years. He abounds with strength, yet I have noticed when you are together, he is as gentle as a lamb. His softhearted manner disguises a warrior's greatest power. And he loves you so much. Many times I have seen the way Rizan watches you when you do not notice. It is most definitely true love."

Zuree bowed her head in apprehension. "He was my first love. The man I wanted to marry when I was a child, but it is just not the same," she whispered in a challenging tone. "That is...Mother, I am not exactly sure that I still feel the same way about Rizan as I did when I was a girl. Oh, I know he is a kind, sweet soul, but I am not so sure that I love him," Zuree cautiously spoke as if she could not trust what she was saying.

The queen gave her a quizzical look.

My heart has betrothed itself to another, Zuree tested the words silently that could potentially free her from the chains that bound her. If she could win her mother to her side, together, they could perhaps sway her father, the king.

The queen looked Zuree in the eye. "What is there not to love? He is the youngest king in the empire, the ruler of Ziyon-topia, the greatest gem in all of Zia."

Zuree rotated her eyes. "I know, Mother. I know." Exasperation filled an expelled groan.

"Have you lost your senses, child?" The Queen's voice was gruff.

Zuree was surprised at the accusation in her mother's voice. *Bare with me, Mother. Let us talk about it more, she thought, so I might make you see why you and Father are wrong.* "I know I care for Rizan deeply, but not in the way a woman should love a man she wants to spend the rest of her life with," Zuree announced.

"It is the custom of royalty to select their spouse objective-ly, and love many times must be a secondary consideration. A successful union sometimes has nothing to do with the sentiments of the heart. You are simply feeling the same jitters I felt when anticipating the approach of my wedding day," the queen said while Zuree considered a new strategy.

Zuree was about to ask that question whose answer might prove contemptuous. Zuree proudly raised her chin and asked,

"Should it not be my divine right to choose whom I love? Whom I marry?"

The queen's brow wrinkled with concern. "Love is not often the main reason for royal marriages." She repeated as if to convince herself as much. She remembered that there had been many times when she had longed to talk to her mother concerning her doubts but had always reasoned her way around it.

Zuree restrained a defeated little grin at her mother's response, but she could not hide the teary mist that shined in her eyes. Things were not going quite as she planned.

"Is there something you are not telling me?" The queen patted Zuree's hand.

Zuree felt she had said too much already. Suddenly the memory of her stolen moments close to Izz in the garden and his shop came to her. Every sight, every sound, every smell, every sensation leaped back into her anew. She suppressed a shudder. Now was the time to speak out, to proclaim what her heart wanted to cry out with every beat. But how could she? The wonder of it all was beyond the bounds of impossible to put into thoughts, let alone explain in words. Finally, she pushed her hair back behind her ear, and she spoke vehemently, "There is no easy way to say this...I have met someone. It was one of the most truly wonderful moments of my life. I have never known such contentment. It is something that I never intended to happen to me, but now that it has, I need some time to think about what it all means."

"Who is this person you speak of, and by what powers has he bewitched you?"

"It is Izz, the carpenter from Zollerzon." Her eyes sparkled as she said his name.

"Izz...! The carpenter, Izz?"

"I know, believe me, I know. If anyone had told me days ago that I would soon be hopelessly in love with a commoner, I would have been exceedingly offended. Instead, now I feel deeply exalted t have met this young man. No one has ever made me feel as happy as I do when I am with him. He kindles my heart in ways that no one else has ever done. It is almost as if we were meant to be together as if he was my soul mate or something."

"I never thought I would ever hear such a confession come from your lips. I can see in your eyes how you feel about the foreigner. But the truth is he comes from a different world, from a rougher, earthier, more common world. The distance between the two of you could never be bridged." Queen Zahra raised her arm around her daughter's shoulder and gave her a consoling hug. "I am sorry if that hurts you. But you have pushed me to say it."

"What you and Father are asking for is a utilitarian merger, not a marriage." Zuree's voice was defiant.

Sensing the tension of an argument in the air and knowing she was helpless to protect her daughter from a broken heart, she tried reasoning with her. "You must understand you were born royal, and that means you can marry only someone of your own class," the queen spoke very matter of factually about such things.

"Is it possible that you do not perceive how unjust, how unkind, it would be to marry someone I did not love with all my heart?"

Zahra considered the question for a moment and then said softly, "I understand, but you must realize that there is absolutely nothing that can be done. If I thought there was even one chance in a million, I would point you in that direction, but you would have a better chance of keeping the sea from rushing onto the shore or stopping the sun from traversing the heavens."

"How important could a vow be?"

"The king's word is his bonding covenant with his people. Royal marriages in countless times past have been arranged in this manner. Your father, the king, has pledged your hand to Rizan before the Assembly of Nobles in the Court of Kings. He might as well have vowed before the whole world of Zia. It is, in essence, an unbreakable promise."

"I am the king's daughter. How could he care more about tradition than he does about my happiness? I cannot just simply erase the things I feel."

"I have no answers," the queen said. "I try not to have any questions either. I do know without a doubt that you are the apple of your father's eye. Though he may get upset with you, from time to time, even when he rebukes you, he has only your best interest at heart. Next time you confront your father, you would do well to try charm; it is a weapon women employ very well. But when all is said and done, you must remember that he has given his word. He might just as well have opened a vein and signed his pledge in blood."

"And my father should remember this is my heart," Zuree whispered under her breath, but she knew that the arrangement was a done deal and could not be undone without dishonoring her father before his people. She did not want to face it, but she knew the one thing she wanted most of all, she could not have.

To avoid unpleasantness, she forced her most charming smile. Zuree realized that it would be hopeless to challenge the traditions of the countless generations of her forefathers. It was not meant that she and Izz should be together. In a faint, wavering whisper, she affirmed, "I shall not dishonor my father's name. I will marry whom he wills." She had given her promised vow to Rizan, and was she not obligated to honor that? Her loyalty was as important to her as her integrity and saw plainly now that she could not break her word. Her acknowledgment was so compelling and inevitable that it had the force of doom. Her mother had taught her all too well the honorable qualities a royal princess should possess: taught her by example, not by lecture. Zuree's duty had, at that moment, been set in stone in her hardening heart.

"Child, do not fret yourself. Even if you find that you do not truly love him, he will love you enough for both of you. Rizan is a wonderful man in every way, and even if he turned out to be a mistake, he would be a mistake worth making. But no matter what, I know you are of the sort who gives warmth to everything that you touch. You are the type who loves with your whole heart, and happiness is sure to follow you wherever you may go." Her reassuring tone had always been so full of faith.

Zuree allowed the built up tension inside her to drain away. She knew what her mother said was proper. Her mother's soft spoken words carried with them the truth and wisdom of the ages. Zuree's lips pressed together in a tight line, while those thoughts revolved in consolidating loops in her head. She nodded slowly, "It is best. I see now that I have been acting like a moonstruck child."

"This is your destiny, and you must not tempt the hand of fate. Fulfill your destiny wherever it may take you." Her voice was as reassuring as a proverbial foretelling.

"Sometimes, I think you have more faith in me than I have in myself. I believe that you know what is best for me because you love me more than anyone."

Zuree let out a deep sigh of acceptance as she reassured herself that she would be better off, in the long run, as Rizan's queen. It would be a more secure life, a more satisfying life. After all, she was betrothed to a king and fast was approaching the day of their union. If this was the right thing to do, then why did that thought pierced her heart like an icy barb. A list of what ifs and possible consequences seemed to endlessly bounce back and forth between her guarded thoughts and her heart. Zuree suddenly felt lost, as if she had been cast into a deep foreboding sea a thousand miles from the nearest shore. She covered up every trace of her lack of faith with a crooked smile. She bowed her head and resigned to her fate. Her mind whirled with conflicting emotions as she lowered her head onto her mother's lap, calling on her mother's strength because hers was waning. Zuree continued smiling even though her heart was breaking as the queen smoothed a few loose strands of hair from her face and caressed her cheek, attempting to comfort her resales heart. Inevitably, the deep currents of royal blood that flowed through Zuree's veins pulled her back into a sense of moral obligation to the established standards of her noble lineage. Zuree closed her eyes as if she could hide her heart away and, for the moment, be her mother's little girl once again.

Sixteen

The Lost Crown

The world of Zia turned, and the face of the moon changed, and the prized tree trunk was almost at the end of its long, arduous journey. With just days left to wait, Izz was feeling anxious for its anticipated arrival. It had been days since he had seen or heard from Zuree. One day, unable to sleep, he woke and got up an hour earlier than necessary. He ate alone breakfast, wondering why he was up so early. He needed something to fill the awkward, vacant hour. From time to time, he would take a long walk along the beach to reevaluate his life, sort out his feelings, and reawaken his inner spirit. He packed a light lunch and headed for Edawn's seashore. Maybe a brisk walk along the shoreline would calm his nerves down and help him think things out, help him to make sense out of all that had happened to him recently, and what was happening inside him regarding Zuree. When Izz woke up that day, there was little uncertainty in his mind what had to be done. The answer to what he had to do he had answered for the hundredth time, possibly the thousandth. He had to get over Zuree and get her off his mind. She was beyond him. News of her upcoming wedding to Rizan was already being circulated, and preparations were being made throughout all the empire. Anyway, it was just as well as he was just passing through. He had just gotten sidetracked into taking the long way around his true calling.

He took the path that led down to the shoreline. Just beyond the dunes, the sea seethed and crashed against the shore. Izz reached the beach that day before the first rooster crowed. It was so early that even the smallest of seashells were casting long shadows along the shoreline. Waterbirds were beginning to make their peculiar little tracks on the sandy beach. Before him was the vastness of the open sea, on either side was the shore that stretched away as far as the eye could see between water and sky. Behind him, there were repeating rows of dunes rising one after the other, imitating the crashing waves before them. As he walked, Izz combed the beach for the driftwood he liked to use for the toys he loved so much to make and give away to the children at the orphanage and in his neighborhood. There was no sign of anyone; no other human footprints marked the long stretch of sugary sand that separated the brilliant azure water from the land like a bone white ribbon from horizon to horizon. He picked up a long stick laying across the wavy strips of fragmented shells and seaweed that marked the receding tide from the high tide to the water's edge. The early morning air was clear, and the wind was steady and gentle. Izz took a long, deep breath, filling himself with the crisp, enchanted dawn as the full morning sun shone on his face. Along the dunes, two seagulls bobbed and maneuvered around each other with wings squared and feathers ruffled. The sea glittered in the early morning light as it extended across the southern surface of Zia. There was almost nothing he would rather do than walk barefoot, feeling the white frothed waves lapping at his bare feet and squeezing the sand between his toes.

Izz bent down to pick up a shell among the stick like tracks of birds. *It is beautiful,* he thought to himself. Suddenly, memories that Izz had pushed into the back of his head, the image of Zuree, flashed in his mind. Without thinking, he took his long stick and scrawled out Zuree's name in the sand. The woman was still a puzzle to him. He somehow knew she felt something for him. Izz seemed to be able to see and feel things others could not. He refused to allow any hope for the dread of being disenchanted again. Perhaps she might merely be playing some cruel joke on him, toying with his heart, stringing him along to amuse herself.

"You fell prey to her beauty," he whispered. He took in the fresh salty air; the wind blew through his hair as he thought how he should not have a single care in the world. All his intense feeling faded away into a cold hearted world. When all was said and done, he reasoned to himself, "Why create problems where none need exist." He would just have to take it one day at a time. Even if she loved him the way he loved her, what were the odds that they would ever be together? A little better than zero to none. He kept reminding himself that she came from a long bloodline of crowned heads, and he from the lowest rank of people who worked with their hands. Even so, he did not care. Carpentry was a noble trade, and besides, he loved working with his hands. After all, a dream is only an involuntary whisper of a nameless fantasy. No matter how vivid, they are simply a series of fleeting feelings, emotions, ideas, thoughts, and images that flutter uncontrollably through one's head. Who can know what they mean or where they come from? They are only unbridled imaginations. Believing in them would almost be as ridiculous as believing in Ammiz's Great Conjunction and Creator fairy tales. He respected Ammiz, and a lot of what he said made sense, but somewhere along the way, he had gone off the deep end.

Besides, Zuree's hand belonged to Rizan, a wealthy aristocrat. He was a king, royal in every way, and the emperor/king's favorite. Izz wondered why she was in his thoughts again and again. Why was he once again rethinking the same old story as if the same obvious worn out conclusion was somehow going to change if only he thought it out one more time? He rebuked himself and wrestled with his heart with the last of his resolve to no avail. Trying to forget Zuree was hopeless. It was impossible. The price of love was painful. Everywhere Izz turned his thoughts; there she was: the sparkle in her eyes, the prized sound of her laughter, the touch of her hand, her feminine scent. He might as well have commanded the tides of the sea to turn back. Sure he was grateful for the precious moments, however brief, Izz had shared with the princess, and yes, he was painfully aware that he probably would never trade those special moments for a lifetime of never having known her. Even though having met her might very well have been something he would lament for the rest of his days. He tried to make himself face the truth, but the light behind her eyes would not set him free. Just what kind of spell had she cast on him? He felt she was in some way using him. Loving anyone that much could only bring him deep pain, maybe even kill him, as it had his father.

It was time for him to live his life in the real world, not in the depth of delusion. It was time to let his dreams die, not nourish, and protect them. The future was filled with promise, and he had everything to live for. A far reaching wave spread across the beach, washing away Zuree's name along with the thought of her. He saw the realization of his dream withdrawing farther and farther into the realm of the impossible. He took the beautiful shell and tossed it across the water, between the white capped swells, where it skipped several times before it slipped into the depths. However, without his consent, his heart tucked his dream into a quiet, secret corner, a hiding place where all his impossible dreams were kept suspended between love and hope, fear, and despair. He needed protection from himself.

He recaptured the noise of the seagulls and the smell of the sea. He turned his attention up the sun drenched coast. As the water rolled back, the beach sparkled off the sunlit sand as if so many tiny diamonds had been cast along its length. In the distance, he watched a lone fisherman casting his net from the rocky cragged shore. The surf crashed against the bare rocks, splashing a spray into an outspreading arc in the air. His eyes slid across the waterfront, appraising the great ships docked along the bay. He turned his attention to the sea and saw fishermen on small boats pulling up their nets, flipping them overhead, and then splashing them back into the deep. A pelican dropped out of the blue, spearheading beak first, slamming into the rolling swells. The smells of the oceans beckoned him. The open arms of the sea called him to ride once more upon its waves to unknown lands, to the most remote ends of the empire where his heart could once again be free. He suddenly had an overwhelming desire to merely get in his boat and race to anywhere he had never been before. His life suddenly felt empty.

He had been walking all morning, and his mind was still in a jumble. He gazed mournfully about him. Far off up ahead, Izz spotted what looked like the perfect piece of driftwood. He forgot what he was thinking about and hastened his steps. As he approached, he noticed in the sky a flock of seagulls that were circling above the driftwood like a horde of vultures waiting for something to die. As he came closer to the water's edge, fiddler crabs pop in and out of their bubbling and sputtering holes in the sand. Hermit crabs disappear into their shells, cautiously trying to avoid being preyed upon by seagulls circling overhead.

As he came closer, he thought he caught a glimpse of something golden reflecting in the water or had his eyes been deceived by the drifting mist. No, he could see that it was a creature, but not an ordinary sea creature, not like any he had ever seen, for it glistened like the purest of gold, fracturing the light as it sparkled in the sun. His breath came short, and his heart began to pound. There to Izz's astonishment, in the silt laden water, almost buried in a mound of seaweed, was the most amazingly beautiful golden fish he had ever seen. The fish was entangled in a fisherman's net, which was caught on the driftwood. From the marked line of seashells that had formed around the fish, he knew it had most likely been there all night. The fish's breath was shallow, its presence seemingly weak and powerful at the same time. There were peck wounds all over on the fish's shiny back that showed it had suffered several attacks from impatient seagulls, which would have eaten the fish alive if Izz had not found it at that very moment. It was a miracle, almost like fate, that Izz had happened along when he did. Izz drew his dagger and began to cut the fish free, as marauding seagulls shrieked and dove within inches, attempting to reclaim their prize.

The fish half opened its lusterless, light blue eyes and looked up at Izz, and he could have sworn he heard the golden fish ask, "Are you going to eat me? You will not like the way I taste."

"You are much too beautiful to be eaten," Izz found himself thinking out loud as he wondered why he had answered. That was an eerie feeling; hearing the fish speak out was like being in some-one's thoughts. Once cut free, the fish seems too weak to fight, too weak to swim. It completely surrendered as Izz gently gathered it into his compassionate arms. He carried the golden fish into deeper waters, till he reached the open blue sea where pounding waves wrapped around him and pulled away out to sea. The fish began to revive in the cooling waters and started to squirm in Izz's arms. It opened its light blue eyes again; they were no longer dull. There was a faint gleam like light glowing brilliantly deep within. Once the fish realized that it was being set free, its spirit quickened and hastily splashed out of Izz's grasp. When it had reached a safe dis-tance, the most unexpected thing happened: it turned around and stared at Izz for the longest time. And Izz heard in his mind, *I will see you again someday.* It was the most uncanny feeling of all, which came over Izz. It was the weirdest sensation of being in the fish's mind. And although he did not consciously hear the fish seemed to be speaking within his thoughts, as if their souls had suddenly, for a measureless time, melted into unity. It seemed to be thanking him or something, and then with one mighty swish of its tail, it vanished into its underwater world. Izz stood there for a moment and saw only white flecked bubbles, wondering what had just happened, as the never ceasing waves rolled in regularly and pounded against him like a great pulse with a life of its own hear beating a rhythm that seemed to echo his own pulse.

Izz continued to stare at the spot where the fish had disap-peared then he turned his gaze out to sea toward the horizon. *He tilted his head up and casually scanned the darkening southern skies. His eyes narrowed and considered the changing skyline as lightning flickered over the distant sea.* Izz focused his eyes be-yond and saw a mass of black clouds gathering in the distance. Its red lined glow filled the southwestern sky. Beyond that, he saw more ominous dark clouds rolling in from the most southern point. The darkness stretched across the sky, casting jagged, threatening shadows as if some supernatural force had flung a black cloak across the heavens. It looked like a massive storm, yet the winds were still and offered no indication of the brutal deluge that was bearing down. It was the calm before the storm. Izz felt an uneasy, foreboding feeling coming over him, for he knew these were the days in which the king was en route from his trading venture.

Far out at sea, Emperor Ozzdon and King Rizan were on their return voyage from the Norticlan territories. The king's voyage thus far had been ideal, and the trading venture—a risky diplomatic campaign based on a shaky truce with the Norticlan tribes of the Noragore Mountain range—had been mutually beneficial. The trade talks could have, at any time, taken a turn for the worst. For Darkon, the brutal leader of the ruthless Norticlan tribes could have been capable of any unexpected betrayal. He was one of the most cold blooded killers one would ever hate to meet. His name alone made kings and prince quake. Numerous murders had stained his path to the throne of the Norticlan tribes. Legend had it that Darkon was one of three brothers born on the same day. It was believed, by their pagan priests, that the triplet birth was a bad omen. The three infants were taken into the nearby mountains by the light of the evil star that overshadowed their birth and left to die, only to be taken in and raised by a renegade pack of wild mountain dogs. Toughened by the struggle to survive among the bloodthirsty carnivores, the three grew strong and fierce. The Norticlan nomads roamed from one mountain to another, never settling, eking out a wretched existence until the three savage hearted brutes united the mountain clans. Once power was solidified, Darkon, possessed by the most powerful spirits of the darkest realms, murdered his two brothers, cut them into pieces, and ground them into the dust without a pang of conscience, for he did not want to share power with anyone. He became the sole law unto himself with the courage of a lion, the instinct of a weasel, and the soul of a jackal.

The trading mission that might suddenly have turned to war had ended favorably, yet on shaky ground. King Ozzdon had led the delegation, meeting personally, face to face, with Darkon and the leaders of surrounding territories and tribes in which he negotiated for trade, peace, new laws, and territorial rights. The campaign altogether had been a resounding success. New avenues for the free transfer of goods and products to and from the major markets of Zia had been established.

The ship's hull was heavy laden with tributes from their neighboring new brothers. They carried ornament and utility: articles of gold, silver, copper, and bronze; unique fabrics; exotic spices; and a collection of exotic animals for their estuaries and gardens. The king was on his return trip from yet another enterprising triumph for which he was well known for. It almost seemed as if everything that King Ozzdon touched turned to pure gold.

By the navigator's reckoning, they were thought to be less than midway out from the shores of Edawn. The watchman from the crow's nest in the upper part of the mainmast was the first to spot the approaching weather system. For a moment, he studied the rolling, red rimmed clouds sweeping up over the southern horizon and reported it down below to his overseer.

"It looks like we are in for a bit of unfavorable weather, Captain."

The captain shaded his eyes from the sun and surveyed the situation. He took a moment as his eyes swept from side to side from one end of the horizon to the other. At first, all he could see was a distant slither of blackness poking up over the horizon. But he did not like what he saw. For the longest instant, he stared at the ominous warning signs that could not be ignored. In moments, it became all too readily apparent to every sailor on deck. The captain ordered, "All hands on deck. Full sail ahead, we will try to outrun it." There was an odd tone of uncertainty in his voice that indicated nothing that might give optimism.

Soon the full crew was on deck, scrambling and scurrying about, tuning the primary fore and aft mainsails and bringing the headsails into the wind. The scent of rain in the air suddenly became heavy with forewarning. The wind and tide were with them, but the tremendous dark thunderclouds were billowing, boiling, and rumbling, pierced by lightning that was cracking the sky. The rigging crew reset the sails to harness the shifting winds. Immediately, the vigorous wind bloated the canvas sails. Long streaks of sunlight lanced through a mass of dark clouds from somewhere above the immense black mass that filled the southern sky. The captain looked carefully at the approaching storm, now a yawning, inky black, spreading like an awning from one end of the sky to the other. Its bottomless reverberating drone was becoming audible.

The lookout in the crow's nest had one eye on the swelling waves and one eye on the ominous darkness that was threatening to swallow them up. The storm was approaching fast—very fast. There was an unusually dry, steady, warm breeze from the South that abruptly and suddenly appeared out of nowhere. From the opposite direction, there was an unseasonably cold, moist wind bearing down from the North. One wind began to mix with and feed the other, creating swirling waterspouts that danced on the face of the deep. The storm was worsening. The sky blackened as if the sun had been swept away. Lightning cracked, and claps of echoing thunder sounded in the distance. The beast then drew nearer, its boundaries lengthened outward like the up and coming point of a broad tip of the spear, widening gradually but surely diagonally across the horizon like a black cloak, reminiscent of a mounting avalanche of blackness blocking out the sky. Its center was as dark as coal. The onrushing wind was saturated with the whiff of an intensifying tempest on its waft. No one could have judged the wrath that was about to descend upon them.

The king came out of his cabin to see what all the commotion was about. His disposition was as turbulent as the weather. His dazzled eyes suddenly made sense of what everyone was anxiously staring at. The encroaching, massive, dense clouds were raging as the winds howled disagreeably. The king was attempting to calculate the full scope of fury that was headed straight for them. As the opposing winds entangled one with the other, the front of surging waters was drawing nearer with frightening speed. Rumbling sounds crackled in the distance and echoed across the thundering skies as electrical discharges of lightning exploded in the atmosphere overhead, while thunder rumbled and wisps of murkiness swept past on a bitter wind. The king knew that many ships caught in such rare, monstrous storms had been lost in the past. Everything that they had worked for so hard, along with their precious cargo, might all be lost in a moment.

The captain called to the king over the terrible moaning of the wind, "Your Majesty, it is not safe out here on deck!" But it was plain that the king was going nowhere.

As the wind fluctuated madly, the king called back, "Perhaps the main brunt of the storm will go around us." His voice was drowned in the thunder and became incoherent.

The onrushing high winds of the approaching storm flapped wildly in the sails, and the waves battered against the halls of the ship, as the overwhelming forces of nature tossed the vessel around the liquid murk of the sea like a plaything. The captain ordered the crew to cut the fore and aft rigged mizzen masts down and ordered that all nonessential cargo be cast into the sea to lighten the ship. Violent sea swells heaved, creating whorls and eddies, which in turn were creating ever rising waves. Then the rain came dancing across the sea. First, it came down in huge globules that cratered into multiple scattering droplets as they struck. Then came the heavy rains that pattered and pounded onto the deck of the ship. Menacing clouds sweep across the skies followed by ensuing torrents of dark slanting sheets of rain that began to fall, pouring down as heavy as thick drapery. The blur of rain cast the heavens into twilight darkness that bore down on the ship. Like a black velvet shroud, the slayer storm was heading straight toward them as though in angry pursuit. A thundercloud dropped out of the sky like a black predator. In another few minutes, it would pounce over the ship.

The captain stayed at the ship's wheel facing into the oncoming waves and trying to ride out the approaching storm. There was a brilliant flash of lightning and a deep throated rumbling clap of deafening thunder followed by a terrifyingly foreboding rush of wind. Suddenly, the full fury of the storm broke over the bow of the ship, and the king wondered how it had come upon them so suddenly. More waves rose and thrashed hard upon them as if the sea had become a diabolical beast intent on tearing their ship to shreds. Over the roar of the approaching storm, the captain of the ship ordered that the vessel's mainsails be cut down. The southern winds rattled the naked masts and booms while the chilling northerly flurries shook the rigs and riggings. The sound of the raging downpour and crashing waves mingled with the flashes of dark and light. Thunder rumbled roundabout the ship on all sides like an all out war in the face of the heavens. It was a killer storm for sure, crashing in on them from all sides. And in another few minutes, its full brunt would engulf the ship. Greater and greater waves began to pummel the ship and tossed it about violently. Beneath them, the surface of the sea surged like the skin of a monstrous killer serpent. Dark gray veils of cloudbursts were descending almost horizontally on tempestuous winds.

The rain pelted down on the king as he struggled against the wind and frightful waves that surged all around him. There was a drawn out bellow overhead as if all the angry gods of the sea had come up out of the deep to vent their enraged anger all at once. His robe was soaked by the spray blowing over the bow and flattening against his body. A shivery and biting gust whipped at the king's face. With a demonic rumble of thunder rolling down from the roof of the storm and the growling of ominous wind in his ears, the king screamed, "This storm will send us all to the depths!"

His voice was swallowed up by the roar of the scowling storm. The king turned and started to make his way back to the perceived safety of his cabin within the midst of a whirlwind that threatened to sweep him overboard. His clothes were whipping in every direction in the shifting squalls when, without warning, a sudden howling gust of wind blew the king's royal crown from his head. The king was filled with numbing distress as he saw his precious crown, the symbol of his monarchy, the source of his wisdom, swept over the side. He saw it splash and disappeared into the enraged sea. His face became a mask of shocked disbelief. He rushed to the railing, hanging on for dear life, and reached his hand out toward the crown as if he could somehow magically recover it. Members of the royal guard, having seen what had happened, quickly stripped themselves of their armor. They heaved themselves up and over the ship's railing, and dove into the water where the king's outstretched hand was pointing. Where he had last seen the final glimmering rays from the crown jewels as it slipped into obscurity. Too stunned to turn them back, the king stood there staring in complete, utter disbelief as, one by one, they disappeared into the darkened waters. All the while the ship was tossed in the storm's immensity, swaying violently in the rising swells, rocking first to one side and then the other.

Rizan, the bravest and most physically powerful warrior on board, had been the first to go overboard, recklessly slicing into the face of the deep, exactly where the king had indicated. He was unafraid as furious waves came crashing in all around him. Intense lightning lit up his strong square face as he entered the chilling water blackened with impending disaster. The king's cries of disapproval rang on deaf ears. As lightning flashes lashed out like forking snakes across the sky, Rizan's eyes adjusted to the murky depths as he plunged—into the yawning unknown. As bolts of lighting arched across the skies, Rizan caught a faint echoing flash of the priceless crown. Without hesitation, Rizan dove downward in pursuit of the glistening beacon of reflecting metal and glimmering stone. Deeper and deeper, the courageous mortal dove into the gloomy abyss. Before long, the lack of oxygen began to take its toll on the relentless diver. Farther and farther down, he swam. His eyes fixed on the gleaming prize, and closer and closer, he came to it. His lungs were aching, and his muscles burned with pain beyond imagination, but the king's champion was not about to let his king, his future father-in-law, down. not now, not ever.

The crown was within reach. Rizan stretched out his big hand with every fiber and touched the rim of the crown to the tips of his thick fingers. Just then, out of nowhere, he sensed the first signs of something dreadfully wrong. He heard an instantaneous whooshing sound and felt the water moving around him at a high rate of speed. Suddenly and without warning, he felt a blow to his right side as violently as if a raging bull had gored him. He did not see the mastodon shark before he felt its teeth sink into his flesh. The killing machine held his left upper body in teeth that were designed to slice through flesh and bone. In a moment of horror, Rizan was staring straight into the beast's right eye. He immediately began to punch the shark on the nose with straight jabs and pokes sharp, quick, and repeated thrusts to its eye. The massive predator rolled its protective eyelids like barriers over its eyes as it repeatedly bit down and shook Rizan violently. Rizan would never give up, never give in. He kept pummeling the shark's eyes and kicking its gills. He would never yield until either he was dead or the shark let him go. Rizan put up a brave fight, but inevitably everything went black as the death grip of a mastodon shark squeezed the life out of him with its powerful razor sharp jaws as the waters turned crimson red.

From the eastern horizon, the sky was split by a flash of blinding light with the scorching brightness of the sun. As the chilling flare discharged, it branched outward, filling the sky from horizon to horizon to horizon. In its afterglow from beneath the stirred up water and on its surface, the bubbles of Rizan's last breath were seen rising from the darkness, sending up small spouts of water. The swimmers on the surface, who had long since given up the efforts to recover the crown, knew when they saw the red stained water ascending from the depths that they had lost their hero, their champion, their friend. Everyone on board was making holy signs and babbling prayers in low stunned voices. In that same moment, a lightning strike, millions of volts in magnitude, struck the mainmast, snapping it in two. The acoustic shock wave boomed as its flash turned everything bone white. Time seemed to stop, and the king's heart gave a hollow thud. Rizan's spirit was gone. The loss was too great. Intense dread struck the king and the ship's crew like the sting of death itself. Swimmers scrambled out from a would-be watery grave as the crown continued its descent into the depths, into the endless utter black darkness, and everyone on board was lamenting Rizan's horrible, untimely death. As the crew struggled hopelessly against the storm, giant waves rose and crashed continuously over the deck as the rain continued to pour down. The ship was tossed about in a whirlwind as it was drawn into the central vortex of the storm of storms. The ship was hurled in the clutches of doom, caught in the fury of the thunderstorm's terrible power, staggering within a dance of death and obliteration. The ship was built to withstand the most powerful of storms but not of this enormity. Long oak, mast timbers buckled and came crashing onto the deck, crushing sailors who clung to safety ropes strung from the bow to the stern. Wide oak planks from the deck splintered like twigs with jagged edges, pinning and piercing sailors in the hull below. Waves as big as mountains continued to rage all around them as furious winds tossed the ship mercilessly with its brutal force. The ship was tossed helplessly throughout the night like a child's toy against a deluge carried on the breath of a perfect storm.

Far away in the palace, Zuree was suddenly awakened. Her gaze was drawn to her bedchamber's southern windows by the crossfire playing against the dome of the distant skies. She loved the rain: its smell, the way the lightning lit up the sky, and the weighty rhythm of it steady drumming. She saw images of herself dancing in the rain when she was a child. She sat up on her bed, slipped her feet into her velvety slippers, and a few quick steps took her to the window. She pulled back the heavy, pleated drapery and opened her windows. She looked toward the horizon, and suddenly the rain did not seem so pleasant. Everything was dim outside. She looked out toward the sea in the direction her father's ship would be returning and froze with anxious eyes when she saw the bleak sky on the horizon. Her face grew pensive, and her eyes were troubled. Her white gown fluttered in the stiff breeze as lightning flickered from afar. It's flashes created radiating highlights in her golden hair.

An unsettling feeling loomed over her as she watched ominous thunderheads swept across from the South like massive black ships enshrouding the southern world of Zia into darkness. She gasped and stumbled back when the entire southern hemisphere suddenly lit up with the fieriness of midday as if a terrifying blazing claw of condemnation had reached out to catch hold of her. She drew the shutters, closed the window, and gathered the curtains, shutting out the unpleasant fury of the storm. But she could not shut out the premonition that something frightfully awful had befallen her or was about to overcome her. Unnerved, she moved to stand by the hearth, but the fire lent no comfort to the chill at her core, nor offered warmth to the curdling blood that ran cold in her veins. Her teeth chattered, and her lips trembled as she tried desperately to get hold of herself. She crawled back into bed and huddled her thick blanket up against herself. An unusual ache throbbed in her heart. Her body shook with deep uncontrolled sobs as she cried herself back to sleep, and she knew not why.

As the sun crept over the curve of Zia and dawn began its pale unveiling, light rain fell like so many teardrops weeping from the sky. Sunbeams pierced each droplet as echoing prisms divided the white light into its seven brilliant colors, creating a mysteriously beautiful triple arched rainbow that hung ominously over the sea against the clearing sky. The nightmare was over, and even those poor tempest tossed souls who had witnessed its ferocity firsthand could not fully believe they had lived through what they had lived through. The full power of the storm had broken. The ship was left floating on a calm, ghostly, glassy sea. The vessel looked as if it might splinter into a pile of planks and timbers if anyone kicked it.

The royal ship had taken the slayer storm's full brunt. It was a miracle that it had not gone down to join the crown at the bottom of the sea. The keel and ribs of the ship hewed from the giants of the forest, with their iron like strength, had held the hull together. The dew was still heavy in the air, and a great stillness swept across the deep except for the usual steady breeze from the South. The only sounds were the creaking of the timbers. The king's tattered banners fluttered, tangled rigging and broken ropes whipped in the wind. The shredded canvas rages moved eerily back and forth in the breeze. The once mighty sails were now beaten to pieces by the wind and the waves. Most of the long oars that dangled from their portals aligned along the ship's port side just above the waterline were broken or missing altogether. The vessel was in shambles, barely seaworthy, barely afloat.

As if coming up out of a daze, the king peered out of his cabin, looking somewhat seasick, feeling guilty for having failed to foresee the coming storm. Why had his crown not warned him? The king was frantically asking himself, "What am I to do, what am I to do?" As he clasped his head and raked his fingers across his face, the unthinkable had happened. He had lost his beloved champion and his priceless crown all within the same tragic moment. He stumbled himself over to the ship's railing, slain with grief. He clung to the railing and let out a low sustained moan. He kicked and stomped his feet and shook his fist at the sky as tears poured down his cheeks. And as the sun climbed over the horizon, a calm came over the crew. But the dark shadows of death remained in the hearts of every seaman. When the ship pulled into port, under the power of the few long oars that remained intact, what survived of the once mighty ship was a frightening skeleton of the glory it once had been.

The news spread rapidly throughout the kingdom: Rizan had been lost at sea and thought to be dead. Upon hearing the news, minds were unexpectedly jarred with anguish and grief. The greatest champion of all time, so well loved by all, no longer walked among them, snatched away in the prime of his life. Gone was the soul whose equal would never be seen again. Many people wept openly, not wishing to hide a single tear. It was an enormous loss for Zia.

It is with the deepest, saddest regret that King Ozzdon approached Zuree, needing to tell her personally of Rizan's death. He had to tell her himself, no matter how grievous, for the better or worse. She had the right to be the first in the palace to know. Tears streamed down his cheeks.

"I have sad tidings, daughter. What I am about to say is so dreadful that I would give anything not to have to tell you. Rizan is...no more. The dreaded denizen of the deep has taken him from us." His head slumped with the words.

"What!" Maybe she had heard wrong. Perhaps she had misunderstood. *No!* Her mind screamed as it rejected what her ears had just heard. *It cannot be true!* But her father's tearful eyes confirmed it was no mistake.

Overcome, Zuree fell toward her father, trembling and shuddering against him. She loved Rizan for his affection toward her. He was like a sweet older brother.

"How can it be? He was so very kind to me. I cannot believe he is gone," she said between sobs. The next few moments passed in mute anguish as they shared each other's deepening grief. A thousand questions she wanted to ask flashed in her mind, but at that moment, she just wanted to be alone. The ache in her heart deepened and began to throb. Zuree's eyes swelled with tears as she broke away wordlessly and turned to run to her chamber to mourn privately. King Ozzdon wished with all his heart that he could somehow bear the heaviness of her heartbreak for her, on top of his own, but he knew full well that she would need time to cope with her grief in her own way.

Behind closed doors in her chambers, Zuree collapsed on her bed in tears, in shock, in numbness, and disbelief. She buried her face in her hands and wept as she deflated in her spirit. She grieved, as any loving person would grieve for a man she admired and loved like a blood brother. Even though she had not learned to love him as lovers do, she respected him without end. She tried to find solace in that thought, but her pain was too deep and too complete. She could not believe that Rizan was dead! But worst of all, she could not stop the guilt welling up within her. Self accusation plagued her soul. She wanted to be free, yes, but not at such an unbearable cost. Not at a price that was beyond heartbreak. Rizan's death marked a boundary ending one chapter of her life—and to a large extent, what she had been groomed for had been left behind. There would forever be a special place in her heart for his dear memory. There would always remain an immense, bottomless, stark void in Zuree's soul that could never be filled. Her heart fell downward deeper into an endless pit of despair. She broke down and wept inconsolably for the man who was positively worthy of her tears.

When Baddlock received the news of Rizan's tragic death, he turned, hiding a smile from the council that had assembled, and said grievingly, "I only hope he is in a better world."

But little did anyone know that at the very moment that King Ozzdon and Darkon were swearing upon their new allegiance, the Wicked Warlock Wizard had ordered Mossca and Pongo to disguise themselves in King Ozzdon's standards. Under the king's colors, they covertly attack a defenseless Norticlan outpost. The staged attack led to the slaughter of hundreds left unprotected due to the absence of their men gathered with King Ozzdon. All were massacred: the old, women, and children alike. Unspeakable atrocities were committed, breaking the ancient carnal laws of war. A handful of survivors were permitted to escape so that they could tell of Edawn's evil cruelties and treachery, of deeds too horrible even for the Norticlan mind.

Filled with sorrow over his loss of Rizan and his crown, distraught beyond the ability to cope, the king fell into a dark chasm of grief. King Ozzdon stumbled to his throne and flopped onto it and sat there motionless. His eyes filled with tears. There was not enough room in all of Zia to contain his pain. The king locked himself in his private chambers and would not see anyone. His last decree had been to dispatch Zandor and Kondor, the twin warriors, immediately with a contingent of elite troops to Ziyontopia to tell Rizan's family of the tragic loss of their favored son.

King Ozzdon did not want to speak to anyone and did not want to be interrupted by anyone. In essence, he had become a prisoner in his own throne room in which the lock was on the inside. Periodically, Ozzdon would stand, and he would pace back and forth, like a caged animal pacing for hours deep in thought, heavy with intensely agonizing despair, reeling with gloom over his irretrievable loss. The king anxiously paced several steps one way and then stopped and paced back the other way, wearing a pathway from one end to the other in his chambers. His heart sank, his mood darkened, and he descended into a profound, bleak state of depression. King Ozzdon sat alone in the middle of his pitch dark room hunched over, looking shrunken, gray faced, and stricken. The savor for life seeped out of him. The expression on his face was one of grief and torment. His forehead creased with worry, bags puffed under eyes that took on a glazed look, and the weightiness of his years settled down upon him more burdensome than ever. He battled inwardly against his hopelessness. Struggling in the grip of his melancholy, the king searched his mind for solace but brought into existence only doubt, dread, and intellectual decay. Dazed by sleeplessness, his mind seemed to be focused on some other universe, a lost soul in some other timeless chasm. The catastrophic loss of his beloved champion and his crown had drained away his ability to govern over his empire and its people. His world was turned upside down, and his mind was scattered to the four corners of the empire. His inability to cope tormented him.

As time wore on, hours and days lost their meaning, and the matters of the empire and those that King Ozzdon loved so dearly seemed to be scarcely of any significance now. The king would not leave his room, confined in a prison of self pity and self condemnation; he was the sole keeper, who held the only key that would unlock himself from his bondage. The king would not even eat and became thin, worn, broken down, and enfeebled. With every passing day, Ozzdon seemed to draw deeper and more profoundly into himself, blocking out the rest of the world, crawling into himself like a snail in its shell. As he lost touch with the real world around him, he became ill tempered, his coldness had turned to ill will, and he refused to see even his loyal Queen Zahra. After a temporal length of several days of self torment and uncertainty, changes began to come over his soul, darkening his heart within an oppressing, choking shadow. His sorrow had become utterly entangled with his kingly duties. His rule seemed to him but a loathsome phantom. The chain of command was severed, and the kingdom orphaned. The nobles sat in council waiting for the king's command. The situation was grave. The empire's administration stumbled without his leadership, and Edawn was falling into turmoil. Rumors were widely whispered that the king was dying.

Concerned for his well being, the queen intruded on his privacy against his wishes. When she entered, he did not even look up. She had never seen the king of her heart seem so old and crushed. His misery had sapped more than his physical endurance. Zahra was close to tears to see Ozzdon fading away a little each day. She wanted to share his pain, ease it if she could. Hiding her pain, she reached out.

"Your people need you, and I need you!"

Grief strike and emotionally exhausted, the king responded with a distant and detached expressionless expression. Without raising his head, he said in a hushed voice, "All is lost. There is no hope. What is the use? What does it matter? Please just...leave me be." His words came in angry, measured tones.

The queen frowned at the resignation in her husband's voice. She had always been his safety net, but now he seemed so incomprehensibly out of reach, lost in despair, and there was nothing she or anyone else in the empire could do to help.

Stargazers looked for the answers in the constellations but were forsaken. Seers attempted to peer into the future but were left sightless. Healers, magicians, and soothsayers kept visuals and uttered unanswered prayers for the recovery of their king. Ammiz, the eldest seer, looked up into the star filled night and thought, *It is ourselves who are flawed, not the eternal truths.*

The king's power over his people was in the gravest jeopardy. King Ozzdon had been the heart and mind of the empire, and the guardian of its being. Without him, the people were left helpless, cut adrift from order and direction. Rizan was hoped to be the king's next in command, pledged to marry Princess Zuree, and in line to be Xylenian's next Emperor-King. But Rizan, the mighty, was no more. The kingdom had never suffered such a loss. The loss was so significant that it shook the very foundations and rocked the pillars of the empire.

Izz had not known Rizan well, but he knew him well enough to know that he was a good man. And now he was gone, perhaps to where the mistress and Ammiz said all good people go, to where his parents waited for him. Who could know for sure? Izz could not be allowed to understand what it meant. And what of Zuree? He wondered what thoughts were going through her mind. He knew he had made a mistake in allowing his feelings for Zuree to have taken a life of their own, but now there was nothing he could do about it. What was the past could not be changed and was best somehow forgotten. But try as he may, Izz could not help believing that he was somehow responsible for Rizan's death. Nevertheless, what crime had he committed? Whatever laws of love had he broken? Had his feelings for Zuree been too hopeful, needy, and wanton? There was no point grieving over what could not be helped. Even though Rizan was gone, he knew Zuree could never be his. She was royalty, he was a commoner, and that was never going to change. Now was not the time to think about his personnel affairs. He could hardly wait for the arrival of the tree trunk, where he sought to find some form of solace. He planned to immerse himself in the king's last command: the commissioning of the table. The trunk was close, so close. He imagined he could almost smell the sweat of the yakoxen and the labors on the waft of the light breeze.

As long as the sun had shone, a feat as monumental, and ambitious, had never been imagined before much less attempted. But as sure as the sun rose at length, finally, the day came when the caravan moving the colossal tree trunk emerged from the forest's edge. Day by day, the taskmasters inched the huge wooden piece closer and closer to its resting place. The main gate had already been dismantled to accommodate the oversized cylinder of timber. New towering gate planks had been split and planed from the upper part of the tree and would replace the existing ones, making this the grandest gate of the empire. The main street was cleared as men and beasts of burden working in unison, testing their wills between the immovable object and the unstoppable force. Yakoxen let out low, prolonged, rumbling "Murrrrumphs," which gave way to deeper wrenching "Maaawwuuuuers" that mingled with the sorrowful groans of men whose muscles were strained to their full extent. The triumph of the will became the deciding factor as well oiled wheels grounded and squeaked in protest under the weight of the immense volume of hardwood. The wooden giant squeezed along the main northern avenue, traveling only a few paces per hour, with the familiar tinkering, clunking, and clattering along the street accompanying the grunts and low bellows of the straining yakoxen. The wagon trundled down the street, wobbling from time to time as the wheels clicked and clacked across cracks along the stone laden street. The enormous flat bedded dray inched along in a slow plotting rhythm as they negotiated the treacherous turns around street corners as the wheels screeched in objection. The massive load crunched down on the axes, moaning, and groaning with loud noises, grinding out fiery showers of sparks. The low loaders wheels clattered in a steady tempo, every turn of the wheel brought the huge wooden trunk closer to its resting place. The iron clad wheels etched the stones and crushed ruts into the crumbly rock as the wagon was drawn forth. The foundation where the table would rest had been completed. The site was next to the palace, where a new throne room would be built around the massive round table. When the entanglement of men and droves of yakoxen maneuvered the wooden trunk to the edge of the palace, all came to a shuddering, clangorous halt. Men sighed in relief, fell to their knees, and rolled to the ground, exhausted. The multitudes of yakox were unharnessed. The sound of jingling chains and clinking leather rings filled the streets. The yakoxen were led away and released onto green pastures for a well earned rest.

The unloading, maneuvering, and placement of the tree base would require precision and patience. The offloading would necessitate the focus and attention of the entire royal staff of architects, designers, builders, and construction engineers. Hours of redundant measurements and discussions of possible methods of accomplishment ensued. The laborers did not mind one bit. The longer their learned counterparts remained in the debate, the longer they could rest and recover. Finally, a workable solution was agreed upon. Wooden derricks were raised using a complex array of scaffolding and ramps. Pulleys and tackles that were powered by large numbers of men were attached to the rings that would be used to off load the wooden prize. While the giant core was prepared to be unloaded, a caravan of carts and wagons hauled in tons of sand that were piled into an offloading ramp and base where the table would rest. Two teams of a hundred men each assembled at both ends of the tree stock. Balancing ropes were manned by small bands of men on either side of the trunk. The hundreds of twisting ropes stretched, and pulleys squeaked as the leading columns of men, on the ground, pulled the enormous block forward and off the wagon. All the while teams on the derricks manned the ropes that ensured the table did not go rolling down the street and crushing everything in its path. The hoist and movable block of pulleys strained as it took up the weight of the wooden giant. The timber derrick, scaffolding, ramps, and pulleys made a succession of sharp, snapping, and crackling noises as everyone held their breath. Thumbs breadth by thumbs breadth, the massive timber cylinder came down, ever so slowly. Hundreds of laborers were flung to the ground in the fierce recoil as the enormous cylinder came to rest in its place, churning up massive plumes of dry debris fragments. As the dust cleared, the workers and disburdened overseers watch their work come to completion and let out a triumphant cheer. All that was left to do was swivel the table and set it in its footing.

Once the cylinder was in place alongside the mountain of sand, the sand was then removed, and the table slowly came down to its final resting place. A yakox hide tent was raised around the gigantic wooden slab. Here is where Izz and a host of skilled woodcarvers would spend a significant part of the day working on their monumental commission.

As soon as the tree trunk was in place, the primary work of building the domed throne room's foundation to encompass the table started. Master quarrymen, sculptors, masons, blacksmiths, glassmakers, stonecutters, mortar makers, and carpenters all began their work to build the most magnificent edifices ever build in Edawn, in Zia.

Hoping to please his king, hoping that this could somehow bring the king out of his worsening melancholy, Izz took up his new task with relentless enthusiasm and zeal—a zeal that consumed him. He had the basic concepts of this project all worked out and held in his head and had created intricate, detailed sketches that he posted everywhere to be referenced by the army of woodcutters under his command. Izz eagerly listened to the many suggestions offered by his talented team of master woodworkers. He filled his days with toil, driving himself feverishly, tirelessly. It was hard work, but Izz was accustomed to such labor. The work on the deep grained wood was intensively demanding, and Izz plunged himself wholeheartedly into it, pushing himself relentlessly. The process was slow, one day followed another, and so the days stretched on. Every day, Izz labored from the crack of dawn to the last glimmering rays of dusk. At the end of each day, he was too fatigued to think, too tired to care about anything else. Izz was a man with a mission, and the table was his labor of love, his only love for the present.

By this time, word had long since reached Darkon of the horrific atrocities committed against his defenseless people. Shock and anger roiled over his face, and he was outraged. To think that with one hand, King Ozzdon had offered peace, friendship, and trade, and with the other hand, he had desecrated those least able to defend themselves. Ozzdon was a two faced serpent of cold, cunning; there were few uglier traits of inhuman depravity. Darkon's anger exploded in volatile wrath. His face twisted with fury as he burst into a barrage of verbal abuses and screams. Darkon trembled with madness and cried out, "If it is war, Ozzdon wants, it is what he shall have. Death to all Edawnians!" he screamed at the top of his lungs as he stormed about, lost in a growing rage of a raving lunatic. And from that moment, the Norticlan world began to prepare for an all out war with the inhabitants of Xylenia.

Seventeen

The Edict

The king's Inner Council of Elder, the most trusted subjects of great thinkers, those charged with the duties of administrating the general affairs of the kingdom during the king's absence, called for an urgent gathering of the most powerful nobility in Edawn. None but the honored, the influential, and the powerful, and special aristocrats were permitted to attend. They came together to devise a plan to stabilize the empire. The Inner Council of Elders had the full authority to act in the king's stead if the king was unable to rule the empire for whatever reason. They were also authorized to select a new king in the event of the death or the inability of the reigning monarch to fulfill his responsibilities. The meeting took place in complete secrecy. It was thought best that the people did not know the seriousness of the situation. Every Elder was present, including a rare appearance by Ammiz. Even though he was still a member, no one expected him to show up.

Dandork, the master of arms, was the king's right hand now that Rizan was no more. He was responsible for law and order throughout the land of Xylenia and was the next down the line in the chain of command. He was seated at the conference table beside Baddlock, who was there as an adviser at Dandork's request. Tigbone, who never left Baddlock's side, was seated next to him, showing what few teeth he had left as he continually swiped drool from his mouth. Baddlock was leaning back in his chair with a sneer on his face as he spoke to Dandork in secretive whispers. Both wore matching self important, conspiratorial smiles. Ammiz sat in the corner, seemingly distracted and looking almost sleepy. The seer inconspicuously turned his head sideways, cocked an eye, and took note of Baddlock and Dandork with a quick, discreet glance that included both of them.

Their smugness was almost unbearable. There was something very suspicious about the pair, and Ammiz suspected that the two men were in league together in some dark conspiracy. Dandork spoke first, bringing the meeting to order. "It is time to consider our options." The crowd in the hall ended their muted discussions, and the room began to quiet down. "We must either figure out a way to recover the crown or consider the obvious—choosing a ruling successor."

The latter provoked a rumbling difference of opinions that threatened to erupt into a full blown interruption of disobedience. There were many gasps of surprise and dismay, for they all loved their king. Men hooted and jeered, grumbled, and whispered among themselves.

"Absurd!" someone shouted.

Dandork restored order, speaking with the authority of one who was accustomed to being obeyed. Knowing that King Ozzdon was well loved and that he could very well be facing a riot, Dandork said, "If you think we can afford to wait. It is then crucial to the survival of our civilization that the crown be recovered, if that is at all possible, and placed back on the head of our noble king."

Murmured conversations quickly came to an end as a tense stillness fell over the room.

"Let it be known that even as we speak, the king's condition worsens," Dandork spoke in a tone of finality, then opened the forum by asking, "Is there any among us who can offer a solution to our dire situation?"

More profound silence fell like a cloak of concern over those in attendance. Never before had so much thought been focused on one single problem, for the ruling class wished with all their hearts that their noble king would regain his normal frame of mind and return to rule over them.

One noble suggested, "Let us offer a treasure twice, nay, three times as big as the one offered for the falling of the tree." No other noble countered. "The task is monumental, perhaps impossible, considering the denizen of the deep. The reward must be of a value that men are made willing to go to the ultimate extreme to win it."

Ammiz, who had remained silent, fully aroused, rose, and tapped his staff forcefully on the marble floor. A surprised hush came over the room as all heads turned to look at the old seer in the corner. The senior seer had been kept in the Inner Council only out of respect for his many brilliant years of past service. Ammiz cleared his throat.

"The solution that we all seek is quite simple," Ammiz exclaimed in a voice that carried to the farthest corner of the room. He unexpectedly paused as if suddenly lost in a vision of revelation; his eyes seemingly focused in some timeless, faraway distance.

"What...what?" The noble next to him reached out and shook him.

The old seer suddenly refocused with a start in much the same way as a night watchman might awaken after being discovered sleeping at his post. The seer faced the group as a smile stretched his lips, and his hazy eyes flashed with rebirth. "Let us offer to whoever will recover the crown—"

"Yes! Yes!" the gathered urged.

"Why not offer up the kingdom of Ziyontopia? With Rizan's death, the kingdom has been left kingless, and anyone able to recover the crown is surely worthy to rule over the gem of Zia. A man could not ask for more than that."

A great consultation of controversy arose through the room. The discussion became heated. The prize that was Ziyontopia has been coveted by many. Its vast fertile farmlands and great vineyards made it the treasure of Zia. On top of all that, it rivaled as the seat of higher learning and expression of the arts. Differences flared, and rumblings of disagreement grew into an unsettling uproar as patience drew to its end. Senior elders entered into a heated argument over the wisdom of Ammiz's suggestion as a distinct tremor ran through the room and erupted with commotion. One noble elder stood abruptly.

"The pride of the empire? The second richest kingdom in Zia? Let us, for a moment, consider the cost, labor, and architectural skill freely expensed for over a hundred years to enhance its splendors. All other kingdoms set side by side are built of mere sand in comparison—preposterous! Purge yourself of the notion."

Recognizing the challenge for the insult it was, Ammiz responded with a long silence. And he would have let the matter drop then and there if Baddlock had not infuriated him with his next callous remark.

"Who but the man of fairy tale books is capable of greater bizarreness?" The wizard's rebuke brought forth suppressed laughter from the assembled. Ammiz avoided Baddlock's long cold glare and then quickly glanced at the congregation dauntlessly, looking boldly at each doubting face in turn. Returning to oneness, he finally spoke again. Ignoring the ridicule, he said, "If you cannot see the obvious. I have not the patience or the inclination to draw you a simplified picture." Then he nodded and folded his arms confidently over his staff.

Baddlock and Dandork were mumbling some muted words, which had the force and sourness of profanity as they furrowed their faces, looking at each other, reflecting their resentment and indignation for the old man. Baddlock stood, making no attempt to hide his distaste for Ammiz.

"Master Ammiz," he hissed mockingly. "We all know your love affair with fantasy." He snickered and then continued, "Why burden yourself with these troubles, which ought never to have vexed you. You are aged, haggard, and as almost everyone knows you are at best, suffering from delusion and seem to be enjoying every minute of it." Baddlock followed his statement with a fixed stare and ghastly grin of condescending contempt.

Laughter erupted among the members. Ammiz's eyes slid over to Baddlock and shot him a blistering counter stare then turned to the assembly and said, "It does not befall me to think all these things through for you, nor need I remind you that it is your duty to forever bear in mind the highest priority for our king and empire."

Whispers of disapproval rippled through the crowd, and Ammiz could hear a multitude of grumbling tones coming from the judgmental faces all around him. A leader of the Inner Council, honored in the courts of the nobles, interrupted, slamming his open hand down hard and loud against the oak table where he was seated.

"No, no! It is brilliant! Ammiz, the Elder, is right. As crazy as it may sound, it is far better to sacrifice something of greater value than to risk the stability of the entire empire." A man could not ask for more than that.

Eyebrows rose alarmingly as a few nearby nobles nodded their silent approval. The laughter suddenly stopped, and even

Ammiz's most ardent critics humbly submitted and fell silent. The reaction was not immediately affirmative, but gradually the spontaneous response of the group was that of overwhelming agreement, which pleased them all. Yes, that is it. Who could resist such a grand offer? Someone started clapping, and the room erupted into applause. And those who had only moments earlier scorned the seer rushed forward, cheering the judgment.

"Send out the edict immediately." Dandork joined in hypocritically, hiding his annoyed expression behind his harsh features. Baddlock clutched at his dagger as he felt rage boil up within him, angered that his attempt to discredit Ammiz's credibility had resulted in his own undermined belittlement. An evil smile lurked at the corner of his mouth at the thought of plunging his blade to the hilt into Ammiz's heart. He whispered under his breath, "I will personally see to your demise and that of your little carpenter friend." His face became a mask of pleasing agreeability, careful not to condemn himself before the council with his arrogance.

The decree was sent by land and sea out in every direction to the furthest borders of the empire, to every kingdom, village, and hamlet. The response was halfhearted at best. There were very few takers. Only the most experienced and hardened divers bothered to show up at all. Rumors of the sea monster that inhabited those waters, where the crown was lost, had spread throughout the empire, growing more ominous along its way. Only the bravest of the brave gathered around the search site. Most people thought they were the craziest of the crazy. The point where the crown went down was well mapped and marked. The would-be heroes began to arrive along with the latest underwater innovations of the day, devices that promised to make them the next king of Ziyontopia.

The first to give up were the sponge, coral, and pearl divers, who dove with little or no equipment. They were divers who submerged into the deep with the aid of ropes to guide them and stone weights to help them descent quickly. Even though they could hold their breath for extended periods, they came nowhere near the bottom. The next to give up hope were the divers that used air bubbles made of large ceramic bells, attached with wooden handles, laced together with brass straps. The air bubbles were then lowered into the deep on long ropes. These divers were barely able to reach the twilight zone. The only divers left were the men experienced in retrieving sunken treasure. These divers worked in teams. The divers themselves were equipped with ceramic helmets that fit over their heads and shoulders. The diving helmet had two openings where the diver's arms fit through, and the front of the helmet was equipped with a thinly sliced piece of polished tortoiseshell, which allowed the divers to look out as they made their descent. At the top of the ceramic helmet, there was a brass plate from which a rope was attached. Along the length of the line ran a long air tube. On its inside were fitted sections of hollow reeds to keep the airway from collapsing, which was then encased with waterproofed sheep's gut. The air was then pumped to the diver through the encased hollow reeds with a furnace type bellow.

The helmeted divers made their last preparation before being lowered into the water. Two men took turns manning the air bellows as the diver was dropped into the deep sea. A group of men lowered the weighted down diver, deeper and deeper, and deeper. The job of the youngest members of the crew was to make sure the airline was not leaking as it slipped into the depths. The diver carried on his pocketed belt three hollow, airtight glass balls used to signal the surface. The yellow one meant he needed to surface, and the orange meant he needed to surface quickly, and the red one indicated that he needed to surface immediately. The crew kept lowering the diver. According to markers on the line, it was the deepest a diver had ever gone. The diver was lowered past the twilight zone and could feel the weight of the ocean crashing down on him. It was not easy to see anything in such dim light, but after a while, to some extent, the diver's eyes gradually grew accustomed to the darkening waters. Down he went into a world that was quickly vanishing into the shadows.

In the murkiness above, the diver saw what he dreaded most, the outline of a huge mass that momentarily eclipsed everything into total blackness. The silhouette was unmistakable. The diver fumbled for the glass balls at his belt and unintentionally released all three balls at once. The giant's savage shadow came whooshing by at an accelerated speed. The terrified diver felt the water being pushed by its massive force as he turned with bulging eyes to see the fin and the side of a giant fish before it faded into the pitch black darkness. It passed so close he could have reached out and touched it.

The crew on the surface, upon seeing the three balls pop up simultaneously, instantly knew something was terribly wrong. Every man on the diving team struggled frantically to pull the line up. Suddenly, the line jerked violently from side to side and then came loose. Everyone that was drawing the line lost their balance and went tumbling to the small ship's deck. They quickly recovered and brought the slack line up to discover that the line had been severed as if by a razor. The thousands of tiny blood laced bubbles rising to the surface made a bubbly sound. The other surrounding crews saw what was happening and rapidly started pulling their own divers out of the water. Yet another soul had been

Skullzome
TOM ICON
GATEWAY INTO THE ABYSS
IZZ OF ZIA

SKULLDOOM
PHANTOMS DEEP
NORTHERN RANGE
ZIYNATOPIA
WASTELAND OF WOE
WOLF DEN
SKYMOUNT
FORBIDDEN ZONE
WARNING TREE
EBONY
FOREST
RING OF GIANTS
BAY OF TRANQUILLITY
GREAT SOUTHERN SEA
THE EDAWNIAN KINGDOM
THE DEEP ABYSSAL
EARTH'S END
POINT OF NO RETURN
N NE E SE S SW W NW

swallowed up by the sea. The estimations of risk weighed against the acquisition played across every man's mind. No amount of reward, not even the kingdom of Ziyontopia, was enough to make it worth inevitable suicide. And thus, the search for the crown was immediately called off.

To be continued in Tom Icon's second book, Izz of Zia, "Skullsdoom."

For more information contact us at izzofzia@gmail.com